NIGHTFALL IN THE GARDEN OF DEEP TIME

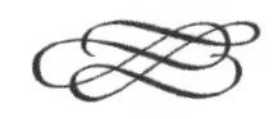

TRACY HIGLEY

ISBN: 978-1-7370579-7-0

Cover design by Alexander Ness at nessgraphica.com

I THINK YOU'LL LOVE THIS FREE STORY!

Hello Reader Friend,
Would you like a free adventure?
When you sign up for my mailing list, you'll receive a free ebook, *Theft on the Nile*. It's a classic murder mystery (about an hour's read) that I think you'll love, my gift to you!

You'll also be in the know when there are free books, new releases, and discounts on past titles.

Get your free ebook right here:
https://BookHip.com/PLRFKJK

The soul lives in such eternally deep time.
We are both driven and called forward
by a kind of deep homesickness.
What appears to be past and future
is in fact the same home, the same call...

~ Richard Rohr

PROLOGUE

LOCATION—FROM THE STREET:

A wasted city lot, hidden behind a blank wall of moldering brick, empty of all but scrabbly weeds grown tree-height and the wind-blown detritus of several apathetic generations. The empty lot presents only a single wrought-iron portal: a gate so rusted one wonders if it ever swung in welcome.

Beyond the gate, the woody stalks of weeds reach for the sky, and for the adjoining buildings, and for the bars of the iron gate, tendriling through empty spaces between the bars until only rusty iron fragments appear through a verdant wall of greenery, admitting no one.

A vacant lot. Abandoned, forgotten, ignored.

INSIDE—UNSEEN:

Life.

Music and Art.

Poetry and Story.

Truth and Beauty and Goodness.

Waiting to be discovered, to be seen.

To be *given*—as benediction. But also as rebuke.

As a means, or perhaps as an end.

Waiting for those with eyes to see, for him who has ears to hear.

Waiting for Kelsey, the unsuspecting woman rushing toward a bookshop, balancing a steaming coffee in one hand, gripping a paper sack of oversized chocolate cookies in the other, writing words in her head...

ONE

When glimpsed through the eyes of imagination, a city on the threshold of spring holds promise and potential in its asphalt fingers, daring the cold weather an attempt to slither back from its recent retreat, marshaling pedestrians who've shed jackets and drivers unrolling car windows as fellow soldiers in the battle toward warmth and leaf and birdsong....

Nah, that's no good.

It's a weather opening. The laziest of all ways to open a scene.

And how late am I?

I force my focus from the cracked sidewalk's dangerous ridges and valleys and rotate my wristwatch to catch the time.

My coffee threatens to spill even though the motion is too gentle to activate the display. It must be nearly three. The students could arrive any moment, with all the inherent impatience of teens. I need this time with them, especially today. For our brief hour together, I can set aside the obsession over my current disaster.

As usual, I've lost track of time while at the Sunny Side

Up Diner, stocking up on chocolate cookies for the bookshop's front counter and brainstorming with AnaMaria about my latest marketing idea, borne of desperation. And it doesn't help that I've wasted time composing a ridiculous ode to spring, slowing my walk homeward.

"Wool-gathering," Gran would call my imaginative notion of the city and its people soldiering together to bring a new season to the world. She'd include a wink and a smile, but still. I have too many real-life problems to fix, to be running down fanciful mental paths.

Imagination doesn't pay the bills.

I've covered three blocks since AnaMaria's diner, through my lovely Lincoln Village neighborhood. I pass the Rhythm & Wonder Music Shop, which has been there since my childhood.

Between the music store and my bookshop stretches the red-brick wall of a vacant lot. I hurry along its blank face, but then pause, seized by an urge to linger at the iron gate, which is nearly overgrown by the weeds inside. I touch two fingers to the bright green growth. A frisson of something—surging life, perhaps—tingles my fingers and raises the hair on the back of my neck like a warning. I twirl a stem around my finger, but the feeling fades, leaving a wake of disappointment.

Move along, girl. You're late.

The Chestnut Street Book Emporium—once-upon-a-time the Chestnut Street Theatre—greets me next. The sculptural facade, looped and scrolled into the cornice over pedimented doors, hearkens back to the building's origins. A muscled Dionysus lounges suggestively overhead, raising a goblet in honor of the merriment of theater.

Switching the white cookie bag to my teeth, I free a hand to drag the door open and set the bell overhead jangling.

"What are you, Kelsey—some kind of Scottish terrier?"

Lisa's nasal voice pierces the spring warmth, followed by Lisa herself reaching to take the bag from my teeth.

"What time is it? Are they here yet?" I retrieve the bag from Lisa and set the cookies and my coffee on the burnished mahogany of the front counter.

"It's only like 2:30." Lisa scrunches her eyes and juts a chin toward my arm. "Don't you look at that fancy thing on your wrist?"

She says "that fancy thing" like she's seventy years old, though she's closer to forty, even if life has aged her unmercifully. Jagged, blunt-cut brown hair hangs in a lank frame around her deep-set eyes and mouth, and today's yellow scarf only accentuates her sallow skin. She looks as though last night went late.

"I was—the coffee—" I shake my head. Arguing with Lisa is pointless. Besides, she's on a punctuality streak, and as my only employee, I don't want to ruffle her feathers.

Instead, I shred open the bag, remove the waxed-paper-separated cookies, then unlatch the glass case on the counter and layer them like cottage-roof tiles along the top shelf, ready for a swarm of hungry after-school teenagers.

Lisa retreats to whatever task she was doing, or avoiding, in the back room behind the counter.

Despite the ticking clock of catastrophe, I take a moment for a mouthful of chocolatey cookie and a sip of Peruvian Blend. I lean against the counter and allow myself the luxury of scanning the bookshop, bathed in the honeyed afternoon sunlight spilling through stained glass windows set high in the wall to my right, above the murals of famous authors. Dust motes dance in sunbeams to the soft strains of Vivaldi, tiny Tinkerbells darting through Neverland.

Yes, no matter what, I'm going to savor this moment in my happy place, grateful for this shop. It's everything I love, stacked and bundled and shelved into one cavernous and glorious space with a hundred mysterious corners. For a girl whose genealogical tree holds nothing but blanks, the shop is home and family and life.

It's been more than sixty years since Gran combined her

love of theater with her love of books and purchased the doomed building to make it her own bookish paradise.

Subtle hints of its former use as a community theater are obvious to those who know the city's history or stop near the entrance to read the captions under the sepia-toned photos. The multiple levels of the shop once served as a stage at the rear of the building, balcony seats running above my head, and backstage rooms with lightbulb-rimmed makeup mirrors and stuffed costume racks instead of bookshelves marked ART HISTORY and INTERNATIONAL PHILOSOPHY.

And it is the books, not the theater, which I adore. From the fresh-ink smell of glossy new releases to the dusty mildew of used leather hardbacks waiting for someone to love them back to life, nostalgia and happiness waft from every book. I never fail to press the pads of my fingers into the sharp corners of recent arrivals or skim my palms over the velvety softness of used volumes with their frayed cloth covers and gilt-embossed titles that cross my desk.

A bookshop holds a thousand portals to other worlds between the pages... worlds of love and longing, joy and sadness, of questing and mystery and destiny. The stacks wrap the walls of the building and the days of my life in an embrace that is both consolation and intoxication.

Sixty years of book lovers patronizing the Chestnut Street Book Emporium.

All of it about to be destroyed by my staggering ineptitude.

The cookie turns ashy in my mouth, and I circle the counter to deposit it underneath, beside the marketing book I'll take to my apartment upstairs after closing tonight to pore over for inspiration.

The bell above the door jangles again.

I turn to the melody, expecting my Tuesday-Thursday group which I've joyfully named the "Creative Writers of Tomorrow."

But the new visitor chases the smile back down my throat where the coffee now sits bitter and acidic.

I say nothing, waiting for him to state his business.

As if I don't know.

He looks down his nose—actually *looks down it*—from behind horn-rimmed glasses he must believe make him look intellectual. Behind the glasses, his eyes are greenish gold, the creepy eyes of a cat in the shadows.

"Ms. Willoughby."

I nod with mock respect. "Charles Diamond Blackburn."

I'm rewarded for my sarcasm by the angry crease between those eyes. But a man who insists on the pomposity of using three names deserves to be addressed thus. And what's with "Diamond"? Did his mother burden him with that middle name? Or is it a fabrication, an affectation designed to impress?

I glance at my watch. 2:57. Unsurprisingly, Lisa's time estimate is wildly inaccurate. The digital second-hand matches my heartbeat. I have three minutes to convince Blackburn to retreat. He absolutely cannot be here when the kids arrive.

I circle the counter, extending a hand toward the glass door. "I'm afraid it's not a good time. I have a class to teach—"

"This won't take long."

So, everything about this man irritates me. His hundred-dollar salt-and-pepper haircut and expertly trimmed matching beard, the tiny white triangle peeking out of the breast pocket of his suit jacket.

I straighten my shoulders, twitching against what feels like bugs crawling down my back. "In fact, it will take no time at all since there is nothing new to talk about."

"Oh, but I'm afraid there is. I've received a fascinating bit of information from the City Tax Office."

I tighten my lips, clamping down on the rapid-fire repetition of unpleasant words in my head.

He smiles, a predatory smile, with a row of capped teeth gleaming like ivory headstones.

"I was greatly surprised to hear of this, Ms. Willoughby, but in my recent conversations with those officials with whom I must deal on a day-to-day basis, I was bound to uncover these facts at some eventual point in time."

Loquacious. It's the label under Blackburn's imaginary Polaroid pinned to my mental cork board, a longstanding habit of hunting for the perfect descriptive term for everyone I meet. I debated between *loquacious* and *verbose* but preferred the sound of former.

"I see from your reaction, Ms. Willoughby, this information regarding the tax situation is not unfamiliar to you."

I grab a rusty polishing cloth reeking of Lemon Pledge from the front counter and crush it into the mahogany as though I'm Lady Macbeth trying to erase guilt. The cloth snags in a scratch along the lip.

"I don't need your help in running my business." I yank the threads from the wood's grip and trace a finger along the fissure. Is the crack growing? Will it spread across the surface like some kind of evil wizard's curse, break the whole counter into fragments?

Blackburn chuckles, the sound as ridiculous as a cartoon villain, while showing all those capped teeth. "Business advice is not the offer I'm making, as you well know."

Yes, I know.

I toss the rag to the counter and face the sooty gray of Blackburn's pinstripes, like a prisoner before a firing squad.

"I've made a promise, Blackburn."

I'm not going to let that sweet woman down. Not after all Gran's done for me, and especially not now. Something like ice hardens the core of my spine.

Gran's entrusted me with her legacy, like someone handing off an injured bird she's been cradling in her palms, asking me to care for it, to nurse it back to life.

If only I knew how.

He chuckles, the sound humorless and condescending. "You're quite young, Ms. Willoughby. If Elizabeth were here—"

"Don't speak of her like you know her. She would never sell."

Lisa emerges from the back office and sidles up beside me, hands fluttering at the black-and-yellow scarf at her throat, which suddenly seems oddly reminiscent of police tape.

"Oh, Mr. Blackburn, I didn't realize you'd stopped by. What a pleasure." Three fingers reach to sweep hair behind one ear.

I suck in a breath through gritted teeth. "I've got this, Lisa."

Lisa runs her fingers over the glass case. "Would you like a cookie? They're fresh baked, and I'll bet you could use a pick-me-up."

"No, thank you, my dear." Blackburn pats his suit jacket buttons. "Watching my figure."

Lisa laughs, a little trill which I have only heard in this context. "Oh, I don't think you need to worry about that."

I step between them and look Blackburn squarely in his cat eyes, one definite perk of my above-average height. "Okay, then, if there's nothing else—"

"Ms. Johnson at the tax office has graciously and informatively given me to know that significant time has already elapsed since your last notification."

The bell clangs again, and a stream of students tumbles into the shop, shoving and laughing.

I pinch his elbow, slide him to the door. "Thank you for your visit, Charles Diamond Blackburn, and for the very many words which you have formulated, assembled, and delivered to kindly and graciously inform me of all the information to which I was already privy. But as you can see, I am quite busy."

I hustle him through the still-open door onto the sidewalk. There's no way I'm letting him speak another word where the students will hear. I've worked too hard to build the fragile trust necessary for them to open up creatively, and if they knew the truth, they'd be gone. Not to mention how much I need the small stipend the school pays for the program.

Blackburn sucks in a sharp breath and raises his tweezed eyebrows at the insult—that of being pushed outside. I doubt he's registered my attempt to mock his delivery. He plants his feet on the concrete.

"Ms. Willoughby, perhaps you should spend less time with books and children and more time focused on your crisis. I'm giving you one last chance at this opportunity. I'm afraid you will soon regret your reticence to make the best of your untenable situation. There are things you do not know—"

"Nothing you could say would—"

"Ms. Willoughby—*Kelsey*—there is nothing sacred about this place. And there are worse things than selling."

Is that some kind of veiled threat?

I fold my arms and stare him down. "Not for me there aren't."

"Ignoring the truth will not make it go away, my dear."

"Perhaps. But will ignoring *you* make you go away?"

I don't wait for an answer. And barely resist the urge for a sarcastic flip of my long hair in his direction. Gran would be horrified at my "cheekiness," but there seems no other way to deal with the man.

The bluster is a fake, though. The scaffolding devouring the row of Chestnut Street stores, mere shadows of their glory days, scream that he's probably right—I'd do better to spend my time on practical efforts than dreamy thoughts of books and beauty and springtime.

Even though the wannabe writer inside me whispers that fighting the Big Bad Hotel Developer is a played-out story line.

Deep breath, Kelsey.
Tell that voice to crawl back into the shadows.

TWO

My assumption is that the story of any one of us is in some measure the story of us all.

~ Frederick Buechner

I ignore Blackburn's retreating figure, paste on a cheery smile for my seven Creative Writers of Tomorrow, and reenter the bookshop to find them waiting.

"Ready for some fun?"

Several of them roll their eyes at my standard greeting.

But I'll never stop reminding them that our time should be enjoyable. More than anything, I want to infuse a sense of playfulness into their writing, obliterate the pressure of perfection.

I wish someone had done the same for me.

So, for today, I'll shove down thoughts of Charles Diamond Blackburn and his threats, give my full attention to these talented students until later, when I can dive back down the rabbit hole.

I grab my coffee and send them off toward my proudest achievement—the entrance to the Children's Section that once made local news for its creativity.

When they're out of earshot, I turn to Lisa.

"I don't want the kids knowing any of—that." I wave a vague hand in the direction of Blackburn's exit.

Lisa frowns. "They're going to know it soon enough. Unless you find a way—"

"I'm aware."

"Well, I don't know how you expect to turn this thing around, when you won't even carry the books people want."

I sip my coffee to stifle my frustration with her frequent unhelpful suggestions. "I think I keep a pretty good selection here."

"Yeah? I know you turned down that big display the publisher wanted to pay for. That bestseller everyone's talking about—*The Starlight Folio*. I still don't understand why you won't—"

"I don't want that book in here, Lisa. I've told you."

"Yeah, but it's selling like crazy! It's totally nuts to refuse to carry it. I know you're kind of a literature snob, but still, it doesn't make sense—"

"I said I don't want to sell that stupid book, Lisa!"

The petulant pitch and volume of my voice is followed a fraction later by the door's bell-jangle.

"What stupid book?"

Austin pushes into the store, polished and perfect in a platinum-gray linen suit, holding two Starbucks cups and raising an eyebrow.

I feel myself color at the childish outburst. "Never mind. What are you doing here?"

He crosses and pecks my cheek with a quick kiss. "Nice to see you, too."

He's cute, just like my former college roommate, Amanda, promised when she set us up. *A good match*, she said. A little taller than me, his blond and blue-eyed features contrast with my darker coloring.

"Sorry." I accept the proffered coffee cup. "Just wasn't expecting you. I have my workshop today..."

"Workshop?"

I sigh. How many times have I told him about my Tuesday and Thursday commitment? True, we've only been sort-of dating for about a month, but he's started calling me his girlfriend, and that seems like a step that should come with an attention to detail.

I glance toward the mysterious entrance to the Children's Section. "My creative writing students. I need to get back to them. What is this?"

"Uh, it's coffee, obviously."

"I mean, why didn't you check with me first? I've already gotten coffee this afternoon."

"If you're talking about that ratty diner coffee—"

"The Sunny Side Up Diner is not ratty, Austin. And AnaMaria makes wonderful coffee."

He shrugs. "Whatever. But I carried these cups five blocks because there's no decent coffee shop anywhere near here."

I sigh again, set down my original coffee, and take a swallow of Austin's. It's lukewarm after its five-block journey. "I prefer to buy local, Austin. It's important to support the neighborhood."

Lisa's not-so-subtle derisive snort turns us both in her direction.

She shrugs. "Just sayin.' Supporting the neighborhood seems like a lost cause."

"Well, AnaMaria has agreed to supply the coffee for our next big event—Free Coffee Friday!" My voice rises into sales-pitch mode at the end, and I glance between the two. "Free coffee with any purchase, every Friday!"

"I don't think free coffee's going to save the day, Kelsey." Lisa eyes Austin as if he is a co-conspirator in her negativity. "Blackburn was here again," she says to him.

"Kelsey, when are you going to admit the inevitable?" Austin tastes his coffee and grimaces at the temperature, which somehow feels like my fault. He waves a hand at my colorful craft table displays. "Even if you manage to keep this place afloat with your free coffee and your little social media posts and your local yarn-weavers and pottery-makers selling their junk during all the construction, that hotel is going to dwarf your shop and put you out of business for good."

I set the cup on the counter with a *thump*. Coffee sloshes through the lid's tiny opening. I flick a droplet off the counter.

Austin has spelled out my biggest fear, as though I'm oblivious. Like that annoying *beep beep* of a near-empty gas gauge when you've already been watching the fuel level drop for miles.

"Besides," Austin adds, "you know you need the money for your grandmother's care."

"She's not my—" I bite off the correction. We haven't shared our histories yet. "You can't be sure of all that, Austin. Maybe the White Orchard Hotel will bring in a stream of new customers once it's finished."

But I'm grasping, and I know it. If I refuse to sell, the luxury hotel Blackburn has been hired to develop will end at the east wall of my bookshop, but its clientele will spend their time on the hotel's opposite side, in the adjoining Convention Center. Not browsing neighborhood bookshops.

"Besides, what good is money to pay for Gran's care if I have to sell the shop to get it? That would kill her."

Austin huffs, a patient and paternal sound of frustration, and rakes a hand through his close-cropped blond hair. "So then, take my advice—business advice from someone who's done pretty well, I remind you—and turn this place into an upscale coffee shop and bakery with a bookstore *theme*. You can make it exclusive and high end, advertise to those wealthy hotel guests who won't drink diner coffee."

I roll my shoulders, no more interested in his idea than the first time he launched it at me. I've seen the kind of place he's advocating—all black and white fixtures with pretentious menus styled on chalkboards, espresso machines whirring, glass displays loaded with overpriced cake pops, fake-vintage kegs of kombucha on tap, all lit by trendy bare lightbulbs hanging from an industrial ceiling. Call me a throwback, but *no thanks*.

I'm suddenly angry, from both the interaction with Blackburn and this conversation.

"Nobody reads anymore, Kelsey. You can't just be a dreamer. You need to be sensible."

Imagine what he'd say if he knew how much *more* I dream about.

"You've gotta sell them what they want." He waves a hand at the shop's inventory. "Keep the books as decoration if they're important to you."

Decoration? Important to me? Yes, only years and years spent with Gran, her introducing me to exciting debut authors, letting me choose my next blank journal from the flowery new arrivals, leaving me bent over my homework with my back against the stacks while she waited on customers...

"I do have other ideas for improvements, Austin. Some new displays—"

"Kels, if financial success depended on your papier-mâché abilities, you'd be golden. But that's not how it works."

Lisa grunts. "That's what I keep telling her. She needs to focus on what's hot. Like that *Starlight Folio*—"

I fling a look like sharp steel in Lisa's direction.

The woman holds up both hands and shakes her head.

"Austin, I need to get to my students. We're still on for tomorrow?"

He sighs dramatically, as if I've foiled his grand plan to

sweep me off my feet with tepid coffee. "I'm only trying to look out for you, Kelsey. You have to live your own life or this place is going to kill *you*." He nods a goodbye in Lisa's direction, then kisses my cheek again. "See you tomorrow."

In under thirty minutes, I've successfully ignored advice from two men who think they know best. I should be congratulating myself. But perhaps my resistance to their suggestions is only stubborn pride since I still feel the word ***FAILURE***, in large font, typed across my mind.

Yes, I should get back there to the students. But all I want to do is run.

I spin away from the jangling door to Lisa, who hands me a stack of today's mail.

"I don't care how good-looking that guy is," she says, "I don't know why you let him treat you like that—so condescending. You deserve better."

I set aside my annoyance at Lisa's protective comment about Austin. She's loyal, which I appreciate. But men treating Lisa badly is a repeating motif. Maybe that's what makes her an expert.

"Thanks, Lisa. And I'm sorry for getting mad earlier—about—the book." I can't bring myself to say the title.

Lisa shrugs. "Something's gotta pay those." She points at the mail in my hand.

Bills, unpaid bills, overdue bills. And I haven't received yesterday's invoice from the plumber yet, an unavoidable expense to fix the leaking toilet in the men's room.

I shove the envelopes into a folder under the counter, one bulging with others of its kind.

Just let me escape to the students. At least with them I feel useful. And I need to be certain they finish their pieces by the end of the year if the program is to continue.

My dark thoughts are interrupted by the old-fashioned ring of the vintage telephone behind the counter.

Lisa grabs up the phone as if she's waiting for a call, so I head back toward the kids.

"Chestnut Street Book Emporium… Yeah, she's right here." She covers the receiver and stage-whispers. "It's the nursing home. She says it's urgent."

I stutter-step a moment and hesitate, my hand dropping to my side. Gran's-health kind of urgent? Or financial-department urgent? I've been avoiding their calls for a week. But I can't take the chance. I circle back, clutch the dinged black handle in one hand, and unravel the kinked cord with the other.

"This is Kelsey. Is everything okay?"

"Hi, Kelsey. This is Jenny at the front desk. The nurses asked me to call. She's not having a great day. Lots of confusion, but she's asking for you."

I glance at Lisa, cover the phone. "Can you watch the students? Close up?"

Lisa shrugs and nods.

"Thanks, Jenny. I'll be right over."

"Great. Oh, and Kelsey? Megan in billing asked me to have you stop in her office when you arrive."

I close my eyes and drop my chin to my chest. "Okay, thanks, Jenny."

An impossible see-saw. That's what I'm managing. With Gran's well-being on one end and the shop on the other. Every time I shift attention to one, the other threatens to fly off into oblivion.

I wish I could take care of Gran myself, but my second-floor studio apartment above makes that impossible, among other reasons.

I jam the old phone into its cradle, severing the connection in that satisfying, visceral way a touchscreen button can't provide.

I haven't told Gran about Blackburn, about the hotel, about the gradual demise of Chestnut Street. Truly, the idea sickens me. And I fear Gran won't survive the news.

But the little money trickling in can only flow one direction—to the nursing home or to the shop. Impossible choice.

And even if I sacrifice the shop—simultaneously losing my job and apartment—eventually Gran will be gone, too.

The woman who raised me, my only family.

I reach for my wallet, phone, and jacket. The spring afternoon will give way to a chilly evening.

"See you Thursday, then?" Lisa waggles her eyebrows at me.

"Huh? Oh, yeah. Okay." Wednesdays are supposedly my day off, and Lisa's always giving me a hard time about showing up in the shop, unable to stay away.

I grab my keys off the hook near the door and head outside. Will I be able to calm Gran's confusion today? It's never easy.

Just the other day Austin made a joke when he nearly stepped in front of an oncoming taxi. "Nobody lives forever." We laughed, albeit a little nervously. But the cliché isn't a harmless one. Or rather, it feels harmless enough—until it doesn't. Like a grinning circus clown you've been watching juggle his bowling pins, until his painted smile and dead eyes suddenly shift your direction, chasing a chill down your spine.

Nobody lives forever.

THREE

The poet's job is not to tell you what happened, but what happens: not what did take place, but the kind of thing that always does take place.

~ Northrop Frye

"Nonsense. That nurse is as big a storyteller as you are, Kelsey."

I arrange the lumpy pillows behind Gran's head on the elevated bed. "So, you didn't insist on a visit to Mr. Perez in 107? Tell him you'd fire him if he didn't learn his lines by Thursday?"

Gran huffs. "That old fart? He couldn't hold onto a line if it were tied to a fishing pole."

I laugh, then drag the scratched wooden chair with its split-open vinyl the color of old pennies closer to the hospital bed, wincing at the *screech* of chair legs against speckled tile.

The incident earlier, prompting the facility's call to the

bookshop, seems to have resolved itself. Gran is calm and lucid, beautiful as always in her favorite shirt—white with red hearts washed out to pale pink.

Maybe we can even discuss the elephant in the room—the elephant with the three pompous names.

I glance at the clock, then cross the room to shut the door against the mind-numbing and unceasing *ding-ding-ding* from the nurses' desk. Only twenty minutes until the five o'clock reprieve, when the billing manager leaves and I'm in the clear.

After signing in at the front desk of AdvantaCare Skilled Nursing, I managed to ninja-sneak past the offices without alerting Megan, the billing manager, to my presence. Now if I can stay under the radar for twenty minutes, I might escape without more questions.

I return to sit in the vinyl chair. I'll need to ease into conversation about the bookshop's crisis. "So, how has your day been, then?"

"Well, you don't see a sheet pulled over my face, do you?"

Gran's berry-blue eyes are sparking, intensified by her short white hair still worn in the springy curls she boasted thirty years ago. We look nothing alike. Her corkscrew lamb's-wool contrasts with my straight hair the color of espresso hanging nearly to my waist. She's petite compared to my above-average height, fair-skinned beside my olive complexion that tans to bronze. No doubt anyone who meets us wonders about the generation between us that turned my appearance in a different direction.

I've often wondered about those in-between people myself.

"No sheet over you, nope. Looks like you're still giving the nurses a hard time."

"Oh, they love it. Spices up their boring day."

"Right."

AdvantaCare is a mixed bag. Like so many of its kind across the country, the facility is as aged and run-down as its residents. Graying floral wallpaper behind Gran's bed defies the wall in peeled strips, the wooden slats on the window blinds bow like a set of bleached rib bones, the bedsprings sag and whine. Everything seems to be headed downward here, as though the elemental pull of gravity leaves every person and object struggling to remain above earth.

But I keep a close watch on the staff's care for her, and they are attentive and mostly kind. I'm thankful they carry the terrifying responsibility of her well-being, which I can't even consider.

Still too cowardly to bring up the bookshop, I stall by starting the playlist I've created for her, then set my phone on the table beside a Mason jar of daisies as the folksy sound of Simon and Garfunkel beats back the TV news blaring from the next room.

"Guess it's time to replace these flowers." I nod at the daisies. Still-bright lemon eyes but petals drooping like wet paper.

I've tried to lighten the decay by surrounding Gran with familiar items. A couple of warm lamps so the fluorescents can remain off, a collection of black-framed photos on the bedside table, Gran's favorite pink blanket nestled at the foot of the bed, and a few cherished watercolors painted by old friends propped around the room.

Gran stares at the daisies, as if trying to process my comment.

"Gran? You with me?" I take her warm hand in my own chilly fingers, which grew cold during the thirty-minute drive to AdvantaCare.

Gran returns her gaze to me, but her smile has gone a bit vacant. Just that quick.

I lean in and rub her hand, as if she needs the warmth. Her skin is gossamer-soft, and I trace the blue-green veins that thread through tawny age spots like the patterns of a butterfly wing. She still insists on the huge garnet ring on one hand and green topaz on the other, worn on her thumb and middle finger now, the only digits still able to keep the rings from slipping off, and those only because of swollen, arthritic knuckles.

"Tell me one of your stories, Kelsey. One of your magical stories."

"Oh, Gran. It's been a long time since I made up stories for you."

"What?" She sinks her head into the pillows. "No, it has not! Remember the story about the purple polka-dot tiger?"

"I remember."

Gran's eyes flutter and droop. "That one came true, you know. I never wanted to tell you, but I saw that polka-dot tiger in the city zoo once."

"Did you now?"

It has been like this always with Gran, long before the passing years began to dull reality. Me telling stories, but Gran telling them right back, bigger and more fanciful, crazier, sillier. She is an actress and a poet and an aging hippie, never content to see the world through pragmatic eyes. She had three books of poetry published, back when such a thing was possible, but of course they earned her very little money and even less fame, though a great deal of respect among her literary friends.

"Stories have power, you know, Kelsey. But perhaps you just need some inspiration. That's what the garden is for."

I blink and tilt my head. "The garden here? At Advanta-Care?" Last month, I wandered the concrete paths between the few flower beds out back when nothing but the winter's browned stalks of sedum and a few blackened geraniums remained. I can't imagine the scraggly beds would be much inspiration, even in full bloom.

"Or do you mean the roof?" In the summer, I keep a few pots of petunias and marigolds on the Book Emporium's roof beside a rickety lawn chair. A sad attempt to indulge my love of flowers, but all I have time for. The effort can hardly be called a *garden*.

Behind me, the wall unit under the window puffs out an initial stale breath and then blows hot and steady on my back.

Gran lifts her head but doesn't answer, distracted by the rolling creak of wheels in the hall.

"That'll be your dinner, right, Gran? What's on the menu tonight?"

"Ha! Your guess is as good as mine."

It's a running joke, if a sad one—the inability to identify at least one thing on each meal tray. I have complained numerous times, with varying degrees of outrage, to no avail. The kitchen staff is apparently overworked and underpaid and not especially worried about offending the refined palates of their guests.

"Don't worry. I've brought you something extra."

Gran's lips quirk sideways. "Good girl."

The tray of food bears the typical fare and smells like old metal cans. I cut the mystery meat, arrange shrunken green peas within reach, smash cold butter into lukewarm beige potatoes, then sit again while Gran eats, trying to find the words I need to say.

She grimaces at the first taste of meat but keeps going. "When is that book of yours going to be published?" she asks between mouthfuls.

I try to smile. "I'm afraid I don't have a book being published, Gran."

"Of course you do. That one about the shop."

The title and cover of that stupid bestselling book Lisa's been so eager to carry flashes across my brain, despite my best efforts—its premise so similar to a story I wrote years ago. A novel trashed by my critique group and shoved in a drawer. I have no intention of repeating that torture.

"Nope, I'm afraid I wasn't quite ready for publication. Maybe someday." I force out the hollow words with a smile.

Gran pauses, forkful of peas halfway to her mouth. "I

know it's very hard, but no one can stop you from telling a story, Kelsey. Except yourself."

It seems the woman will never cease to be my creative mentor.

I choose not to argue about all the other things that can stop me—duty and guilt, lack of talent and time, a vulnerability that is hard to define.

"Well, that's true, I suppose. But right now, I'm focusing on the shop."

"Yes, how is the shop? People will be stocking up for summer reading soon, eh?"

Here we go.

I bite my lip. Gran would rather sink into the earth, like everything else at AdvantaCare, than see the shop sold. But the money from the sale of her house where I grew up is nearly gone, and facilities like this one are outrageously expensive.

"Sure. But they may be stocking up on Amazon, you know. Or loading their devices with ebooks."

"Phht." Gran's disdain for digital reading is legendary. She shoves away the chipped stoneware plate, only half-empty.

"It's tough making a bookstore profitable these days, Gran. Lots of online competition. And Chestnut Street's not the same as it was back in the day."

It's the closest I've come to a confession, and I wait, holding my breath, for the reaction.

"We had Faulkner there for a signing once, you know. Right before he died."

Gran is drifting again.

"Yes. I know."

Gran reaches for my hand, wraps ropy fingers around it. "But you still have the garden, Kelsey-girl. That's your special gift. You'll always have that."

This again.

"What garden, Gran?"

Gran's eyes flick to mine, confused. "Beside the shop, of course. You know."

The vacant lot between the Rhythm & Wonder Music Shop and the Book Emporium?

That same electricity I felt earlier, at the iron gate, shoots across my skin. A feeling somewhere between an omen and a promise.

The lot has been walled-off my entire life. I've nearly forgotten it's technically part of the bookshop's property. Too bad it's on the wrong side of the shop, or we could sell it to Charles Diamond Blackburn and perhaps turn our financial situation around.

"You're taking care of it, though." Gran's grip tightens. "Of course, you are."

"Is—is it something we could sell, Gran?"

Would someone be willing to risk tucking another store into Chestnut Street?

"Sell?" Gran releases my hand and straightens in her bed, then begins to swing her legs over the side.

"Hold on, where are you going? Let me get your wheelchair."

"I'm going to the shop! I need to check on things—I—I don't know what you're doing over there!"

"No, it's okay. It's okay, Gran. Everything is fine." I try to urge her back into bed, hand on her shoulder, another on her arm.

"Let go of me! I need to get to work!"

A passing nurse, or perhaps an aide, leans into the room. "Everything alright in here?"

"No!" Gran shouts toward the doorway. "This nurse here won't let me leave, and I am late for work!"

I meet the woman's eyes, telegraphing a plea for help.

Together, we calm her back into the bed, clear away the dinner tray, pull the fuzzy pink blanket up to her chest.

The aide narrows her eyes at me. "She shouldn't be agitated. We can't have her wandering."

I respond with a nod. I've heard the instructions a million times.

We are left alone. Her eyes are flickering now, sleep coming on fast, as it often does after an outburst of confusion.

I keep my hand on Gran's arm, resisting the urge to hold so tight I'll hurt her, instead gripping the bed frame with my other hand.

Once, when I was about six, Gran surprised me by purchasing a panda-head balloon at the city zoo. Minutes later, I accidentally released my hold on the string. In an instant, the balloon was too far out of reach. Standing there, watching the black and white sphere of helium spiral into the sky where it could never, *never*, be retrieved, a feeling of such loss—irreversible, unfixable—swelled in my chest until I feared I might suffocate. It was a loss of innocence, in a way. My first understanding of grief, of control as a mere illusion. Oddly, I pretended not to be devastated, not wanting Gran to spend money on a replacement. But I've never forgotten that sense of powerlessness as the balloon drifted away.

Now, today, holding the old woman's arm and watching her watery eyes roam the room, the weight of impending loss again presses the air from my lungs. If I could hold more tightly, like a balloon on a string, perhaps I could keep Gran by the strength of my will. But like my six-year-old self, I smile and tamp down the grief, not wanting Gran to see the way it steals my breath.

"Ready to sleep for a bit, Gran?"

She nods, eyelids weighted and lips parted. "Just for a bit."

The outbursts are infrequent and unpredictable. I never know what will set Gran's mind into a spin. But it's always been impossible to talk of selling the bookshop. And now it seems I can add the sale of the empty lot—Gran's "garden"—to my list of taboo subjects.

But with our financial situation worsening, the choice

might soon be taken from my hands. Gran's shop is under attack from every direction, from the unrelenting tax office with its ticking clock of due dates to the betrayal of online shopping. And with Blackburn's hotel project creeping down Chestnut Street like a hungry beast, devouring one local shop after another in its maw, foot traffic is dwindling to nearly nothing. I've already missed a school loan payment when there wasn't enough left after writing Lisa's last paycheck.

And despite my best effort, I cannot help but look further down the road, to a future with no bookshop, no home, no job, and eventually, no Gran.

That hollowed-out feeling. Balloon bobbing against a cruel blue sky. Powerless to change anything.

I straighten the blanket around Gran's shoulders, turn out the lamp beside the bed, and tiptoe from the room.

I refuse to let Gran down.

There must be a way to turn it all around.

FOUR

These so-called children's stories are aware of what many adults have forgotten—that the daily, time-bound world of provable fact is the secondary world,
the shadow world, and it is story, painting, song which give us our glimpses of reality.

~ Madeleine L'Engle

I return to the Book Emporium as the daylight is ending. Across the street, a last exhale of sunlight leaks through the buildings, evaporating as it crosses my path. I hesitate at the front door, my attention caught by the sun's final effort to glint on the few visible fragments of the lot's vine-choked gate.

What was it Gran said?

You still have the garden. That's your special gift.

Did Gran grow vegetables in there once upon a time?

I jog the twenty or so steps to the gate and try to peer through, to the interior.

Then blink, squint.

Something beyond the overgrown weeds inside the gate

seems to shimmer. A wink that flashes once, twice. Is that a trick of the dying sunlight?

That curious feeling washes up again from my toes, the tingle of something impossible.

I wrap a hand around the metal gate and pull. Nothing.

But no, the gate is meant to open inward, it seems. I try the latch, but it is locked. The keyhole is large, old-fashioned, and a memory floats behind my eyes of a big iron key hanging on a peg.

There, again. A glint, just beyond the edge of my vision.

An abandoned bicycle, reflecting the sun?

I lean my forehead against the cold iron, peering through the greenery. With my body blocking the little remaining sunlight, there is no chance of a reflection from some abandoned metallic object.

But then, the light is gone now, isn't it?

Once more, I shift my field of vision to the side. And once more, I sense the faint incandescence at the periphery.

Again, the delightful shiver.

Not just excitement. Something else, like the deliciousness of waking up on Christmas morning. Or the breathless suspension of waiting past a lightning flare for the inevitable crack of thunder.

I laugh at myself. A twinkle that is only visible when you aren't looking at it? It's an invitation as clear as any fictional call to an adventurous quest.

"Can't remember the last time I saw that gate open."

I jump and gasp at the sudden voice at my ear.

"Oh, William! You scared me!" I grip the arm of the man behind me.

"Sorry, girl. I thought you heard me walking up."

William Jackson, owner of The Groove—the vinyl records store on the other side of the Chestnut Street Book Emporium—has owned his shop nearly as long as Gran. He's just turned seventy and is technically young enough to be

Gran's son, but they socialized as peers, and he's been like a friendly old uncle to me.

I put a hand to my pounding heart. "No. No—I was just looking through the gate—" I drop off, suddenly shy about sharing my childish excitement over nothing. "Do you know if there's a key somewhere?"

William shrugs. With his short-spiked hair, long ago turned pure white and set in beautiful contrast to his deep-brown skin, he reminds me of an aging musician from a century ago, still spinning his records. "Your Gran would know." His wide smile falters. "Well, she *would've* known, at least."

I nod and return my gaze to the wild jungle beyond the gate. The shadows are deepening, leaving it shrouded. "I wonder what's in there." I can't keep the wistfulness out my voice.

"Nothing I've ever seen." He chuckles. "But it kinda reminds a body of that mysterious secret garden, doesn't it?"

I turn on him sharply. "What garden?"

"Come on, girl. You're the one with all the books, the one who loves a good story. That one about the orphan and her cousin. *The Secret Garden.* Made it into a movie a bunch of times if I'm not mistaken. My Sara loves that movie."

The orphan girl, and her secret garden. Once more, I feel it, the longing.

What is this sense we sometimes get in our skin, in our blood? The invisible pull—of grief-tinged joy, or some bright sadness haloed by mystery? I inhale deeply, chest rising in response, and reach fingers through the bars.

William does not know, cannot know, how intrigued I have always been by invitations into secret places.

I have glimpsed these ordinary-looking places, whispering of portals, many times in my life. And always, always felt that strange lightness mixed with dread, the delight of longing for something just out of reach. The desire to be *there,* not *here,* without knowing whether this other place even exists. Stirred by unnamed emotions that seem to hint at unknown, yet important, truths.

"How is Elizabeth these days?" William's voice is tinged with regret. "Sara and I need to make a visit."

I shake my head, more to clear the mental cotton-candy than in response to William. "She—she has good days and bad. But I know she'd love to see you both. Well, especially, Sara," I add with a wink. William's wife is one of those women who brings life into every room she enters.

"Oh, you don't have to tell me she's the better half." William laughs. "Because she's been telling me herself, for fifty years!"

I grin and wrap my jacket against the evening wind, picking up and biting.

William glances toward the Book Emporium. "You holding strong with Blackburn?"

I nod. "That hotel has to end somewhere."

He shrugs. "And The Groove is as good a place as any."

William told me weeks ago he'd decided to retire, to sell the shop, let it be razed for Blackburn's White Orchard Hotel, and start spending winters in Florida. I can't blame him, but it doesn't mean I have to join him.

"Listen, Kelsey, you let me know if you need me to chain myself to the bookshop or anything, to stop the bulldozers. You know I will."

I laugh. "I do know. I remember your Vietnam protest stories. Between AnaMaria willing to spit in his coffee and you chaining yourself up, seems like I can't lose." I turn my back into the wind, and my hair blows across my face.

"You go on up, now, girl. It's getting cold." He gives me a little side-hug.

I lean my head against his shoulder, a brief point of contact, then nod. "'Night, William."

I force myself to continue to the bookshop without gaping into the empty lot.

Upstairs, I grab a protein bar, change into some paint-spattered yoga pants and a college hoodie, and then drift to one of my crowded bookshelves, my hand finding the slim volume without hesitation.

Francis Hodgson Burnett wrote *The Secret Garden* in 1910, the beautifully redemptive story of orphaned but selfish Mary Lennox who comes to live with her stern, disfigured uncle and his invalid son. Only the garden, hidden for years, left to grow wild but still full of beauty, restores them all.

I glide my hand over the hardcover edition with its gorgeous illustrations, a gift from Gran on my seventh birthday.

And I know what I'll find tucked into the front cover of the book.

I take the book and my pathetic dinner, switch on a floor lamp, and settle into the well-worn leather couch that forms the back of my "living room" and divides the studio apartment from the area where my bed and dresser form the bedroom.

The light does little to beat back the lengthening gloom. With windows along only two sides, overlooking Chestnut Street and peering across the roof of The Groove, my apartment is dim until noon and pulls in only a bit of the city lights after sunset. The deep wood of my bookshelves, exposed brick wall, and hardwood floors absorb most of the light, but I love the space, knick-knacked with faux souvenirs from trips I haven't yet taken and antique furniture I've hunted over the years.

Austin's first impression of the apartment replays in my mind. "It's like you drilled a hole in the bookshop's ceiling and let all the same stuff evaporate into the upstairs."

Well, okay. So what?

In the cozy saucer of yellow lamplight, I unwrap the protein bar, bite off a third, then lay it aside and nudge open the book, resolutely setting aside the folded pages of wide-ruled paper, ripped from a spiral notebook, that are tucked into the front cover.

I skim to Mary's first glimpse of the garden, soaking in the passage of description.

It was the sweetest, most mysterious-looking place any one could imagine. The high walls which shut it in were covered with the leafless stems of climbing roses, which were so thick that they were matted together...

Mary had thought it must be different from other gardens which had not been left all by themselves so long; and indeed it was different from any other place she had ever seen in her life.

"How still it is" she whispered. "How still."

But it was not stillness that gave me that strange feeling downstairs at the iron gate. More a sense of consciousness, wakefulness. As if something alive dwelt within all that wild greenness, waiting for me to meet it.

I let myself slip into Mary's story for the few minutes it takes to finish my dinner, then set aside the book and lift the folded notepaper. It's been years. Do I want to revive any of this?

I unfold the stack of sheets—perhaps ten of them—and read the first line scratched clumsily on the first page with a half-dry fountain pen. I remember that instrument, the feel of it in my ten-year-old hand, a gift from Gran from the case of expensive pens on the Book Emporium's front counter. My first sense of being a "serious" writer. How many pages did I fill with that pen?

Once upon a time, there was a young orphan girl, raised by a grandmother who was not her grandmother, who did not know who she was, but was meant to have many adventures in many secret places.

Enough. I crease the pages sharply, shove them back into the book, and toss it to the other end of the couch. As though I can rid myself of the stigma I still feel all these years later.

Ridiculous, with the real-life problems facing me, to be

wondering about mysterious shimmers in an empty city lot and old stories left unwritten.

Once I loosen the reins on my imagination, it's a quick hop to seeing things that aren't there. It's always been this way with me, despite my attempts to tamp down my wandering, irresponsible thoughts and focus on the practical. I can hear Charles Diamond Blackburn in my head. Perhaps I should spend less time with books and children.

I wonder where that gate key is now.

No, enough. I need a different book to read for the evening. I left one under the shop counter this morning, but it still sits there, along with my uneaten cookie. I don't have the energy to go down for it. I replace *The Secret Garden* and skim my fingers over other beloved books, looking for something different. A book nothing like the royal blue hardback Lisa keeps mentioning, with its mocking, starry yellow title.

In the end, Netflix wins the day as I settle back into the couch, disgusted with myself. But forty-nine minutes later, I exit the app before the next episode auto-streams, toss the remote to the floor, and lean my head back into the overstuffed pillow.

I'm tired, cranky, and vaguely depressed.

My phone buzzes with a text from Austin.

Sorry about the cold coffee earlier. Should've walked faster.

Sigh. A pattern is beginning to emerge with this guy. Compliments that feel like disguised insults. Apologies that beg for affirmation and assurance.

I use one thumb to reply. *Don't worry about it—I appreciated the eff—*

No, delete that. Back, back, back.

Good thing I got a hot cup from the diner!

Ha.

I hit send before I can second-guess my snarkiness.

Once upon a time, there was a young orphan girl, raised by a grandmother who was not her grandmother...

The faint sound of music drifts across my consciousness. I glance at the TV—did I leave it on?

No, the music's coming from outside my apartment. A rhythmic syncopation, fingers dancing across a keyboard accompanied by a plucky bass beneath and the *swish-swish* of a brushed drum. I enjoy jazz, but I'm no aficionado, and don't recognize the particular tune.

I relax again, following the wandering melody, reaching out for the sound nearly too delicate to hear.

I glance to the east side of my apartment. Why are there no windows on the side of the building adjoining the empty lot? I've never thought about it. None on that side of the bookshop downstairs, either. There must have been a building there once, sharing a wall with the shop and precluding windows.

What kind of place was it? And why does it no longer exist?

What's in there now?

The music picks up, the tiny crash of cymbal and a more insistent beat, volume sliding upward.

It's coming from the empty lot.

Somehow I know this, without understanding how I know.

My feet swing from the couch, nearly of their own accord.

It's fully dark now, and if there is activity behind that gate, it's likely drug activity—buying, selling, using. Masking their activities with music?

But my feet are moving toward the steps, down into the darkness of the bookshop. Phone-flashlight turned on, I unlock the front door and slip out into the street.

I smother the light against my thigh and shiver against the cold wind tunneling down Chestnut Street. A dozen steps and I'm at the iron gate. That same prickle of premonition runs down my spine.

In the darkness, the shimmer I witnessed earlier is undeniable. Light twinkling through the stalks and vines. And music, still as faint as it was from my apartment, but spilling through the gate as definitively as the light.

Almost without thought, and certainly without logic, I lift a hand to the gate's latch again, pushing the metal tongue downward, knowing it will be futile.

The latch *thunks* under my touch. The gate inches inward. Just a tiny movement, but enough.

Unlocked.

Unlocked and waiting.

FIVE

How can I search for beauty and truth unless that beauty and truth are already known to me in the depth of my heart? It seems that all of us human beings have deep inner memories of the paradise that we have lost.

~ Henri Nouwen

The gate does not willingly surrender.

I push with one hand, then pocket my phone and use both. A gentle shove before finally I put my shoulder into it, blood pulsing.

The vines resist, backed by weeds so thick they've morphed to shrubby wood.

I advance through the gate by degrees, drawn like a child to the faint scent of the pied-piper tune beyond the bars. Somewhere within lies an answer, though I do not yet know the question.

Half in, half out, I wince as the iron presses my chest. Am I mad to be forcing this?

One final thrust, and I slip through, silk-smooth leaves kissing my face.

Behind me, the gate snaps shut like an iron jaw. I am inside.

Phone-light back on and heart hammering. Will I encounter a group of the unhoused warming their hands beside a bucket fire? Or something more sinister?

I use my free hand to split the river of weeds and branches and plunge into the emerald-black tunnel I've created. The pinprick of light from my phone dances on the underside of leaves like a firefly finding its way home.

The music's volume rises, and the shimmer I saw from the street deepens to a warm luster somewhere beyond. I thumb the flashlight off and tuck the phone away, led by the distant glow. Using both arms to sweep aside the overgrowth, I duck to avoid back-snapping branches and low hanging vines. The weedy tunnel smells of wet loam and new life, like a greenhouse in winter, and I fill my lungs with the wonderfully humid, peaty smell.

And then, at last, I am borne into the edge of a wide and grassy lawn, expansive as a park, yet intimate as an embrace.

A lightheaded vertigo sweeps from my toes to my hairline. I reach to clutch at something, anything, for balance, and wrap trembling fingers around a slim maple branch no thicker than a magician's wand.

"What—what is this?" The words escape through numbed lips, an exhale prompted by a vision so startling I cannot take a new breath.

Where to look first?

A massive tree dominates the center of the space—it must be a live oak, the only evergreen oak species, deep green leaves massed along its heavy limbs despite being only early spring.

Though it does not feel so early now… the air suddenly so much warmer.

A few feet above the earth, the cinnamon-brown trunk of

the oak divides into multiple trunks, each leaning a little this direction or that, spreading outward and lifting generous arms up and over the rest of the open space, a canopy enfolding, a mother protecting her young. Through the patchwork spaces between the leafy boughs filters a peach and cobalt twilight.

But it is the area under the tree that draws my eye.

A multitude of hollow iron spheres hang from cords of various lengths. They are globes, each the size of a melon, with a flicker of ruby-white firelight trapped inside yet escaping around the dark silhouettes of continents, like fire at the earth's core. Beneath these, the globe-lanterns illuminate a table draped with a powder-white linen cloth generous enough to brush the grass. Swags of greenery, heavy with pink teacup roses, festoon the sides of the table. Across the top is laid what looks to be a feast of all the good foods one could imagine.

Other objects crowd around the base of the tree, but it is the *people* who surprise me most.

A crowd of perhaps fifty dressed in period costumes—but what period?—mills around the evening garden party, drinks in hands, talking and laughing in congenial little clusters or sitting at round, cloth-covered tables with centerpieces of cut-glass bowls brimming with floating flowers and candles.

"Unbelievable." Still a whisper, as I would not break the spell for anything.

I rub my arms, a frisson of pleasure raising the flesh, then spin slowly in place to take it all in.

The fabric of my own clothing catches my eye.

No more yoga pants and hoodie. I run a hand down the butter-soft knit of a dress I've never seen. An ivory background highlights tufted blooms of amethyst-purple wisteria on seafoam vines twining around a flared skirt. On my feet, a pair of shell-pink strappy-heeled sandals. A light breeze plays on my neck, and I put a hand to my hair to find it upswept into a sleek French twist, a few petals tucked above my right ear, where earrings dangle.

The feel of elegant sophistication blends with a sudden swell of childlike innocence, and I am all at once twirling, twirling, watching the great blooms of wisteria fan out in a lavender-and-ivory blur.

Laughing. Tickled by a strange sense of déjà vu.

Lightheaded and weightless, I catch myself before I fall off my heels. I glance behind me, where my leafy tunnel of weeds should be. A black-veined white marble bench, backed by a white magnolia tree, sits ensconced among waist-high terracotta pots that spill over with candy pink bougainvillea which tumble from beneath plumes of astilbe in riotous shades of cranberry and champagne gold. Tucked behind the pots, a torch blazes above the height of the flowers.

A few wobbly steps backward, eyes focused again on the party, I slide downward onto the marble bench, chest expanding and then releasing. All my tension seems to flow to a faraway place.

Under my heels, dove-gray slates fit like puzzle pieces to form a patio of sorts, the cracks filled with meandering moss. The scents of honeysuckle and white jasmine hang in the air, and I can nearly taste their sweetness on my tongue. The sound of water, both a gentle trickle and a splashing, filters from somewhere I cannot see and blends with the hiss and pop of the torch burning beside me.

Why have I only nursed a few sorry pots of humdrum annuals on the bookshop roof these past few years? Since the sale of Gran's house, I've given up my love of gardening. Given up the tangible cultivation of beauty which, once upon a time, fed my soul and brought me life.

I am seized with a powerful desire to plunge my hands into dirt.

No one at this otherworldly garden party has yet seen me. How long can I remain tucked away, hidden and observing? I want to remain unseen, and yet I also long to engage.

Will they ask me to leave? Clearly, I do not belong.

How can this place exist? This garden within the walls of the empty lot is more expansive than it has any right to be. Even the magnificent live oak would be seen from the street.

I watch their interaction, the laughter and light, the camaraderie around what most certainly must be witty and intelligent conversation. Exquisite food and flowing wine, abundant life within the shelter of the tree.

Innocence. The word plays across my thoughts, not as opposed to *corruption* but in contrast with the dash of cold reality that hits us young and steals our childlike wonder, our belief in the extra-ordinary.

Then the music draws me. Beyond the brimming feast, shadows play across three faces gathered around instruments. A black man taps a staccato on drums, taut strings across the wood glow of a tall bass are plucked by a mustachioed man who looks to have Latin roots, and a white woman—heavy set with spiked gray hair and wearing a man's dark suit and skinny tie—pounds a jubilant version of Cole Porter's "Night and Day" on a piano. She wears a smile that could light the night. Beside her, a white man in dark-rimmed glasses grins and nods like a pleased tutor.

This, then, is the music I have been following. And these lanterns, spangled across a dusky twilight, are the light I have glimpsed.

I close my eyes for a moment, my senses so fully awake, so exposed, it is too much to take in, these waves of ethereal scent and kaleidoscope color and joyful melody. A warmth infuses me, a serenity filling empty spaces in my soul and washing away worry.

I return to watching, holding stillness within and observing from the outside but with a connection that feels like a golden thread stretched from my heart to the tree, a connection which includes every person at this impossible party.

Now I see more objects scattered at the base of the tree—

several paint-splashed canvases on easels, a sculpture luminescent in the fire glow of the lanterns. A small table with stacks of something—books and papers, perhaps?

Can there truly be a place of this much unsullied beauty in the world? I am dreaming, I must be, and yet this moment feels closer to realness, if such a thing exists, than any moment of my life. A settled feeling of... of *belonging*... grounds me utterly in the present moment. How can this place, which I have never before seen, feel like my true home, like some forgotten past?

I lift a hand to my cheek and find it wet with tears.

The movement seems to catch the attention of one of the men, who turns his head from his conversation. His partner, a petite woman dressed in a 1930s-style flapper dress, complete with cropped haircut curving to tiny points on her alabaster cheeks, glances toward my bench. The man half-smiles at me, with the air of a friendly question in his eyes and the crease of his forehead. With a nod to the woman, he heads toward me, stopping at one of the scattered round tables to empty a crystal decanter into two wine glasses.

I use both hands to swipe the tears from my face, then pull my spine erect and lift my chin in a smile. Perhaps with the dress and the shoes and the hair I do not look so out of place.

He smiles as he approaches with the wine. The torchlight plays over his face. He is older than me, in his forties, with pale skin and full, dark hair slicked away from a sharp, off-center part. Attractive, though with quite prominent ears. His gray wool suit, white shirt, and dark tie make him look like a banker.

"There you are, Kay," he calls. "What are you doing hiding yourself over here?"

SIX

The poet's eye, in fine frenzy rolling,
Doth glance from heaven to earth, from earth to heaven;
And as imagination bodies forth
The forms of things unknown, the poet's pen
Turns them to shapes and gives to airy nothing
A local habitation and a name.

~ from *A Midsummer Night's Dream* by William Shakespeare

The man who's mistaken me for someone he knows approaches my bench, hands me one of his two wine glasses, then sips the sparkling garnet-and-rubies liquid from his own.

Still sitting, I cradle the wine glass in my palm, the stem cool between my fingers, and try to smile at his misidentification. Should I play along? Nothing makes sense here, so why try to clarify?

I cover my discomfort with a drink, then extend the glass to study it. I am not a connoisseur, but it is the best wine of my life. Have I been missing something this exquisite, or does nothing like it truly exist?

He's still looking down at me with raised eyebrows, the question of why I've been hiding hanging in the air, not rhetorical, it seems.

"I—I wanted to see the party from this distance. So pretty."

Well, that was lame.

He turns to follow my gaze. "The still point of the turning world."

The quiet words wash up against my heart like a tidal swell, settling into the rocky places. I say nothing.

"Sorry." He laughs, a quiet, refined sound that seems suited for drawing rooms and parlors. "Waxing a little philosophical, I suppose." He points to where I sit. "Any room on that bench for an old poet?"

"Of course." I slide over.

He lowers himself to sit beside me, crosses one leg over the other, and leans on a forearm.

Our shoulders brush, and the warmth is comfortable.

"This music is wonderful." I smile in the direction of the jazz trio.

"Isn't it? Her playing improves with every tune."

Across the grass, another man in conversation is eying us. He's closer to my own age, dark hair, beard trimmed close to be nearly stubble, and a wide smile. His muscular shoulders fill out a white shirt, sleeves rolled to his elbows, and a black double-breasted vest gives him a classy-but-casual flair. He holds a small plate in one hand. When he goes back to speaking with two others, he uses the other hand in broad sweeps of expression, as though his topic is a passionate one.

I almost ask my companion if the man's a friend of his, but perhaps I am supposed to know everyone.

"Looks like someone has an admirer."

"What?" I glance sideways. "I—what?"

My bench-mate laughs. "Oh, come, Kay. Don't tell me you can't tell when a man is interested."

I opt for silence. Perhaps the muscled guy is Kay's boyfriend. Or a stalker.

"Have you brought it?" He sips his wine. The question seems casual, yet somehow intimate.

Uh... "Brought...?"

"Your story, silly girl. Is it finished? Is it on the table?"

Okay, this is officially getting weird. My doppelgänger, Kay, is a writer?

"No. Not finished yet." Seems the safest choice.

"Well, what are you waiting for? I hope you're not being shy about it. Everyone else's gifts are pouring in." He lifts his glass in the direction of the tree.

Gifts? Does he mean the artwork and sculpture? The stacks on the table?

"I've been told it isn't... good." I've somehow switched from answering as the mysterious Kay to answering as myself.

"Good? You have a responsibility, Kay, you know that." The tone is chiding, though friendly and even sympathetic.

"It... needs a lot of work. A total rewrite, perhaps."

He waves away my objection.

"What might have been is an abstraction
Remaining a perpetual possibility
Only in a world of speculation."

He quotes the lines like poetry. And he did refer to himself as a poet.

Dramatic. It's probably too soon to define him, but the clothing, the poetry, the intensity of his voice all give me the sense that he'd be comfortable on a stage.

"Something you wrote?" I smile encouragingly.

He shrugs. "Trying it out still. Seeing how it feels in my mouth. It's probably no good."

"I like it." I do like it. It has a familiar pull, like something I've read before.

He bumps my shoulder with his own. "You're always a good audience." He juts a chin toward my so-called admirer. "But perhaps you'd better play audience to someone else. Looks like your fellow is not giving up."

There is no denying that the guy across the grass is looking at me. His face and body remain turned toward his companions, a man and woman, head nodding as if listening, but his eyes are trained on me.

How long has he been watching? Did he see my childish twirling?

At my return glance, his mouth lifts in a half-smile and he holds my gaze for a long moment before turning back to his conversation.

My breath hitches in my throat. I drop my eyes, even though he's no longer looking at me. A flush builds at the base of my throat and travels upward.

"I think I'll stay here. It's peaceful."

"Hmm. Playing it safe in work *and* in love, I see. It's no way to live, Kay. You need to finish your story."

"I'm afraid I have more pressing concerns and can't be wasting time on hobbies." The words spill out, oddly hostile.

His shoulders stiffen and he turns on me. "Hobbies? *Hobbies?*" Disdain drips from his tone, as if I've struck him with a deep insult.

"I—I only meant for me—I don't have the talent to be a professional writer, so anything I write is only—"

"*Professional?*" The same horrified disdain.

I hide a smile by looking the other direction. I feel him shaking his head.

"I thought better of you, my girl."

I've lost my footing in this conversation. Where to go from here?

"I'm sorry, I didn't mean to cause offense. It's just that I need to survive, to take care of normal life, you know?"

I half-expect him to say "*Survive?!*" but he only sighs.

"Yes, there is that. Survival. Striving. It is a losing proposition, is it not? We seek to survive but then—bitter irony—we instead become deadened and hopeless."

Is it true? Am I destined for hopelessness if I continue to focus only on the practical?

He turns on the bench, facing me with an earnestness that seems almost like concern. "You must see that there is also the embracing of more—waking up to truth and beauty and life—while you speak only of death. You are imaginative. And so you must find your true self in that still point, Kay. The still point of the turning world."

"And what is that?"

"Except for the point, the still point,
There would be no dance, and there is only the dance."

More enigmatic poetry, still slightly familiar, but not an answer.

"It's just that there is never enough time."

He shrugs. "And yet it is always the present."

The little group of three, with the bearded guy who keeps glancing my way, is breaking up, and it is the woman who heads our direction. She is not a beauty but wears a pleasant expression. Like the others, she wears period clothing, a curve-hugging black satin dress brushes her ankles. Her short dark hair is styled into a 1930s look, with Marcel waves that curl just above her ears.

My seat mate stands at her approach, perhaps only in gentlemanly custom, but I stand with him.

"I've come to rescue you, my dear." The newcomer smiles on my companion. "I see Tee monopolizing you over here, keeping you in the shadows." She holds out a jeweled hand. "Come, you must join the party and eat something."

I glance at the man beside me.

He shrugs, as if guilty of the charge. "You've caught me, A. You know I can't resist a willing listener."

Tee? And... A?

Ah, these must be letters. No first names at this party,

apparently. Everyone uses only their first initial, it would seem.

A chill runs across my neck.

Not Kay.

K.

As in *Kelsey*.

Am I known here? Truly known?

"I wish you'd use my real name," I blurt. "If you know my true name, that is."

T. laughs. "I'm afraid that's a question you first need to answer for yourself, old girl."

A. is still extending her hand to me, waving her fingers impatiently. "Come, you must add some nibbles to that wine."

I leave behind T. and allow myself to be led past the clusters of conversation toward the feast table itself. Along the way, I run fingers across the blushing tips of golden dahlia petals, touch the rough twigs of dwarf cherry trees. Everything here, including me, is so extraordinarily alive.

The gaze of the man who's been looking my way follows my movement, but I don't make eye contact. One new person at a time is enough.

We reach the magnificent Tree, where streams of water flow in all four directions like rippling sidewalks. Each of the four meandering streams is bordered by white pebbles, as glistening as summer hailstones. I trace the course of the stream at my feet, as it flows through the chattering crowd, under a tiny footbridge near what should be Chestnut Street, then gathers in a wide pool before cascading over an edge to perhaps another pool beyond.

This place is peculiar and crazy and all-wrong. And yet, perfect.

The table is indeed laden with every good thing. Platters of grilled chicken with a pineapple relish, silver tiered stands piled with feta and spinach wrapped in puff pastry, porcelain bowls of salad overflowing with cranberries and tiny orange slices, a mountain of spicy couscous. I breathe in the fragrance of Moroccan curry and leeks, and brush my fingers across the linen, strewn with glossy emerald magnolia leaves.

A. is pushing a small china plate into my hand, pointing out her favorites.

"Thank you," I whisper, slipping a few grapeleaf-wrapped dolmades onto my plate, piling on a mix of multi-colored Greek olives.

"Nothing to it, my dear." A. waves a jeweled hand in the vague direction of the party goers, lamplight glinting from her heavy silver rings set with sapphire and jade stones. "We storytellers must stick together, you know, amongst all these others."

Here it is again, this lovely inclusion, however mistaken, into their midst. Yet the recognition of "storyteller" draws something deep from within me, like a tiny sprout suddenly uncovered, green and alive but so tender, so vulnerable. Emotion clogs my throat and I sip the wine—glorious—to gain control.

"They are not all writers?" I scan the heads of the crowd, some standing and others sitting at the round tables.

"Goodness, no. Far more than storytelling is needed, is it not?"

"Needed... for what?"

"To wake us up!" At this, she snaps her fingers a few inches from my eyes, like a hypnotist bringing his subject back to the present. But if this place is a product of hypnosis, it will apparently take more than A.'s finger-snap to remove me.

"The world is half-asleep, my dear. It will take all the mystery and beauty we can conjure together to make a difference." She shakes her head and breathes deeply, as though ridding herself of a difficult subject. "But I am remiss—where is your lovely E.?" She bites into a canapé, then closes her eyes, head tilted back as if in ecstasy at its flavor.

I bite my lip, scrambling for an answer. "E.?"

"Don't be foolish. The woman who raised you." A. scowls at my apparent daftness.

But her words stun. Could she mean *Elizabeth*? Gran?

You still have the garden. That's your special gift.

I have not thought of Gran's strange words since entering this magical place.

Is it possible Gran has shared this experience?

But that would mean I am not dreaming.

A. pats me on the shoulder. "Not to worry. I would guess T. has *her* in a corner now, deep in a discussion of their poems. But you know me." At this, she winks and leans in, her voice droll. "Give me a good old-fashioned murder over a poem any day."

Murder? A tingle of danger runs across my arms. But she must mean a mystery novel.

"E.—she hasn't been well." I bite my lip at the confession. Will it make sense in this place? I cannot believe they're speaking of Gran, but cannot miss the opportunity, just in case.

"No! Don't say it! Such a kind woman. Taking you in, after all that—well, she is a dear. You tell her that we will brook no argument—she must feel better immediately!"

"Who must feel better?" This from another man helping himself to some of the canapés. He wears a tan tweedy jacket, sports an impressive mustache, and studies me over gold-rimmed glasses.

"Why, K.'s dear E.—you know, the lovely woman to whom you signed one of your first editions. She is unwell." A. lifts an eyebrow in my direction. "F.'s first edition is going to be worth quite a tidy sum one day, you will see."

The glass case of Gran's first editions, unopened for as long as I can remember, flashes across my mind, cloth-bound books in fading brick red or navy-turned-denim. Gilt-lettered, fraying spines.

Are these real people?

But the thought is chased a moment later by the return to A.'s comment about Gran taking me in. After… what?

"Tell me more about E. How she took me in. Why did she do it?"

A. studies my face for a moment. "Why does anyone do anything? For love, I suppose." Her gaze drifts beyond my shoulder, and her eyes light. "Why, is that G.? I must go and say hello."

And she's gone, leaving me holding food and wine beside the table. I give F. a quick glance. Can I ask his real name?

He smiles on me, as though encouraging me to ask, but speaks before I have a chance. "It's nearly time for you to leave, I expect?"

I exhale, deflated. "Leave?" Has he figured out I do not belong here? "It's so… radiant. I'd love to stay."

"Yes, that's always the way, isn't it? On the threshold of something new and suddenly the old seems too wonderful, too perfect, to be abandoned."

Does everyone here speak in riddles? Or only the writers?

"Threshold of something new?"

He lifts his glass in the direction of a remote side of the garden, opposite the bookshop, beyond another set of flaming torches. Where the wall of the Rhythm & Wonder Music Shop should stand. "Of course. This party is just the beginning of it all. You must go through."

I squint past the torches to the edge of the garden, or what should be the edge.

I see only shrubbery and flowers and a winding gravel path lined with gray stone statuary. All of it dissolving into unknown darkness.

"Where does it lead?"

"Hmm. That is the question for each of us, isn't it? But of course the imagination is everything."

I smile. "You sound like E. But I tend to see things more practically."

Which is a lie. Or maybe a wish.

"Nonsense! What do you suppose gave us the steam engine? The telephone? The automobile? These things had to be dreamed before they became realities. The imaginative man or woman is most apt to create, to invent, to foster civilization!"

"Perhaps you're right." I pop an olive into my mouth and bite down on the salty tang.

"No 'perhaps' about it! To fully live, we must each walk through our own portal into somewhere more marvelous, more wonderful, than we have ever known. Opportunity. Destiny. These are not to be taken lightly."

I take a deep breath, at a loss.

"Go along, then." He nods toward the gravel path and darkness.

"Excuse me?"

"You must go through."

So, not metaphorical, then.

But this is all getting to be too much. Despite my love for secret paths, there is no way I am going to walk into a dark wood, regardless of the fact that a brick wall should be in its place.

"I—I think I need to..."

F. *tsks* at me. "Do what? What could be more important?"

"It's E. Not well, as you know. I must check on her. And the shop—the shop's not doing well either—"

He tilts his head, a slight scowl creasing his features.

"That's because you don't know who you are."

My lips part, but I can think of no reply. Does this man somehow know me? My parents, even?

"When you don't know who you are, it allows others to take from you. To take what you've already been given." He touches my shoulder, nudging me toward the dark edges of the garden. "You'll find the answers here, answers to all your questions. If you have the courage to go deeper."

Will he force me into the woods?

For the first time since I entered this unreal place, I feel the clutch of fear, the need to flee, though everything else within me craves what I've found.

"I must go. It was... so nice meeting you—I mean seeing you again."

I whirl away from F., away from the table.

Where is the marble bench, the place I entered?

I hurry across the lush turf but partway to the bench my heel catches and I stumble, lose my footing.

In the twinkling candlelight I catch a last glimpse of my wine glass spinning through the air, past the wide-eyed gaze of the man T. called my "admirer."

And then, darkness.

SEVEN

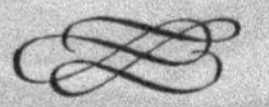

Love is the waking life, you are the dream.

~ from *Word in the Wilderness* by Malcolm Guite

From within the darkness, the call of birdsong, faint but melodic, tickles my ear.

Wakefulness comes slowly, eyes still closed, feeling my way through a fog of unconsciousness.

Remembering. The garden. I am in that magnificent, glittering Garden.

My eyes flutter open to search for the birds who sing me a morning greeting. Perhaps from the boughs of that grand live oak?

But the yellowing ceiling of my apartment fills my vision.

One downward glance reveals paint-crusted yoga pants and my college hoodie. No wisteria-covered twirly dress.

And the birdsong is only my phone alarm, gradually gaining volume from its cradle on my nightstand.

I groan, fumble for the phone, and shut down the alarm.

A dream. All a dream.

I press the heels of my hands against my eyes. Against the hot, unexpected tears.

Why am I crying?

Because it was so real. And so… restorative.

Strange word, but the first to pop into my mind.

The embracing sense of being recognized as a "real" writer. A community centered around beauty and creativity. My people. Like stumbling across an oasis in the desert. The exquisite feast, the gifts offered, the sense of timelessness.

The Garden was everything I love. An alchemy that might have sprung from my very veins—nostalgia and elegance, mystery and curiosity. Joy and belonging.

But I know exactly from whence it came.

I roll from the softness of my bed, cross into the living room, and pull *The Secret Garden* from the shelf once more. Then remove the folded sheets of notepaper from the front flyleaf. The fringed edges of the pages, where they were once attached to the wire rings of a spiral notebook, curl and fall to bits in my hand.

I sink to my couch where just last night I read the first lines—was it only last night?

Once upon a time, there was a young orphan girl, raised by a grandmother who was not her grandmother, who did not know who she was, but was meant to have many adventures in many secret places.

And the first of these places, where she discovered her True Self, was a very magical garden, with magical people who loved her.

Again, the tears. I lay the pages aside and rub stiff fingers against my forehead, trying to erase the lunacy that must have broken out in my brain while I slept.

The well-loved story of orphan Mary's secret garden. And these pages from a ten-year-old version of myself. Plus, William's mention of the story as we peered through the locked gate. Even Lisa's reminders of that bestseller, *The Starlight Folio*. All of it must have combined to create a delusion, a place to escape and be someone I am not. Crazy, crazy Kelsey.

But such a dream! I have never experienced one like it. Filling up my senses and my emotions, connected and solid. Not at all the elusive fragments typical of dreams.

More like waking up.

I have to know.

I shove my feet into a pair of Chuck Taylor hightops, leave the laces loose, and jog down the stairs, through the bookshop. Unlock the front door, dash the twenty feet down to the iron gate, and push against the bars with both hands.

If hope and desperation were all it took, the gate would have flung itself wide.

Instead, my body crashes into the bars.

I remain there, head pressed against the cold metal, swallowing bitterness.

But there must be a key. Perhaps it was only unlocked last night, and someone has locked it again.

I'm still delusional. It's the only explanation. The only reason I would run back to the shop, turn circles near the front desk, eyes closed.

Where have I seen that key? On a hook somewhere.

Where, Gran, where?

The Children's Section.

I flip the master light switch and the Book Emporium floods with the hiss of halogen.

A moment later, I'm pushing through the secret entrance, into the back room where my young writers bring their own spiral notebooks to fill with dreams that may or may not be true things.

There, on the wall, a display of "curiosities," she called it. Two or three dozen items curried from antiquing and theater storage chests and sixty years of the Chestnut Street Book Emporium's history. Gran herself hung the rusted iron key on a hook there.

"You never know what this might open," she'd said with a mischievous grin.

Did you know what it opens, Gran? Do you still?

I grab the key from the wall, reverse my course back through the bookshop, then to the street.

My fingers tremble as I slide the key into the gate's keyhole, breath suspended.

It fits. It turns.

It clicks.

The gate is unlocked, and I am once more pushing through the overgrown weeds and vines, shoving my way toward the magic.

But there is no magic.

There are only weeds and more weeds. Trash and more trash. Wrappers and papers, windblown and rain soaked. Beer cans, tossed over the wall by half-drunk teens laughing their way down Chestnut Street for decades. Near the center of the empty lot, one impossible rusted Maytag washing machine has landed here, who-knows-how.

I cross my arms over my chest and turn slow circles, a deep sadness rolling over my soul. But what did I expect? To find that sense of home here, among the weedy trash?

You don't know who you are, the man, "F." said last night.

No kidding. And no wonder "home" has always carried a hidden question mark.

Not that I haven't tried. Peppering Gran with all those questions about my adoption over the years, never answered. Lots of adolescent fantasy—rich parents who accidentally lost me and searched for me still. Or perhaps I was abducted royalty, left on the Book Emporium's doorstep by a conniving usurper to a far-off throne. I imagined tearful reunions, lavish birthdays of glitter-wrapped packages tied with curly red ribbons.

And then later, The Letter. Which I can still see, tucked away but not forgotten.

So this emptiness, here in an empty lot, is not new. It is an unresistant look full in the face of an alienation which has been with me all along.

I fight my way out of the noxious jungle, re-lock the gate, slide the key into my pants pocket. It sits cold and sharp against my thigh.

Is it better to be given a taste than never to have tasted? Better to have loved and lost, as they say, than never to have loved at all?

Last night in the Garden I returned to life after the soul-deadening focus on financial disaster. How can I now return to all this hopelessness?

It's a question for another day, for today there is only the gut-wrench, the breath knocked from my lungs. The gritty burn of more tears I refuse to shed.

Thirty minutes later, stepping from a steamy shower, a remembered line from last night's dream surfaces.

F.'s first edition is going to be worth quite a tidy sum one day, you will see.

The glass case downstairs, sealed and locked against onlookers, holds treasures.

Would one of them—maybe all of them—be enough to stave off disaster? The case does not get much attention tucked against the side wall of the shop. But what if I put them up for sale online? Surely someone, somewhere would pay a good price.

I jump into jeans and a T-shirt, then head down to the shop, despite it being my day off.

Lisa is just entering. She frowns. "The front door was unlocked. That's totally unsafe."

"It's fine. I was outside a few minutes ago. Didn't bother to lock up again."

"Still, I don't like the idea of you being here alone without it locked. There's valuable stuff in here."

I smile at the concern, though it seems to be more about the merchandise.

"Good day off?" Lisa punches the unlock code into the front register.

I slow my rush toward the glass case of old books and raise a hand in surrender at Lisa's sarcasm over my inability to take Wednesdays off. "I know, I know. I just want to check something."

Lisa shakes her head. "No, I was asking if you had a good day off yesterday."

I laugh. "Today is Wednesday, Leese. Two more days until TGIF, I'm afraid."

Lisa frowns, glances at her watch, and starts toward me. "I'm not that hung over. It's Thursday, for sure. Besides, you were gone all day yesterday."

My heart staccatos over itself, and I pull out my phone. Besides the glaring "Thursday, March 31" under the time, I also have a series of unread text messages, sent through the evening last night, from Austin.

Where are you?

Then, *Are you coming?*

Did you forget about Les Trois?

Seriously?

Finally, *Leaving now. Text me when you get this. Hope you're OK.*

I reach out for a shelf, breath tight. I have lost an entire day? To a dream?

I scan my memory. Did I drink too much? Do I have a fever?

"You okay?" Lisa folds her arms. "You look sick."

"Do I?" I press the back of my hand to my cool forehead. "I—I don't think I am."

"Maybe you should take another day off. I've got things here."

"No! No, I'm fine. I—I think I'll just go to my office for a bit."

With the door closed, surrounded by my messy stacks of uncatalogued books, I drop my head to my desk.

Think, Kelsey. How is this possible?

It's not. It's not possible.

There are no explanations, and there is nothing to be done.

Lisa knocks once, then leans through the door. "Mail's here. This one looks like a problem."

"Thanks."

Alone again, I rip open the letter from the City Tax Office.

Unsurprisingly, it's another Delinquency Notice, with the interest piling up. This one has a bit more information, however.

Unless I agree to a Confession of Judgment by April 15, they can seize and auction the property.

A nasty image traipses across my imagination, Charles Diamond Blackburn waving an auction paddle, a look of glee on his face.

A Confession of Judgment—awful term—basically means I agree to a slow, ten-year payback of the delinquent taxes while remaining current with all future payments. But if I default, the city has the immediate right to take over the property and I have no recourse to appeal. I've resisted this deal up until now. But April 15 is only two weeks away.

Enough about mystical gardens in empty lots. It's time to get busy.

I shove the letter into a drawer and head back out into the shop. Weave past floor spinners and through a series of tables set like square quilt blocks, heaped and labeled with NEW RELEASES, BEST OF THE YEAR IN HISTORY, and FAVORITE FICTION.

But I can't help myself, I slow at the wall of framed vintage travel posters from the 1920s and 30s, indulging a favorite moment of fantasy. The posters invite me to "Spend an Elegant Summer!" on Italy's Amalfi Coast beside the fashionable raven-haired beauty balancing a long-tapered cigarette holder in one hand and a martini in the other. Or promise an escape to the camel-dotted stretch of bronze sand leading to the Giza Pyramids, "Mysterious Wonder of the World!"

What is it about *other* places that calls to us, begging us to explore?

How many times have I imagined quitting my job at the shop and running away to tour the world, gaining enough experience and inspiration to perhaps one day write something worthwhile myself?

Lisa teased me once about my fascination with the posters, accusing me of being too timid to do it. The comment stung. But I can't abandon the shop. And I won't abandon Gran. For now, it's enough to escape into the pages of other people's books.

Almost.

In response to my ever-present wicked impulse to answer that call, jump on a plane, and forget my responsibilities, I nod to the posh travelers on the posters, acknowledging their superiority and my longing.

Life is a series of options, I've found, each one of them a voice with a particular cadence and charm. Sometimes the choices who whisper most urgently, into the deepest parts of us, are the most dangerous.

I find Lisa organizing a shelf near the glass case of first editions. "I've been thinking. What do you suppose we could get for some of these?" I cross to the case, skimming the titles.

Faulkner's *As I Lay Dying*. Alice Walker's *The Color Purple.*

L. Frank Baum's *The Wonderful Wizard of Oz*.

Frank, as in "F."? Or would he be "L."? My chest pangs and I push the sharpness aside. No more craziness.

But on an impulse, I pull out my phone, Google *L. Frank Baum,* and hit the "Images" link. A checkerboard of grainy black-and-whites pops up. I pull my phone close and squint.

A buzz of recognition begins at the base of my neck. He's older in most of the photos, but, that's the man I met at the table, the one "A." claimed gave "E."—Gran?—a first edition. Isn't it?

"Well?" Lisa's at my shoulder.

I hide the phone against my chest. "What?"

"That good, eh?" She nods at my hidden phone screen. "Afraid if I see what they're worth, I'll demand a cut?"

"What? No, no, I wasn't looking up their value. Just searching for… Frank Baum. One of the authors." I point at the red, white, and green volume in the case.

Lisa lifts her eyebrows. "Let's see."

I show Lisa the photo I've clicked. There is the squared chin, the full mustache, the kind eyes behind gold-rimmed glasses.

"Huh. Kinda cute, I guess. In an old-fashioned sort of way."

I shake my head. "One of the most popular writers of the nineteenth century and that's your comment."

"Hey, I call 'em like I see 'em!"

The doorbell clangs, and Lisa moves toward the front of the shop.

I study Baum again, pulse back to stuttering.

Back to Google, a new search: "The still point of the turning world."

The memorable phrase seemed familiar last night. My conversation companion said he wrote it, but maybe I've read it somewhere…

Holy quotes. The poem, the poet, his picture, it all materializes onto my phone screen at once.

And there is my new friend T., exactly as he looked last night.

T. is short for Thomas. Specifically, Thomas Stearns Eliot.

Popularly known as T.S. Eliot.

The phrase is from the poem "Burnt Norton," the first of his "Four Quartets," which I remember reading in college.

I skim the rest of the poem, finding his other lines:

What might have been is an abstraction
Remaining a perpetual possibility
Only in a world of speculation.

I could not have known these lines, not so well as to have dreamed them, despite their vague familiarity, could I?

Who else?

My fingers shake. I glance toward Lisa, but she is occupied with our first customer. The breath catches in my throat.

Who else?

The attractive guy who kept looking at me—the one with the rolled-up sleeves and black vest. But I have nothing to go on there, no initial. Nothing.

The woman who led me to the table—A.

What do I know about her?

You know me. Give me a good old-fashioned murder over a poem, any day.

A murder-mystery, I'd assumed last night.

I look up, toward the MYSTERY section of the shop, on the upper level that was once the theater's balcony.

But there is no need.

Any book lover in the world could tell you the name of a female mystery-writer beginning with A.

I can even picture her from her autobiography cover, although the photos in my memory bank are of a woman in her later years.

My fingers barely cooperate on the tiny screen-keys of my phone, but I manage another search.

Plenty of images.

Scrolling for one taken in her early days of fame.

When a younger photo appears, I nearly drop the phone.

I clutch it against my chest once more, whether to protect the truth or deny it, I can't say.

But there is no doubt.

Last night, in a totally impossible Garden party, I met Agatha Christie, *grande dame* of British mystery writers.

EIGHT

For this is quite the final goal of art:
to recover this world by giving it to be seen as it is.

~ Jean-Paul Sartre

Gran insists on visiting the flower beds of AdvantaCare, despite the sooty clouds scudding across a pewter sky.

"The bulbs are coming up, Bertie told me. You know I can't resist spring bulbs."

I maneuver the wheelchair's chrome-and-rubber wheels until my back is to the double doors leading to the so-called gardens, then try to shove the door open with my elbows.

An alarm sounds.

I'm trying to tamp down my frustration at the unplanned field trip. A stroll among spring flowers is not the reason I have come to AdvantaCare.

I've sent apologetic texts to Austin for skipping out last night, and we've rescheduled dinner at Les Trois for tonight.

And after a morning of researching the value of the first editions in the bookshop's glass case, I've already listed a printing from 1900 of *The Wonderful Wizard of Oz* by L. Frank Baum, one of the most valuable of the old books, on multiple online auction sites. And prematurely promised the finance department of AdvantaCare that I have money coming any day now. But even though Gran signed over medical power of attorney to me years ago, and I can pay the bills and sign the checks, I don't technically have legal *carte blanche* over her finances. She still likes to be kept in the loop, though we are way past the point where that should have ended, I know.

And if I'm being honest, I have a few other little questions about a certain empty lot beside the bookshop. Though I have all but decided my excursion was some kind of insane blend of subconscious knowledge bubbling up from my useless college Lit degree and too much anxiety over money.

A staff member rounds the corner in the wake of the alarm. "Let me punch in that code for you." The twenty-ish woman tilts her head at Gran. "Can't have our guests wandering off at all hours, can we?" The tone is patronizing.

Gran's shoulders straighten. She is still upright and elegant in a plum turtleneck that sets off her white hair.

My lips twitch at Gran's self-restraint. This sing-song condescension is just the sort of treatment she despises. Hopefully the aide won't call Gran some diminutive name like "sweetie," or the restraint might break out into a tongue-lashing.

"You sure you want to go out here, Gran? I think it's going to rain any minute."

"Oh, I gave up caring about getting wet a long time ago." Her veined hands grip the wheelchair's handles. "And I'm going stir-crazy in this place. As long as we're back in time for lunch."

Outside the facility, the air smells tropical—warm for this early in the year and laden with moisture. A single bird chirps lazily from the stand of trees that blocks the highway from view.

I direct the wheelchair toward the rectangular beds laid out like cemetery plots between a grid of cracked pavement.

"Can't you pick up the pace, girl? I'm not a toddler, for heaven's sake."

I laugh. "Have you seen this sidewalk? Any faster and the first deep crack would toss you out flat on your face!"

"Then do that backwards-thing again, like you did at the doors."

"You're crazy." But I do it—spinning Gran's chair around, pulling her backwards toward the flower beds as quickly as I can manage.

Gran lets out *whoop,* like a kid let out of school early, pumps a fist in the air, then grabs the handrest again with a squeal as the rutted sidewalk jolts her, as predicted.

"Happy?" I laugh and slow, turn Gran around to face the frilled heads of canary-yellow daffodils, their necks bent as if in prayer, before a lavender-throated chorus of crocuses.

I park the chair beside a bench and set the brake.

Gran reaches for my hand as I sit. "Happy, yes." Her smile is for me, not the flowers.

I grip Gran's hand, not too tightly, and fight the sudden tightening in my throat. This connection and belonging are on borrowed time. As challenging as it sometimes was to grow up with a woman in her sixties and seventies as my only maternal figure, Gran has always accepted me fully, for exactly who I am. Who will do this when she is gone? Lisa? Austin?

And is it my fear over impending loss that has me creating nonsense in my head about being welcomed into a party of dead authors?

I point to the bulbs. "Looks like you can't keep life down, even in a place like this."

"Hmm. Yes." Gran's eyes travel the length of the beds, still largely dormant under last year's death. She reaches a frail hand toward the nearest daffodil. "Gardens are like that, aren't they? Putting flesh to beauty, even when we are indifferent. Reminding us that all our man-made art is only a reflection of something greater. All the gardens in the world, perhaps all connected to the same archetypal original garden. Some fractured bits of Eden, still lingering in the world."

"That's beautiful, Gran. You've not lost your gift for poetry."

She laughs, quiet as a breath. "Perhaps." She turns her gaze back to me. "But what about you and your stories?"

I look away, focus on the gray-green blades of iris leaves, cutting through the dark mulch. Somewhere, an early bee buzzes against a flower.

"Not much time for that these days, I'm afraid."

Gran pulls herself upright again, studies my eyes. "That's foolishness, and you know it, my girl." Her lips tighten to a slash.

"It's okay, Gran, really. That was just something I did when I was a kid—"

"You've done it much longer than that!"

"Well, yes, but—"

"So when will it be published? That's what I want to know!"

"It's not that easy, Gran." Well, technically, these days it *could* be that easy—there was nothing stopping me from putting my finished novel out into the world.

Nothing except that stupid bestseller with nearly the same premise. I'd be mocked for being pathetically derivative if I self-published the thing now.

"Oh, you silly girl. Of course it's not easy. Who ever said it would be? You still haven't learned that you must join the fight!"

"What fight?" I regret the question as soon as it's asked. She is getting agitated.

"The fight against the deceitfulness of evil!"

Okay, if I want answers on anything today, I don't have long before exhaustion pushes her beyond lucidity.

Her eyes wander back to the double doors. "Do you think it's lunch time yet?"

"I need to ask you something, Gran. It's about the first editions in the glass case at the shop."

Gran nods. "You want to sell them."

I exhale against the back of the bench. "They're worth quite a bit more than their old price tags at this point. The Oz book could… could really help."

"Help? You need money?"

I bite my lip. I hate to give Gran cause for worry. Or cause her to fear I can't handle the shop on my own.

"We do need money, yes. The property taxes are a bit late. And we've had some plumbing issues. The Oz book could cover the taxes, as well as a few months here."

"Well, that's your fault, then, for giving up on your stories. You're acting like a coward!"

I close my eyes against the anger in Gran's voice.

The bird has stopped singing and the world hushes as it always does before a storm. Behind the stand of trees, the hum of traffic seems to increase.

I take a breath, lick my lips. "We don't get as many customers these days."

"The shop's just having a downturn. It'll pick up soon."

"I hope so. But in the meantime… do you mind very much if I sell it?"

"I don't mind. But don't tell Bobby. He's been salivating over that book for years. Frank gave me that one himself, though it's so long ago now he probably doesn't remember. I think he would understand."

Here we go again. I have nearly talked myself out of bringing it up. But now…

I choose to skip over "Bobby" and go directly for the more intriguing name she's mentioned.

"Frank—gave it to you himself? Frank Baum, the author?"

"Of course, who else?"

"But he... died. Before you were born."

"They were always so helpful to me. So giving, when you were young. Perhaps you should ask them for the answer. Certainly, they would help us now. They know it would break my heart to see the shop in trouble."

"Who, Gran? Who was helpful?"

"In the garden, of course! They knew what it meant to me, the day you came into my life."

My chest sags under the blow of this new information. Something about my past, my parentage, is part of all this?

But no, this must be Gran's aging mind creating fantasy. I'm not letting myself buy into it, even if it's best to play along, to keep Gran from getting upset.

"Tell me about that day."

Gran's eyes crinkle and she puts a finger to her lips. "We all have secrets, Kelsey-girl."

The first raindrops trickle from the sodden clouds, spattering the beige sidewalk with circles the size of copper pennies.

Gran lifts her arm, studying a splat of water on her sagging skin. "It's raining." Her voice has a sudden edge to it, something like fear.

"Yes, time to go inside."

"Why did you bring me out in the rain? Are you trying to kill me?"

"No, of course not. I'll take you back right now." I turn the wheelchair for shelter and navigate the cracks carefully.

"I'm getting wet!" She tries to turn in the chair, her eyes fiery.

"I'm sorry, Gran." I fight to keep the tears at bay. "I'm sorry."

These bouts of confusion, like someone has replaced Gran with an evil clone, are getting more frequent. The staff warned me this would happen as her mind begins to fail and her body follows.

"And now you've made me late for lunch!" Her fury has swept in more quickly than the storm.

"No, not too late." I push the chair faster. "We'll get your lunch now."

We leave the garden behind, under a curtain of rain.

I have more questions than answers and a heart as broken as the sidewalk.

NINE

The primary job that any writer faces is to tell you a story of human experience—I mean by that, universal mutual experience, the anguishes and troubles and gifts of the human heart, which is universal, without regard to race or time or condition.

~ William Faulkner

I struggle through an afternoon of invoices, deciding where to cut back on purchases and Googling for ideas on how to run a successful independent bookstore—the top recommendation being to choose a high-traffic location.

Perfect.

But at least the fruitless research forces my mind away from the repeated phrase: *They knew what it meant to me, the day you came into my life.*

It's insane, all of it. To think that the Garden is a real place, that Frank Baum gave Gran his first Oz book, and, most of all, that the people I dreamed up inside that Garden —all dead, mind you—could have any information about where I came from or how to save the Book Emporium.

Even if I did believe that learning my identity would yield answers, why would I search for that information inside a Garden rather than public or agency records?

Just before my Creative Writers are due to arrive, a bike messenger enters, requiring a signature for receipt of an official-looking envelope.

"What is it?" Lisa lifts to her toes behind the counter.

I rip open the envelope. Are things like this ever good news?

I skim the single sheet inside, typed on city letterhead.

Then return to the top of the letter, throat seizing and eyes blurred.

"What is it? What's happening?" Lisa circles to look over my shoulder.

"The city is taking the bookshop." The words are barely audible, as though I've lost the strength to speak.

"How can they—" She looks over what I've read three times. "Eminent…?"

"Eminent domain. It means they can take property from private owners if it's for city use. They have to pay for it, of course, but they can take it."

"What's the city going to do with a bookstore?"

I read it again, as though it will say something less horrifying. "Nothing. They're going to sell it to the hotel developers since the hotel is in the best economic interest of the city. Apparently, that makes it legal."

"That's—"

"Outrageous."

This must have been what Blackburn warned me about a couple days ago. My last chance, before something worse happened.

When you don't know who you are, it allows others to take from you. To take what you've already been given.

No, I'm not going there. Too weird that L. Frank Baum might have warned me as well.

"You have to fight it, Kelsey. There must be a way to fight it."

"Right. With all the extra cash I have for legal fees."

I slide the single sheet of paper back into the envelope and place it behind the counter.

All I want to do is hit the internet and start researching this latest disaster, but my students are jostling into the shop.

I herd them past the travel posters, and then the papier-mâché "There and Back Again Tree" calls to me next with empty promises.

Last year's students helped create the tree, an homage to *The Hobbit.* Its shire-inspired trunk and branches are molded from favorite pages of the book, each page torn from a used paperback version, then stained walnut with strong coffee and plastered with glue. My fingers skim the bumpy texture of my favorite quote, too long to read as I pass, but I don't need to read it to hear the taunt.

There are no safe paths in this part of the world. Remember you are all over the Edge of the Wild now, and in for all sorts of fun wherever you go.

Maybe someday, Gandalf. Maybe someday.

As if in answer to Gandalf's warning, the line of students reaches the secret entrance to the Children's Section, my proudest achievement since taking over the decor of the shop a few years ago.

The teens balked at first, at meeting in the Children's Section for their after-school sessions. But within weeks, my renovation worked its charms.

An unused section of the theater at the end of a long, cramped hall languished for years as dusty storage until one day, while antiquing, I spotted the massive wooden wardrobe.

I solicited help to haul the thing to the shop, sawed off its worn pedestal feet so it rested on the floor, and positioned it to block the head of the hallway after cutting a wide opening out of the back. The wardrobe doors hang always-open, an assortment of fake fur coats, reminiscent of the costume racks of the old theater, hanging inside. Most of the time, the coats are shoved to both sides revealing the doorway cut in the back. But on Tuesdays and Thursdays I draw the coats into the center, forcing the teen at the head of today's pack to sweep them aside so we can enter.

I bring up the rear, bending to half my five-foot-eight height to get through.

We pass into a hall covered in a glossy purplish-black. The light from the room beyond illuminates the murals painted by a local artist.

This hall is a tribute to my lifelong passion for secret paths into unknown—those just-around-the-bend places and the ordinary-looking portals that invite us into them. Here, shadowy, leafless trees edge a wintery wood, bone white snowflakes fall against a wrought iron lamppost, and a tawny-furred faun in a red scarf, carrying parcels, bends to speak to a dark-haired little girl.

I had a tough time convincing the fire marshal to let the whole thing stand, even though there's another exit, a back door out of the Children's Section that leads to the alley between the bookshop and the art museum behind. We squeezed past his inspection only after I fastened the wardrobe doors so they were impossible to close.

But the effect is, well… magical. And even the teens admit there's no better way to fire up the imagination than to first cross into Narnia, to escape from reality and wrap ourselves in that magic.

For me, nothing is better than seeing their creativity spring to life. They feel secure here, away from others who don't understand, able to safely share their dreams.

I push away the panic that surfaces whenever I think of letting them down.

Fairy tales are for babies. The memory's still a bruising, nearly twenty years later.

I settle the kids at tables, then clear my throat in my best scolding-librarian manner. "Now who has finished their assignment?"

I'm met with wide eyes and silence.

I smile, to relieve a bit of their tension. It's supposed to be fun, after all.

"Come on, you know I'm counting on at least one of you becoming the next Fitzgerald or Hemingway. Minus the alcoholism, of course."

A ninth-grader, Saanvi Mehta, raises her hand.

I lower myself to the wooden chair at the head of the table. "You don't have to raise your hand, Saanvi. We're friends here, writing stories."

Saanvi runs a self-conscious hand down her hair, silky as a raven's wing. "Oh. Okay. I was wondering—you haven't told us what *your* story is about."

The innocuous question lands like a heavy fist on my heart, then pounds at my lungs and compresses my breath. My Tuesday-Thursday group is supposed to be the bright spot in the week, not remind me of missed opportunities.

"I'm just here to help you guys with your creativity." I scan the table full of potential—lovely kids who probably don't fit into the social milieu of their middle school any better than I did. Hopefully none of them have been as scarred as I have. "I'm here to help you become the geniuses you can be, because it's important that you write the masterpieces I know you have inside you."

"Why?" Lily plucks at the rings of her spiral notebook. "Why is it so important? What happens if we don't?"

Good question.

At the end of the table, Alejandro leans in and growls, "End of the worrrllddd..."

I laugh. "Well, maybe not that dramatic."

"Miss Kelsey, don't you have a masterpiece inside you?" This from Jae, whose thick-lensed glasses and floppy hair both seem too large for his head.

Maybe. Probably not.

Past experience has taught me that any story inside me is likely too optimistic, too full of childish wonder, for the bleak and depressing hopelessness that tops the bestseller charts these days. Part of the reason I haven't written a word in more than two years.

Without the talent for commercial success, creativity and storytelling quickly became a waste of time, an escape from reality. But I'm not about to discourage these kids with the truth, not while it's unknown which of them might have that talent.

"Miss Kelsey? Hello?"

"Sorry. Wool-gathering." I smile, thinking of Gran, then fight my way back to positivity. "Maybe we've all got masterpieces up here." I tap my temple. "Or more accurately," a hand over my heart, "in here. But you can't know until it's right here." I lay a hand over the cover of Lily's spiral notebook between us, inked with labyrinthine swirls in violet Sharpie. "Even the greats didn't know they were great until they started getting the words down. If Gran were here, she'd tell you some stories."

These kids have never met Gran, but they feel they know her from the word-pictures I've painted of the spunky old bohemian, fighting "the man" with her poetry.

"She knew some of the best writers of the twentieth century. Some of them even did book signings here. William Faulkner, Isaac Asimov. Even Roald Dahl."

"*Charlie and the Chocolate Factory?*" Lily grins. "I loved that book when I was a kid."

"Doesn't surprise me." I elbow her. "You're a little odd."

"Were you working here when they signed books?" Alejandro seems serious.

"Ouch, Alejandro! How old do you think I am?"

He grins and shrugs. "Twenty?"

I laugh. "Well-played, my friend. No, I just turned twenty-nine last week, if you must know." The confession scratches a bit at my heart. Thirty looms, taunting me to do something bigger with my life. "And all of those men were dead before I was born."

"What about women? Any famous women writers?" Saanvi's leaning forward, as if the answer means the world.

"Of course, there've been many famous women writers, but I'm not sure any have signed books here. I guess you'll have to be the first, Saanvi."

The girl's dark eyes flash. Challenge accepted.

"Miss Kelsey, did your parents know famous writers, too?"

My muscles tighten. "Hmm, well, that's something you don't know about me." I waggle my eyebrows. "I don't have parents."

The table goes silent.

I wink, an exaggerated gesture to break the tension. "Mysterious, eh? Was I hatched? Did I arrive here from another planet?"

Uneasy smiles all around, as if they understand they'll get no more out of me on this topic.

But my mind has drifted to Gran's desk drawer. The Letter, tucked in the back...

I've barely assigned their first writing prompt before Lisa is waving me out of the Children's Section.

"Be right back," I tell the seven future writers before I join Lisa at the head of the hall, hands on my hips. "We just started, Lisa—"

"Yeah, well, I've got a live one for you. Needs your special touch."

I glance at the students, all scratching pencils on paper. They'll lose steam quickly without me.

"Keep writing," I call, then follow Lisa.

Her scuffed beige flats, literally down at the heels, catch

my attention, and her rainbow sweater's last purple stripe is ragged. The sight pinches me a little, even though there's no way I can pay her more.

My "special touch," as Lisa calls it, is the ability to find the right book for a picky customer. Lisa thinks it's some kind of uncanny gift rather than a basic skill necessary to work in a bookstore. A skill Lisa notably lacks—along with several others, such as punctuality and organization. But Lisa's employment, like the shop itself, is a promise made to Gran, and one I intend to keep. Though I've never been able to get the reason for it out of either one of them.

"Can I help you, sir?"

Lisa's "live one," a stocky, mustached man in a black wool pea coat and Kelly-green beret, turns a watery smile on me before launching into a description of the book he's looking for—part history, part conspiracy-theory—about the likelihood of aliens building the pyramids.

Interesting, as I was just looking at the travel poster for Egypt.

We wend our way through NATURE and LANGUAGES to a narrow shelf under the wall of windows where the pseudo-archaeology books are shelved.

Just for fun, I turn to him, grin, and squeeze my eyes shut. "Let's see if I can find it." I run my hands down the shelf vertically, find the correct row, slide my hand across the spines to sense their trim size, spine width, cover finish. I stop about halfway down, tilt a book outward, and open my eyes.

"How did you do that?" He's clearly impressed.

I shrug and hand him the white hardcover sporting a pyramid topped with the all-seeing eye.

He runs a hand over the volume. "You must have read it, then."

"Not this one, I'm afraid."

"Author's a genius, if you ask me. But, of course, the scientific world wants to keep it quiet."

"Of course." I smile, hopefully without condescension. In truth, I wish I had this guy's belief, wish the world were a more mysterious place than creditors and past due bills. Lisa calls me "whimsical," which never sounds like a good thing when she says it, and despite my weakness for travel posters and Narnia, I'm attempting to be more practical these days.

I should get back to the students, but the customer wants to keep talking, so I shift to a walking discussion, leading him back toward the register.

"Is there anything else I can find for you?"

He waggles the hardback in the air triumphantly. "No, I've got what I came for."

"Wonderful. Lisa here will ring you up."

He shifts his comments to Lisa as he pulls out a leather wallet. Another talkative one.

But one advantage Lisa has is her way with people, and she has him smiling his way out the door before I've finished straightening a few hardbacks knocked askew on the HOBBIES table.

She points to the man's retreating figure. "That's the kind of stuff we should be featuring, to get more customers. Controversial. Not all these boring books." She waves a vague hand at the BEST OF THE YEAR IN HISTORY table. "You know, like that bestseller—"

"Don't say it, Lisa." I return her grin. "Don't say it."

The workshop hour ends all too soon. The students retrieve their backpacks, and I follow the train of them back out of Narnia, into the real world, and out the front door. I side-hug each of them with reminders to have their current writing prompt finished by next week.

Quiet and serious Olivia holds back. "Miss Kelsey, I have a question."

I tilt my head, waiting.

"How can you have a Gran if you don't have any parents?"

I pinch the bridge of my nose. The beginning of a

headache presses behind my eyes. "Story for another day, Olivia."

When the door closes after the last student, I turn to find Lisa jamming trash into a black bag.

"I don't know why you don't just tell them the truth."

"That is the truth."

TEN

Writing is a process in which we discover what lives in us.
The writing itself reveals to us what is alive in us.

~ Henri Nouwen

Five o'clock hits, and I flip the hanging sign in the front door from "Once Upon a Time…" to "The End" and lock it with relief.

I haven't had a chance to research the eminent domain situation yet and am regretting my earlier rescheduling of dinner with Austin, but it seems rude to cancel. Maybe I can cut the evening short and get back in time to start figuring out solutions.

Lisa has quit a few minutes early to take her final smoke break on the roof before leaving for the day.

I climb the stairs to my apartment, then continue to the roof entrance to ask the question that's bubbled up through the haze of disasters.

A midday rain shower ended quickly, with the sun

making a reappearance in the afternoon. The tar-and-gravel rooftop surface still holds some of the day's warmth.

Lisa leans against the parapet, looking over the city.

Before I join her, I cross to the east side of the building and lean over the wall to survey the empty lot.

As expected, nothing but weeds and trash spreads below me, all the way to the Rhythm & Wonder Music Shop's crumbling wall opposite the Book Emporium's. Chestnut Street is on my left, and the museum's back wall and alley on the right.

I push away and head toward Lisa, barely glancing at the pathetic pots where I grew a few marigolds and petunias last year beside the decades-old lawn chair I kept when we sold Gran's house. After the richness of my dream-Garden, the scraggly annual flowers seem to taunt me with the failure of half-efforts and forgotten passion.

Lisa turns her head at my approach and holds out a box of cigarettes.

"No, thanks."

She shrugs, pockets the box in her scraggly cardigan, and exhales a thin stream through her nose. "I guess if you're ever going to start, today would be the day."

I brace my forearms on the wall and scan the city. The low hanging sun is across the street, streaming across the rooftops, setting them aflame.

Lisa shakes her head. "Wish I had money, for you to get a lawyer or something."

"I appreciate the thought."

Lisa's a good person, despite the way life's challenges have worn her down. How many of her forty-ish years have been happy?

"So, I've been thinking. Your mom and Gran were really close, right?"

Lisa drags deeply and exhales again. "Yeah. So?"

There's a bit of defensiveness there. Probably because it's long been obvious that Gran has kept Lisa as an employee—

nearly seven years now—for some reason besides her stellar work performance. It's actually been more like on-again, off-again employment over the years as Lisa has struggled with alcohol, a series of deadbeat boyfriends, and even a few months of homelessness. Gran's generosity, no doubt out of loyalty to her friend who passed away years ago, has often seemed misguided to me.

"So… did she ever talk about me? Your mom, I mean. Ever talk about my adoption?"

"She was dead before that."

"What? Oh, I'm sorry—you must have been so young when she died."

"Fourteen, yeah."

"Wow."

"Why are you asking about your adoption?" Lisa stubs out the cigarette on the stone wall and clears her throat in a concerning smoker's cough.

"I've just been wondering. About my parents, I guess."

"Elizabeth never told you anything?"

I shrug. "Not really. The name of the agency, that's about it."

"And you never tried to find out?"

I hesitate.

The Letter.

It's a painful memory. My childhood curiosity deepening to an angst-filled *need* to understand myself and where I'd come from.

"I did once, yes." I breathe out, easing the pressure in my chest. "I wrote a letter to the agency requesting information when I was sixteen."

Lisa crosses the front of her cardigan against the spring chill. "And?"

"I never got an answer. At the time, I assumed it meant they wouldn't, or couldn't, tell me anything."

She shrugs and studies the rooftops across the city. "I don't really know how all that works."

"Then two years later I found the letter, unsent, in one of Gran's drawers."

The confession tumbles out, sounding far less like a betrayal than it felt at the time. Than it still feels.

Lisa frowns. "What?"

"She must have retrieved it before it went out and kept it. Never sent it."

"Did you ask her about it?"

"I did. She said, 'There are some things better left unknown, Kelsey.'"

The memory burns. Gran's disappointment in me. The cryptic, ominous words about The Letter. The feeling that there might be something truly awful about me, about my past or my parents.

"She's right."

I turn toward Lisa, waiting for more.

"Gran's your mother, Kelsey. She raised you. That's all that matters." Lisa's typically rough edge seems to soften. "You should be grateful to have been raised by a woman like that. Not everyone is so lucky."

I nod. "I know. You're right. But sometimes it's hard. Not knowing." I run my fingers along the crumbling stone, and my voice drops. "When I was a kid, I used to make up stories, about my past. My identity."

"What—like you were switched at birth or something?"

I laugh. "Something like that. Yes."

"Well, you always were a storyteller, Elizabeth says." There's condescension in the tone. "Always trying to escape to someplace else in those books."

"Yeah, I guess it's pointless. Besides, any mother who would give me up isn't someone I want to know anyway, right?"

She shrugs, pulls out another cigarette, lights it. "What has you thinking on all this now? Seems like you have bigger fish to fry."

She's right about this as well. Time spent worrying about

my biological parents, or my fictional secret Garden, is time *not* spent on figuring out solutions to the present crisis.

"You're right. I'm not a storyteller. I'm a bookshop owner. And I'm fighting to keep my small, indie store alive in the face of corporate greed, online depersonalization, and mindless algorithms."

Lisa smiles, the expression amused but sad. "Wow. You just can't help yourself, can you? Managed to make even that sentence sound like Don Quixote tilting at windmills."

"Was that a literary reference, Lisa?" I grin. "Is the Book Emporium finally worming its way into your brain?"

"Don't get too excited. A customer said it today, and then she had to explain it to me."

"Well, I'm not counting myself out yet. I still have fight left in me."

"And this thing about your parents? You gonna pursue that?" Lisa's voice is casual, but her body seems tense. Did her mother perhaps know something after all? Something Lisa's keeping a secret out of loyalty to Gran? Or worse—some kind of blackmail to keep her job?

And why hadn't I ever tried again? It's been more than ten years since I found The Letter unsent. In all that time, I've accepted Gran's caution and stayed away from the topic. But now, with Gran fading before my eyes…

I shake my head and push away from the wall. "No. There's nothing to pursue. And I have a bookshop to fight for."

ELEVEN

The writer operates at a peculiar crossroads where time and place and eternity somehow meet.
His problem is to find that location.

~ Flannery O'Connor

Thirty minutes later, waiting inside the doors of the dimly lit Les Trois restaurant for Austin to show up, I'm beginning to feel sick over the latest developments.

Les Trois is a bit pretentious, not my preference for dinner. Tonight, I'm craving some comfort food, maybe a warm panini or some lobster mac and cheese. This place is more likely to serve *boeuf bourguignon* and steak tartare. But it's Austin's invite and he enjoys taking me to fancy places, so I should be grateful.

A quick Internet search for eminent domain on my phone on the way to the restaurant gave me nothing hopeful. There are many precedents for what is formally called a "taking." The term seems ridiculous and brings Frank Baum's warning to mind once again. I've already started capitalizing it in my head, getting ready for my Epic Battle Against the Taking.

It seems the city has legal strength on its side. All the court cases I skimmed that settled in favor of property owners only resulted in more financial compensation for the owners. Never any success in keeping their property from being confiscated.

I don't want financial compensation. I want to keep the Book Emporium. My home.

And for that, I'm going to need a lawyer.

I'm still fighting thoughts of the Garden and Gran's hints that the mysterious party guests might be helpful. They did, after all, give me the idea of selling the first editions. But I don't have time for blind alleys.

I glance at my watch. 6:40. Austin is ten minutes late. Is this his retaliation for ghosting him last night? Maybe he didn't believe my lame explanation of a headache so intense that I forgot to contact him.

Five more minutes and then I'll go try that gate again. It'll be nearly sunset by the time I get back there. Just about the time I first saw that shimmer of light.

What am I thinking?

A couple enters, whispers their name to the hostess and are smilingly escorted into the dining room. I return to my phone, searching for better examples of businesses fighting the Taking.

Only two more minutes and then I'll go back to the shop, to the empty lot. Should I change my clothes first? I've put on a dress for tonight, floral and soft. Interesting… I hadn't realized how similar this dress is to the one I was wearing in my… dream.

"Miss?" The girl from the hostess desk is touching my arm.

"Hmm?"

"I think your friend is here."

"What? Oh."

Austin is standing by the entrance into the main dining room, head cocked and brows drawn together in a question. "Are you coming?"

"Sorry. Didn't see you come in."

What does it say about our relationship, that I'm disappointed he showed up before my deadline? Or maybe it's not about us as much as it is about my insane obsession with a mythical Garden.

I catch up. He kisses my cheek quickly before we follow the hostess.

"You look beautiful."

I smile. "Thanks, you too."

Once seated at the candlelit table and with orders placed, I try to bring my attention to the date. "So, how was your day?"

Austin snaps a black cloth napkin and lays it carefully across his lap. "Fantastic."

I sip my ice water. "Sounds intriguing."

But it isn't. At least, not to me. Austin does something with finance, something I can never quite get curious about. My thoughts are focused on that messenger-delivered disaster as Austin tells me about the lucrative deal he put through today. I pull myself back, guilt snagging me on the way. I need to find a way to be interested in his work, just like he takes an interest in the bookshop.

Our Caesar salads arrive. I push the lettuce bits around, getting them well-coated in grated parmesan and anchovy dressing before taking a salty bite.

It's a break in the conversation, so I change the subject and briefly outline news of the Taking.

"And so, according to the letter, on the seventeenth there will be a hearing where I'll get to present whatever argument I manage to come up with. Then they'll make the final decision."

"That's less than two weeks from now."

"I'm aware."

"You should have put the Book Emporium in your name years ago, Kelsey. It's going to be hard to fight this while it's still owned by Elizabeth. Besides, if the assets were in your name instead of hers, she'd get more financial assistance for her facility care."

I sigh. "Should-haves are not helpful right now, Austin. An ownership change for the bookshop never seemed necessary since she's named me in her will."

"Hmm. You can never have too many safeguards. But maybe this is a good thing. Maybe the city'll give you top dollar for the store—more than Blackburn would have. And you'll be able to do something else with your life."

"It's my home, Austin. I'm going to fight for it with everything in me."

He shrugs with an eyeroll, as though he expected me to say something this dramatic.

"I can recommend a few attorneys."

"Great. Thanks."

How about if I ask mythical party guests inside a vacant city lot for some help? What do you think of that idea?

"Austin, have you ever had an experience you couldn't explain, you know, in natural terms?"

He chews slowly, seems to be thinking. "You mean, like a miracle or something?"

"Yeah. I guess. Or something that feels supernatural."

He chuckles. "I knew that old bookstore was going to be haunted one of these days. Between the theater and the shop —too many old ghosts revisiting their glory days, eh?"

I swallow a crouton too soon, and it scratches on the way down. "Do you really believe that?"

"Believe in ghosts? Nah." His eyebrows quirk upward. "Do you?"

"I don't know. Maybe. Or maybe in... magic."

Austin snorts. "Didn't see that coming."

The conversation stalls as we continue with our salads, but then Austin leans back. "Actually, I probably did see that coming. I'm beginning to realize how... imaginative you are. Lisa told me you want to be a writer. Why haven't you ever told me that?"

Because I'm ashamed.

Wow, where did that come from? Do I actually feel ashamed? Of what?

Of my lack of talent.

Hmm.

I shrug and push away the salad plate. "Imagination without the ability to pull it off is basically just a hobby."

"Yeah, that makes sense."

My fingers curl into the napkin on my thighs, tight and painful. But did I expect him to disagree with me?

I smooth the napkin. "Some people would say it's worthwhile to pursue artistic things, even if you don't have the talent to be great."

"Really? Seems like a waste of time to me."

The entrée course arrives. I pick apart tiny fragments of my smoked halibut even though I could probably polish it off in three bites.

"I think I may have seen something... impossible."

Why did I say that? It feels like some kind of test, which is unfair. Will I really knock points off Austin's boyfriend-score if he doesn't believe something I myself can't quite believe?

"Impossible, how?" Austin spreads butter over a crusty roll, eyebrows lifted.

I resist giving him the whole truth. The Garden feels private. As though it belongs to me alone. The restaurant's soft music fills the interlude.

"Like something you glimpse one moment and then the next moment it's gone, like it was never there."

"Sounds like what they call 'magical thinking' to me."

"I—that's not—that's not what *magical thinking* means, actually."

Austin frowns and bites into his roll. "What do you mean?

It's magical and you're thinking about it, so... magical thinking."

I clear my throat and take another bite of fish. Again, is it fair to think less of him because he doesn't know the definition of the psychological term referring to finding links of causality between unrelated events?

"Well, whatever." Austin shrugs. "I know you like all that stuff—artsy stuff, I mean. But it seems better to focus on the numbers, to keep your eye on the prize, as it were, and quit being a dreamer. That's why I kept telling you to turn shop into a high-end café. But I guess it's too late now."

He is still talking, but I'm not hearing.

Storyteller. Imaginative. Dreamer.

All words in the mouths of Austin and Lisa, all tinged with condescension, disapproval.

But Agatha Christie called me a Storyteller. And T.S. Eliot said I was imaginative.

From them, the words seemed more than a compliment. They'd felt like a high calling. A gift.

I make it through the rest of the meal with forced focus.

Austin walks me to the bookshop entrance and seems surprised when I don't invite him up.

But I need to think.

Because something has to change.

I wait on the street with Austin for the few awkward minutes it takes for his Uber to slide up to the curb.

"I'll text you the names of those lawyers," he promises, ducking into the car.

I lift a hand and smile. Watch the car drive west on Chestnut Street, then make a right.

A moment later I'm at the gate, checking my watch. It's 8:30. A bit earlier than last night—no, Tuesday night—when the gate was unlocked. But I saw the flickering light earlier than that, at sunset, when William startled me. Will I see it again?

I am far from decided about venturing into the empty lot

again, even if I find the gate open. The loss of an entire Wednesday still sets my stomach churning.

But one push on the iron bars assures me the lot is inaccessible, just like this morning.

Wait, yesterday morning? No, that was this morning.

Gah, get a grip, Kelsey.

I touch my forehead to the cold metal, squint through the greenery and overgrowth, eyes roaming for even a hint of warm candlelight.

Nothing.

Because I'm crazy.

TWELVE

If you look the right way, you can see that the whole world is a garden.

~ from *The Secret Garden* by Frances Hodgson Burnett

Still at the gate, I sigh, stretch the tense muscles in my neck and roll my shoulders. Dinner with Austin has left me feeling anxious.

And hungry.

It takes me half a second to turn my feet toward AnaMaria's diner, always open late. Time for some real food.

The Sunny Side Up Diner manages to be both retro and a product of its time. Its decor is an artifact of *the way things were,* a place to forget for a moment that fast food and fast life have won the day. A place where black-and-white checked tiles, red vinyl on chrome counter-stools, and a Plexiglas turntable of fresh pies speak of Mom and Americana and all we romanticize about a bygone era.

Yet running alongside all this 1950s feel-good flag-waving is its owner, AnaMaria Ortiz, second generation out of Puerto Rico, setting the diner's playlist to match her heritage, adding tostones and empanadas to the sticky plastic menus, and calling instructions to her staff in equal parts Spanish and English.

AnaMaria's hair shows no hint of gray despite her age. She wears it tied into a messy bun, which she uses to stash a ball-point pen for taking orders. Her grandson sits at the end of the counter, head bowed over homework, while his mother, AnaMaria's daughter Lucia, runs the kitchen. "You sure that's all you want?" AnaMaria's dark eyes narrow over a frown.

I lean on the counter, tapping my fingers in anticipation of my plastic foam to-go container.

"Yeah, just need some comfort food. I saw Blackburn a couple days ago."

The older woman shakes her head. "That man comes in here, I will spit in his coffee. But you—you need to take care. You'll have a heart attack before forty with that diet."

"I ate a fancy dinner earlier." I smile at AnaMaria's worried expression. "But thanks for looking out for me."

In truth, it's the date with Austin that has me wanting to escape into the hot saltiness of AnaMaria's famous Adobo yuca fries.

Why do I feel so negative? Austin's a perfectly nice guy, just like Amanda, my former college roommate, promised when she set us up on a blind date five weeks ago. Great-looking, successful, sweet.

It's not Austin. It's me.

Maybe more accurately, though, it's *life*. Everything. All of it. Gran's failing health, the dying bookshop. Charles Diamond Blackburn and the fire-breathing tax office and now, the Taking. Leaky toilets, skipped paychecks. That stupid bestseller, *The Starlight Folio*.

At this last item on my list, with its royal blue and starry yellow cover, my soul feels like it's on its last breath, as though some part of me has lain dormant for years, waiting to be awakened, and instead is now being suffocated. A mental image of Sleeping Beauty, awaiting the kiss of rebirth and instead having the life choked out of her, is enough to make me suddenly nauseated.

There is also the embracing of more—of truth and beauty and life—yet you speak only of death.

T.S. Eliot's words, in the Garden.

Yes, that crazy, illogical Garden, with its roaring, all-encompassing vitality, somehow spawning morbid thoughts of my soul suffocating.

All the weight of a lost bookshop and lost dreams and losing Gran—all of it piled on one side of a scale, and that Garden on the other, with its promise of creativity and life and finding my true self.

No contest.

Even though the Garden draws me, promising the chance for answers—perhaps even a mentor who could help me find what I lack—if it's not real, I am in some serious mental health trouble.

And if it *is* real, and time passes differently there, then I have no control over what I'll miss. Could I return to find the Book Emporium seized by the city?

Could I return to find Gran… gone?

"Everything okay?" AnaMaria pushes my foam container across the counter.

"I'm good, thanks."

But I slide onto a stool and open the container, unwilling to leave the comfort of the diner just yet.

I can't risk trying to get back into the Garden. Not for some existential crisis over my creative self. Besides, there was that creepy conversation with Frank Baum pushing me to go into the woods.

AnaMaria takes in my expression. "Despite what I said about your diet, you look like you could use some pie."

I swallow against the heat in my throat. “No pie tonight. I just want to sit here. Thanks, though.”

Her eyes are warm, but curious. “You take all the time you need.”

I nod, unexplainable tears welling as she returns to the kitchen.

Really? Am I crying at her simple kindness?

No. It’s everything. All of it. Like a pile of pebbles that’s been slowly crushing me, topped today with one huge boulder.

But as the list of crises rushes back, so do Gran’s words about the help I might find in the Garden—help to save the shop. And Agatha Christie’s hint about the first edition Oz book, which proves there is real-life help to be found there.

I hold Gran’s words—about my own past and where I came from—at a mental arm’s length, focusing instead on the solutions to my bookshop problems.

Could the people in the Garden tell me more, perhaps something that could be the key to saving the place?

Is trying to enter the Garden again the best chance I have?

Or am I grasping, trying to rationalize a decision I've already made? The push-pull tug of war is exhausting.

The Garden is illogical, and of course I’ll also pursue legal action, but desperate times call for desperate measures, right?

You’ve always been a Storyteller.

Whose words this time? Gran’s, with that twinkle in her eye? Lisa, or Austin, with a tinge of mockery?

I have two weeks to save the Chestnut Street Book Emporium or break Gran’s heart. And if there’s a chance the answers lie behind that iron-gated brick wall, I have to find out.

I toss a few bills on the counter and close my half-empty container.

I resolve to analyze the marketing efforts of the

surrounding stores as I walk home. Free Coffee Friday probably won't move the needle fast enough to pay the bills, the taxes, and Gran's care. Assuming the Garden is a delusion, what else can I do?

Like AnaMaria, all the residents of the Lincoln Village neighborhood look out for each other. It's one of the things I love best about living in the city, along with the ability to walk everywhere. I love the streets that branch into theaters, museums, parks, and gardens. The architecture of its buildings, from utilitarian to fanciful. The intriguing people I meet and the vibrancy of it all.

Though *vibrant* may not describe Chestnut Street much longer. And this evening I ignore all I love, my thoughts bouncing over a multitude of frustrations and non-solutions, like a street pigeon refusing to light.

The springtime sun will set soon, and long shadows stripe the streets, dark reflections of tall buildings. I button my jacket against the chill, stuff a few spicy fries into my mouth, and study the shops and businesses as I wander.

Okay, figure this out, Kelsey.

How have these stores kept revenue going in a world that is tipping into big boxes of stores and a river of online everything?

Or have they? If one looks, the cracks are beginning to show. The first telltale fault lines forecasting the shift that will likely bring these retailers to their knees. Peeling paint. Outdated signage. Rusty railings. Like Gran, the neighborhood is aging. Somewhat gracefully, but trending down.

I approach the neighborhood pharmacy, The Dispensary, its stenciled name artfully faded across the broad brick storefront, with "est. 1978" added to the name as if it were 1778. Like the Sunny Side Up Diner, it's attempting to evoke nostalgia as a marketing ploy. Is it working?

I slow at the display window. What products does the pharmacy find best to entice passersby?

Three identical stacks of hardback books, fanned like

three tiny spiral staircases built for book sprites. The yellow title on a royal blue background screams at me before I even attempt to center myself before the display.

That book again. *The Starlight Folio.* Everywhere. Taunting me.

I shove in a few more fries, chew furiously, swallow too soon, cough.

I've heard a bit about the book's author—Selena Manning. Apparently a mystery, a recluse, no interviews, keeping to herself. How nice for her, the luxury to remain in an ivory tower, dropping her stories like flowers tossed to a waiting crowd below who snatch and devour them while other writers toil like factory workers, churning out substandard cogs and widgets useful only to plug holes on bookshelves.

The front door of the pharmacy opens. A white-haired man exits, keys jangling in his hands.

"I'm about to close up, but if you're thinking of buying that book, I can tell you, it's fantastic—"

"No!" The word jumps out to bite the poor man. "No. Thank you, though."

"You sure? You sound like you could use a reminder there's still beauty and goodness left in the world."

"No. Thank you."

He shrugs, locks the front door, and waves a goodbye.

The jealousy is uncharitable, of course. My own mediocre talent is not the fault of this book, this author. And even if my talent could be improved, if I have more inside me waiting to be released, it would need to happen at the expense of more important concerns. And this I won't allow.

But I'll admit, I've spent an evening clicking through to some of the book's 1-star reviews, enjoyed a little of the naysayers' nastiness before shutting my laptop with guilt over my pettiness.

Another thirty minutes of walking and studying the

neighborhood. My fries are gone, a chilly wind rising, and sunlight has abandoned all efforts to reach the streets.

Time to give up, with no fantastic ideas to save the shop.

I've wandered far from Chestnut Street, but my inner compass turns me westward, directing me down Maple, then a left on Elm for three blocks.

A fantasy version of Lincoln Village tugs at the edges of my thoughts, prompted by the diner's 50s vibe and The Dispensary's historic feel. I fight it, but imagination pokes at me, calling to me, offering itself like a painkiller with promises.

I yield to its pull, this need I have to create other worlds, just for a moment...

In my head, the angry honks of cars transform into the quick toot of *hello neighbor, hello*. Cracks and fragments and flaking paint are filled in and smoothed. The constant whine and hum of heating units and truck gears becomes the happy whir of industry in a city of success.

I reach Chestnut Street in a haze of unreality, passing the Rhythm & Wonder Music Shop, forcing down an urge to wave a neighborly greeting at the owner inside. Despite our proximity, with only the empty lot between our two stores, I've spoken with him only once. An unfriendly guy in his forties, he took over for his mother years ago. I haven't seen the mother for more than a decade. Is she still alive?

I push away yet another reminder of the decay of time and start past the brick wall of the empty lot.

And impulsive as it seems, I try the iron gate once more.

THIRTEEN

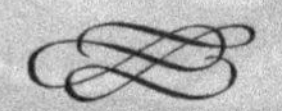

Time past and time future
What might have been and what has been
Point to one end, which is always present.

~ T.S. Eliot

A tentative push on the gate, then a forceful shove.

I am unsurprised when it doesn't give way.

Magic is never that easy.

Think, Kelsey. How did I achieve it the first time?

Standing at the gate, with twilight in the air, I saw the slight flicker of the hanging lanterns through the weeds.

Twilight.

The Time Between Times.

A shiver runs up my back and across my arms at the Celtic notion of liminal spaces, liminal times. Blurry thresholds where two things exist in one place, where the past, present, and future become one thing… The narrow space of borderlands. The turning point of a new season, of a new year. The misty moment when day gives way to dusk.

It is during the time-between-times, supposedly, that the veil between worlds becomes so thin you can, perhaps, step through it.

Is this the secret? My first glimpse was at the edge of the day, a moment of magic, reminiscent of the lights of the Ferris wheel and the Tilt-a-Whirl buzzing to life down the length of a beach pier, the washed-out ordinary color of the day fading toward the velvety, mystery-holding darkness, promising adventure.

I love the twilight, the threshold of nightfall, the hushed pause as the world holds its breath, waiting.

Two nights ago, I came back down in the dark, drawn by the music of Cole Porter drifting into my apartment.

And then the next morning, with the metal key from the Children's Section, but even though the gate opened, the Garden did not.

I check my watch. Already 9:30, later than when I entered the first time, and much later than sunset. Must I wait until tomorrow?

I give the gate another useless shake, as though my will alone will conjure something.

Upstairs, I resist the temptation to change into my paint-spattered pants and hoodie. Certainly magic cannot be triggered by something so prosaic as yoga pants.

Besides, the date-dress I'm wearing is better for a party.

Am I really thinking this is going to happen?

I sink into an upholstered chair in the dark, beside the west-facing windows overlooking William's shop. The sagging chair was an estate-sale purchase and still smells faintly floral, of rosewater perfume the elderly woman must have worn all her life.

What else? What more can I do? Is it anything I must *do*? Or perhaps something I must think, or feel?

Can these people teach me to be a real writer? Perhaps I

simply haven't had the right support and affirmation. Gran has always been encouraging, but it wasn't enough. My literature profs gave me good marks, but I never found the courage to write more than term papers for them. And after the Critique Group Incident, just after college, I haven't shown anyone my work.

Maybe the story I began as a ten-year-old, before the first mocking began, could finally be turned into something worthwhile.

Or perhaps the authors at the party could simply be honest with me. Tell me—gently, one would hope—that my efforts would be better spent elsewhere. Even that brutal truth would be better than the uncertainty of these past few years. I've been in a liminal space myself, or perhaps *limbo* would be a better word—in the medieval theology sense, of a place of waiting, between.

The possibility that I might be rejected out of hand if I attempt to claim any talent whatsoever sets me back in the chair, eyes closed.

Will I be laughed at and mocked once again for wasting my time? Reminded that the storied world of creativity and art is reserved for those born with a special endowment, the ability to create connections between the ideals of Truth, Beauty, and Goodness and the rest of us mere mortals?

I cannot know.

But I must risk it. Not only for myself, but for answers about Gran, for a way to save the shop.

The only question left is *how*. How am I to get back in?

I pull myself to standing, cross the apartment in the light of only the streetlamps, and reclaim the folded sheets tucked into *The Secret Garden*.

Those few lines at the start of my scribbling, about my own orphan girl stumbling into another place... those words were on my mind when I first heard the music.

I return to my rosewater-scented chair, pages in hand.

In what direction would my story have turned if I had continued past these few sheets?

Eyes closed again, I allow my imagination to wander down mysterious paths. To hear the gravel crunch under my tentative footsteps, smell the soft caress of pink roses eddying around me, the taste of summer on my tongue, with its languid, drowsy warmth and a hint of far-off rain…

And then it is there. Delicate and tenuous as spider-silk, ready to blow away if I listen too closely. The *ting-ting-ting* of a far-off piano.

Trance-like, I rise from the chair, barely opening my eyes, not wanting to break the spell, afraid to sever the connection.

I slow at my kitchen table, eying the rusty iron key.

But no, if I'm to be granted entrance, it will be through an act of faith alone. The old key unlocks an empty lot, nothing more. There is no key to the true Garden.

My hand skims the handrail on the way down, my breath grows shallow.

I do need a key, however, to unlock the front door of the shop. I drift around the counter, ears still trained to that elusive melody, and pull my spare ring from a plastic bin under the register.

Once the door is unlocked, I stand inside the shop a moment, key ring in hand, not wanting to take it with me into the Garden.

I toss it back onto the wooden counter. Lisa would kill me for leaving the door unlocked and the keys in full view. Oh, well.

On the sidewalk, in the dark, I fill my chest with night air. The music is no louder here on the street than it was upstairs. Is it possible it's only in my head? Am I the only one who hears it?

Should I wait for someone passing by, ask if they hear the faint tune of "You'd Be So Nice to Come Home To"?

Not sure what the point would be. Either I'm crazy or I'm

not, and right now, affirmation of either seems unimportant. The only thing that matters in this moment is whether that gate will be unlocked.

In fact, I feel my whole world centering down on that gate. As if the very existence of the Garden will negate the reality of everything else. As if the Garden is the only real thing in the world.

Twenty steps from shop door to gate. I take them slowly, still savoring the piano melody, now undergirded with the pluck of bass strings and steady *thwump* of a soft drumbeat. These instruments have only just joined the piano solo. The music grows no louder as I approach.

With fingers wrapped around the gate's bars, I pause. Try to take a breath, but it hitches in my throat like a strangled sob. I fight the urge to whisper some kind of prayer.

Why do I want this, so very, very much?

This moment here at the gate, on the threshold, unknowing what—if anything—awaits... it is every bit of joy and sadness and longing for something just out of reach I have ever known.

Sehnsucht, the Germans called it, and the paucity of English has no comparable word. That indefinable craving for something astonishingly perfect and yet beautifully intangible, a yearning that lifts the heart and mind from the awareness of the present into a bittersweetness where time does not exist and symbols become more real than the ground we walk. How many poems and melodies, books and films, have been composed around this longing for a place—a *Home*—we can never seem to find?

And here at the gate, I feel all of this, all that I have ever felt in my whole life. And in some way, I suspect all I will ever feel. It is a longing for something past, something I have abandoned or forgotten, wrapped in a soul-deep desire for a mystery I have not yet known.

Once upon a time...

I push.

It yields.

Breathless, I slide the gate forward against its aged creaking, but it gives way without resistance this time. I ease it closed behind me.

I brought no phone to light my way, trusting myself to the weeds. Hoping for the lanterns.

The dense growth brushes at my arms and face. Not scratching, more like leafy fingers encouraging me forward, touching my shoulder in encouragement.

I push ahead, heart hammering, arms burrowing.

It's taking too long. Shouldn't I have reached it by now? The life at the center?

But the music... now the music is more than smoke on the wind. A voice has joined. *You'd be so nice, you'd be paradise...* And I hear laughter. The clink of glasses. The hum of conversation.

Oh, mercy. It is truly here.

The last of the weeds sweeps from my view, and I am present in the Garden again.

The still point of the turning world.

I emerge from the growth and pause, feeling gawky as a newborn calf.

It is all the same, and yet it is different.

The same feast-laden table, the flames flickering inside globes hanging from the bent arms of the stately live oak. The scent of lilac and rose, peat and new growth.

The party guests, mingling and chatting, dressed in the clothing of their time.

My own dress. I touch the soft fabric—not the dress I wore to meet Austin. No, I'm draped again in lavender and white wisteria, ready to twirl my way through the Garden.

The clothing of their time.

Now that I'm here, I allow myself the question I've been refusing to ask.

Not only *what* is this place, but *when*?

Even if I can accept the notion of portals into the past, my quick research into the three authors I met the other night has revealed an incongruity.

Although T.S. Eliot, Agatha Christie, and L. Frank Baum were all alive at the same time, Baum's *The Wonderful Wizard of Oz* was first published in 1900. Christie's first novel did not hit stands until twenty years after that, and it would be yet another twenty years before the lines Eliot quoted from his "Four Quartets" were written. Not only that, but Baum was dead before either of those works were published.

This place, whatever it is, does not exist in a single historical era.

I set aside questions of time period and scan the Garden for what feels different. My little marble bench, where I chatted with Eliot, is still tucked against the cottony blooms of the magnolia tree. Behind the magnolia, I can just make out the dance and leap of a fountain, lit from beneath.

Tonight, I notice other light, besides the globes on the oak and the blazing torches stuck into the grass. Lanterns glow at the base of many smaller trees, uplighting limbs and flowers as though placed by a master landscaper. Along the border of the open space—not the Garden's final perimeter, which lies in shadows, but simply the edge of the party—a series of stone columns gleam, also with lanterns sheltered at their bases, creating pools of light in the blades of grass.

I approach the nearest of these columns, touch the vines and tendrils curling in hungry loops around the granite, follow the height of the column toward the sky. Surprisingly, far above me, the column joins a stone arch, which curves high and lovely over the central Garden and spills down cascades of wisteria blossoms that match my dress.

Were these columns here the other night? I don't remember them. Now that my eye is trained to see, I follow their path in a square around the huge Garden. The entire space is like an open-air courtyard. But no, not a courtyard. Each of the columns is joined to its opposite across the wide lawn by a stone arch that spans the space above my head, though open between, to the night above.

I turn a slow circle, eyes skyward.

Is this place a forgotten and broken-down cathedral slowly transmuting into wildness as it is reclaimed by nature?

Or was it firstly a lush garden, now being tamed into something that is both wild *and* sacred?

Whichever, the Garden seems a place where the mundane and the holy touch their fingertips to each other, like Adam and his Creator reaching across Michelangelo's Sistine ceiling. Where heaven seems to invade earth for a particular moment, in a particular space.

And now I notice the torchlit gravel paths lead deeper into the wildness of the Garden. These deeper places are like naves and halls, lined with benches half-shaped into wooden pews but also clinging to their former roughness as hewn logs.

The previous urge to create living beauty surges in me again. To plant something, to cultivate, to water and fertilize, prune and harvest. To take delight in the participation of a living, tended miracle.

I am tracing the vines of the living column with gentle fingers, still gawking at the luxuriant architecture and a row of topiaries shaped into blunt-topped green pyramids, when Agatha Christie appears at my elbow, champagne flute in hand, smiling as though we share a private joke.

FOURTEEN

The earth itself tells a good and true story through its shifting seasons. And this ancient and enduring story of spring, summer, fall, and winter is itself woven into numberless other tales. It is an archetype, a recurring motif that has yet to lose an ounce of its power and meaning.

~ from *Garden Maker* by Christie Purifoy

"Now you're ready, perhaps?" Agatha nudges a delicate china plate of strawberries and cheesecake tarts into my hand then lifts her champagne flute toward the Tree, toward the table groaning under its feast.

We stand with our backs to the column, the light at its base twinkling around our feet.

I take the plate, studying the woman beside me.

It's truly her. I've peered over dozens of old photos of her on my laptop. Same oval face, same languid eyes.

She wears the same ebony satin dress as the other night, the long strand of pearls and sparkling rings.

Is this version of her I'm meeting *before* or *after* her inexplicable disappearance in 1926? Gone eleven days, and decades later, it's still a mystery where she went, what happened to her. Even her autobiographical books skim the incident without mention. Do I dare ask?

Or perhaps she's already remarried to archaeologist Max Mallowan, and we're between their dig seasons in Egypt and Syria.

Forceful. That's my word for her, at least for now. She seems a force of nature to me. Smart and determined, successful and confident.

She laughs, a demure and elegant little laugh, and smooths fingertips over her hair. "Has something gone amiss? You are examining me quite intently."

"No! No, I'm sorry." I turn my gaze back to the party. Are there more people in attendance tonight? They mill about the grassy lawn, conversing under trellised arches of rambling roses and along brick pathways that lead to the shadowy perimeter.

I don't see T.S. Eliot or Frank Baum, but there are so many it would be easy to miss them.

I do, however, see the muscled guy with the great smile who kept glancing my way the other night.

He is laughing, head thrown back, at something a petite woman with radiantly dark skin is saying.

She joins his laughter and nudges his arm with her shoulder.

Agatha touches my hand. "You are nervous?" She nods. "We all are, at first, but you needn't be. F. told me how you ran off a moment ago. I hope he didn't frighten you. He can be very fanciful. Absurd even, at times."

A moment ago?

I glance at her dress again, and my own, identical to my last visit here, two nights ago.

Despite losing an entire Wednesday on the "outside," have I returned to the Garden only a moment after leaving?

Across the party, the piano-bass-drum trio is still playing, sliding into "It Don't Mean a Thing If It Ain't Got That Swing." The man in horn-rimmed glasses still stands like some kind of hipster jazz-age music teacher over the older woman with the spiky hair as she plays, that same abandoned grin on her face, wearing the same man's suit and tie as the first time I saw her.

"My dear, you are very quiet. Something is troubling you?"

I inhale, so full of questions I don't know where to begin. "Miss Chr—" The name lodges in my throat, caught there like a hand has cut off my air. I panic, unable to breathe, then suddenly the invisible grip is gone and I exhale the letter *A*, as if I never intended to call her anything else.

"Yes?"

"I want to know more about E. More about my adoption."

This is the question I have asked first? When this Garden is still so inexplicable? I've summoned the courage to return, despite the fear that I might be missing for an unknown span of time from a place and people who need me, because the risk seems necessary to get answers about saving the bookshop from the Taking. And yet my first question is about my adoption?

"Try the strawberries, dear. They are absolutely perfect."

I lift a huge berry, nearly the size of a plum, and take a bite to accommodate her. If I eat, will she talk?

I'm momentarily distracted by the taste of the strawberry. It's as if all the strawberries of my life have been an imitation of this perfect berry, which here in the Garden has ripened into what strawberries have always meant to be.

Like those blissful sips of wine as I sat beside Eliot.

"There," Agatha smiles on me. "Are you fortified now? Ready?"

The second time she's asked me this. My entrance into the Garden distracted me the first time, but a clutch of fear follows this repetition. Ready for what?

I finish the strawberry, use my tongue to ensure there is nothing stuck in my teeth, and shake my head. "Ready?"

Agatha tilts her head in mock exasperation. Or perhaps real exasperation. "To leave your gift on the table, of course."

This again.

T.S. Eliot believed I was writing a story and planned to place it on the table under the Tree.

"It's not finished yet, I'm afraid." The excuse seemed to make sense to Eliot.

A cloud passes over Agatha's features, and she returns her attention to the party-at-large.

Something about her expression tickles a new bit of anxiety. I don't want to disappoint someone I respect so greatly, but what I saw in that moment, that flash of expression, was not disappointment as much as something else. It looked like fear.

"I—I'm sure I'll be finished soon. It only needs a bit of —reworking."

Agatha says nothing. An almost-imperceptible nod of her chin is the only indication she heard me.

Should I leave and return with something written?

Sure, Kelsey, just run home and whip something up.

The hours of writer's block, no the *years,* mock this impossible idea.

Not to mention, I have no assurance I'll be able to return. Or even how to leave this place, for that matter.

"It won't be anything as good as your stories, though. I've always loved them."

Her lips twitch into a slight, sad smile, and she does not look at me. "That is lovely, and I do appreciate it. But when it comes to creativity, comparison will not serve you well. It spawns competition, which can end in only pride or pessimism, both of which have no place in an artist's world."

"But isn't it better to face the truth? To be realistic about one's ability?" *So you don't waste anyone's time,* I almost say.

At this, Agatha turns an incredulous expression on me.

"Wherever did you acquire the notion that you could be realistic about your ability?"

The words reach into the silent spaces within me, and I find I have no answer, so I avoid her gaze, turning to stand at her side and nibble on the cheesecake from my plate. A pink puff of blossom escapes from a tree and drifts to our feet.

"People will forget, K. They will forget and begin to accept the lies. It is our responsibility to remind them of the mystery, to love them back to life through the generosity of our work."

And yet, the intimidating perfection of everyone and everything in this place makes the idea of bringing my work to be welcomed or praised or respected completely ludicrous.

"I'm wondering if you can help me." Finally, I am pursuing the reason for my visit. "It's about the shop."

I realize in this moment how thin a thread I have followed to this question. My previous visit gave me some vague information about someone named "E." who received a first edition of *Oz* from L. Frank Baum himself. Yes, Gran has one in her glass case, and *Elizabeth* begins with the right letter. But that's all I have. Do these people even know about the Chestnut Street Book Emporium? About the Taking? Am I crazy to think they can help?

You believe you're standing in a magical garden. You are crazy, period.

But Agatha's kind expression is fixed on me once more. "Is there a problem with the shop? You mentioned that E. is unwell, but I hope it is nothing serious."

Ok, then. So far, so good.

Agatha points to the jazz band. "Odd that E. took ill so quickly. She was just here, dancing the Mashed Potato with P."

Wow.

My gaze drifts to the band in the leafy shadows of the

lanterns. I imagine a younger version of Gran—how young? —snapping her heels in and out, kicking her legs into the air.

How long has this party been going on?

Probably better not to mention Gran's age, or her decline.

"The shop is in some financial trouble, I'm afraid."

I've finished off the dessert but still hold the empty plate, fingers shaking a bit, at my waist.

"When I was here last time—when we talked a little while ago—you mentioned F. giving her the first edition. We've decided to sell it, to help offset expenses. But it won't be enough, not for long."

"You're—selling it?"

Uh oh. It has not occurred to me that the sale might be frowned upon. "Yes, as you said, it is worth—"

"You are selling F.'s work, and bringing none of your own?"

I inhale against a tightening chest, and my eyes flutter closed. I'm botching this whole thing, badly.

It's as if I'm ten years old again, ridiculed for trying to be a writer. Standing on the outside. Waiting to be rejected.

This Garden is beginning to feel like a test. One I am failing, mostly because I don't understand the questions. Can I gain helpful answers only if I bring a good story? But this place boasts novelists like Agatha, and Frank Baum, and a poet like T.S. Eliot. How in the world am I supposed to offer anything of value to this group?

I am still searching for a reply, eyes closed, when Agatha touches my arm.

I turn to face her, feeling an embarrassed flush creeping up my chest into my throat.

"I don't mean to criticize, my dear. I—I am only worried, you see. We rely upon—that is to say, the Garden relies upon —well, you understand. The paths are only open when we all work together, not simply to seek, but to build."

Could she be any more enigmatic?

"I don't understand, I'm sorry."

But she is shaking her head, lips a tight slash. "I've said too much already. I must go and find C. He will know better what is to be done."

But her fingers are still on my arm and her grip curls around me, tightening uncomfortably. She leans close and whispers. "Be careful."

And then she hurries away, throwing a faux smile to someone across the grass, leaving me with a chill and a foreboding unease.

The paths are only open...

Am I trapped here?

FIFTEEN

The artist is someone who is full of questions, who cries them out in great angst, who discovers rainbow answers in the darkness, and then rushes to canvas or paper.

~ Madeleine L'Engle

Standing alone at the edge of the lawn, the empty plate in my hand, I feel foolish, my legs restless.

I thread my way through the groups of guests who talk and laugh like age-old friends to the flower-swagged table under the globe lanterns. Hanging between the lanterns, crystal teardrops shimmer on invisible gossamer threads and catch the firelight as they spiral in the slight breeze. The musical trio continues to play, something a bit tamer now, a song I don't recognize.

I would prefer to fade into the periphery of the Garden, to observe from a safe distance. But I can't waste this chance if there's a way to get help for the shop.

And so I tap into my second-best party strategy.

I have always relied upon food at any social gathering to cover my awkward sense of being an outsider. Tonight, I load the floral china plate with roasted new potatoes and grilled asparagus, then add something that looks like a curried meat with cashews from a vine-covered ceramic dish. A three-tiered tray of seared scallops swimming in browned butter draws my eye and I add a couple of those. The table is weighted at either end with mountains of desserts, but I'll save those for later.

Loading my plate is not just for show. The cheeseburger at the Sunny Side Up Diner feels like hours ago.

There is an urn of steaming, deep-roasted coffee, but I allow a smiling young woman to pour me a glass of white wine. She is tiny and dark, almost elfin in appearance, with bright green eyes.

Now, who looks likely to have information that could help me?

The "gift table" under the arms of the gnarled Tree is piled higher than I remember. I circle to take a closer look.

Leather-bound books, but also looseleaf manuscripts—in progress, perhaps? Stretched canvases of finished and unfinished art in the impressionist style, others surreal or abstract. A sheaf of sheet music stands propped against an exquisite violin. Smudgy pencil sketches, rainbow-hued pottery, black-and-white woodcut prints, and on the grass beside the table, a delicate marble angel spreads her wings. The display is a visual feast to rival the food, a jumble of prodigious talent and astonishing beauty.

Someone behind me jostles my arm, nearly spilling my wine.

I turn, smiling, to a man slightly shorter than me, his face narrowing to a sharp chin softened by a reddish beard. He wears a heavy wool coat over a high-collared white shirt and carries a canvas, aiming for the table.

"Excusez-moi, excusez-moi! Je ne sais pas où j'avais la tête!" He shakes his lowered head, as though humiliated.

I know very little French but get the idea. And I am reminded, oddly, of A.A. Milne's character of Piglet, with his tendency to apologize and catastrophize everything that happens to him and Winnie the Pooh.

"No harm done."

"You are too kind." This in English.

"I am glad it didn't spill," I lift my wine glass, "since I would not want to see your canvas ruined."

"Ah, this, yes." He holds it up in both hands and tilts it left and right, as if seeing it for the first time.

I suck in a breath. It's a beautiful piece. And a recognizable one.

Café Terrace at Night.

And if I'm right, then that would make my new friend... Vincent van Gogh.

"I've always loved this one," I say, not thinking how strange it might sound.

"Have you?"

If there's a lack of logic to my recognition of his painting, he doesn't seem to notice. Of course, he was known to be a bit mad.

My glance flicks to his left ear, then the right, since I can't remember which one he cut off. Both intact, thankfully. Or intact *again*? I would not be surprised to learn this place has the power of restoration. And I still haven't worked out if the Garden exists in any actual time. Van Gogh's presence seems to confirm my suspicions about the timelessness of this place. I don't remember much from Art History 101, but it seems like he was before Agatha's time.

Van Gogh studies his work a moment longer. "I am glad you like it. But perhaps you will be the only one." A quick, embarrassed laugh. "Though of course it does not matter what they think. Only what they feel."

He places the canvas, cockeyed, into the midst of the jumble and stands back, stroking his beard and biting his lower lip. "This piece makes you feel something, I hope?" He glances at me, then breaks eye contact, as if he is not brave enough to hold it.

"It does, indeed." The pulsing golden stars in a blue sky tempt me to stroll beyond the café to the end of the cobblestone street and into the darkened buildings in the background. "I would very much like to visit France and walk these streets at night."

"Yes, I often think that the night is more alive and more richly colored than the day."

Compelling. The perfect word to describe my new friend.

I set my glass and my plate, still piled with delectables, on the edge of the food table and cross to the table of art. "May I?" I glance back at him, indicating my desire to pick up the piece set so casually askew among its peers.

"Of course, of course."

I begin with *Café Terrace at Night* but cannot help shifting several other canvases before moving on to some of the books and papers, then sketches and pottery. Within sixty seconds I have arranged the entire table as if it's a display at the Book Emporium, with asymmetrical lines, balanced proportions, and color palettes which at some points contrast and others complement.

I stand back, head tilted, reminiscent of Van Gogh's examination of his masterpiece.

"My dear, you are a genius!"

I laugh, more amused than he can possibly know, considering the man who has said it, and shrug. "I've always had a knack for merchandising."

But this is not merchandising, is it? This display is not to attract buyers. What is it for then?

"You are too modest! The way you have arranged everything—it is art in itself!" He turns to face me. "We have never formally met, I do not believe, though I have seen you here often." He extends a hand, the nails spattered with the hardened paint of a hundred canvases. "I am V."

Of course you are.

I take his hand in mine. "And I am K. It's wonderful to meet you."

"Yes, K., lovely. You are E.'s girl, are you not?"

I nod.

"Ah, we were so happy when you were given to her."

I breathe, in-and-out, over that comment, but let it go.

I am determined to first broach the topic of the bookshop needing help.

I leave my plate untouched on the table but return to another sip or two of wine. "What is it all for?" I wave a hand toward the artwork. "Why do you bring it?"

His brow creases for a fraction of a moment—that same look of consternation I saw in Agatha. "Because we must."

I clasp my arms around myself, suddenly as chilled as the wine still balanced in my fingers.

Is there some higher power at work here in the Garden? Something forcing people to bring their work, like sacrificial lambs, to offer at the base of the Tree? I look up into its reaching, spreading branches. The water running in streams below reflects on the underside of the limbs in rippled waves of bluish-white.

"Someone is… demanding that you bring your work?"

"Of course not. We give freely. We choose to offer our gifts because of the enemy."

Oh, mercy.

I scramble for a response, feeling my pulse throb in my neck.

"There is an enemy?"

Again, the flicker of concern on his face at my ignorance. "There is always the Enemy."

I hear it with a capital "E," like a storybook villain.

"K., you must never forget there is always and forever an Enemy to all generative work. One who would destroy all life-bringing creativity. One who can wreak destruction if the circumstances are ripe for it."

"Destruction, here?" I sweep a glance to encompass all

within the granite columns which embrace the wide lawn. "This place seems like perfection."

"Ah, but in every story perfection is under constant threat."

True. And also true there are many unexplored and darkened areas beyond what I can see.

Van Gogh turns back to face the party with me, as if watching for this Enemy to approach even now. What are the right circumstances for such a thing? Or is he simply paranoid?

Be careful. Agatha's whispered warning.

"*Trompe l'œil.* You know this term?" Van Gogh asks.

"Yes, I've heard it. Those optical illusion paintings that make you think part of the painting is real, right? Like a scene beyond a window when even the window is part of the painting."

He smiles. "Very good. Yes. *Trompe l'œil*—'fool the eye' it means. But this is all of life. Everything is a flat stage prop, a *trompe l'œil* horizon to fool us into believing the lie that all we can see is all that exists. When there is so much *more.* And as an artist, you tell them this truth."

"Do you know everyone here?" I point my chin to the clusters of guests. "Are you all… artistic?"

"We are all *creative*. But then, everyone is creative in some way, would you not agree?"

I bite my lip, hesitant to disagree. Because… *Van Gogh*. "Well, I know many people who are not artistic, or musical, or gifted with words."

He nods. "Of course, these are the arts that receive the most attention. Though perhaps not the most money." He half-bows toward his painting with a small laugh. "But are there not a thousand ways to be creative?" He spreads a hand to the table. "What of the chef who prepares a feast for the eyes and the nose as well as the palate, and the host who spreads it for us?" Another gesture, to the party beyond. "Or the gardener who transforms a field into a paradise?"

"I hadn't thought of creativity that way."

"Everywhere there is beauty, my dear. And those who draw our eye, our ear, any bit of our attention to this beauty are the artists among us. Whether the beauty is a sculpture or a piece of jewelry. A sonata or a sitting room. A well-told story or a well-proportioned building, or even a well-oiled machine. Let us never minimize the gifts of those who bring us beauty in whatever form they are skilled to bring it."

I'm pondering his words, savoring them, really, when an approaching figure catches my eye.

My "admirer" as T.S. Eliot called him, who has been at the fringes of this crowd. Stubbled jawline, wide shoulders, still wearing the shirt rolled to his elbows and black vest. His eyes are on mine as he nears.

I tuck an errant strand of hair behind my ear. Good thing I left my piled plate of food on the table.

"Hello, hello." Van Gogh nods furiously.

After all the looks and glances this guy has given me, a sudden thought sets my pulse racing again. Am I'm supposed to know him?

Van Gogh extends a hand and grips the man's upper arm. "Good to see you. Good, yes." He turns to me. "You've met S.?"

I take a chance and shake my head in the negative.

The newcomer smiles that big, joyful smile I've already noted.

"Well, S., this is K."

So many letters. But, okay, this guy is "S." How can I figure out what that initial stands for? He seems to be a friend of Van Gogh's, but I don't know enough history to guess who it might be.

"It's nice to meet you, K."

I resist the urge to ask why he's been looking my direction so often.

"Nice to meet you, too."

"S. is a sculptor," Van Gogh explains.

"Oh, wonderful." I try to be appropriately impressed, still having no clue. A couple of the Ninja Turtles were sculptors, right? Michelangelo, Donatello, maybe? Nothing with an S. "Do you have a piece here at the Tree?" I glance over and realize there are at least a dozen sculptures in various spots in the grass, between the streams running out in four directions from the trunk. Molded, cast, and carved, though I'm not even sure if that means they are all considered "sculptures." I smile at him, awaiting the identification of his piece.

"Yes."

Ah. Okay, then.

"K. is a Storyteller." Van Gogh seems to be playing matchmaker.

I can think of very few weirder things.

"Where is your work, K.?" Van Gogh asks, his Dutch accent heavy on the words.

"I—haven't brought anything. Yet."

Van Gogh turns to S. "She is E.'s girl," he says. As if this is some explanation for my lack of offering.

Well, perhaps I'm only here on a guest pass, and it's really Gran who deserves to be here, bringing her poetry.

But S. says nothing in response to this explanation.

"I will leave you two to discuss." Van Gogh half-bows and backs away.

I lift a hand, as if to detain him. I've gathered no usable information.

But he's gone, and I've been left to "discuss" something, though I have no idea what, with an extremely good-looking stranger I should probably know but do not.

I resort to another sip of wine.

SIXTEEN

You use a glass mirror to see your face; you use works of art to see your soul.

~ George Bernard Shaw

The man called S. turns to stand beside me, and we watch Van Gogh's retreating figure in silence for a moment.

I search for something artsy to say. About sculpting. Or anything. I need to break the ice somehow, before starting to grill him with questions about saving the Book Emporium.

S. inhales deeply, stretching the buttons of his starched white shirt across his chest, then turns to me. "You are not eating? The food is wonderful."

"Oh, yes. I—I set my plate down." I wave a hand in the direction of the table.

Why did I say that? If I return to that mound of food, he'll likely think it's the only reason I'm here.

"Come," he inclines his head toward the table, grinning. "I don't believe in being a starving artist."

"Ha! Well then, you'll love what I'm eating."

I retrieve my plate and brandish it with a shrug.

He looks it over, bends to examine it. "Are those... *scallops?*"

I lift the plate. "Have one."

Still bent, his eyes flick up to mine, as if to assure himself I've offered him food from my plate. His blue eyes are a breath away, his lips serious.

He plucks a scallop and pops it into his mouth in a single bite. Then closes his eyes and tips his head back as he chews, the way Agatha did with the canapé.

Yes, the food here is that good.

I watch him, the sharp angles of his jaw, the full eyebrows and generous mouth.

Who is this man?

I can trace just the tiniest bit of an accent in his speech. Something European—the uplifted final syllable of Italian, perhaps. His clothing—the gleaming white shirt under the shiny black vest—it could be from practically any era.

"I must have more of these." He turns to the table, takes a china plate from the stack, and begins to fill it, beginning with the scallops.

Van Gogh and I were blocking his path to the food, weren't we? While it appeared he was eagerly joining us, perhaps he was only headed to the table. Sure, he's been giving me looks, but he hasn't approached until now. Maybe I'm way off.

An image of Austin across the table at dinner, elbows propped and hands clasped over his meal as he earnestly lectures me about my business practices, floats at the periphery of my thoughts.

I push the image away. This guy—S.—is either long-dead, a figment of my imagination, or part of a vivid dream. I refuse to feel guilty.

He returns to my side with his plate heaped higher than mine, a thick filet of pecan-encrusted salmon topping the pile. He lifts the plate in my direction, as if to toast our mutual gluttony.

"Would you like to walk?"

"Sure." I set my wineglass—now empty—on a nearby round table laden with a tray of empty glasses.

S. ambles away from the Tree, away from the center of the Garden, toward the shadowy outer edge where Chestnut Street should be.

We follow one of the four streams until it reaches a larger pool surrounded by lantern-lit trees, rimmed with mosaic tiles in charcoal, silver, and white. The pool stretches oblong into the shadows, then spills off the far edge with the *sploosh* of a short drop to another pool.

In the distance, a tiny light seems to be set waist-high, illuminating a whiteish grid around it. A window?

"It is so beautiful here. I keep discovering new areas."

S. leads the way as we skirt the pool and continue beyond the drop. "Indeed. There is much to discover."

We descend a few brick steps to a gravel path leading into a jumble of trees. In unspoken consent, we drift onto the shadowed path. The borders of pink orchids and yellow lilies give way to frilled ferns and the pebbled purple leaves of coleus.

I pick at my asparagus and curried chicken as we walk. The engraved design of twirling vines in my heavy silver fork sparkles in the torchlight. I am still searching for some comment about art that will sound intelligent.

But S. speaks first. "So, you are a Storyteller? What is your story wanting to say?"

I chew my chicken. What an unusual question. He hasn't asked what my story is *about,* the only thing I've ever been asked when people hear that I'm trying to be a novelist.

What is my story *wanting to say*?

As if my story is alive, asking me to give it voice.

I shake away the image, because… because there is no story.

"I'm afraid it's too small to say anything just yet."

"Ah, still just an infant-story, then."

I laugh. "Yes, something like that. But I'd rather hear about your sculptures. What are they wanting to say?" I nearly laugh again. I've finally found something "artsy" to talk about, even if I'm only parroting him.

But S. is not laughing. We walk for a moment in silence along the edge of the stream.

"My sculptures. They are saying… *see us.*"

The words have emerged from him like a secret. Quiet and hard-edged, like he has been clenching them in his palm and has only pried his fingers open for a moment to let me glimpse his pain.

I slow on the path and look up into his startling eyes, hooded with an emotion I can't identify.

Unthinking, I put a hand to his arm, warm under my touch. As if I can heal his wounds.

He covers my hand with his own.

Something like electricity, like fairy tale, like coming home, runs through me.

I pull my hand away.

This place is dangerous.

I continue toward the trees, feeling him follow at my heels. The white-glowing gravel crunches underfoot, masking the silence between us.

On either side of the path, the ferns thicken into trees, until we are more in the woods than a Garden. Still the path winds on, the distant light growing only slightly brighter.

We should probably turn back. But my curiosity pulls me forward.

The light is indeed a window, the rest of the structure coming into focus as we walk.

"Is that—a cottage?"

I slow, and S. draws to my side.

We both take in the sloped roof with tiles like gingerbread, the fat stacked-stone fireplace complete with wispy smoke curling into the night air, the arched window resting on a flower box overflowing with petunias in jewel-tones of amethyst and ruby, and tiny blue cornflowers.

How can this place be here? It is like wandering to the edge of a high-class botanical garden in the city and finding the entrance to a hobbit's shire. My mind tries to shift around the new information, but it is too much.

We walk toward the cottage, and I wonder, briefly, if we will meet F-for-Frodo inside.

But on the narrowing lane that leads to the wood-slatted door is someone more like Gandalf than Frodo. He steps into our path.

Gray-haired and gray-bearded, he holds a sword with both hands, just above the hilt, pointed to the ground.

I half-expect him to growl *You Shall Not Pass!*

But he does not wear the wizard's cloak or hat. He is in silver chain mail with a sapphire-studded golden crown resting on his forehead.

"This is not for you," he says simply, his eyes piercing.

I can't tell if he is speaking to me or to S., or perhaps both of us.

We hesitate, as though we intend to argue, which is, of course, laughable.

S. turns toward me, eyebrows lifted, then continues his slow spin to face back the way we came.

We walk away, toward where the path at the perimeter of the Garden branched into this shadowy forest.

"Any idea who that was?" I whisper to S.

He glances over his shoulder. "I'm not certain. But the sword—did you see it? Two fire-breathing chimeras on the hilt."

I shake my head. Medieval swords are not my thing.

"I think the sword was Excalibur."

I slow down, pinch the bridge of my nose, and close my

eyes. I have come to this place to get advice about how to save Gran's bookshop. Instead, I've rearranged Van Gogh's artwork, flirted with a sexy sculptor, and been turned away from an enchanted cottage by King Arthur.

"Are you—are you alright?"

I sigh. "A little overwhelmed, I suppose."

We cross a tiny stone bridge to the far side of the cascading pool.

I bend to dip my fingers into the eddying current as we cross. The crystal water bubbles around my fingertips, cold as a mountain stream.

At the edge of the pool stands a round, stone pavilion, like a miniature temple—known as a "folly" in the English countryside. As wide across as a small patio with a dome supported by ten pillars and three steps to reach its platform, it is architecture created as purely decorative, serving no other purpose than to be seen at the far edge of an estate, strolled toward, then lingered upon as one takes in bucolic views.

S. extends a hand, and we ascend the folly's steps and turn, from this angle able to see the sheeting water drop from the first pool, with lights glowing from behind the fall. We sit on the top step, in a world alone.

I've been resisting giving S. a descriptive word. It's a habit usually reserved for casual acquaintances, and I'm wishing for something more than casual. Besides, "swoon-worthy" is technically two words, isn't it?

I set my empty plate beside me. I'm full and just a bit lightheaded. Probably too much to drink.

We watch the party in silence, arms resting lightly against each other as we sit on the step. Comfortable, except for the heat running through me. It feels like the first night, sitting with T.S. Eliot. And yet nothing like that.

"Can I—" I turn to him, hesitating. "May I know your name?"

It's not just about wanting to Google him later. There is

something too distant about only using abbreviations. And I find myself wanting very much to close the gap between us.

He smiles. "It's S—" The word cuts off in the same way I could not speak Agatha Christie's name.

He shakes his head and shrugs.

"It's fine. S. is fine."

"Perhaps a clue?" He looks around, surveying the guests. "I do not think he's here, so perhaps I can say his name… You know the poet, Coleridge?"

I smile. "You mean S—" But "Samuel" sticks in my throat.

We both laugh.

"Looks like you've got it."

I lean into him.

So, the same first name as the poet, Samuel Coleridge. Doesn't tell me who he is, but at least I have a first name, though I think I'll call him Sam. Since it's only in my head, anyway.

"Your turn," he says. "A clue."

That's a tough one. I can't think of a single well-known *Kelsey* born before the twentieth century.

I smooth my wisteria-covered dress over my legs. "No famous versions, I don't believe. It's an Irish name, which I think is supposed to mean 'brave,' if that helps."

"And are you brave, Irish-girl?"

I laugh. "Not particularly. I'm not even Irish. That I know of." I lift an olive-skinned arm as proof.

"Hmm." He rubs his chin. "I suppose we will have to stick with letters, though I do not think we can do without bravery."

I nod my head toward King Arthur. "Thinking of facing down Excalibur?"

He laughs. "Nothing so headstrong as that. But still, I have found it takes courage to face the inevitable if I am to create."

"Inevitable?"

He shrugs, but his tone is not casual. "Failure. Disappointment."

I want to ask *then why do it?* But I know the answer.

The conversation lulls, but it's a lovely space. We gaze across to the wider lawn in the distance and the foreground of abundant flowers and vines nearby—fringed and ferny, in spikes and cups, fuzzy as lamb's ear and diaphanous as silk. The air is an intoxicating blend of gardenia and hyacinth. In truth, I could sit here for hours, basking in the green hush, the twinkling lights with matching stars above, the scents of gardenia and jasmine infused into every breath.

But I have a mission, one I can't ignore.

"When we spoke with V., he told you I was E.'s girl." I broach the new topic tentatively. "Do you know E. well? I'm hoping to get some help with a problem she's having."

"What kind of problem?"

My answer is interrupted by a woman standing at the far-off buffet clinking a fork against a glass.

"Attention, attention," she says, in a lyrical accent, which somehow carries all the way to where we sit.

I raise my head, surprised. It's the first announcement of any kind since I've entered the Garden. Somehow, I thought my experience thus far was all there was. Just a wandering about, eating and drinking. Has this only been the preamble to some kind of program?

"What happens now?" I whisper to Sam.

He spreads his palms and lifts his shoulders, as if as baffled as I.

We stand in unison, step down out of the folly, and cross into the central area of the Garden, to be part of whatever is going on.

"It is time," the woman calls over the slowly quieting crowd, "for one of our favorite activities."

She's a strikingly beautiful Indian woman with a gold-dotted headscarf over her dark hair and a coil of gold armbands circling her forearm.

The partygoers begin to drift toward the central oak from all corners of the Garden.

"Yes, yes, come closer. Do not make me shout." She smiles over the crowd, like a beneficent queen.

Who knows? Perhaps she is.

Sam and I stand amidst a copse of green bamboo which runs in a narrow band at least two stories high. The sturdy stems and leafy branches, uplit by spotlights, sway and flutter in a soft breeze. We squeeze in among stone urns filled with rounded gray-green succulents and lush palms the color of ripe kiwi. Even the smell here is tropical—I would swear to the scent of coconut and citrus in the air.

"Wonderful." Our hostess claps twice. "Now, for our next guided conversation, we will join in groups of three."

Immediately, the crowd begins shifting, a dance for which everyone seems to know the steps.

I look to Sam in a bit of panic, smiling to cover my ignorance.

He takes a half-step toward me, as if to claim me for his own.

A thin, middle-aged gentleman nearby, sporting a long beard and dark hair beginning to recede, catches my attention and raises his brows in inquiry. He wears a velvet jacket the color of red merlot over a starched white shirt and black bow tie. He looks like he should be smoking a pipe.

I nod assent, smiling. His face is familiar, but I'm not placing him yet.

He joins us, bouncing on his toes at my side. "Thank you, my dear. One is always nervous about finding compatriots for these things, you know." He bows in my direction. "I am C. And you are?"

"K., and this is S." I'm finding the letters less awkward as time goes on. Perhaps there is something enjoyable in the anonymity.

Though I am sure I know this man from somewhere. A

blurry version of his face—a little older perhaps—dances at the edge of my memory.

"Yes, well, S. and I have surely met, but I am quite pleased to make your acquaintance, K., for whatever jollity A. up there has planned for us next!" He jabs a thumb in the direction of the woman at the front, then punctuates it with a grin and another bounce.

Congenial.

We've chosen our third partner well, I think. Someone to fill any conversational gaps. And I'm happy to meet yet another guest who might have answers to my problem.

At the base of the Tree, the woman, apparently another A., is clinking her glass again. "We are ready, then? Groups of three? Well done, all. Now. We all are much aware of the nourishing power of our little artistic community here. One of our functions is to encourage each other's work, regardless of his or her place in the creative journey. To remind each other of the extraordinary generosity that must be summoned to do this work. Without each other, as you know, we are likely to forget our power, to forget our roles, to allow the deception to fester."

She lets these words linger over the quieted crowd.

Those nearest me are nodding, smiling. As though she has spoken what they are all thinking, what they would say if it were one of them at the base of the Tree.

"With that in mind, we will speak some creative encouragement around our tiny circles, each one speaking to the person on their left."

She twirls her hand in the air.

"And... Begin!"

SEVENTEEN

EMILY: Does anyone ever realize life while they live it...every, every minute?

STAGE MANAGER: No. Saints and poets maybe...they do some.

~ from *Our Town* by Thornton Wilder

Despite the safety of being tucked into our little bamboo alcove, my throat goes instantly dry. What can I possibly say to either of these men whom I know nothing about?

Sam glances at me and clearly perceives my panic.

"I can start."

I breathe out relief.

Although he doesn't know me, either. What can he possibly say?

But Sam turns to C.

"Your work has had great impact on my life." He smiles, a self-conscious sort of smile with a dip of his head. "Imaginative, of course. For the boy that I once was, enough ghostly apparitions and spooky graveyards to keep me intrigued. For the adolescent, confirmed in all the feelings and trials of growing into a man, and all the... *expectations*... which that brings."

At this, they share a knowing smile, some secret code I'm missing.

C. appears a bit choked up.

"And, of course, as I matured, understanding your great passion for the impoverished and ill-treated, seeing the inequality you brought to light." Sam's hands punctuate each point in his expressive way. "I'm only one person, of course, but for me, your work has been delightful, encouraging, and challenging."

C. grips Sam's upper arm and bows his head briefly. "You have given me a gift, then. For no one is useless in this world who lightens the burdens of another."

And, *click*.

Just like that, the face of the man before me transmutes itself to a framed, fake-vintage oil painting on the wall of the BRITISH LITERATURE section of the Book Emporium, with the very words he just spoke emblazoned as a quote on the picture's matting.

Hello, Charles Dickens.

C. releases his grip on Sam's arm, but at the same moment I reach out to Dickens myself, grabbing his free hand before my usual reticence kicks in.

"I am so happy to meet you." The words gush, but I don't care. *Great Expectations, A Tale of Two Cities, A Christmas Carol, Oliver Twist, David Copperfield...* I can't stop the flood of works through my brain, all of them favorites at some point in my life. "You—I love your work."

Unexpectedly, he pulls me to himself, into an embrace.

His beard tickling my cheek, and I close my eyes against unexplainable tears. He smells of ink and old paper, just as he should.

"Thank you, my dear," he whispers before releasing me. "And now, it would appear to be my turn to speak to you."

This cannot be happening.

"But since we have only just met, I will need a bit of enlightenment—"

"She's a Storyteller, as well." This from Sam, his eyes on me.

"Ah, wonderful! I look forward to reading your work soon!" Dickens claps his hands together, then presses the tips of his fingers against his bottom lip and lowers his head to study me. "But until then, I will tell you some things..." His eyes narrow, as if reading my secrets.

I study the grass at my feet. I don't want him to feel obligated to say untrue things simply because he has been assigned this strange exercise.

"Yes, I see. It is like that, is it?"

I return my gaze to his. What does he see?

"You are still early in your journey, I suspect. Still questioning. Perhaps even... refusing?"

He waits as if for some affirmation from me.

I nod, a little unsure of what I'm admitting.

"I wonder... " His voice tilts into a musing, inquisitive tone. "You feel it, but you sometimes push it away. Perhaps to focus on surviving. As we often think we must. Or perhaps... you have been deceived into believing you will find happiness elsewhere, in lesser things."

A cool breeze ruffles my hair, and the tears threaten again. This Garden is such a strange place.

Dickens takes my hand in his own, envelops it with his other. "I fear the touch of God has been buried by some trauma, my girl. Voices from the past which discredit you in your search for something *other*. Because of this, you have embraced pragmatism until you have become... benumbed."

Is this man a novelist or a psychiatrist?

I clear my throat against the rush of hot emotion and look away.

"Oh, but what have I done?" He leans toward me. "Our wonderful community is meant to be encouraging, and I have only made you cry."

"No." I return my attention to him. "No, I appreciate what you've said. I will need to think more on it."

"Don't think too long, my dear. Refusal is a dangerous thing."

So I've heard.

But now it's clearly my turn to encourage Sam in some way, impossible as that seems.

I smile on Dickens, pull my hand from his warm clasp, and turn to Sam.

He is looking at the grass.

I know how that feels.

His earlier words, about his sculptures, return to me.

They are saying... *see us*.

"My turn," I say brightly, drawing his attention to my face.

"You don't need to—"

"Nonsense. If C. here can encourage me, having just met me, then certainly I can do the same."

Sam inhales, lifts his chin, and nods.

"Okay. I think you worry, maybe even you *fear*, that unacknowledged work has no value. And because you are, at your core, an artist, you therefore fear at times that it's *you* who has no value. You long to create art that touches people, that moves them. Just as you spoke of C.'s work doing for you."

His jaw is tight. Clenched against my words, but not in anger. It seems I've hit a nerve, and he's working hard to stay controlled.

"I think you need to reawaken to beauty itself. To become alive again to the value of your own creativity, to its purpose in the world. Regardless of the recognition the work may, or may not, receive."

Where am I getting these words? They pour out of somewhere deep within me, as if I'm channeling Dickens but also as if they've always been there, though I have not been listening.

"You are discouraged. You are tempted to quit. But you cannot quit. The world needs what only *you* can bring to it."

His breathing is heavy, his chin lowered.

"You are important, S." I take his hand now. Wait for him to meet my eyes. "And I *see you*."

He returns my grip with such fierceness, like a man being pulled from the abyss.

I try to smile but find myself choking back a sob instead.

Wanting to remain here, in this moment, my hand wrapped in his, for a very long time.

A *clink-clink* again, from the front of the crowd.

Our hostess of the moment extends a gold-bangled arm over the crowd as though bestowing a blessing. "Perhaps you are finished now, perhaps you are not. We will soon have someone to sing for us, and you will enjoy it so very much." She turns to the jazz trio. "But first let us thank our dear friends, J. and E., and of course B. on the piano, for granting us such pleasure."

Enthusiastic applause and a few hoots circle the crowd.

The older woman at the piano, B., pushes to her feet with a bit of a self-conscious flush. She ducks her head in a few directions, acknowledging the little groups of applause.

Beside me, Dickens has drifted, or been pulled, away. He chats with others nearby, as though our time together, while enjoyable, was only a small part of his evening.

Sam, however, remains at my side.

But not for long.

The Indian woman who led our group activity appears. She is even more beautiful up close. "S., you simply must meet D. and H." She smiles at me. "You will not mind if I steal him for a few moments?"

She tugs Sam's arm without waiting for my response.

He meets my eyes, an unreadable expression on his face.

I choose to believe the expression is regret at being separated from me. I nod, waggle my fingers, and half-turn away, to give him permission to abandon me without feeling rude.

"I'll be back," he says, eyes on my face. "Soon."

I feel the words, warm as the wine, in my chest.

He disappears with the woman into the crowd.

I am at a loss for a moment, with hands empty and standing alone. I left my plate of food in the stone folly, but glancing back, I don't see it. There seems to be an invisible staff taking care of the pesky details of cleanup.

I twist my fingers together at my waist. Are people watching me fidget like the unpopular girl at the party?

I need something for my hands, so I head back to the food table. Maybe dessert.

But my stomach is twirling with the emotion of the past hour, and not even the dark chocolate tart drizzled with caramel holds appeal.

I take an already-filled champagne flute. I've had plenty to drink tonight, but it's an easy prop for jittery fingers.

I float through the crowd, attempting to look confident and available for conversation and not too pathetically alone. A party trick not easily accomplished, I have found over the years.

Perhaps I should explore a further edge of the Garden I have not yet seen? Maybe someone will approach me with a conversation-starter, making it easier to probe for answers. Thus far, I've gotten nowhere with my questions.

I wander past large and friendly debates, shared group jokes, heads bent together in intimate conversations, even a few couples silent and observant.

I push farther than I've yet been, toward a lighted area that's been obscured by the bamboo copse.

A huge pergola appears, the underside of the latticed roof strung with fairy lights amidst the green hearts and white blooms of moonflower vines. Gauzy fabric the color of clouds is tied at each corner. At the far end, a warm blaze burns in a stone fire pit.

I approach from the side, unnoticed by the two people who converse quietly on a sumptuous white couch. I hold back in the shadows, beside the pineapple-bark of a slim palm tree.

I run my glance over them both, as opposite as seems possible. A heavyish black man in a black tux, white shirt, and black bow tie holds a trumpet loosely at his side. His companion, a rail-thin woman so white she seems nearly alabaster, is swathed in a complicated arrangement of pearly fabrics, like some kind of Greek goddess.

It's very little to go on, and I have no expertise in the arena of trumpet players.

I listen for clues, curious.

"Perhaps if I speak to her," the woman is saying.

He shakes his head. "She needs to come to understanding on her own. She's not ready for you, yet."

"But did you hear about the book, L.?"

I lean against the palm trunk feeling only a little guilty for eavesdropping.

So, the man is L.

I scan the memory banks… Louis Armstrong? Seems like a good guess, but maybe only because I've got jazz on my mind.

L. nods. "Yes, I heard. *Selling* it. And she's brought nothing of her own."

My fingers convulse around the champagne flute. I switch it to my other hand, as if the act will save it from being shattered.

They are talking about me.

I shift behind the palm, further out of sight of the pergola, only half my face exposed so I can watch them speak.

"Why does E. do nothing?" The woman's question seems to stem from sadness more than aggravation. "It's dangerous to allow it. You know the threat as well as I."

L. shrugs. "Someone has said E.'s unwell, but it does seem odd."

The Greek woman sighs. "And she had such a promising beginning. So... eager."

"But of course, she's not legitimately E.'s daughter, so that may explain—"

The woman waves off L.'s explanation. "What difference does that make? I've inspired a thousand creative minds with no genetic connection to any prior genius."

I'm breathing through parted lips now, trying to stay quiet enough to hear over the pounding in my head.

"This girl is different," he says. "She doesn't know the truth about herself. Perhaps it's—clouded—things for her."

"She doesn't know the *facts*, perhaps. But there is still truth in her. Give her time. She'll understand better after she's gone deeper, understands all that is required."

"I only hope it won't be too late."

From the faraway center of the Garden, the music picks up again, this time an ensemble of strings in that pleasant cacophony of instrument-tuning that precedes an orchestra performance.

The two I've been eavesdropping on turn together toward the music, lift their faces in smiles, as if the instruments are warm sunlight on their skin, then stand and leave the pergola behind, walking together toward the Tree.

I step out of the shadows, heart racing, hand on the wooden post.

Unthinking, I put the champagne flute to my lips, tilt it backward. Find it already empty.

Between the alcohol and the overheard conversation, my head is as dizzy as a mad teacup ride.

Be careful.

I need to get out of here.

I stumble to the right, past a free-standing living wall crumbling at the edges and tangled with English ivy, toward what feels like the direction of my bench under the magnolia.

There, there it is, the bench, like an *Exit* sign.

I'm blinking too much now. It's impeding my vision, which is blurring at the edges and bursting with little flares of light in the center.

Where is the tunnel of vines and weeds I've emerged through twice?

I thrash at the thick shrubbery, push past a weeping willow—champagne flute gone now, I have no idea where—deeper, deeper into what should be my leafy tunnel, but nothing feels familiar and the dizziness is starting to get bad. Really bad.

And then I am flat on my back, eyes squeezed shut against a hot glare, and someone is shouting my name.

EIGHTEEN

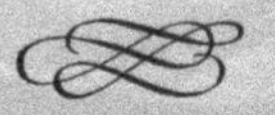

Art brings things to light. It illuminates us. It sheds light on our lingering darkness. It casts a beam into the heart of our own darkness and says, "See?"

~ from *The Artist's Way* by Julia Cameron

I force my gritty eyes to open.

Find myself in my bed.

"Kelsey!"

I grab at sheets, brain pummeled with stimuli.

My bed. Ceiling above me.

Someone yelling.

Sunlight, harsh and bright from the window. So … afternoon. Late afternoon.

I've lost time again.

"Kelsey, if you're up there, I'm coming up."

Lisa's voice, followed by the clomp of her Birkenstocks on my stairs.

"Kels?"

"Here. I'm in here."

I swing my legs over the side of the bed, then wobble to my feet, which are bare, despite the fact I'm still wearing the dress I wore to dinner with Austin.

I touch shaky fingers to the watch on my arm but don't have time to look at it before Lisa's at the top of the steps, across the open expanse of my apartment.

She grabs the half-wall at the top of the steps, then cocks her head at the sight of me standing forlorn beside the bed. "You sick or something?"

"What? No. I mean—I'm not. Yes, not feeling great today."

She raises her eyebrows at my dress. "You look like you're going out."

I run two hands across my waist, down to my thighs, then return my attention to her. "Did you need something?"

"Oh, right." Lisa gives a little shake of her head and rolls her eyes, as if she's almost forgotten the reason for climbing my steps. "Yeah, sorry, there's someone downstairs looking for you. It's about that Wizard of Oz book you listed online."

I exhale, then try for a longer intake of breath, in through the nose…

It feels like three minutes ago that I was listening to Louis Armstrong and an ancient Greek woman discuss their outrage over my selling this very book.

"Okay, thanks. I'll be right down."

Lisa narrows her eyes, gives my dress another once-over, and shrugs. "If you say so."

As soon as she disappears down my stairs, I check my watch.

It's 2 PM, which doesn't surprise me, but I'm more concerned about the day—the date. I was in the Garden much longer for this second visit. How much time have I lost?

But my watch assures me it's Friday afternoon.

So… I've missed less time after more hours in the Garden

than when I skipped an entire day during my shorter first visit?

I set aside the lack of logic for now and take two minutes to drag a brush down the length of my hair, swipe a little color onto my lips, and slip on some low-heeled sandals. I'm thinking people selling first editions for thousands of dollars probably shouldn't look as though they've just rolled out of bed wearing last night's outfit. The dress is a fabric that doesn't wrinkle, so I leave it.

After a shaky descent to the shop, in which my balance still feels a little off, I cross to the front counter.

A white-haired gentleman in an expensive suit is chatting with Lisa, who stands behind the counter, all smiles and leaning in.

"It would be great for the shop, I think," he is saying. "Bring in dozens of new customers."

Lisa straightens at the sight of me, looking strangely guilty. "Here she is." She nods toward me. "Kelsey, this is Mr. Dumas. He says he knows your Gran."

I hold out a hand, palming the other, too damp, against my leg. "Kelsey Willoughby. You know Elizabeth?"

He returns my handshake, firm but not overbearing. He's nice-looking, in his sixties perhaps, but still in good shape. *Distinguished.*

"I do indeed. Well, I did know her, 'back in the day' as they say. It's been many years. I was hoping to see her."

Over his shoulder, Lisa shrugs, her mouth a flat line, by which to say *I didn't tell him.*

I like Dumas immediately, though wish he would have chosen a better time to visit. I'm feeling waves of heat and cold in the sharp transition from Garden to bed to bookshop. I desperately need to be alone, to process the past few hours, and figure out how to fight the Taking, since my trip into the Garden was no help at all.

"Elizabeth's not in today, I'm afraid."

"Oh, too bad. I saw she was selling the first edition Baum, and I'd love to acquire it."

I extend a hand to the end of the counter. "Why don't we step into my office."

A flicker of surprise crosses his expression—perhaps at the *my office*—but he follows the direction of my hand, around the counter.

I step behind him, stumble over my own feet, then right myself, ignoring Lisa's raised eyebrows. She knows a hangover when she sees one, of course. Perhaps I did drink too much in the Garden, but it's not my body rebelling, as much as my mind.

"This way, Mr. Dumas." I circle him and lead the trek into my cluttered office.

"It's Robert, please."

"Not Alexandre?"

He smiles at the literary reference. "Afraid not. Although *The Count of Monte Cristo* was, of course, my favorite book as a boy, and I dreamed I was a distant relation."

"Have a seat, Robert." I nod toward the wooden banker's chair in the corner. "Oh, let me just—" I totter over to collect the toppling stack of books and papers from the seat of the chair and deposit them on the floor.

"I've been very busy..." The excuse for the chaos is weak, so I let it die and crumple into my own desk chair.

"Perhaps I should come back at a better time? When will Elizabeth—"

"I'm sorry." I grab a ballpoint from my desk, to give my fingers something to do, and click it on-off-on-off. "I'm afraid Gran—Elizabeth—won't be coming back to the shop. She's living at AdvantaCare Skilled Nursing now. She's ninety-four." I add this last bit for Gran's sake, as if to explain why her absence from the shop should not be held against her.

"Wow." Robert sits back in his chair. "Yes, of course, that makes sense, but where do the years go?"

"You two were close?" I curse the question as soon as it's out of my mouth. I want this guy to be on his way so I can *think*, not sit reminiscing about Gran's good old days.

"Yes, I suppose you could say that. I was getting my start at the publishing house, just a junior editor back then, and we were part of a creative group that met together frequently. Some collaborations, a bit of mentoring, that sort of thing. She was always such an encouragement."

I replace the pen on the desk and nod. "That sounds like her."

"I remember you. When she adopted you. We were all so..."

"Surprised?" I supply the word with a wry smile.

"I was going to say *delighted*." He laughs. "But you are right. We were surprised. She'd been on her own for so long and didn't seem the type to—" He shakes his head.

"Raise a child. I know." I spread my hands, as if to present myself for inspection. "But as you can see, she did an excellent job." I try for a self-deprecating smile, but it feels forced and awkward.

"Yes, that much is clear. Good for her. And for you."

I nod.

The stack on the floor beside his chair collapses, three books sliding to rest at his feet.

I stare at them, unable to think what should be done. My brain is paralyzed.

Robert picks them up gently, places them on my desk.

"Did you know the details? Of my adoption?"

Lisa chooses this inopportune moment to poke her head into my office.

I jump, startled at the sudden interruption.

"Sorry, just a quick question. Did you get that shipment from Turner Books yet?"

"Not yet."

She glances at Robert, nods, and backs out.

"I apologize. She's... anyway..." It seems odd to ask the

question again, about my adoption. As though I'm fishing for details more than making conversation. Which is true.

But he hasn't lost the thread. "We never heard much, no. Just one day, there you were. And she was happier than I'd ever seen her." He smiles past me, as if seeing the baby I once was.

"And you said you're an editor?"

"Yes, publisher now, technically, at Sparrow Books. Which leads me to another question, which I will ask in a moment. But first, is the *Oz* book still for sale?"

A parade of faces marches through my mind—Agatha Christie, Charles Dickens, Louis Armstrong—the disapproval and the warnings.

But running parallel is the AdvantaCare Finance Department, Charles Diamond Blackburn, the letter from the City Tax Office shoved into a stack of unpaid bills on my desk. And above all, always, that horrifying single sheet of paper announcing the Taking.

"Yes." The word emerges cold, to the point of being hostile. "I'm sorry. I—I don't really want to sell it, I'll admit. It means a great deal to Gran, I think. But..." I rub at a sharp pain in my left temple and close my eyes. The desire to unburden myself to this stranger needs to be resisted.

"I think I understand." He chuckles, the sound rueful. "I'm in the publishing business, after all. I know how hard it must be to keep a bookstore this size profitable these days."

I only nod, eyes still closed, fighting the sting behind them.

"But actually, that brings me to the other question." His voice is kind. "I know it's not a solution, *per se*, but I do have an idea that might help give some visibility, even prestige, to the Chestnut Street Book Emporium."

Yes, wasn't he saying something of that nature to Lisa when I first came down?

"I'm definitely listening." Which is only partially true, because my mind is still deeply embedded in a nighttime

Garden Party. I glance through the grime and metal bars on my window to the street. It's already late afternoon. Can I get back into the party in a few hours?

"You've read *The Starlight Folio,* I'm assuming?"

"What?" My attention snaps back to his face.

"*The Starlight Folio*. You must have noticed how the Book Emporium feels very much like the bookstore in the novel."

I roll my shoulders and tilt my head until my neck cracks. "I have not read it. But I've heard about it." And yeah, the similarities.

He laughs, good-naturedly. "I'm too close to it, I suppose, since we published the book. I'm always thinking everyone has read it by now."

"You're the publisher?" Seriously?

"Yes, lucky for us. It's leading the revenue this year. But here's my idea." He waits, as if needing my permission to launch it.

I nod, though I don't want to hear it any longer, whatever it is.

That stupid book again. It's as if the writing-gods keep throwing it in my face to remind me of my failure. My own attempt at writing a story set in a bookshop much like this one, in which the adventures of my shop owner never made it past Cora Oberman and her poisonous critique.

"Well, there's a bookstore in the novel. And I hadn't thought of this place in years—lost touch with Elizabeth about a decade ago, probably—but as soon as my assistant showed me the listing for the *Oz* book, and I saw the location of the seller, all those memories flooded back, of our Friday nights in that unused back room, eating and drinking, reading our work aloud to each other, making suggestions, encouraging. Sometimes disparaging, all in the name of excellence and always with kindness..."

He seems to have drifted into his memories.

"And then I realized, how the Book Emporium could be a

sort of stand-in for the shop in *The Starlight Folio.* And the idea seemed obvious."

I give him another nod, which he seems to need. I sense I am somehow a proxy for Gran and the insecure thirty-something junior editor has made a reappearance.

"Well, the hardback's sold nearly fifty thousand copies, and we're about to release the paperback version."

I cross my arms in front of my chest and feel my lips flatten out.

He leans forward, hands clasped over his knees. "I'd be happy to host an event here. A celebratory party, of sorts. Invite the public, have refreshments, that sort of thing. We'd need to put it together quickly since the release date on the paperback's in a couple of weeks. But the store would likely sell quite a few copies, plus gain some real visibility. We'd promote it heavily for you. I can see it already, people lined up around the corner, waiting to see the shop, buy the book..."

He seems to run out of steam. As if he's piled on all the benefits he can think of, waiting for my enthusiastic response, which still has not arrived.

"You want to have a party to celebrate *The Starlight Folio.* In my store."

"Yes, on the seventeenth. I think it could really help."

The seventeenth. The same date as the meeting where I'll have my last chance to fight the Taking.

"Sorry, I'm busy that night."

NINETEEN

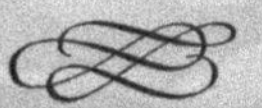

Literature takes reality and human experience as its starting point, transforms it by means of the imagination, and sends readers back to life with renewed understanding of it and zest for it because of their excursions into a purely imaginary realm.

~ Leland Ryken

Robert Dumas rocks back in his chair after my curt refusal and steeples his fingers against his bottom lip. He looks a bit like he's praying. Or begging.

Why does he care so much?

"Sparrow Books would, of course, donate the paperbacks to be sold that night, pay for all the expenses, if that's your concern—"

"No, I'm just not interested. But thank you."

"I—if it's not a good time, perhaps we could—"

"It's not the timing. I would just prefer not to stock the book here."

I silently curse my chattiness. I wasn't planning to admit that little fact.

His mouth drops open slightly. "You're not stocking it? At all?"

I fidget with a stack of junk mail on my desk, straightening the corners. "I'm trying to retain Gran's high standards in selection. A book's popularity does not necessarily signal its quality. I've heard it's being called a 'rocky debut' by some critics. Not going to win a Pulitzer, obviously."

I risk a glance at Robert's face, expecting anger, but finding something more akin to pity.

He sighs. "As much as it might pain us, Ms. Willoughby, bookstores—and publishers—cannot survive selling only Pulitzer-winning novels. Yes, popular books are not always of the highest quality. But sadly, a book's *quality* does not necessarily signal its *popularity*, either."

He thinks my literary snobbery is dragging the bookstore into financial ruin.

Perhaps he's right.

"And despite its flaws, it's a beautiful book. And I don't say that because it's one of ours. Entertaining, yes. But heartfelt, with a transcendent feel to it. And even imperfect books have the power to help us make sense of our own lives, give meaning to our own stories, shape our perspectives—"

"Would she attend?" I gather scattered paperclips and drop them into a little box in my top drawer.

"Who? Elizabeth? If she—"

"Selena Manning. The author. Would she be attending this soirée you want to hold here?"

He crosses one leg over another and straightens his shoulders. "I'm afraid not. She's very private, as you may have heard."

Yes, I've heard. Stuck-up little narcissist-princess.

"Ms. Willoughby—Kelsey—I really do want to help. For Elizabeth's sake, and for yours. Perhaps you can think about it."

I shrug one shoulder, feeling highly unprofessional. Bratty, even. I need to get this jealousy thing under control.

"In the meantime," he uncrosses his legs and leans forward, "let's talk about that first edition Baum."

It turns out Robert is a collector of rare first editions as well as an Oz fan since childhood, and he had his assistant scouring the internet for any that surface. He would have sent Cherise herself, he tells me, if she hadn't mentioned the Book Emporium. He references the price I listed online, and though I'd inflated it somewhat, assuming the buyer would want to negotiate, he asks if the price is still acceptable.

It's a pity-move, I suppose, or at least a nod to Gran's influence in his past, but even if I'm refusing his book party, I'm not too proud for this offer.

We walk together to the glass case, halfway to the back of the shop. I'm highly conscious of the odds and ends of estate sale shelves and tables we've cobbled together for the shop. Does it look classic and vintage to him? Or just shabby?

I may never be in this close proximity to a big-shot publisher again. I should have a thirty-second "elevator pitch" ready, to see if he's interested in my book.

Yes, my book that sounds like I ripped off the very bestseller he wants to celebrate here.

Right.

"I have a few others here," I say as we approach the case and I unlock the top. "If you would be interested."

I pull *The Wonderful Wizard of Oz* from its resting place and hand it to him.

He takes it reverently, opens the hard cover with one finger. "It's in perfect condition, as you said in the listing. I wonder who had it first, keeping it so pristine."

Well, apparently its entire journey was from the empty lot next door directly into this case.

He glances over the rest of the books. "I'll keep these others in mind. For now, this is my birthday gift to myself."

I smile. "Happy birthday, then. And, thank you."

I ask Lisa to ring up his purchase—surely the store's largest ever—on our faux-vintage cash register, and he swipes a card as if his credit limit will not be an issue. Which it's not.

"Think about my idea, Kelsey," he says as Lisa wraps the book carefully in tissue paper. "But let me know soon." He hands me a business card from his wallet. "That's my direct number, call me there."

I take the card, my vision tunneling to the black letters on ivory cardstock. His name, "Editorial Director" under it. The big guy, then. Submitting a piece of my writing to him would be like calling the President of the United States with a complaint about a neighborhood stop sign.

Still staring at the card, I feel words spilling out, words I know better than to loose. "I—I do a bit of writing myself." My chest feels hollow, like my lungs are collapsing. Why does he hold so much power over me?

"Do you now?"

His tone is not unkind, if a bit patronizing.

"Perhaps you'll want to show me someday." He takes the bag from Lisa with a smile of thanks, then touches my elbow. "Perhaps even at that event we spoke of."

I bite my lip, exhale, and try to smile. "I'll let you know."

I watch him exit, my legs beginning to tremble. I really, really need to get some time alone. It's all too much.

But I've sold the Oz book. The relief is palpable. It's not enough money to solve all my problems, not by a long shot, but it'll relieve a little pressure somewhere.

Where, though?

I can send it to AdvantaCare and cover another couple months of Gran's care. Or I can commit to the Confession of Judgment, pay the first installment on the tax bill and then catch up on the rest of the overdue invoices before they turn the lights off. But then I'll need to keep up with future double-payments on the taxes. Meanwhile, the city's ready to swoop in like a vulture on roadkill, and I need a lawyer.

I put a shaky hand to my forehead. How long has it been since I've slept?

Yes, I woke up in my bed an hour ago, but it felt like I'd been asleep only a few seconds. It's Friday afternoon, and I've been awake since Thursday morning, but that doesn't account for whatever time I lost while in the Garden, so... how many hours is that?

"You okay?" Lisa is frowning over me, where I stand with one hand on the counter and the other on my head.

"Yeah. I guess."

"Still feeling sick?"

"Yeah."

"Uh oh."

I glance at Lisa, but she's looking at the front door.

The bell clangs. I don't want to turn around.

"Ms. Willoughby."

Charles Diamond Blackburn.

My chest does a funny little thing, like I'm panting, dog-like. Is my tongue hanging out?

I turn slowly, eyelids fluttering. Spots appear at the edges of my vision.

"I can't today, Blackburn. I really can't."

I don't even have the energy to use all of his many names.

"I'm not feeling—"

"Then I will get right to it, Ms. Willoughby."

Will he, though?

"For some time now, I have been under the understandable and yet mistaken impression that the vacant lot here beside your little store, which was once a floral shop, I am told, before it was demolished because of water running under the foundation, is owned by the unpleasant fellow who runs the musical supply establishment beyond it."

This is Blackburn, being concise. I sag against the counter, willing it to be over.

"I have, however, in making inquiries into the history of your location—and its current and past tax situation, I might add—been surprised, and I must say a bit intrigued, and even delighted to hear that my assumption was, in fact, incorrect. And to learn that, in very fact, the available space actually belongs to you. To your grandmother, that is."

I exhale but say nothing. Obviously, there is more.

"I'm prepared to triple my offer, Ms. Willoughby, if you'll also sell the empty lot."

Oh, mercy. This man is the devil.

"I would beg you, don't be a fool, Ms. Willoughby. Your business model is obsolete. Your building, with its ridiculously ornate facade, is grossly outdated. That lot next door is nothing but an eyesore and a danger to the community. And I have been informed that you have been informed that the city will exercise its legal right of eminent domain if you do not sell. Is it not time to cut your losses and accept the financial recompense? You could start over, do anything you want, go anywhere."

Of its own accord, my head turns toward the travel posters, toward their silent and continual invitation.

Gran is ninety-four years old and failing. There is nothing I can do to keep her with me forever. When she is gone, it will be only her memory that obliges me to this place. Am I truly willing to struggle to keep it going forever? This opportunity—to walk away with a windfall—would provide the best care possible for her and would give me a future.

"Your neighbor, Mr. Jackson, has made the wise choice."

Yes, but William is seventy years old and ready to walk away from The Groove and head to warmer climes.

"And I would daresay that printed books are as outmoded as vinyl records." He smooths a hand over the back of his head. "This offer will not last forever, Ms. Willoughby. Decisions must be made and, once finalized, cannot be revoked."

"Not the empty lot. I can't sell that."

The words spring unbidden, but true.

"My dear, don't be—"

"If you call me a fool again, Charles Diamond Blackburn, you'll be on the street before you can say Mephistopheles." I pull away from the counter, spine straightening.

"Mephi-what?" His eyebrows shoot up, as if I am insane. "I don't—"

"Mephistopheles." I sigh and roll my eyes. "The demon who offered Faust his perfect life in exchange for his soul."

The metaphor is not lost on Blackburn. His jaw sets and he lifts his chin, silent for once.

"Don't be too offended." I try to smile. "You're not the only demon running around town." I flick a glance toward the street. "*In very fact*, there are far too many of you running all around this country. With your Walmarts and your national hotel chains and your massive publishing houses eating all the smaller publishers until nothing is left for anyone, no independent thought or a creative idea or opportunity to be the master of their own fate. It's all selling-out and folding-in and mergers and acquisitions and gatekeepers and power."

I was on a roll now, the fatigue forgotten, a decade of resentment welling up.

"You think because you have money, you can decide everything. Control everything. That with enough zeroes on a check, the people who've put in the sweat and sacrifice to create something of their own can simply be bought off, made to fade into the sunset, like... like an old gaming system or an MP3 player that's outlived its usefulness in your world of concrete and glass."

He's dropped his chin onto his chest, his eyes closed.

I know I should probably feel bad about my condemnation. I don't.

But wait... is he *laughing*?

Lisa is at my side now. Actually, standing a bit in front of me. As though she fears I might get violent.

Blackburn lifts his head, his shoulders shaking and teeth

bared in hilarity. He pulls off his glasses to swipe the knuckle of an index finger across the corner of his eye.

"Oh, my dear." He replaces the glasses, shaking his head. "How I wish I had a recording of that performance." He glances toward the corners of the shop. "You don't have cameras in here, perchance? No? Too bad." He chuckles again. "Seriously, it is very clear who raised you. You are like a throwback to some earlier time. Shaking your fist in the face of progress, advocating for the 'little guy.'

He air-quotes around those last words.

I want to kick him in the shins. Is that wrong?

"Perhaps my father, in his time, would have been offended, Ms. Willoughby. Would have defended himself against your accusations of heartlessness and corporate greed. But the 1980s have come and gone, my dear. You are a cliché. A sad, antiquated cliché." He tosses a glance around the shop as if to include the books and all the wonder of the Book Emporium in his dismissal. "It's time to wake up."

"Mr. Blackburn," Lisa takes a step toward him, her tone respectful, "perhaps it would be best if you came back—"

"I will consider your offer, Blackburn." I shoot a look of death at the man, but some part of me knows he is right. "And I will give you an answer by Monday."

I push past him to the stairs, use the rail to haul my shaky legs upward, and escape to my apartment.

TWENTY

Fairy tales do not give the child his first idea of bogey. What fairy tales give the child is his first clear idea of the possible defeat of bogey. The baby has known the dragon intimately ever since he had an imagination. What the fairy tale provides for him is a St. George to kill the dragon.
~ G.K. Chesterton

I toss Robert Dumas's business card onto my nightstand and collapse into my bed with a searing pain behind my right eye.

Lisa will have to handle things for the rest of the day.

Between my staggering around the shop and my insane rant with Blackburn, she's probably figured this out.

Curled up like a snail in a shell, I pull the grass-green of my favorite fuzzy blanket over my head.

In the mossy haze, the pain behind my eyes subsides the tiniest bit. Perhaps I'm having some kind of stroke, or aneurysm, or psychotic break, or seizure, or hypoglycemia, or anything that might explain losing a day and half to an impossible nighttime Garden Party in an abandoned city lot that is bigger on the inside.

But now, finally alone, finally granted a moment to think, my thoughts drift immediately to Robert and his willingness to buy the Oz book—how best to use that money? And his offer of a splashy publicity-generating event held at the Book Emporium—should I do it? And Charles Diamond Blackburn with his triple-the-money temptation if I sell him the empty lot—not possible, right?

I moan and pull the blanket tighter around my eyes, blocking the afternoon sunlight, wishing for darkness. For twilight. For the time-between-times.

Slowly, gently, the memories of last night return, displacing the past hour's emotional rollercoaster.

My time there is not finished. I know this somehow.

I will sell all the first editions I possibly can, use the money to hire a lawyer, and fight the Taking with everything I've got. But I am not finished seeking answers in the Garden. Answers for the shop, but also for myself.

Although, there remains a significant problem.

The guests have made it clear. I will have nothing but their disapproval if I don't bring them a story I've written. Especially after I've sold the Oz book. Will I run into L. Frank Baum again and need to explain my decision to sell his gift to Gran?

Regardless, I've felt enough of their censure to refuse myself another entry without bringing what they want. Something for the table. A gift, as they say.

Sure. I'll just jot down a few words, then casually slip the pages in beside *Café Terrace at Night.* Who could possibly notice that my talent is anything less than Van Gogh's?

But I have to try. Or I have to give up the idea of ever going back to the Garden.

And that is not an option, I realize in the hot confines of my green cocoon.

Slowly, I lower the fuzzy blanket to my chin, blinking in the light.

They insist upon a manuscript? Fine, I'll give them one. Hopefully nobody inside that Garden has read *The Starlight Folio*. Because the only thing I have is that early attempt at a real book, stashed in a drawer somewhere after Cara Oberman and the Critique Group Incident. A manuscript which would only be considered derivative at this point.

First, though, I have some arrangements to make.

I scrabble to a sitting position, back against the wall behind my bed.

Dumas's credit card transaction will post at midnight. Since it's Friday, the money won't be in the Book Emporium's bank account until Monday, perhaps even Tuesday. But if I do this old-school and drop a check somewhere later today—AdvantaCare or tax office?—I can probably count on it sitting on a desk until Monday.

I'll use the rest to retain a lawyer to fight the Taking, one of the names Austin texted.

My skin itches at cutting it so close to an overdrawn bank account, but living this near the financial edge has worn me down.

There are more first editions in the case downstairs, of course. But even if I were to sell each of the books, the funds would only be a temporary bandage on the financial hemorrhaging of the shop.

Selling the property to Blackburn or letting the city take it would be an amputation.

They were always so helpful to me. Perhaps you should ask them for the answer.

Gran's words, about her friends in the Garden.

If I'm not crazy, that is, and Gran has actually attended this preposterous party.

Enough wallowing.

I swing my legs over the side of the bed and rise to a tottering upright position.

I'm not out of this thing yet. I have Dumas's money to stave off immediate disaster. I have the possibility of the guests at the Garden Party to help me somehow. I have a few more first editions and the name of a good lawyer.

I glance at the white rectangle on my nightstand.

Robert Dumas. Editorial Director.

I'd be crazy to pass up this free publicity for the Book Emporium, which could help reestablish it as a destination for book lovers.

Perhaps I'll call Robert on Monday and agree, with the condition that I won't be attending the party since I have an important meeting that night. A legitimate excuse, but a convenient one. I'm still too petty to celebrate that book.

My phone buzzes from somewhere muffled. When was the last time I even saw that thing? It's a wonder it's still charged.

I scan my bedroom as though I barely belong here.

There. In the little cross-body purse I wore to dinner with Austin a hundred years ago. Last night.

And it's Austin who is texting me.

TGIF! I was thinking Recollections tonight. Yes?

We've been to Recollections a few times. I like the dark and smoky jazz club, mainly the music, though the inevitable comparison between the crowded Recollections and the jazz trio I've heard at the base of the Tree next door leaves me longing for another open-air performance.

Don't think I can do it tonight. Have some things I have to get done.

I stand in the center of my bedroom watching the pulsing three dots that signal a forthcoming response. Then nothing.

Sorry, I add. *Maybe tomorrow?*

Three dots again. Waiting.

Then, *sure.*

This relationship could definitely be going better, and I know it's my fault. He's a nice guy, and I can tell he cares about me, even if his ego tends toward the grandiose. But I'm not perfect either.

I resist the urge to apologize again.

I have only a few hours before twilight.

Now, where is that manuscript? I turn a slow circle in my room, then stop, close my eyes, and form a mental image. The stack of printer paper. The title— *House of Dreams*— printed, bold and overconfident, in the center of the top sheet.

Coming home from the critique group meeting… but not here, not to this apartment above the shop.

Gran and I still lived in her Tudor two-story a few miles outside the city. She was healthy and independent and sharp, and I was a couple of years out of college and full of hubris over a future literary career.

The replay of that night continues behind my closed eyes. Shoving the manuscript into a drawer—the half-moon shaped antique side table in the entry hall—the first place I reached after running into the house, desperate to get the stupid thing out of my sight.

Where is that table now?

The house sold three years ago, just after Gran's ninety-first birthday, when she entered AdvantaCare after a serious stroke.

Hard as it was to sell the house, we believed the money would ensure good medical care for her for the rest of her life. But the money went faster, and Gran lived longer, than either of us expected at the time.

And with the house went most of the furnishings… but not that table, right?

I try to mentally follow its progress through the changes to our lives.

We kept it, brought it to the shop, tucked it somewhere amidst all the other lovely pieces collected over the years. Stacked it with something… *gift sets*! Yes! That is it.

I race down the steps, fatigue forgotten, and rush through

the main section of the shop, past the tables of NEW RELEASES, toward GARDENING and COMPUTERS.

Just before the shelves of PHOTOGRAPHY, the little side table hugs the wall, heaped with gift sets of fancy pens, boxed together with flowery journals.

I have the drawer open before my feet stop moving.

Then exhale and drop my shoulders.

Empty.

Eyes closed again, I will my brain to remember removing the manuscript from this drawer, placing it somewhere else.

Come on, Kelsey.

Nothing.

All I can remember is the grim sense of defeat each time I passed this little table in the entry hall of the house, until eventually the sharp pain subsided to a dull ache that had no particular focus.

And it takes me no time now to remember the old laptop on which I'd typed my masterpiece. And the knocked-over latte a couple of years after the manuscript sat yellowing in a drawer which drowned the insides of the machine. I'd been careless about backing up in those days, feeling there was little of value on my computer.

So, no digital file. No hard copy. All of it, gone.

I curse my rotten luck and slam the little drawer shut.

Lisa makes eye contact from the front counter, her brows drawn together.

She starts on her way toward me, but I meet her halfway, headed to my steps.

"What's going on? I thought you were sick. What's wrong?"

"Nothing. I'm—I'm going to visit Gran. You okay here until closing?"

Lisa wedges her fists against her hips. "Kelsey, I gotta be honest, you've got me a little worried."

I squeeze her arm and smile. "Thanks, Lisa. I appreciate

the concern. I'm fine, just have a lot on my mind. I think a visit will do me good."

She nods, as though still unconvinced. "Tell her I say 'hello.'"

"Will do."

I escape upstairs, retrieve my keys, phone, and checkbook, and am back out of the shop a minute later.

My thoughts have started to form a coherent plan:

One, call the lawyer on the way to visit Gran, setting up an emergency appointment as soon as possible.

Two, ask Gran where she put my manuscript and give Megan in billing at AdvantaCare a check for partial payment, with lots of promises of more to come.

Three, drop off a check at the tax office for the first payment and agree to the Confession of Judgment. Can't give the city any more ammunition.

Four, take my old manuscript inside the Garden with me tonight as my "gift" and hope no one reads it and deems it unworthy of joining the offerings on the table.

Five, once I'm approved by the party guests again, get the geniuses there to help me find a way to save the shop.

Lastly, on Monday morning, call Robert and agree to the publicity event for *The Starlight Folio*.

Oh, and probably in there somewhere, spend some time with Austin before he starts to feel ignored.

Simple.

Forty-five minutes later, I'm sitting in the Common Room of AdvantaCare, Gran in a wheelchair and me beside her. I'm holding her hand, and she's watching her "neighbors" take turns with mini golf clubs, trying to putt-putt neon orange balls into red Solo cups laid on their sides.

"Gran, you must remember. The story I worked so hard on all those years. It was in the drawer of the French *demilune* table in the foyer. We moved the table to the shop when the house sold."

Gran nods. "Yes, yes, your story about the orphan girl and the garden."

I close my eyes and drop my forehead to the back of her hand. "No, that was a story I wrote when I was a little girl." My voice is muffled against the sleeve of her sweater. "I'm talking about the one I wrote after college."

Should I remind her why the book got shoved in a drawer? She was there that night, bustling around the kitchen island where I sat crying, making me a cup of tea and insisting my critique group was a bunch of ignorant hacks.

"I always knew you'd tell your story one day," she says now, patting the back of my head with her free hand. "About finding the garden. How much you loved it."

I half-expect her to start calling me Mary Lennox and asking about my childhood in India before coming to Misselthwaite and finding the Secret Garden with my cousin Colin. She's confused me completely with Burnett's novel.

Her confusion is devastating.

And my plan is disintegrating.

How can I attempt to enter the Garden Party again and ask for help from such esteemed artists without bringing a manuscript, as they've insisted I must?

But the manuscript is gone, that much is clear.

I watch Mr. Mason waggle his mini-golf club in triumph over the sinking of his putt and fight a sudden urge to grab the club and start smashing the Common Room knick-knacks.

It's not just the thwarting of my plan to re-enter the Garden. It's the lost manuscript. Something I made, created, labored over. Simply gone. Never able to be recreated.

All these elderly people, waiting here to die.

My panda-head balloon, drifting away, irretrievable.

My chest is leaden, but my eyes are dry. I can think of only one option now. And at the idea, my insides quiver, the flutter of pages in a breeze.

I need to start writing again.

TWENTY-ONE

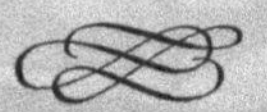

You owe it to all of us to get on with what you're good at.

~ W.H. Auden

"I've found you, finally!"

I turn to the words, recognizing the voice even though the two of us haven't spent long in conversation.

I'm standing beside the marble bench, where I first spoke to T.S. Eliot, gripping a canary yellow folder stuffed with a dozen sheets of paper in my sweaty hand.

It's Sam who greets me first, crossing the grass to join me at the edge of the party. Eliot is nowhere to be seen.

Behind him in the Garden, little has changed. The lantern-globes still swing in a gentle night breeze, tossing bits of light like confetti over the table's unending banquet. Groups of well-dressed men and women talk and laugh and drink in clusters. The gnarled live oak still spreads its arms over all the party, and beside it, in the shadows beyond the hanging lanterns, I can just make out a small group of musicians, tuning their instruments.

Still tuning up? Have I been gone only a few moments, then?

"I finally broke away from A. and her friends, but then I couldn't find you." Sam's forehead is creased, his eyes intense, his head tilted as if waiting for an explanation for my absence.

He seems angry—no, worried.

But why worried? For him, it's not been a missing weekend—a weekend spent holed up in my apartment, researching eminent domain and attempting to write a short story that would measure up—it's only been a missing few minutes since I slipped away to the far side of the Garden, to the pergola where I overheard a conversation that sent me running home.

"I was just… wandering." I smile, but it feels like all teeth and no heart.

He points to the folder in my hand. "What's this?"

I look down at it, lift it waist-high, study the blank cover. "It's—it's a story."

His shoulders seem to lose their tension as he nods in approval. "So you did bring something for the table."

"It's not very good. Still a rough draft." I meet his gaze. Yes, it's still rough, despite the many hours poured into it, the words flowing much less readily than I'd expected. Hard work, for sure. "But you never showed me the gift you've brought."

A cloud passes over his eyes. He re-rolls the white sleeve up his left arm where it has slipped. "Perhaps later." He holds out a hand. "First, your story."

I lower the folder to my side, then move it slightly behind the falling waves of the wisteria fabric of my dress. "It's—I'm not ready for you to read it yet. I only brought it for the table. To have something to bring." My voice trails off. I bite my lip. Why do I sound so terrified?

"I understand."

He doesn't seem offended. Perhaps he truly does understand. He's being cagey about his own gift, so maybe he's as reluctant as I am. Even Van Gogh seemed insecure about his canvas.

From the corner of my eye, a woman hurrying across the grass toward us catches my attention.

Agatha Christie.

"There you are, my dear. I've been searching for you." She nods to Sam. "And you, as well, S."

"Hello, A." I feel a surge of warmth for one of my favorite authors.

Can you teach me to write a good story?

But no, I'm here to find the bookshop-saving solution.

The yellow folder at my side seems to be screaming. I am nearly crumpling it in a death-grip between my fingers.

"Have either of you seen C.?" She casts a worried glance back and forth between us.

The single-letter designation is too vague to answer definitively. I look to Sam, who thus far seems to know everyone here.

But didn't Agatha mention this "C." earlier? After learning I'd brought nothing for the table? She ran off to find him, saying he would know better what was to be done. About me, I presume.

Sam is scanning the partygoers. "We were just speaking with him, a few minutes ago..."

"Yes, yes, I saw that. He was with both of you when we circled in groups of three."

C. is Charles Dickens?

I join Sam in peering into the darkness, looking for the beard and Victorian clothing.

Agatha twists her fingers together, eyes darting from guest to guest. "I wanted to speak with him. But then, after, he—he seems to have disappeared."

Something in the way she says the word touches off a

flicker of fear in my chest. Implying something more than a guest who's ambled off to join a conversation in the shadows or gone home early without saying goodbye.

Disappeared. Her tone more sinister than confused.

But it is Agatha Christie we're speaking with, after all. Perhaps she is always expecting foul play and rounding up suspects.

"He must be here somewhere," I say, having absolutely no idea whether this is true. Does this party go on forever, as it seems to? Does no one ever get tired? Leave? But where would they go? Maybe everyone has a leafy tunnel leading back to their own iron gate outside their home.

I smother a laugh at the thought since Agatha seems truly distressed.

"Yes, yes, I hope so." She glances between Sam and me, as if trying to read a villainous motive in our expressions. "Well, if you see him..."

Sam touches her arm and meets her gaze. "We will be sure to send him to you."

Am I imagining some kind of unspoken understanding passing between them?

Agatha hurries off.

I turn to Sam, but what to say?

"You should take that over." He points at my crinkled folder.

A small tremor runs through me, something like the age-old bad dream of getting up to speak in front of a crowd and finding you've forgotten your clothes. I press the folder against my abdomen with both hands.

It took most of the weekend and some significant effort to create these few pages. Every time I started to write, all I could see was writers and artists I've met here, each bringing their own work to the table. What story could I possibly generate that would deserve to rest in the same space as work by Van Gogh and T.S. Eliot?

Sam is watching me. "I'll walk over with you." His tone is sympathetic.

Who is this guy? Does he suffer from this same terror?

Over the weekend, needing to procrastinate these pages many times, I did some random Googling for sculptors with the first name of Samuel. I didn't come up with many, and none that looked like a football player with a side hustle posing for billboard ads. Maybe his name isn't really even Samuel.

I clear my throat and take a few steps toward the welcoming oak, the feast spread before it and the heap of gifts on the table behind.

The instruments have finished tuning and a melody begins, plaintive and sweet on a single violin, like a woman crying over lost love.

Sam and I both slow, arrested by the beautiful sound.

Other instruments join, then a woman steps out of the shadows and lifts her chin to the night sky.

She is beautiful, waves of blonde hair and full lips, and when she lowers her head to smile on her audience, her eyes are so expressive it feels as though she has seen only me.

And then she begins to sing.

I have always enjoyed operatic music, though I know almost nothing about it. I've been to a few opera performances and loved them. Created a playlist of popular arias as part of the rotation of music we play in the bookshop each week.

But this… to stand so near a woman of such immense talent as she pours forth Italian as though the language is her own, words set to music that builds inside your heart until you are near to weeping…

"Come," Sam says in my ear, "you need to bring your story."

He tugs on my arm.

I must forcibly pull my attention from the soprano to move toward the tree.

We circle the food, resupplied with teeming platters and mounded dishes as abundant as ever, and approach the table of canvases and manuscripts, music and instruments and sculptures and books.

The yellow folder in my hand is the grade-school type, three sets of metal prongs poked through the sheets of paper and pried open to secure them. I fished the thing out of an old box at the back of a closet last night. I probably bought it a decade ago at a dollar store.

"Ah, thank goodness." A familiar voice behind me.

I turn to Agatha.

She's smiling at my folder.

Do I dare ask her to read the story? To tell me whether it has merit?

I've been asking myself this question all weekend. In truth, the possibility of an opinion is the only reason I've written it, and the main reason I've brought it, despite trying to tell myself it was to gain access to the Garden and get help to save the shop.

"Go ahead, dear. Leave it there." She nods toward the table.

Others have left little stacks of unbound manuscripts, and even without covers they seem somehow more professional than my dollar-store folder.

"Let me just take it out of this." I lay the folder on the table, bend over it, and open to the title sheet. I can have these prongs open in only a moment—

But the first page is blank.

What? I'm certain I printed a title page.

I flip to the next page.

Blank.

I'm rifling through all of them now—empty, empty, empty. A little gasp escapes my lips.

"What is it?" Agatha steps beside me, looks over my shoulder.

I meet her gaze and am only half-surprised to see something like fear there.

"I—I don't know what happened. It was in here—"

Her lips tighten, brows drawn together. "Why did you bring it?"

Sam towers beside Agatha, his own expression dire.

"What? You told me I needed—"

"Yes, but why? What was *your* reason?"

I exhale, searching both their faces for a clue as to what answer they want to hear.

I settle on the truth. "I was hoping you could tell me if it's any good. If I have talent. If I should continue…"

But she's thrown up her hands, as if my answer is the worst news I could have delivered. And now she's massaging manicured fingers against her temples.

I press the folder to my side and try to slow my breathing. This reaction from Agatha, and even Sam, is my worst fear, realized much sooner than I anticipated. To face rejection even before my work has been read hits me somewhere deep and feels like affirmation of a truth I've instinctively known since the first night I stepped into this place.

I do not belong here. Do not deserve to be here.

TWENTY-TWO

It is the mark of a good fairy-story, of the higher or more complete kind, that however wild its events, however fantastic or terrible the adventures, it can give to child or man that hears it, when the "turn" comes, a catch of the breath, a beat and lifting of the heart...

~ J.R.R. Tolkien

"I'm so sorry." I look between Sam and Agatha. "I don't know why the pages are blank—"

"Because you did not bring a gift!"

I drop my head, study the folder. Should the presentation have been fancier? Did others bring their work wrapped and ribboned?

Agatha purses her lips and shakes her head. "The Garden is not immune to danger, my girl. You have brought your work for the wrong reasons, and there will be consequences." She looks behind her. "Perhaps there already have been."

"She's not ready, A." Sam leans into the conversation.

I sense that he is on my side, though his answer seems only to frustrate her.

"Then she must become ready! We are all of us still learning, still fighting our own resistance, but we are all needed. If she's not yet willing, she should not be here."

I drop the folder on the table and square off, facing Agatha. "I'm sorry I've disappointed you. Perhaps it is time for me to leave."

I nod to Sam, turn, and head back toward the bench that is always my entry point, though I've yet to successfully navigate my own way home from there.

This whole thing was a bad idea.

"K., wait."

Sam is on my heels, jogs to catch up and walk at my side. "You can't leave."

I slow and glance at him. Does he mean this literally? Am I trapped here?

"Why not?"

I am still racing toward the marble bench, with its hint of spurting fountain beyond.

"Because—because I am enjoying talking with you." He grins and shrugs.

"I'm not meant to be here, S. I don't fit with these people. With you."

"Did you write something to bring?"

I stop and huff, hands on my hips. "You know I did." I jut my chin back toward the blank folder, still laying on the table.

"Then you belong."

The white magnolia and marble bench are just where I left them.

"How can you say that? The pages are blank."

"But only because you brought your story for validation. Because you didn't believe it deserved to be here."

"Because it doesn't! Because I don't! And do not try to

convince me otherwise—you've never read anything I've written!"

He rubs at the stubble along his jaw and sighs. "I know. It's difficult to understand. Perhaps it's about going deeper."

More of this *going deeper*, which was mentioned first by Frank Baum, then by both Agatha and Sam, and even by the trumpet player Louis Armstrong when whispering to the Greek woman.

There is more to the Garden, obviously. Something beyond the lantern-lit central courtyard with its encircling marble columns. More than the cascading azure pools, the gleaming stone folly, and the vine-draped pergola. Many paths lead into darkness, but who knows what lies out there? The Hansel-and-Gretel cottage, for one. Is that where I'm supposed to go to learn something I have not yet understood?

I glance at the fountain beyond the white magnolia. Is that a glint of reflective glass from somewhere farther still? Impulsively, I circle the bench, push past the lemony-scented magnolia until I feel the spray of the fountain on my face. A tiny glass conservatory, lit from within, is tucked into the trees beyond the fountain.

What does the Garden need with a greenhouse? I approach slowly, feeling Sam at my heels and music still in my ears. The narrow door opens freely. We step into the warmth, to shelves and tables of infant-sized flowers and plants and the humid smell of soil and roots.

The far end of the greenhouse is glass, but it is a stained-glass masterpiece, an intricate web of vines in turquoise and sage, with flowers in champagne gold and pinks, the color of ballet slippers.

"K., you need to try again. To bring a gift." S. stands at the greenhouse door, arms folded over his chest.

I drift along a table of tiny coral bells and asparagus ferns. "Listen, S., if I'm being honest, I'm glad the words evaporated, or whatever happened. I don't think I could take being critiqued by the people here. This whole thing feels like some sort of test that I'm doomed to fail."

"Because it *is* a test." His hands are upraised in that expressive way he has. "But it's not a test of quality, as you seem to think." He spreads his palms, as if offering his own gift. "It's a test of bravery."

"What does that even mean?"

"I don't fully understand, myself. But I know there are risks. Many of them. And we must persevere, despite these great risks."

"Well, I've been there, done that. And it didn't end well." A wisp of hair loosens from my French twist and floats across my eyes. I swipe it away.

The sound of arguing slips into our greenhouse, drawing our attention.

Outside the glass, near the marble bench, two men are engaged in a discussion that sounds both friendly and contentious at once, though I can discern nothing of the topic since they are not speaking English.

I indicate to Sam that I want to leave, and he steps aside.

Perhaps the arguing men can provide a distraction for Sam while I try to find my way home.

The divine soprano beside the Tree finishes her piece on a high, sustained note, and in the silence that follows this moment of rapturous conclusion, the voices of the two men beside us seem too loud.

Heads turn in their direction.

They both sense the attention at once, cease their good-natured argument, and smile at the crowd looking their way.

I slip out of the shadows and stand beside them.

One of them looks like Father Christmas, with his long white beard. If Father Christmas wore a medieval-looking black cape and squishy hat.

The other, a man in a twentieth-century suit, with a long, rectangular face and full mustache, steps up beside me and waves his hand toward the musicians, like a conductor signaling for the next piece to begin.

As if taking their cue, the little orchestra at the Tree begins again.

The blond soprano is joined by another singer, a huge, dark-haired man with a full beard and a wide smile.

I reach for Sam's arm, forgetting my own distress in a flash of recognition.

"That's Lu—" Not surprisingly, the name sticks in my throat.

As ill-informed about the opera scene as I may be, I have no doubt about this man's identity. That barrel chest and charming, infectious smile. He is one of the most recognizable tenors of recent history.

Luciano Pavarotti.

And then they sing.

First Pavarotti, declaring something to the woman. When she joins the duet, her high soprano soars over his tenor like a bird that's taken flight and glides on an invisible breeze.

The piece builds and swells and in the beauty of the music I forget my own failures and my conviction that I should escape this place where I don't belong.

"What is it?" I whisper to Sam. "What is the name of this piece?" I need to know, need to be able to look it up once I am home. To hear it again and again and again.

Sam shakes his head. He does not know.

"O soave fanciulla." This from the more contemporary of the two men beside us, the one who seemed to direct the musicians.

O soave fanciulla. I whisper the phrase, trying to commit it to memory. I cannot take my eyes from Pavarotti and the soprano. "It is—it is so lovely." My words feel entirely inadequate, and I blush with the juvenile sound of them.

The man chuckles and turns to his white-bearded companion. "You see, L.?" He is speaking in English now, perhaps for my benefit. "When have you ever seen a beautiful woman stand and weep before one of *your* pieces?"

I wipe at the tears I didn't know I'd shed. "Did you write this?"

He shrugs and smooths his mustache. "It is part of a greater work, yes. About those tragic Parisian artists doomed in their bohemian lifestyle."

"*La bohème*? It's from *La bohème*?" I know only a bit about this opera. But enough to know… I must be speaking with the famous composer Puccini.

"Ah, there, you see that, L.?" he asks his companion again. "We shall tell this to the critics who say my opera is unsophisticated—that at the very least, the music can make a woman cry."

His friend waves an impatient hand, as if my emotional response to the transcendent beauty filling the Garden is of no consequence.

I am falling, falling into the music, their voices, wanting it to never stop, to prolong the feeling of the breath in my chest, sharp and exquisite.

Puccini turns back to me. "You are E.'s girl, are you not?"

The question steals my breath.

Gran knows Puccini?

I nod, still unable to find my voice.

"Where has she gone?" He scans the Garden's shadowed edges. "I saw her just a few minutes ago."

"She… is not here."

"Hmm." He smiles. "She is a bit of *la bohème* herself, yes?"

At this, I am able to laugh, and the sound releases some of the tension of the past few minutes held tight between my shoulders, ever since the words in my yellow folder vanished.

"Yes, she always has been that."

"And you? Are you also *la bohème*?"

"I—I wish I knew how to be."

Puccini glances at Sam, who has remained silent through

our exchange. "Perhaps you must sacrifice, in your desperation for love and beauty."

"But sacrifice what?" I grasp at a possible answer to the mystery of this place. "Must I sicken and starve, like your Parisian artists living in poverty?" I turn my eyes toward the table of abundance, which seems to negate Puccini's idea of sacrifice.

"Ah, but the enemies of feasting are rarely so simple as poverty, are they? The lack and the scarcity—these are not of money. It is our *time* we are unwilling to risk, perhaps. Or our good name. Or that most dangerous enemy within, the belief that we ourselves are inadequate."

Puccini speaks of feasting as though we talk of music or art or writing. Are they somehow all the same? Is the abundance of the food and wine and conversation here tied inexplicably to the beauty brought to the table full of gifts?

The music rolls on, carrying me into a wave of sadness and longing. "I hate to think of enemies in this Garden." I can't take my eyes from Pavarotti and his duet partner. "In all this beauty and perfection."

"Mmm." Puccini folds his hands at his waist. "Gardens can be perfection, yes. They can also be rebellion. Sometimes surrender. Hopefully, restoration."

As if in strange response to his litany, a four-legged creature of some kind slips out of the shadows to my right and crosses before us. Lantern-light falls on the sleek, oversized cat, tawny with dark spots.

I retreat backward. "Is that—is that a leopard?"

The animal's muscles ripple under its fur, powerful enough to make a midnight snack out of one of us, but it keeps moving, and the light catches at a jeweled collar sparkling at its neck, like that of a pampered housecat.

I glance at the three men with me—am I the only one who saw this animal, which should be wild?

Sam smiles and nods once, confirming I am not hallucinating. But none of them seem to find the leopard's appearance odd.

"You find the idea of sacrifice repugnant, my dear?"

Puccini isn't letting me off the hook.

"No, no, of course not. I understand it will take hard work, and time, and even the possibility of rejection."

He bows at the waist in my direction, as though acknowledging my hard-won concession.

"But I am not certain..."

"Yes?"

"I'm not certain that I'm up to the challenge."

He nods and looks away. "*Amator*. You know this Latin word?"

I duck my head, fighting the flush on my skin. "I assume it is *amateur* in English. But I never claimed to be more."

Puccini chuckles, a small and quiet laugh that seems paternal, not mocking. "Yes, the meaning has shifted, sadly. As though only work rewarded with money is worthwhile. But in Latin, this word at its beginnings is *amare. Amator,* it means *lover.*"

I lift my head, study the composer.

He smiles. "Yes, I see you understand. To create something, we must love. We must love the work," he extends a hand toward the singers, "and love the audience," he takes in the party guests with a wide gesture, "and we must create with love, always, and nothing more, until the work is done."

To be an amateur, then, is perhaps not such a bad thing.

Pavarotti stands behind the soprano now, his arms wrapped around her, as they finish the piece, a heartbreaking *amor, amor, amor,* the last notes of love spinning in triumphant whorls into the waiting arms of the Tree.

A momentary hush, then the partygoers erupt in applause and the pair takes their bows.

I need to get away. To think on what I've heard, to ask myself if I can love enough to create again.

I turn toward my magnolia.

But Sam tugs at my arm, leading me toward a column at the perimeter of the open lawn.

He turns his full attention on me. "Tell me, what risks have you taken?"

I frown, say nothing.

"Earlier," he says, still looking into my eyes, "you said you've taken risks, that it didn't end well. Tell me."

Does stepping into this place count?

I should leave. Focus on preparing for my meeting in a few days with the attorney I've called.

Instead, I scan the outer edges of the visible Garden. "Can we—can we sit there?"

We settle on a log-hewn bench just beyond the column with tall stone urns of overspilling vinca and phlox.

I watch the guests, at tables and milling around, unsure where to begin.

Unsure I even *want* to begin.

Sam softens the start for me. "You have always wanted to be a writer?"

"I wouldn't say it quite like that. To 'be a writer' was never a goal, never a career path I'd planned. Writing stories has always been something I simply... do. It's always been part of me."

"Ah, yes, that is quite different."

"Is it?"

"Of course. There are many who aspire to create something, many who plan to do so, many who believe they will one day create. And then there are those, like you, who have always created. Those others"—he waves a hand to his left, as if to indicate the first group—"they can learn, perhaps. They can produce. But you are a *born* artist, one to whom the Muse has always whispered."

"No." I twist a bit of wisteria fabric in my fingers. "That isn't true. I mean, I've always wished it were true, always wanted to write something wonderful, but over and over I've been told that I'm not good enough."

Sam stares out at the lawn, inhales a huge breath, expanding his chest.

I'm surprised he doesn't pop the buttons of his shirt.

He lets it go slowly, shaking his head. "Why are we so very fearful?"

"I appreciate the 'we,' but I'm guessing your talent doesn't suffer from the same criticism as mine."

He laughs, a little sniff as if to say I know nothing. "Tell me about all this criticism. Over and over, you say."

I shrug. "Since I was a child."

"Tell me."

I close my eyes, unwilling to travel back to that time, that place, where the shame seems to have taken root.

Sitting here in this place, *taken root* is a good metaphor. As if, instead of beauty and life, something dark and grim reached its fingers into me and took hold of all that I loved.

TWENTY-THREE

In speaking of this desire for our own far off country, which we find in ourselves even now, I feel a certain shyness. I am almost committing an indecency. I am trying to rip open the inconsolable secret in each one of you... The secret we cannot hide and cannot tell, though we desire to do both.

~ C.S. Lewis

"I was ten." The words are quiet, like a released breath.

Sam leans toward me slightly.

Do I want to share this confession with him?

"Ten years old. I had a story, written over a period of time, I don't know, maybe a year or two. I hadn't told anyone, not even Gran." I blink up at him. "Gran is—the woman who raised me. She's not my grandmother, she's actually my adoptive mother. I never met my parents."

"Mmm." Sam's response comes from deep in his chest, and there is empathy there.

"I brought my story to school one day. Planned to show it to a favorite teacher, to ask her to read it. I told myself I wanted her help, to make it better. But of course, I really wanted her to tell me it was perfect."

I can feel him nodding beside me, even though my eyes are on my hands.

"I didn't have many friends back then. I was—a little odd, perhaps? I'm not sure. But there was a new girl in school who seemed to like me. We were beginning to gravitate toward each other."

I brace my hands against the log bench, expecting a splintery surface but finding it smooth.

Sam is quiet, waiting for the rest of the story.

"I had the story in a folder."

I pause, seeing a folder nearly identical to the one I'd brought tonight. I hadn't thought of that until now. The parallel leaves me slightly nauseated.

"Some of the other girls in class got hold of it, without my realizing. Outside, in the schoolyard, my new friend and I were walking and talking, and suddenly I heard one of the girls—Ashleigh, her name was, a nasty, sarcastic little thing—reading my story aloud to four or five others."

Sam sighs, as if he can tell where the story is headed.

"They were laughing, of course. And when they saw me, they all turned on me. Ashleigh waved the folder in the air. 'Here she is, the great author herself!'

"'She thinks she's Mary Pope Osborne or something!' This was from another girl, Erica."

I half-turn to Sam. "Mary Pope Osborne is a famous writer for children." I still have no idea when this guy lived or whether the name would mean anything to him.

His hands are clenched together, forearms resting on his knees, and he says nothing.

"I tried to take the folder back, but Ashleigh kept it from me, kept reading the story aloud, with all of them laughing and saying, 'Fairy tales are for babies!'"

"And your new friend?"

"Said nothing. And was never my friend after that day." I rub my fingers against my forehead, where a little stab of pain throbs behind my eyes. "For the rest of the year, they mocked me. They ridiculed me for trying to be famous, dismissed everything I said as "silly storytelling," and told everyone I lived in a fantasy instead of the real world."

"They shamed you. For being yourself."

"Yes."

His succinct response incorporates everything I have felt for nearly twenty years.

I sit with the feeling, and the acknowledgment, for a moment. It feels heavy, like atmospheric pressure.

"But this was only the first time you experienced this shame?"

I nod. "It took me a long time to show my work anywhere again. I went to a nearby university and after graduation joined a local writers' group. We met weekly and shared our works in progress."

"It is good to have a community of others who are also creative."

"I thought so at the time. But when it was finally my turn to bring my work, and it was a novel I'd been writing for years by then, it was... not well received."

"What did they say?"

The image of Cara Oberman, with her narrow nose and widow's peak hairline, is burned into my memory. The sarcastic twist of her lips as she spouts phrases like "saccharine-sweet" and "unbridled idealism." The embarrassment, wanting to get out of that circle of folding chairs as quickly as possible.

"They said it was too hopeful, not real enough."

"Ha!"

I glance at his grinning profile.

"That's funny?"

"It is madness. Beauty is hope, above all other things. You

have taken the highest compliment and turned it into a criticism."

"It wasn't meant to be the highest compliment, trust me. Every single one of them tore my story apart, said it might have been popular a hundred years ago, but I'd never find an audience for it these days."

"And these other writers in this group… their works are all well-loved by many readers?"

"No, it wasn't a group of professionals. Just aspiring writers."

He tilts his head, his eyebrows arched with an obvious comment.

"You're thinking their opinions might not be worth much."

"I am thinking you are listening to the wrong people. A true community of artists will encourage you to pursue excellence, dig deeper. Not make you want to abandon your craft."

My gaze travels over the Garden Party guests. "That's what you have here, isn't it? A true community." A stab of longing leaves me breathless.

Sam follows my glance. "And you are part of it."

"No, I'm not. At least not yet. Not unless I can bring something worthwhile."

"You still don't understand, do you?"

"Help me, then. A. said my words disappeared because I brought the story for the wrong reasons. What did I do wrong? And what is the right reason?"

"K., every artist, every creative person, plays a critical role in the world, to help awaken others to what is Other. To the truth and the beauty and the goodness in the world. All of us know it is there, sense that something Other exists. But we've forgotten. It is only the *artist* who can create work which binds up all that is Other and delivers it to our senses, to our spirits. And so we create… not to be affirmed in our talent, but to serve. We create, regardless of the limits of quality or the reception our work receives. We create, because we must."

He rolls his shoulders back and studies his own hands, as though he's spoken the words as much to himself as to me.

"I suppose I said as much to you, earlier."

"You encouraged me with this truth, K., when we spoke with C. in our little circle of three. But you must also believe it for yourself."

"And the table?" I lift my eyes to the Tree. "The gifts?"

"Our work is brought as just that—a gift, a gift we give to others, a gift that is not about us. A gift we give, simply because it is our responsibility to give it."

"I think I understand."

And perhaps I do. My yellow folder was stuffed full of angst and insecurity, hopes and wishes for affirmation or even correction. It was definitely not brought as a generous gift to the community. In short, it was all about me.

I lean back against the wood of our bench. "But you spoke of risks, and of bravery. So you know there can be rejection like I've experienced."

"Tell me the rest of your story of rejection."

"The rest?"

"You said you've been told over and over that you do not have talent. Thus far, I have heard from a bevy of cruel ten-year-old girls and a circle of unproven hopefuls with no qualifications. Who else?"

I rub my palm with my thumb. "No one else, I guess."

He looks at me again with that cocked eyebrow. "This is your 'over and over' being told you're not good enough?"

"When you say it like that..." I half-smile.

"Listen to me, K." He takes my hand in his own, as if we are old friends. "For this Garden, this community, you must bring your work as a gift and nothing more. No comparisons, no jealousies. But this is a special place. The rest of the world will not be so kind, it is true. And that is where the great risk lies. Because rejection of your work is only the beginning of what you risk."

"Great. So I'm hung up on Step One."

"Perhaps. But even the first step must be taken before you can proceed."

"So maybe it's better to focus elsewhere rather than waste time trying to make myself into something I am not and ending up with only pain. In fact, I do need some help figuring out how to save the bookshop—"

"That depends on what you mean by 'better.'"

I frown, shake my head in confusion.

"You said it's *better* to focus elsewhere, to save yourself the pain. Is that really true?"

"I—I don't know."

"Tell me about a time when someone encouraged you to write your stories."

"Well, Gran always said nice things, of course."

"Not 'of course.' She was not obligated to do so. But who else?"

I close my eyes, calling up a distant memory, nearly too fuzzy to grasp. "There was someone once, an older man—a friend of Gran's, I think. I feel like he was a writer of some sort. She introduced me to him at a party, I think. Some kind of event happening outside in the evening. I don't remember his name. But she had given him a story I was writing. I must have been about seven years old." My eyes snap open and I look down. "Wow."

Sam waits, smiling.

"I just remembered, I was wearing a dress very much like this one. White. With wisteria blossoms." How strange.

"Interesting. What did this writer say to you?"

Even now, the warm glow of his words is like a banked fire in my creative spirit, one I've kept burning, despite the harshness in the years that followed. "He said I had a gift. That my story was charming, and I should most definitely finish it."

"Well, there you go."

I laugh. "One positive review of a young child's story from an unknown reader. It's hardly an endorsement that will have publishers knocking on my door."

Without warning, Sam stands. "Enough sitting. Let's walk. Perhaps meet some better friends."

I rise from the bench to stand at his side, looking out over the meandering walkways and groupings of people. I've talked with or seen so many famous creatives already. Who might Sam introduce me to next?

And why am I still here, lingering when I should be leaving?

But he takes my hand and threads it through his bent arm, linking us as we stroll at the lighted edge of the Garden, just inside the vine-covered marble columns.

I glance into the shadows. What lies in there?

The warmth of his arm seeps into me as we walk in step with each other. I could come here every night, I think, for a never-ending evening with this guy.

"Tell me who you are, S. Give me something about the work you've done, something I would know about."

He is silent. "Not yet. Nothing yet."

Does he mean he's created nothing I would know? Or that he won't tell me yet?

"How about you?" He squeezes my linked arm against his ribs. "How can I know more of you?"

I snort a little laugh. "I think it must be obvious by now that I don't belong—"

But the little squeeze gets tighter, meant to cut off my words.

"I meant to say, I'll be writing something very soon that will have the world talking."

"There you go." The corners of his eyes crinkle in a really attractive way.

We've circled the Garden's torchlit border until we're directly across from the Tree, near the musicians' platform.

A harpist is settling herself behind her instrument. Her long fingers caress the strings, making no sound yet.

Just ahead, on another bench carved from a single tree, a woman sits tapping her fingertips on her knee. It's the older woman with the spiky hair and great smile who was playing the piano when I first arrived. She senses our approach and looks over at us.

"Hey there, S., who you got with you?" Her smile jumps to me.

"This is K." Sam nudges me forward a bit. "K., this is B. She's—"

"The piano player. I remember. I loved your music."

"Did you?" Her eyes widen, as though I've shocked her. "I'm only an amateur."

I smile. "Yes, I can see how much you love it. And it looked like you were having a great time."

She nods and takes a deep breath, her attention going back to the raised platform. "I think I'm finally waking up. Realizing I should have pursued it long ago. Should have pushed through the resistance. Not been so fearful."

"What were you afraid of?"

"Ha!" Her laugh is a chest-deep huff, as though my question has opened Pandora's box. "Everything. And nothing. What if I'm not good enough to make it? What if I am?"

No-nonsense. Two words, but sometimes I cheat.

Beside me, Sam is nodding.

"Maybe it doesn't matter." I want to see that fabulous smile again. "Watching you play, it... it brings joy. Makes people feel something. Maybe that's all that counts."

I glance at Sam. Is he proud of my newfound confidence in the sacredness of creativity?

B. shrugs one shoulder and nods slowly. "Perhaps. But it's not something to be messed around with." She looks up at both of us. "Have you heard about C. disappearing?"

Sam scans the Garden's central grassy area, as if he'll be able to spot Dickens. "A. mentioned it."

B.'s eyes darken. "Well, I overheard A. talking a few minutes ago." She leans in, as if her whisper is a sober secret. "She seems to think C.'s gone because of someone here. Because he was speaking with someone who's refusing to bring a gift."

TWENTY-FOUR

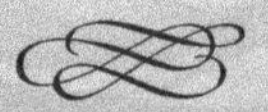

Beauty and sadness always go together.
Nature thought beauty too rich to go forth Upon the earth without a meet alloy.

~ George MacDonald

Guilt is a powerful thing.

It can lead us upward, if we accept our part in whatever damage has occurred, like a gentle priest escorting a penitent into the arms of reconciliation. It can be a swirling maelstrom that sucks us downward into the grip of hopelessness. Or it can feel like a black tally mark under our name, a strike we are determined to erase.

I've always had this third reaction to guilt. In situations where some people repent and others despair, I get to work trying to fix whatever's broken.

The thought that I've caused Charles Dickens to disappear, in some metaphysical way I don't understand, from this metaphysical Garden which likely does not exist, is intolerable to me. It must be repaired.

I'm stalking away from B. and Sam before B. finishes speaking.

"K., wait!"

I cannot fix everything by bringing a gift, this I know. Not unless I leave this place to write a decent story and return with all my past issues somehow healed so I can give my work without fear.

That's not going to happen.

So I'll do the only thing which seems to promise an answer.

Sam catches up and matches my pace across the lawn. "Where are you going?"

"Deeper."

"This isn't the way—"

"It's the only way I know."

I'm flying now, eating up the grass with long strides and weaving through draped tables and clustered party guests like a heat-seeking missile with a tiny target.

My peripheral vision snags on faces turned toward me, eyes widening, lips parting.

I ignore the censure I read in their expressions. The piano player, B., must be the only person at this event who does not know that I'm the one who erased the greatest novelist of the Victorian era.

"K., you don't know what you're doing."

Sam's still at my side, like he's attached there. His voice is low and urgent in my ear.

"You got that right."

But what else can I do? I've heard it from the mouths of too many at this party to ignore the obvious challenge. For some reason, I must go *deeper* into this Garden to qualify myself to be here. Thus far, I've only succeeded in being accused and perhaps shunned. And if I've made Dickens disappear simply by speaking with him, who knows what will happen to Sam?

My heel catches in the grass. With a sickening fear that I'll trip and wake up in my apartment, I reach for him, clutch at his arm like the earth's opened up to swallow me.

"I've got you." He grips my hand, circles to block my forward motion, and pulls me to his chest.

I feel the cords in my neck, strained and shuddering. Sam smells like cinnamon and pine needles, but I refuse to relax into his embrace, much as I long for it. My heart rate and body temperature skyrocket. I set my jaw and pull away.

Sam is still holding my arms. "K., listen to me. I don't think you're ready—"

"Don't try to stop me, S." My vision has tunneled to the little cottage at the end of the forest path, where a light still pulses in a window. "That's the only deeper place I know in this Garden where something for sure exists to be seen. I need to get into that cottage."

He glances over his shoulder. "But it's blocked."

"I know." My voice is steady and low, and I have my feet planted firmly now. "Don't you see? It's like *every* story. Guardians stand at the threshold of adventure, blocking the way."

I look up at him, a stab of uncertainty in my chest. Is *Sam* meant to be one of my obstacles? A great-looking distraction, intentionally placed here to test me?

How have I not seen this next step and what needs to be done? I pride myself on understanding literature, and yet I've dawdled in this in-between place for ages, refusing the real call.

I twist from his grasp. "I have to battle through anything that stands in my way. Fight to cross over into whatever is next for me."

I don't know what's in that cottage—it could be two lost children with nothing but breadcrumbs, or a witch with a hot oven—but I need to get in there.

I expect Sam to grab me again, force me to execute some kind of ninja-move to escape his guardian-clutches.

But he only nods once, his attention pinned on me. "I'm coming with you."

My sprinting heart slows to a fast run. "Let's go."

A shadow still crosses back and forth in front of the cottage, presumably King Arthur with Excalibur at his side. As obstacles go, he's one for the books.

But we won't take the pebbled path to the cottage. I signal to Sam, and we slip into the storybook forest to the right.

The fallen leaves deaden the sound of our footsteps. The mossy tree trunks saturate the air with a humidity that clings to my neck and forehead.

Sam follows at my heels, though I get the sense he'd jump in front of me if the Big Bad Wolf suddenly appeared in the darkness.

We are nearly even with Arthur now, but his attention is fixed on the gravel path he guards. I slow, placing my feet with care, mindful of fallen twigs. The light spilling from the front window is not the only illumination. A small side window, high in the cottage wall, offers another entrance. My best chance of getting inside that tiny locked-up box without encountering Arthur or Excalibur.

What test will I need to pass to bring Charles Dickens back?

"K., stop." Sam's whisper is harsh, grating.

I halt, wanting to *shush* him, but not wanting to chance Arthur hearing.

I raise my eyebrows in his direction, but it's probably too dark for him to see my face.

He brings his lips to my ear, his stubble brushing my hair. "You'll never get in there without his seeing."

I turn my face to him, use a hand to shield my mouth to respond, close to his ear. "I'm going in the side window. You're going to lift me up."

The whites of his eyes widen at this announcement. "This is a mistake."

I ignore the warning, shove aside the ridiculous nature of this stunt.

I creep deeper alongside the cottage, then emerge into the tiny clearing. My attention is on Arthur's back.

Thankfully, his attention is on the path ahead of him and the distant party in the Garden.

The soil around the cottage is damp and spongy. This close, the structure reveals cracks between the stones and crumbling mortar. The roof pitch is sharp, with the eaves sloping down to cover the upper third of the high window.

For once, I'm glad for my too-skinny build. One look at Sam's shoulders makes it clear he can easily boost me to the window, and if I can get it open, I'm sure I'll fit through.

Enough light filters through the window above us that Sam's skeptical expression is obvious.

We spend an awkward moment looking at each other, at the window, at the ground, trying to agree on a plan in silence.

Finally, Sam laces his hands together and bends low, nodding permission for me to place my foot in his grasp.

I slip off my heeled shoes, step one foot into his hands, and touch tentative palms to his shoulders for balance, then give up and grip him with my fingers.

One wobbly boost and I'm fumbling at the glass, one hand braced against the stones and the other searching for a latch. And very aware that I'm wearing a dress, with a guy I don't know standing below me.

Slivers of rotting wood poke my fingertips. The window hinges outward toward me, squeaking as it rises.

I hesitate at the noise, but from here the cottage's guard is unseen, and Sam's grip probably can't last forever. I need to move.

The window's at forty-five degrees, with nothing to prop it open.

I'm going for it.

I grip the frame with both hands, then haul myself through the narrow opening, trying to at least keep my legs from splaying outward. Halfway through, the jagged ledge digs into my belly. Hopefully it won't rip my dress.

There's no time for observation of the interior. My right hand flails for something, anything, to grab.

Beside the window, a rickety hutch leans against the wall, its paint peeling and faded. I grasp the top of it. It seems unlikely to hold my weight as I pull myself through.

But a moment later, I'm dragging my lower legs in and swinging them down to the floor, unsure how I've accomplished it.

Sam's on the outside now, with no way to join me.

I take a breath and steel myself for whatever challenge awaits.

The inside of the cottage is so much like what I imagined, I wonder if I've somehow created it myself. I would swear I smell a waft of warm gingerbread. The rustic table is ready for children—or perhaps a tiny witch-woman—to pull up one of the diminutive chairs huddling around it, carved with scrolled backs and uneven legs. The hutch that aided my entrance holds stacks of dusty plates and chipped stoneware cups hanging from tiny hooks.

All of it seems like it's aged here for centuries. Except for that pervasive, just-baked, gingerbread smell. And the glowing embers in the iron-doored oven at the rear.

A chill snakes up my back. Has someone been here, perhaps only a moment ago? I scan the perimeter of the single room. There is no door but the front door, no windows but the one I saw from the gravel path and the one I've slid through.

And now what?

What am I doing here?

I've snuck past a legendary hero, into a fairy-tale cottage, with the help of a famous sculptor, and I have no idea what I'm doing.

Where is my test? I've gone *deeper,* as everyone keeps telling me I need to, but it feels like a dead end.

I'm turning circles now, at a loss, fighting tears. The single-minded focus that drove me into this cottage is evaporating. How am I supposed to fix the disaster I've caused?

Isn't this the moment when a mentor should appear? Where is my fairy godmother or my Yoda or my Professor Dumbledore, or *somebody*?

On cue, the front door slams open.

I expect Excalibur.

I get Agatha Christie.

Though to be fair, she's got King Arthur at her back.

"What are you doing in here?" Her words are a hiss, her brows drawn together. She holds a champagne flute in one hand but does not look like she's in the mood for socializing.

"I—I am trying—"

"You need to leave. Come. Now." She motions with her hand, with a quick glance over her shoulder, as if we're going to sneak past the medieval legend in the doorway.

A fraction of a moment later, Sam's face appears behind Arthur's shoulder.

I plant my feet. These must be my threshold guardians, all three.

"I'm going deeper, " I say to Agatha. Half-expecting her to be impressed by my awareness of my quest, or at least by my determination.

But she's at my side, grabbing my arm, pulling me toward the cottage door. "This is not for you."

The same words Arthur muttered the first time Sam and I tried to approach the cottage.

Tonight, though, it occurs to me that perhaps this cottage is not for me in the sense that it's for someone else.

I let her escort me outside. Should I be fighting harder to stay?

She doesn't stop at the entrance of the cottage.

Arthur steps aside. She keeps driving into the darkness, hand still gripped around my forearm.

I stumble along beside her, mouth cotton-dry and feet still bare.

Sam follows, my sandals dangling from his fingers.

Does he know what's going on?

Halfway down the gravel path to the center of the Garden, I manage to loose myself from her grasp and plant my bare feet.

"Enough! Where are you taking me?"

TWENTY-FIVE

There must always be two kinds of art: escape-art, for man needs escape as he needs food and deep sleep, and parable-art, that art which shall teach man to unlearn hatred and learn love.

~ W.H. Auden

Agatha whirls on my refusal to move, glaring. "I'm taking you to someone who will explain why shortcuts are unacceptable."

I've committed some sort of Garden heresy, then.

I grab my shoes from Sam, slide them on, and regain my balance.

Her hands are on her hips. "You need to come with me."

I could make a run for it, probably, but I'm too curious.

Or perhaps too invested in seeing where all this takes me. Seeing if I can still, somehow, get information about my real identity or how to save the shop. And I'm feeling a little more confident after my run at the cottage.

Following Agatha, I glance at Sam.

He nods, as if assuring me that he's got my back.

We draw close enough to the Garden to hear the music, a light classical tune on the piano, more like background music in a hotel lobby than a performance. The grassy expanse of lawn is still crowded with party guests in their ever-continuing conversations and laughter. They don't seem to have missed me.

We reach the end of the path and Agatha veers sharply right, with a glance in my direction, to make sure I'm still following.

We skirt the central Garden area, the shadowy edges leading to unseen depths on our right. Move past a flaming torch embedded at the border between grass and wildness, its oily black smoke coiling upward, and then another torch, farther on.

Ahead, a small structure—smaller than the cottage—takes shape in the twilight haze. Boxy and wooden, it looks like a potting shed at the edge of a country estate.

A tiny window reveals a single illuminated bulb hanging inside.

Agatha barrels toward it, opens the door without hesitation, then sweeps her arm in my direction, inviting me to enter.

"I'm right behind you," Sam says in my ear.

We step into the building, which is crowded with shelves of trowels and shears, hand rakes and a tumbled assortment of terracotta pots in various states of wear. Larger shovels, hoes, and rakes lean in the corner, mud-caked and well-used. And in the center, an older man bends over a worktable, using his fingertips to tamp soil around the roots of a small potted aloe vera plant.

Agatha brings up the rear and shuts the door behind us.

Silence holds for a moment, and then the man looks up.

His eyes are kinder than I expect, given the circumstances. He is unremarkable in one way—medium build, average height, hair going white. But there is something almost *too* general about him. I can't guess at his ethnicity, even. As though he is everything and nothing at once.

I breathe a little, readying some kind of response, or perhaps excuse.

"She tried to go through the cottage." Agatha states my infraction in a weary tone, as though I am a frustrating and recalcitrant child.

He nods once. His eyes flick to Sam but without acknowledgment.

I note Agatha's use of the word *through*. Could I have gone farther into the cottage somehow, to a deeper place? Should I have tried?

"That is not for you."

I nearly laugh. "So I've heard." My tone sounds a little snarky, and I wish I could pull it back.

"Where were you going?"

"I don't know."

"Then why did you try?"

I shake my head. "I don't really understand any of this."

"You don't understand yourself." The words are tinged with pity, not accusation.

Unexpected emotion pricks behind my eyes. "That's probably true."

"Then you are getting ahead of things."

Agatha turns to me. "I must get back to the party. Pay attention to the Gardener. He can help."

The Gardener. Wow.

It's the Wizard behind the curtain. Maybe I've finally met my mentor?

Agatha pushes past Sam and escapes the potting shed.

I grab Sam's arm before he can think about following her.

He curls his fingers around mine, warm and reassuring.

"Am I trapped here?" I study the Gardener's eyes, watching for deception. "Unable to leave?"

He laughs, low in his chest. "You keep asking this question. On the contrary, my dear. You are in danger of being expelled before learning your true identity."

"That's what I'm trying to do! I—I kept hearing people talk about going deeper. About bravery and taking risks. I thought the cottage must be the place—"

"I applaud your determination. You have felt and heard the whisperings—the hints—that you must come alive to something *more*. You have listened and followed. But you still have many things to overcome before you are ready to even *begin* taking risks."

"Okay. So, tell me. I'm ready."

But am I? Everything feels mixed together in this place—my identity as E's girl, my identity as a wannabe writer, even my identity as a person, adoption and all.

The bare bulb above my head still sways in the breeze of Agatha's exit, and my attention jumps to some rough-stenciled wording on the wall of the shed, above the Gardener's head.

What you can do, or dream you can, begin it.

Boldness has Genius, Power, and Magic in it.

The Gardener notes my scanning of the words and smiles.

"Who said that?" I see no attribution beneath the lines.

He brushes the soil from his fingertips. "It's complicated. The short answer is that it's from a translation of Goethe's *Faust*."

I was just speaking of Faust and his deal-with-the-devil-disaster to Charles Diamond Blackburn.

I waggle my head, trying to shake loose the perpetual confusion of this place. It's time to focus on whatever needs to be done to fix the problem I've caused.

"Why has Ch—why has C. disappeared?"

He turns, leans back against the shelf, crosses his arms over his chest, and one ankle over the other. His white hair glows under the bulb, but his physique is anything but frail. He is the picture of casual wisdom about to be dispensed.

What's my one word to define him? To contain him into something I can understand? I can think of nothing.

Undefinable.

"You have not brought your gift."

"So then, it *is* my fault? But why him? Why C.?"

He tilts his head, as though speaking to a child. "Did he not encourage you? Challenge you?"

"Yes, but I'm the one who failed! Not him. Why should he suffer, instead of me?"

The Gardener smiles. "It would appear that you *are* suffering."

"What do I need to do, to bring him back?"

"You already know."

I look away. "I'm not ready. I tried, but I can't."

"Exactly."

I huff, glance at Sam, and pick up a muddy trowel from the worktable, turn it in my hand.

Do I have to play this game? Can I wait him out with silence?

He inhales deeply, his chest expanding as though with all the words he is about to deliver, and his gaze takes in both of us.

"An artist has many things to overcome before he or she can even consider the risk of bringing work to the world. You must first get past all the distractions that would keep you from the work—both the distractions of mere survival and those of empty amusements."

I bristle at the accusation of wasted time. "I have responsibilities. This 'survival,' as you call it, can't simply be ignored."

"Yes, it is impossible, isn't it? The choice between duty to family, obligations and commitments to practical concerns, and the charge to be truly yourself and to express the beauty asking to be revealed through you."

He has encapsulated the problem without offering any solution.

I can think of nothing to say.

"And then," his white head shakes slowly, his chin lowered, "there is such trauma from the past, so many hostile voices that keep the artist chained and afraid." He steps toward me, gently takes the trowel from my hand and returns it to the worktable, but still holds my hand in his. "And all this, before you even face the arduous task of creating, or find the courage to confront all that must be risked."

"So what am I supposed to do?"

He smiles the sad, slight smile of one who brings difficult news.

"You must bring your gift."

"Why is *my* gift so important? You have plenty of amazing works at that table out there."

"Because it is only when the work is multiplied, coming together, that the journey back can begin. And because you cannot know your true self without honesty."

I toe a pebble on the floor of the shed, kicking it forward a few inches. I'm tired and frustrated and feeling responsible for a disaster I couldn't have guessed I'd cause. But if these people know something about my adoption, about my biological parents, about saving the bookshop, I cannot walk away.

The Gardener crosses to the shed's door and flattens a palm against the wood.

"I'm afraid humanity has taken a tumble, my children." He speaks like a wise old sage on a mountain. The tone is sad, but so full of love. He turns back to us.

"We've all gotten a little fractured and bent in the process. But pursuing the True, the Good, and the Beautiful is the beginning of our journey back. Some of us are meant to help lead the way, to pursue the mystery and the reality of something bigger than ourselves, to lead others out of the deception of this false time-bound world and into reality."

Van Gogh and his *trompe l'œil.* Wasn't he saying the same thing?

The Gardener nods, as though reading my thoughts. "We've been deceived into believing our tiny sliver of years is the sum total of reality. That the things we can touch and buy and use and feel are all there is. But every once in a while, there is a reminder. The nostalgia returns—the hint that we are living in a false world, and we've forgotten the true."

Yes. The very thing I felt, the first time I entered this place.

He opens his arms as if he would embrace me, but raises his eyes as though seeing past the low roof of the potting shed. "All Beauty has the power to remind us. That slash of pinkish-orange sky above a purple ridge as the sun sleeps. The dark pine pillars in a white forest after a silent snowfall. All the Beauty of the natural world." He gestures beyond the shed, indicating the Garden. "But also music and stories, art and dance, and so much more. Beauty which is imperfect in its execution but still able to stir the soul, whether through the soaring notes of music, the touches of paint on canvas, or marvelous language woven into thrilling story."

He lowers his gaze, pins me with it. "Sunsets and forests are the art of God. The rest—the rest is the art of man, given skill to sub-create. And astonishingly, gifted to stir the same longings."

I am breathless, weightless, suspended in his words, which fit like missing pieces into the puzzling experience of my struggle.

He shares a smile for both Sam and me. "I wonder if you feel it, my friends? Feel that we live in a shadow world, and we have been trying to find our way back to the real, since we took our first breath and somehow sensed that we were meant for more?"

"Yes." Sam and I answer as one.

I glance at Sam, but then must return my attention to the Gardener.

He lifts his hands, palms stretched toward us, like a

benediction. "You are part of a critical work, and you must be generous enough to love the world in this way. This is what you have been given to do, and it is what you must do."

Sam and I are silent. The Gardener's words seem sacred, like a prayer offered over our heads.

The silence lengthens, but I finally break it. "I still do not know how—"

He steps forward and places a warm hand on my shoulder. "The Garden is not an end unto itself. It is only an entrance into what you truly need."

I sigh, tilt my head back to study the low ceiling, as if answers will be plainer there.

But the Gardener is waving his hands outward now, as if to sweep us from the potting shed. "Go now. The way will be clear to you."

With that, he turns back to his little pot of aloe vera, and we are dismissed.

Outside the shed, Sam and I stand side-by-side.

"That was..." I cannot choose a word.

Revelatory? Inspirational? Frightening?

"Yes."

We take a few slow steps toward the party, away from the shed.

What do I sense I have found in this moment? As though so much has been clarified, distilled, answered, even though nothing has changed.

Peace.

I turn to Sam. Does he feel it, too?

He meets my glance, stops walking, takes my hand.

There is no conversation, only a knowing as we study each other.

Sam looks me up and down. "Your dress." He touches a fingertip to the torn fabric across my waist. "You've ripped it."

I follow his glance, watch his hand as he traces the gash

across my skin. I cover his hand with my own, feeling exposed.

His eyes lift to meet mine, intense. His ever-present smile has fled.

When he bends his head to mine, tilts my chin with his other hand, I am not surprised and yet I am astounded, all at once.

His kiss is otherworldly, as it should be. But it is also grounded in the physical and so very, very real.

I rise on my toes to meet him halfway, in a return of emotion that is both perfect and foolish.

I'm not thinking about practicality now, not now, with his hand cradling the back of my head and the kiss deepening to be more than an experiment, more than an introduction, so much more than casual. I'm only wrapping desperate arms around him, wanting this moment to remain suspended, as all other moments in this wonderful place have been apt to do.

We pull apart, finally, and I am breathless, smiling, nearly laughing with the impossibility of it. I look into Sam's eyes, but his attention has shifted to beyond my shoulder.

I turn to follow his gaze, taking in the guests, the tables, the lanterns and food at the center of the Garden.

Something is wrong.

Nothing is changed, not that I can see, but all seems... dimmer. The conversations are quieter, heads bent together in uneasy whispers rather than intimate laughter. The music has ceased, though a man still sits alert and watching at the piano, as if his fingers still hover over the keys.

Has someone else disappeared? Is it my fault?

I look for Agatha, who seems to always be ready when I need her, but she's nowhere.

Have I erased Agatha Christie?

My stomach lurches.

That first night—standing at the table with Frank Baum —what did he say about my going deeper?

Something about the party being only the beginning. That I must "go through." He'd indicated the darkness, not in the direction of the cottage, but back toward where the Rhythm & Wonder Music Shop's brick wall should stand. I could see nothing in that inky direction of that path.

So I'd run from his words, tripped, and awakened from this impossible dream, because I didn't want to heed his instruction.

A man approaches, the candlelight at his back and his face shadowed.

I wait, sensing he is coming for me.

"K." He glances at Sam, but his attention on me.

"Hello, T." T.S. Eliot, my first friend here.

"You've heard?" His face is somber, mouth downturned.

"About C.? Yes. I don't—"

"C., yes, but it's worse now."

I take a deep breath and steady myself against Sam's upper arm. "A.? Is she gone, too?"

"What? No, no, she's over there." He waves in the vague direction of the pergola. "No, it's the Garden."

"The Garden?" I scan the nearby flower beds, the Weigela shrub-lined path leading toward the center, the grassy lawn. Is it… is it *wilting*?

Eliot nods and steps closer to me, grips my hands in his. "You must be brave, K."

I pull away and rush to nearest marble column twined with climbing vines of blooming clematis. Even in the dark it is obvious. I run my fingers over the violet starbursts… closing, bending, browning at the edges. The leaves between the petals droop, beginning to curl in on themselves.

Everything in me wants to curl up like a tight fist as well. Lay down here in the dewy grass, knees drawn up and head tucked away from death and loss. All the perfection in the world is dying, or being Taken from me. All that feels like home, that promises love, that whispers of something more.

Eliot is at my side.

"This is me? I have done this?"

"I know it is difficult." His eyes are kind, sympathetic.

I appreciate the understanding, but it's not going to save the Garden. And I'm not letting it go, any of it, without every bit of fight in me.

I nod once, clarity hitting like a dousing of ice water. "I'm going."

Sam reaches for me, but I'm already moving.

I don't know where, or how, or even why, but I need to take that path into the unknown—the one Frank Baum indicated. The cottage was a distraction. That statuary-lined path is my *deeper*. And I'm going.

Each cluster of conversation goes silent as I pass, as though I'm spreading a ripple of death as I cross the grass.

I reach the feast table, ignore the temptation to stuff supplies into a napkin, and circle the food. Past the table of gifts and its clusters of accompanying artwork.

And then Agatha is there, hurrying along beside me.

Why her all the time? Has she been assigned as my chaperone? My mentor? My warden?

"K., where are you going?"

"Deeper."

She keeps pace, but she's silent. No mention that this direction is "not for me." As I suspected, and have too long ignored, this is the exact direction I need to be headed.

The absence of Sam, who has been my near-constant companion in this place, hits me in the chest, but I keep moving.

Two statues of full-bearded centaurs border a white-graveled path that winds into darkness. I pause for only a moment, touch the horse's flank of one, as if to gain some good luck.

"K., listen to me."

Agatha is still beside me, her tone quiet, but urgent.

"You haven't yet brought your gift."

"Enough!" I spin to face her. "I'm sick of the mixed messages, the whispers, and the accusations."

She pulls back, lips parted and eyebrows raised.

I wish I could believe her reaction is surprise that I've stood up for myself at last, but it probably signals some sort of madness on my part.

Once, when I was about eight years old, I spilled a blue raspberry Slushie on one of Gran's favorite books. I slaved away at extra chores for a summer to make up for the guilt. This thing I've done here, bringing some kind of death to this beautiful place, feels like a blue raspberry Slushie spilled on the Mona Lisa.

I force my shoulders back and my voice to a reasonable pitch. "I don't have time for stories, A. The Garden is dying. I need to go."

With that, I spin toward the unknown path, push past the two centaurs, and head into the darkness.

The path bends into the shadows, and the pea-sized white gravel fades to a carpet of pine needles, barely a path but for the opening between close-growing boxwood now scratching at my arms. I forge ahead slowly into the darkness filled with the sharp scent of pine sap. I should have grabbed one of the tiki torches burning around the garden to wave in front of me. Like Indiana Jones entering a forbidden cave.

Something gleams ahead, whitish in the starlight. More statues lining the path?

I take baby steps, eyes trained on the mystery, ears tuned for wild animals. My pulse trips over itself, tingles through my fingers.

Closer and closer, hands lifted in front of my body as if to ward off some kind of attack.

My eyes are adjusting, and two images coalesce out of the darkness—two pale lions, sitting on their haunches, paws forward.

I draw back, sucking in a breath, heart stopped.

No, not lions. They each have the head of a man in full

Egyptian headdress. Marble sphinxes, guarding the entrance to a stone footbridge.

This is it, then. A bridge. Its iconic guardians. I've found the place where I must dive deeper into the Garden.

I'm pulling in breath like I'm storing it for winter. All my attention focused on where the bridge curves upward at the middle then disappears into parts unknown. Hands fisted at my sides.

I stride forward purposefully, refusing the hesitation I've shown thus far. Everything in me says I must be determined here, resolved, hardened into action.

The blocks of the bridge are chiseled into perfect squares, fitted close and smooth under my feet. I skim fingertips over the railing as I walk, picking up speed and peering into the darkness beyond.

Where will this next adventure land me?

Three steps from the apex of the bridge.

Two steps.

Only a footfall away from crossing the midpoint, which feels like no return.

I lurch into the final step, feel a smile tug at my lips. The sure and steady knowledge that I am exactly where I should be.

Then a bone-jarring smash into an invisible barrier, and darkness.

TWENTY-SIX

This joy... is not essentially "escapist," nor "fugitive." In its fairy-tale—or otherworld—setting, it is a sudden and miraculous grace: never to be counted on to recur... giving a fleeting glimpse of Joy, Joy beyond the walls of the world, poignant as grief.

~ J.R.R. Tolkien

The birdsong doesn't fool me this time.

Even with my eyes closed, the feel of my bed under my hip bones is nothing like the stone bridge that ought to be there.

I groan, reach for my phone on the nightstand, and smash the *stop* button to silence the mockery of the false birds.

I take a moment to breathe, reorient my senses to the idea of home and bookshop and not-deeper.

Anger and frustration ball the sheets in my fists but bleed out of me just as quickly, leaving a hollow exhaustion. Despite the early morning hour, I know I have not slept.

I roll to my side and fumble for the phone again, chest heavy with an unnameable sadness.

What day is it? I've spent longer inside the Garden on this last visit than my previous entries. Have I lost a day? A week? A month?

Nine hours.

It's early Monday morning, just nine hours after I pushed open the gate last night.

It seems the longer I stay inside, the less time I miss in the real world.

Or at least what I've always called the real world. Who's to say?

I flop back to the pillows, eyes on the yellowing ceiling.

Have I been ostracized from the Garden forever? Even if I reenter, will there be a Garden still, or have I managed to kill it?

The image of that yellowing clematis vine curling into a fetal position like an animal waiting to die rakes across my heart. I coil into my own cocoon of rumpled sheets, fighting useless tears.

Every fear, every whisper of mockery and criticism, every certainty that *not writing* would be so much better than *bad writing,* roars into my head. Why did I ever try to bring a story into that Garden? Did I truly think my drugstore folder with its metal-pronged pages would find a place among the literary greats on that beautiful table?

It's a blessing my words disappeared. Much better than to have them read by someone like T.S. Eliot, or L. Frank Baum, or Agatha Christie. Each of them so different, but still, each with *something*—some special quality which makes their work perennial and weighty, popular and delightful. It's a quality which cannot be achieved through pretense or mere effort.

You either have it or you don't.

I exhale the futility and let reality roll over me, like a heavy hand crushing me flat.

Alright, Kelsey, enough maundering thoughts of self-pity.

I have only two hours until my cross-town meeting with the only lawyer who agreed to meet me on two days' notice. Eminent domain, the basis of the Taking, he tells me, is no joke. And my chances are slim.

And so, I shoehorn myself into the day, running a hot shower, dressing without thought. Then trudge the three blocks to the Sunny Side Up Diner. It feels like AnaMaria's TexMex omelette with a sticky bun on the side is my only reason to move forward.

AnaMaria is behind the counter when I enter and blesses me with her usual gleaming smile and one finger held up to signal she'll be with me in a moment.

I slide into the nearest empty booth, set my phone on the table face-down, and study the slow build of Monday morning traffic on Chestnut Street.

In the congestion and diesel fumes and traffic of the city waking up, the Garden feels a million miles away. No, not even that. It feels like a different plane of existence, a place outside of time and space.

So how can the disappearance of a writer who's already dead and some shriveled shrubbery inside a fantasy feel like the end of my world, *this* world? The world where taxes are due and developers are eating the other end of the street and Gran lies in a nursing home bed barely clinging to her memories. What possible difference can anything occurring in that verdant, twilight world make to me here, in this one?

I need to focus on fighting the Taking, and my promise to myself to call Robert Dumas, publisher at Sparrow Books.

"Your Gran okay?" AnaMaria's at my side, head tilted in concern.

"What? Yes, she's—I mean, she's not great, but not much different."

AnaMaria purses her lips. "Okay. You just look like you're carrying the world on those shoulders this morning."

I sigh. "Then I guess I'd better eat." I order the omelette

and pastry, and AnaMaria fills my stoneware mug with steaming coffee before she puts my order into the kitchen.

I run cold fingers over the spidery cracks on the glazed surface of the mug, fissures that will one day deepen and render it useless. I blow across the surface of the coffee before taking a scalding sip.

Waiting for the food, my thoughts run backward through the evening in the Garden. My ill-advised detour into the cottage, the meeting with the Gardener. And even before all that—meeting Puccini while Luciano Pavarotti sang his heart out, his duet with the blonde woman tunneling into my soul.

What was that piece? I flip my phone over and tap out the phonetic spelling of what I remember. Google does the rest, guessing at the correct spelling.

O soave fanciulla. Pavarotti. Duet.

Plenty of links, including videos.

I swivel to check my surroundings. The diner is filling up with the breakfast crowd, so I pull earbuds from my jacket pocket before thumbing to a video link.

My phone screen fills with a live performance, and there they are—Pavarotti and the blonde. Mirella Freni.

And then they sing.

There are subtitles, but I ignore them, first watching only their expressions, their lips, their eyes, as they pour out their hearts, then closing my own eyes and traveling backward to the performance I witnessed firsthand last night.

This piece, this music, this heaven.

Puccini's composition and the blended genius of Pavarotti and Freni... it is too much. A longing like nothing I have known, and for what, I do not know, skims caressing fingers across my soul with a pain so poignant it feels more like pleasure.

What is this desire? Is it a yearning for a *La bohème* version of passion between two people? In a moment that is disloyal but not at all surprising, it is Sam's face at the periphery of my thoughts, not Austin's.

But the tears—and I am near to sobbing now—are not for love. Or perhaps, not simply for love.

The truest I can say is that I cry for wholeness.

I cry for a person or a place or a sense of being which I know by now can be called nothing better than *home.*

Some fundamental and missing piece which I am not sure this world has within it to ever satisfy. And so I cry not only for wholeness but for the impossibility of it, for a thirst that can never be slaked.

Though the Garden has surfaced this deep longing, it has also ruined me, made it impossible to return to suppressing and denying. How can I ever go back to pretending there is nothing more than spreadsheets and profit statements?

And then AnaMaria is there with my eggs, clanking the stoneware plate to the chipped Formica table, eyes widening at my tear-sodden face.

"Honey, what is it?" Her hand falls warm and heavy on my shoulder. Her head bent to study my eyes.

I shake my head, yank out the earbuds and drop them to the table. "Nothing. It's nothing. Just some sad music."

She cradles the back of my head briefly, then brushes hair away from my eyes.

The touch is so affectionate I have to marshal back the tears once more.

"You are exhausted, Kelsey." She points to the food. "Eat, yes. But you need to take better care of yourself. I know it's hard, and your Gran needs you. But I think you need a day to do nothing but rest."

I nod, give her a watery smile, and lift my fork, not trusting myself to words.

She retreats, stopping by again for only a moment to bring my sticky bun and refill my coffee.

I swirl a plastic thimbleful of creamer into the coffee with a tarnished spoon, then catch my reflection in the back of the convex utensil. Haggard, even in miniature.

AnaMaria is right. I need sleep. And probably need to stop spending my nights in a place that has no bearing on my reality.

Yes, that might be better. But ignoring the Garden, the blocked footbridge, the call for me to bring a gift—is it even an option anymore? Can I set aside the only part of me that feels real in order to fight the inevitable?

I twist the spoon left and right, stretching my reflection.

Who am I if I continue to deny this part of myself? This need to *create*, to *make*, to *express*. If I save the bookshop but lose myself in the process, what will I have left?

And if I lose the bookshop… All the other losses tumble into that widening crater—the neighborhood, this place, friends like AnaMaria and William. My home, my job, my purpose. Soon Gran, my only family.

There is no way back to the person I was. There is no way forward to what I need.

I set the spoon on the table, close my eyes to the rising buzz of diner conversations, and inhale a deep breath of the truth.

You win, Garden.

Three simple words spoken only in the quiet of my heart, but the concession is the letting go of clenched fists, the surrender to a fierce wind I've been fighting.

It may take a lifetime to write a story I am ready to bring, but I will do it.

I will bring it to the table of gifts, and then I will walk with head held high all the way across that blasted footbridge, to whatever deeper understanding of myself lies on the other side.

I will.

In the meantime, I will do all I have left to save my life as I know it.

Decision made, I dig into the sticky bun, gulp down the

rest of the coffee, and prepare to face immediate matters. Once today's bookshop crisis is dealt with, I'll have a clear head, the freedom for creativity.

So. First. Time to face down irrational fears and ridiculous angst over a bestselling novel that resembles something I wrote a million years ago. It's time to call Robert and agree to his publicity event, which can only bring benefit to the Chestnut Street Book Emporium, even if it dings my ego in the process. Besides, I'll be at the city meeting during his party, fighting the Taking.

My phone's been auto-playing the video of another operatic aria, but when I pick it up to call Robert, it starts vibrating.

"Hey, Austin." I can hear the weariness in my own voice. It feels like a lifetime since I've seen him, between evading him all weekend while I wrote my disappearing story, then spending so much time in the Garden.

"Hey. I'm surprised you picked up."

I bite back *I'm surprised you called,* since texting is more his thing.

"Sorry. Been a busy few days."

"Sure, yeah. Can you catch dinner tomorrow? I'll be down that way."

Austin is another item on my immediate to-do list. If this thing between us has a chance, we need a bit more honesty. "Yeah, dinner would be great."

"Around six, then. And I won't bring Starbucks."

I try to laugh, knowing he expects it, although I do appreciate the concession, especially sitting here in the diner.

Disconnect, push away the plates of food. One last gulp of coffee.

What else?

A few people coming into the shop to look at the first editions for sale, the meeting with the lawyer, phone calls to make. The ticking clock on derailing the Taking is counting down in a rapid blur.

Yes, I've plenty to occupy my time, pushing the writing of a new story to a pleasant, untroubled distance.

After all, time seems to stand still in the Garden when I'm gone. The party doesn't feel like it's moving toward an end. It's always a party at its peak, when the conversation and food and wine are flowing, and no one has yet said "I've got to get going," and everyone senses, even if they don't leave immediately, that it will soon be over.

So then, what harm can it do, to wait?

TWENTY-SEVEN

Everybody knows in their bones that something is eternal, and that something has to do with human beings. All the greatest people ever lived have been telling us that for five thousand years and yet you'd be surprised how people are always losing hold of it. There's something way down deep that's eternal about every human being.

~ from *Our Town* by Thornton Wilder

With the Tuesday afternoon sun slanting through the front windows of the Book Emporium, seven Creative Writers of Tomorrow tumble through the door.

I'm waiting with a smile that's only face-deep.

"Ready for some fun?"

Can they sense my despair as we trudge back to the wardrobe?

Yesterday's meeting with the lawyer was a billable hour of bad news. The city is willing to pay for the property in the Taking, sure, but since the White Orchard Hotel development is already a *fait accompli,* our compensation for the shop will be based on the expected value *after* the hotel effectively blocks most of the traffic and drives it to bankruptcy. Not good. My new attorney is not optimistic about my odds in fighting the Taking and thinks I'm crazy for not jumping on Blackburn's previous offer.

As if all that weren't enough, in the middle of this circus, the Book Emporium has garnered the attention of the city's Zoning Board, which has informed me the shop isn't zoned to have an apartment on the upper level. Terrific.

Three people were interested in first editions after my postings last week. I sold two of the books, but for far less than I'd hoped. I might as well have told the buyers to write their checks directly to the lawyer.

I have about ten days to pull a magic answer out of the air, to find a way to stop this thing, or both Lisa and I are going to be looking for new jobs. And maybe I have a better chance than Lisa, with her spotty employment record and ongoing "issues," but neither of us are exactly a recruiter's dream.

As if on cue with my dark thoughts, the dramatic blare of sirens screeches into the Children's Section.

And a moment later, Lisa.

"Kels, you gotta get out here. There's a problem."

Has there been an accident on the street?

"Be right back, kids. Work on your prompts."

I follow Lisa through the hallway. "What's going on?"

"The street's flooding."

We reach the front door, and indeed, water is gushing down Chestnut Street, only an inch lower than the curb.

"What—Where is it coming from?" I run outside, Lisa at my heels.

Farther up the street, a fire truck's siren wails, and fire fighters are unloading from the truck.

I suck in a breath and turn to check my building, then

The Groove, even the partially dismantled Vietnamese restaurant on the other side of William's shop. Is there a fire?

William is on the sidewalk.

"Water main," he yells. "Hotel construction broke something, apparently."

A moment later he backs into the entrance to his shop as the water starts pouring down the sidewalk.

The deluge makes a run toward the Book Emporium but then diverts into the first window well of the basement.

I dart to the window, peer down the galvanized metal half-circle. The water fills the well, as it does every time it rains. But this is too much water, and the seals on the window are decades old. A minute later, the water in the niche begins to drain as more continues to gush in from the street level.

"The basement!" I jump for the door, hearing Lisa's footsteps behind me.

The steps to the lowest level are at the back of the shop, and I am out of breath by the time I reach the dungeon-like storage area beneath the building.

Where did Lisa go?

I shelve my annoyance and run for the front, where water is already pouring down the wall and spreading an oil-slicked film across the floor. It reaches slimy fingers for the bankers' boxes full of records and old documents—some from the Book Emporium and some dating all the way back to the theater days.

I start grabbing at boxes, pulling them back, away from the water. There are no shelves, no higher ground. Hopefully someone out there will shut off the water soon.

Moments later, a sound like thunder reaches me from the back, and seven teens plus Lisa are at my side.

"What do we do, Miss Kelsey?"

"The boxes! Take them all the way to the back of the basement—as far as you can go."

The bottom of one of the boxes disintegrates when I lift it from the dirty floor, dumping sheafs of yellowed papers.

Jae and Saanvi grab at the papers with me, gathering them safely away from the water and carrying them to the back of the room.

Photographs of the acting troupes over the years and newspaper clippings with reviews of old shows. I run a hand over the top photo. Would a historical society want some of these? Gran and I probably shouldn't have let them mildew down here for years.

Twenty minutes later, the water has slowed to a trickle and the boxes are safe. The group stomps back up the stairs.

I try to avoid thinking of the cost of repairs, and engage the kids in the remaining time, asking again for volunteers to read their work.

Olivia waggles a few fingers above the tabletop.

I smile at the quiet girl I usually need to encourage before she's ready to share. "Thanks, Olivia. I can't wait to hear what you've written."

She ducks her head and pinches at her bottom lip as though she's reconsidering.

Saanvi leans into the table. "I'm sure it's great, Olivia."

The others nod and murmur agreement.

Despite the solid lump of desperation in my chest, a little burst of pride blooms there.

To hear them affirm each other, to see Olivia's creative growth—this is why I run this workshop.

Each of these students has a fighting chance, I hope, to step into their own creativity without fear.

There is such trauma from the past, so many hostile voices, that keep the artist chained and afraid.

The Gardener's words, spoken in the strange little potting shed at one edge of the Garden.

He's right, as I well know. Perhaps I'm doing my part to negate some of those voices for these kids.

Olivia squirms in her chair, clears her throat, glances around the table.

"This is a totally safe place, Olivia." I catch the eye of each student. Another reminder never hurts. "It's safe to bring your creativity here. We don't criticize or judge. We only encourage. If you want to brainstorm some suggestions for improvement, we can do that. But only if that's what you want. And that goes for all of us who read our work, right?"

Nods all around.

Olivia swallows hard and begins.

It's a short story about a cranky old woman whose pets begin to challenge her attitude which takes Olivia less than ten minutes to read. The narrative contains a few genuinely humorous pieces of dialogue and a touching ending.

When she finishes, the table erupts in applause, and even a few hoots.

Olivia beams.

"That was awesome, Liv!" Alejandro claps the girl on the back, knocking her forward, and the other five laugh.

"Really great, Olivia." I give her a thumbs-up. "What would you say—any of you—is the theme of this piece?"

Various answers pop out.

Old people can still change.

Don't be mean.

I agree with all of them. "I would add that Olivia's story has a theme of 'redemption.' Does anyone know this term?"

Wide eyes and silence.

"I'll give you an example of another story with this same theme, one you all know. Olivia's story is somewhat like *A Christmas Carol*, isn't it?"

Jae frowns. "Like... 'Joy to the World' or something like that?"

"No," I laugh, "not the kind of Christmas carol we sing. I'm talking about the story. Ebenezer Scrooge, Tiny Tim. How does Olivia's story have a similar theme?"

The blank expressions persist.

"Come on, I know you've all heard of Ebenezer Scrooge." I resist the Gran-like comment of *what are they teaching kids these days?*

"The Ghost of Christmas Past, of Christmas Present..."

Still nothing.

"God bless us, every one." I quote the line in my best Tiny Tim voice, but it fizzles out at the end because a terrible thought worms its way into my brain.

I jump to my feet, shoving my chair over in the process.

"Be right back," I call over my shoulder on my way out, leaving the chair where it fell. "Figure out who's next while I'm gone."

Out through Narnia, pushing through the wardrobe, racing to the CLASSICS section.

I don't need to find *A Christmas Carol*—maybe we don't even have it in stock. Any title by Dickens will reassure me.

I scan the shelf... alphabetical by author... Anderson, Byron, Chekhov, Eliot.

Can't be true.

I jog to the front of the store, into my office.

Lisa's lips part as I rush by, but she doesn't ask.

Three clicks and I've accessed our store database.

Dickens, I type into the search bar.

Emily Dickinson comes up as a result, along with some other lesser-known writers. No Charles.

No one is useless in this world who lightens the burdens of another.

The quote under the framed and matted photograph on the wall of BRITISH LITERATURE.

Running back to that section. Scanning the wall.

There is the frame, but inside it, the Romantic period's leading poet, Lord Byron, has replaced Dickens, with a new quote engraved into the matting:

There is pleasure in the pathless woods, there is rapture in the lonely shore, there is society where none intrudes, by the deep sea, and music in its roar; I love not Man the less, but Nature more.

"Lisa! Come over here, please."

She's at my side in a flash. "What's going on?"

"This picture. Didn't it used to be Charles Dickens?"

She frowns and tilts her head. "I think it's always been this Byron guy." She shrugs. "I don't pay much attention, I'll admit. But who's Charles Dickson?"

No, no, no. Not possible.

I lean into the shelf below the picture, grab it with my fingertips, unsteady and nauseated.

"What is it, Kelsey?" Lisa's hand is warm on my back, an uncharacteristic display of sympathy.

"I think I'm losing my mind."

"I doubt that."

Those wide-ruled pages, scrawled with my ten-year-old handwriting, squirreled away in the front cover of *The Secret Garden*. Did I bring all this about, bring the Garden into the "real world" somehow?

"Have you ever wished for something so hard, that it came true, even though it was impossible?"

"Maybe you're wishing so hard, you only *believe* it's true."

Yes, I've fought to believe that my storytelling is more than a waste of time.

But maybe it's worse than that.

Maybe it's actually dangerous.

Once I've wrangled the students out of the bookshop, there is only one logical place to go.

I reach AdvantaCare by four-thirty, but Gran's dinner tray is already arriving. I take the tray from the aide in the hallway to deliver it myself.

"Kelsey-girl!" Gran's in bed, but her smile lights the dingy room. "I wasn't expecting you today!"

I slide the tray onto her wheeled bedside table and swing the arm over her bed.

Gran struggles to pull herself higher.

"Well, I know you like surprises." I help her reposition to

better reach the tray. Her lucidity is encouraging. I'm going to need her as sharp as possible today.

She lifts the gray plastic dome from the top of a dinner plate and wrinkles her nose. "Not this kind of surprise."

"Hmm. I'm afraid I didn't bring any substitutions today. But maybe I'll run down to the vending machine after you finish."

She grins. "Clean my plate, and I'll get a treat?"

"Sorry. Didn't mean to make it sound like you're a child."

"Don't apologize. I'll take your bribe."

I pull the vinyl-covered chair closer to the bed and sit. "I need to ask you something."

Gran lifts a forkful of carrots and raises her eyebrows, waiting.

Where to begin?

I've spent days only half-believing the Garden is real, then slowly becoming convinced that I can't be *this* crazy, dreaming the whole thing into being. Still, somehow I believed it was mine, a private world of my own making or created for me, or.... I don't know.

But the disappearance of Charles Dickens from the world puts a new spin on everything and tempts me to believe something larger than me is at work. Something, perhaps, that includes Gran.

"It's about the empty lot beside the shop."

Is that a smirk I see, between her chewing of her vegetables? A knowing smile?

"I've—I've found the key. Been inside."

Gran is silent a moment, still chewing. Then nods. "Quite a mess in there, isn't it?"

Is she testing me?

"No, actually. It's not. It's... full of beauty."

Her eyes are on mine, steady and clear. "Is it now?"

"And I think you know that."

She sets the fork down, takes up a napkin to dab her lips.

Sips from the waxed carton of apple juice. Looks at me. "You said you had a question?"

Oh, I have more than one.

I want to begin with a question about my parents, whether the guests in the Garden know more than I know. But she's always been resistant to those questions, and I don't want to upset her, risk this moment of clarity.

So, let's get the basic question answered.

"Gran, have you ever been to a party inside... inside the empty lot?"

She smiles and tilts her head. "Have you?"

I inhale, gripping the arms of the chair. "You first."

"Yes. Many times."

I let go of the breath, sag against the vinyl back. I knew it. "So have I."

"Yes, it's your turn now, my girl."

"What does that mean? What am I supposed to do there? I—I think I may have destroyed it already!"

Gran reaches a frail, veined hand toward mine.

I clasp it like I'm drowning.

"I don't have any answers, but you will figure it out. As I said, it's your turn now."

"But I can't do what they're asking."

"Which is?"

Go deeper.

No, that isn't true. That's not what is being asked of me. Not yet.

"Bring a gift. Only as a gift, and not as a need. Without worrying about how it is received."

"Ah. Yes. That is difficult." Gran returns to her plate, this time shredding off a bit of pale chicken. "But of course you must."

Again, the enigma. Do the impossible thing.

The Gardener said I must set aside the distraction of survival and responsibilities, at least for a time, in order to step into the creative place that calls to me. Perhaps I can do that. But to also get past the fear so firmly embedded from past attempts… how can I?

"The Garden is a safe place, Kelsey."

Gran's words are so quiet, spoken around mouthfuls of chicken, I nearly miss them.

"Say that again."

She smiles. "The Garden is a safe place. You can bring your gift."

I rock back in my chair, mind spinning, heart swelling.

It's been only a couple of hours since I spoke those words to Olivia and the rest of my Creative Writers of Tomorrow.

I've asked those kids to trust me. To trust each other.

Can I do the same with the Garden?

Perhaps, as Gran says, I must.

Inside that Garden, perhaps *deeper*—whatever that means—is the chance to find answers about my parents, to get an idea of how to save the shop. Not to mention saving the Garden from dying and restoring Dickens to his rightful place.

But only if I can embrace what those in the Garden have said is my true identity.

Storyteller.

Do I dare hope they are right? Despite the words of others and my own doubts? Must I open my hands and accept the gift the Garden has offered before I can create a gift of my own?

Gran pushes the plate across the tray and leans her head back.

"Too much food tonight?"

She half-smiles but says nothing.

"Gran? Do you want something from the vending machine?"

She shakes her head slightly. "Just tired."

I've worn her out, perhaps, with all my questions.

She's drifting, eyes already half-closed.

I pivot the tray table away, then use the corded control to

lower the top half of the bed, the back of my hand against her warm cheek as she descends.

"Thank you, Kelsey-girl," she whispers. "Tell them I said hello."

I will tell them, Gran. If it's not too late.

TWENTY-EIGHT

Fantasy is escapist, and that is its glory. If a soldier is imprisoned by the enemy, don't we consider it his duty to escape?... If we value the freedom of mind and soul, if we're partisans of liberty, then it's our plain duty to escape, and to take as many people with us as we can!

~ J.R.R. Tolkien

Midway Park at sunset is only a fragment of what the empty lot's Garden has become to me, but it reflects the magic of the Garden, distorted yet still beautiful. Like an image in rippled water. Which is why I suggested Austin and I walk here tonight.

This evening, with more than an hour until darkness, clouds with ill-defined edges scud across the sky, and the air is heavy with moisture.

I do love this park at sunset, when lampposts flicker to life along the asphalt walking path, one by one, in the wake of the vanishing daylight. Not quite the globe-lanterns I've come to love, but still transforming, elevating the newborn maple leaves into vaulted cathedrals of spring green.

But tonight it looks like it will only be a fade-to-black in what promises to be a rainy evening.

Does it rain in that other Garden? The one where I managed to rid the entire world of Charles Dickens?

I have to go back inside as soon as possible. I know that.

Even though time seems to stand still in that place—and perhaps all the guests will be simply frozen, waiting for me to return Charles Dickens to their party, to revive the wilting foliage— the knowledge of Dickens missing from my world changes everything.

The knowledge that Gran has seen the Garden also changes everything. Does it mean I can take someone else in with me?

I've already decided on more honesty with Austin. Wouldn't his response to this secret be the ultimate test of our compatibility?

In the early evening gloom, I trail slightly behind him, watching a mother and daughter toss nibbles of bread from a hot dog bun into the water, where a frantic paddling of ducks competes for each soggy morsel. The little girl giggles in unison with each bobbing duckbill.

"Pulled pork?"

Austin's question, tossed over his shoulder to where I lag, refers to Uncle Chuck's Smokin' Mexican BBQ—Austin's favorite food truck and his choice for dinner after I suggested the park.

"Whatever. Sure. And fries." I slow further, watching the little girl with her mother.

"Fries? Their chips and guac are legendary."

"Fries."

Austin moves on, saying nothing.

I can feel his frustration even from this distance.

We settle with our sandwiches on a bench near the food

truck. I balance the red-plaid paper dish of crinkle-cuts on my lap and set my Coke on the ground.

"You gotta try these, Kelsey." He pushes a styrofoam container of piled-high tortilla chips in my direction.

I shake my head. "Allergic."

"To chips and guac?"

"To guacamole. Well, avocado, technically."

"Hmm. Weird." He digs in, but a few moments later, takes a deep breath, as if in preparation.

Here it comes. The breakup conversation, which I will not fault him for. My sandwich, halfway to my mouth, dips a fraction in its journey.

He clears his throat. "So… how's your grandmother doing?"

I chew and swallow.

"She's not my grandmother." I lay the sandwich on its rumpled paper wrapper and glance at Austin.

"What?" His brows form a tiny V in the center.

"She's more like my mother. She adopted me, raised me. I've never met my birth parents."

"What—I—why haven't you told me this before?"

I take the time to chomp a French fry, then shrug. "I don't know. It just never seemed like the right time to bring it up, I guess."

His attention is on his BBQ, and his nod is slow, as if he sees some truth I do not.

"Well, that makes her situation harder for you, I'm sure. I'm sorry."

"Thanks, Austin. I appreciate that."

Am I trying to force a breakup? Dumping secrets on him in the hope that he'll get angry at my reticence to share my life?

"I guess that's why you've been so distracted lately? So… unavailable?"

In a month-long relationship, I'm not sure what constitutes "lately," but I'm also keenly aware that much more than Gran's failing health has preoccupied me for the past week.

"I'm sorry about that. Yes, lots on my mind."

"It's okay."

He really is a nice guy. Sure, a little full of himself, but he does care about me, I think.

"It's more than Gran, though. There's something else. Something really, well, I guess you could say strange. Amazing." The words are tumbling now. Is this crazy?

The young girl and her mother stroll past, a plastic bag clutched in Mom's hand, now empty of hot dog buns. The girl is looking and pointing and talking, at the trees, the lake, the grass, a bird. Filled up with the wonder of Midway Park, as if it contains all the beauty in the world, which perhaps it does.

"I'm listening." Austin's tone is amused, already a bit skeptical.

Oh, just wait.

"I've found something. Something rather impossible. I'd like to show you."

It's a test, I know it is. Some part of me wants to see if he will believe me, if he will—or even *can*—push through the iron gate with me, see what I see. A test he must pass to be deemed worthy, and yet who am I to be deeming anyone? It's me who has been distant and vacant.

"Can I finish my BBQ first?"

I shrug. "Yes. You can finish. Actually, I can't show you for another hour. At sunset, just a little after, perhaps."

Austin glances at his watch, a heavy gold thing his father gifted to him when he graduated from university. "Sure, I can do that. Are you going to give me a clue first?"

Yes. Yes, I am, Austin. And we will see what you do with it.

"I've discovered a garden, a magnificent and vast garden, so big I haven't yet seen the edges of it."

"Okaaayyy...?"

"It only appears after sunset. And I'm unsure whether anyone can see it but me."

Am I really telling him the truth? Is this some kind of self-sabotage?

Austin chuckles, shakes his head, and wipes sauce from his upper lip with a tan paper napkin. "Wow."

"There's more. The garden is filled with dead people."

He shifts on the bench, mouth downturned. "That's not funny, Kelsey. I don't get what you're trying—"

"Not dead people like corpses. They're alive in the garden. But they're people who have already died. Famous writers, artists, musicians. That sort of thing."

Austin crumples his sandwich paper into a ball, munching the last of his chips, as if he's getting ready to bolt.

"Like that Woody Allen movie?" He inhales the last of his drink through the straw. "What was it—*Midnight in Paris*? The one where the guy goes back to the 1920s or whatever and meets all the famous people?"

"Yes, actually. Very much like that."

A tickle of apprehension troubles the base of my neck. I've seen this movie, years ago. Has the forgotten film entered my imagination, coalesced with my childhood version of *The Secret Garden*, and emerged as some kind of dream or fantasy or hallucination?

"Kelsey, please tell me this is a book you read or some story your Gran told you or something. You're freaking me out."

"It's real. And I'm going to show you."

TWENTY-NINE

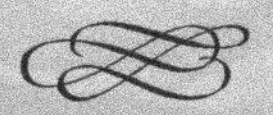

Though nothing can bring back the hour
Of splendor in the grass, of glory in the flower;
We will grieve not, rather find
Strength in what remains behind

~ William Wordsworth

Austin waits for me to finish my sandwich and fries while staring silently into the middle distance, where a guy skims a Frisbee through the heavy air to an eager yellow Lab.

On the walk back to the bookshop, I try to reassure him.

"I know how it sounds, Austin. I know you think I'm crazy. Doesn't it count for something when a person *knows* they sound insane?"

He blows air through tight lips and only shakes his head.

"But you're willing to suspend your disbelief? Give it a try?"

"Listen, Kelsey, your creativity is one of the things I

appreciate most about you. The first time you walked me through the Book Emporium, showed me that papier-mâché tree and the wardrobe entrance to Narnia, I knew you were special."

"That's—that's really nice—"

"I know you could do something really creative with the shop, turn it into some kind of business that would do well. Or you could get a job anywhere using your merchandising skills to bring creativity to stores or libraries or something. You could be truly successful, escape all the stress of trying to make the bookshop stay afloat."

The orange orb of the sun dips lower than the cloud layer now, beaming the last of its strength across the city, warming the air but falling fast. I leave Austin's suggestions hanging without comment, too filled up with the thoughts of introducing him to the Garden.

We round the final corner, pass the Rhythm & Wonder Music Shop, reach the bookshop.

Beyond the Book Emporium, William is pasting a hand-lettered sign on the glass window of The Groove. *Everything Must Go.*

"Kelsey, I think you need to make a better plan, before—before the stress—"

"Makes me snap?"

He exhales again, says nothing.

I round on him, blocking the entrance to the shop.

"Just keep an open mind. Until you see the Garden. Then we can talk about my mental health. I promise."

He nods twice, his jaw locked in the serious, concerned expression of a doctor assessing a terminal patient.

Am I making a huge mistake?

My painful departure from the Garden leaves me little hope of reentering… and to bring an uninvited guest?

But we won't get that far. I'll only take Austin to the little marble bench beside the magnolia, far enough to see the massive live oak and the table bent under its feast, the flickering globes spangling everything and the dozens of party guests. Then we'll leave—back out the way we came, surely it's possible—and then he'll understand why I've been so odd and distant, and I'll see if he has any imagination, or at least enough to be someone I could truly share my life with.

Yeah. I guess that's a lot.

I run into the shop long enough to grab the iron key, though we shouldn't need it, then join him outside, heart hammering and the metal key cold against my palm.

He points. "I'm parked on the next block. Do you want to take my car—"

"We aren't driving." I inhale the evening air. "It's..."

I want to say *right here, it's right here, Austin, in the empty lot beside the shop, where you've passed a dozen times,* but something akin to panic stops me.

After my multiple trips through the gate, I've gotten a sense of what it takes to open this place. Not only sunset, this time-between-times, but a certain feeling, a particular attitude of creative openness and willingness, the very opposite of the skepticism I see written large on Austin's face.

"It's what? Where is this 'garden'?" He air-quotes the final word.

I wince. "Just give me a minute. Stay here."

I pace away from him, glance barely darting to the iron gate, as if I'm only walking the street, thinking.

Imagine the Garden, Kelsey.

The cascades of candy-pink bougainvillea, the powdery scent of lilacs. The clink of elegant silver on glittering crystal and fine china. My very own secret garden, like the orphan girl Mary Lennox, a garden bringing life—*don't think about yellow leaves curling*—encouraging so much creativity—*don't think about blank pages and Charles Dickens missing*—all those lovely people—*best to avoid thinking of Sam the Sculptor and his dazzling smile*—the soaring, heart-rending music...

"Okay," I turn to Austin, bring the key to my fingertips, just in case. "It's time."

My eyelids flutter in a half-prayer, and I push against the gate.

It resists.

I push again, but it's not moving.

Hope fading, but unwilling to give up, I fit the key into the gate's lock.

I'm avoiding Austin's expression, which must be open-mouthed, eyebrows-lifted, all that concern playing out at once.

The gate opens with the key, and I push forward against its weedy resistance, squeeze through. Listen for the sound of a glorious Garden Party, but the blood pounding in my ears deafens me.

"Come through," I beckon to Austin.

He stands on the street, staring at me through the iron bars.

"You've got to be kidding."

"Just come through." My hand is tiring holding the gate open against the overgrowth.

"This is your 'magnificent and vast garden'? This vacant lot?"

I'm working hard to stay in the creative zone, to hold on to whatever bit of the fantastical I've had to embrace to be able to enter this place, but he's not making it easy. A cinder of frustration over his resistance burns somewhere deep in me, and I work to cool its heat.

"Will you trust me?"

My words find their mark—how can he say no?—and he pushes against the gate and slides through, careful not to let the rusty bars snag his button-down shirt and pleated khakis.

The sun is gone now, the last light filtering weakly through the tall weeds. I push into the shadows, every emotional nerve attuned to the other side of this growth, to the magic and the beauty…

We move forward, and forward. Hope insists on rising.

"Is that a *washing machine?*" Austin's voice behind me is part-incredulity, part-laughter. "How in the world—"

I draw up short, cutting off his amazement when he rams into me.

"It's not here." I swallow against a hot tightness in my throat.

"Uh, yeah. Obviously."

Is it Austin's presence? Or have I been ejected, no longer welcome because of the damage I've caused?

Or—worst thought of all—have I killed the Garden completely?

"Go back." I turn to face him, and we are nearly nose-to-nose.

He doesn't move.

"I want to go back!"

He holds up two palms, shakes his head, turns and shoves a path backward to the entrance, through the gate, to the sidewalk where he stops and waits.

I keep going, to the bookshop entrance, into the shop, hands braced on the mahogany front counter, breath coming in brief gasps between heartbeats.

The bell rings a moment later, and I feel Austin at my back.

"I don't know what that was about, Kelsey. Don't know if you are joking, or if something is really wrong, but I don't think I can handle whatever this is."

I nod once, eyes focused on that crack, that terrible crack in the counter which I am sure has widened, deepened, in the past week.

"I'm not—I'm not saying goodbye or anything like that."

Not breaking up with me, then.

"I just think you need some time, maybe with your grandm—your Gran—or to get some rest. Maybe... see someone? Like a therapist or something?"

"I get it. Thanks, Austin."

I can't turn around, can't face him. Just want him to leave.

He touches my arm. "How about I call you in a couple days?"

"Right. Sounds good. Thanks."

And then the bell rings again, and I am alone.

Free to collapse against the counter.

The loss of Austin's respect, even possibly the relationship, is peripheral.

The loss of the Garden, unbearable.

THIRTY

Some day you will be old enough to start reading fairy tales again.

~ C.S. Lewis

After Austin's exit and my moments of self-pity, all I want to do is escape.

Upstairs, the remnants of last night's mac-and-cheese dinner congeal on the kitchen table, and the fraction of light left to the day seeps through my apartment window and is swallowed by the dark furnishings and floor.

But I can see well enough to find the couch, so I don't bother with a lamp.

I need to write. Must create something I can bring, to try again, to get back inside, to see it all recalled to life.

Why do I feel like summoning creativity is the one thing I cannot do?

Sprawled on the couch, I fish the remote from the cushions and then I'm searching for the movie Austin mentioned, *Midnight in Paris,* even though I'm afraid to watch.

No luck finding it streaming for free. Of course. And I'm unwilling to pay.

Another old movie catches my eye, though.

You've Got Mail.

I was a young child when this movie came out—six years old, I see from the date on the description. The title brings to mind a paper-sleeved DVD in the mailbox, popcorn and candy with Gran on Movie Night.

I've committed to the procrastination now.

I hit Play, in a mix of nostalgia and self-destruction, knowing what I'm in for.

And the movie does not disappoint my expectations.

I remember Gran ranting. Hating the movie despite its popularity, shaking her fist at the so-called happy ending. Meg Ryan's character, Kathleen, closes the doors to her bookstore, The Shop Around the Corner, in the face of unbeatable competition from Tom Hanks' character, Joe Fox, and his big box store, Fox Books. The underdog story ends with a sweet romance but a shuttered shop—not Gran's idea of happy—and she declares Joe Fox a manipulative jerk and Kathleen a weakling for giving up the fight.

The credits roll as I lean my head back in the darkness.

Charles Diamond Blackburn is right. I am a cliché.

"A sad, antiquated cliché," to be exact.

The little shop around the corner, fighting the big, bad developer.

And my fight is as doomed a battle as Kathleen's. Except without the romance at the end to soften the blow.

Unless you count Austin.

Which for some reason, I don't.

I shove away thoughts of Austin, and another guy with a great smile and wide shoulders, toss the remote to the floor, and wander to the kitchen to forage in the cabinets for something salty.

Is it a losing battle, trying to fight Blackburn's project? Maybe the hotel is destined to swallow the Chestnut Street

Book Emporium. Don't they always say *you can't stop progress*?

Can I turn the shop into something else? A trendy café, as Austin suggested? Or perhaps a high-end store for first editions… like an art gallery for books?

Or is the shop a relic, one that has served its purpose, seen its day, and needs to be let go?

I settle on a near-empty box of stale cheese crackers.

I really need to start eating better.

I drop into a kitchen chair in the dim light of the endless rolling credits on the TV and scrounge the depths of the box for crackers, eating the broken bits.

Okay, what would it look like to sell the shop to Blackburn? Lose my apartment and job, but have enough to pay for Gran's care and get another place for me, keep me from being homeless until I found another job?

And what would it do to Gran if I told her we must sell?

Would she allow it if I promised to sell only the store property and keep the empty lot?

I don't articulate the disloyal thought, even in my mind, that when Gran is gone, I am her only inheritor and any money left from the sale would go to me. Because she is not gone.

But the flicker of that alternate life dances at the edges of my thoughts.

Eventually… to have the money and the time to travel the world and earn some life experience, to learn to write well.

You can't wait that long, Kelsey-girl.

I know. Yes, I know.

And yet, the starting… why is it so hard? Such hard work, to simply *start.*

I slip downstairs to wander the darkened Book Emporium, lit only by the exit signs and streetlights visible through the front windows.

What am I looking for, here in this favorite place of mine?

A book to help me escape my thoughts? Great works to inspire me?

I roam to the WRITING HELPS section and run my fingers over the spines of books on the craft of writing. Many of them I've already studied. I tilt an unfamiliar title toward me and skim the cover.

But a gut feeling tells me I've studied enough "how-to" books to at least get a start. I'm sure there will always be more to learn, but at some point, does the learning get in the way of the creating?

What I need is an idea. Some "what if," the germ of a story. An intriguing hook I want to explore.

Where does creativity originate? In the mind? Or externally—a flame lit by a stray spark that lands at the right moment?

I am trailing fingertips everywhere now, as if through my touch the shop can transmute meaning and imagination into my body and my mind.

The tree—*There and Back Again*'s coffee-stained pages. That particular idea landed when I saw a papier-mâché globe hanging in a library at the same time I was looking for something to fill this empty wall.

And the passageway to the Children's Section? It was the wardrobe at an estate sale which set that idea aflame.

Nearby, the series of vintage posters, mounted above TRAVEL, have always fired my imagination. I slow now to absorb each one in turn. How often I've wished each one could absorb *me*.

What if...

Yes, yes—the dry tinder has caught, there is a flame here, small but growing. The story of a woman who wishes to escape into aging travel posters, wishes it so much she makes it happen...

It's time for sleep, but I'm sprinting up the steps to my apartment, snatching my laptop from the couch, tumbling into a chair at the dining table.

Three hours and two chapters later, I have the start of something, and I can't keep my eyes open. I drop into bed, still dressed, and sleep a few hours, waking to remember it's Wednesday, my day off.

I stretch and smile like a kid waking up on her birthday, roll out of my bed to the coffeemaker, and am back in my chair in minutes, a steaming mug at my right hand and fingers flying over the keyboard.

This, this thing I'm doing—it silences the voices of little Ashleigh and nasty Cora Oberman. It ignores the well-meaning warnings of Austin and Lisa. And in this little stretch of time, I am able to set aside the worries of the bookshop. There will be time enough to fret over "real life." Here, in this place, I am doing what it feels I was born to do.

I am coming back to life.

She doesn't get herself inside all of the travel posters, my protagonist. Not this time, in this story. Just the first of them, the most fascinating to her—the pyramids of Egypt. I'll need to research more about Egypt, of course, but the story's only just getting started. I'll be happy to rework and revise once I have my main character to her first moment of stepping through the poster into another world.

I take a mid-morning break to stare at the intermittent clouds that promise rain and scarf down a protein bar and more coffee. I do a bit of online research about Egypt, then I'm back at it, pushing through until early afternoon, when my energy suddenly flags and I'm drooping over the keyboard.

How much? How much is enough before I can bring this work to the Garden? Van Gogh's *Café Terrace at Night* is finished, and the pieces of statuary are sculpted, but the sheet music? The manuscripts? Are they all complete? Or is it enough to bring the best of one's self to date and lay it there on the table?

I haven't seen that stupid yellow folder since the night it went blank. I scan my apartment as though something else will jump into view, something suitable for bringing my work.

I don't want to simply bring a printout, not this time. A gift is meant to be special, to honor the one receiving it.

A sudden burst of energy compels me downstairs. I wave at Lisa, who is helping a customer behind the counter. I feel her eyes follow me past the front tables. Hopefully she's not noticed I'm still in yesterday's clothes.

A moment later, I lay my hands on what I'm looking for. A plastic-wrapped blank journal with a moss-green cover, embossed with a gold filigree tree.

Perfect.

It takes me the rest of the afternoon to copy the first three chapters into the journal. My fingers are cramped and swollen when I finish. But I clutch the book to my chest, eyes welling with unexpected emotion.

I can do this. I can bring the beginning of this story as a gift because it feels like a gift first given to me. A rare and precious thing that is part of me, but also apart from me. It is flawed and yet beautiful. Amateurish—no doubt—but poured from my heart.

The afternoon bleeds away, the clouds regroup to smoke out the sun, and time seems to hang suspended and unmoving. My attention buzzes around the wall clock in my kitchen a hundred times, a thousand times.

The days are lengthening now, so I check and recheck my phone's weather app for the time of sunset and the few minutes after—last light—as if I've forgotten since the last time I looked.

Finally, exhausted by waiting, I set a timer for thirty minutes and curl up in my bed for a quick nap, the journal at my side.

THIRTY-ONE

When poetry has done its important work of revealing and describing the hidden hell we carry and perpetuate, it also has this power and privilege to cleanse and renew our vision, and set us on the right road again.

~ from *Word in the Wilderness* by Malcolm Guite

The nap refreshes me, along with a quick shower. I feel new, reborn in some strange way, like one of those women in the surprise makeover reality shows. The fear and angst over bringing this gift are gone, leaving only a sense of joy in their place.

I dress in jeans and a T-shirt, but will I be wearing my wisteria twirly dress soon?

I take my apartment steps lightly, with only the journal in my hand, then out to the street and to the gate as the final shafts of sunlight drop away.

Will they read it aloud? I hope so. Not because I'm

looking for praise—I have no idea if the story is any good. No, only because something created is meant to be shared.

Through the gate. Through the weeds and underdeveloped trees.

Do I imagine the way seems wider, more clear of shrubby hindrance tonight?

And then classical music and flickering lanterns, party-laughter and twining wisteria and my marble bench beside the white-blooming magnolia.

I hold the story journal wrapped in my arms, held to my heart as though a precious treasure.

But a treasure I am ready to share.

A dark-haired woman of about forty is sitting on my bench, clutching a glass filled with amber liquid. She glances at my arrival through the weeds.

"Hello." She nods absently. "I didn't see you there."

"I've just arrived."

Confusion flits across her face, then clears.

Perhaps no one arrives or leaves this Garden, in the usual sense. Have I always been here, then?

"Well, I hope I haven't taken your quiet spot." She glances down at the bench. "I needed a moment to breathe."

"May I join you?"

"Of course."

I slip onto the bench, just wide enough for the two of us, still holding the journal against my body. "I'm K."

She raises her glass in my direction. "Of course you are."

Her voice is deep and a bit slurred.

She's not introducing herself, so I turn to study her, pulling back to get a better look.

Judy Garland. I'm hanging out with Judy Garland.

"You're J., right?"

She half-smiles, shrugs, takes a sip of her drink. "Well, honey, I am now."

I've watched Renée Zellweger's stunning, Oscar-winning performance in the movie *Judy*. I know the child star of *The*

Wizard of Oz was harassed and controlled, and between her pill-pushing stage mother and predatory studio executives, was led down a yellow-brick-road of drugs and alcohol. It's a sad and cautionary tale about stardom if ever there was one.

And notably, she's the first person I've met here whose talent and creativity seems to have been a curse rather than a blessing.

"You're ready, then?" She nods in the direction of my journal.

I lower it to my lap, trace the raised gold paths of tree branches with my fingertips. "I'm ready."

"That is good news." She sighs. "I understand, of course. It took me some time, as well."

"*You* were afraid to sing here?"

A sarcastic huff of a laugh. "Honey, I'm afraid to sing everywhere. But enough about me. You'd best head over to the table." She tilts her head backward, indicating the magnolia behind us. "As you can see, there isn't time for messing about."

I follow her glance to the glossy leaves of the tree, then to the cup-like white blossoms, many-petaled, like open roses.

Each petal is browning at the edges. Some have fallen entirely, carpeting the flagstones at our feet and leaving their yellow stamens bereft.

A wave of nausea weakens me.

"This is—this is because of me?"

She smiles, the movement of her lips quick and sad. "We all struggle."

Her comment is simple, but I ponder the possible truth of it.

The struggling artist is so stereotypical that perhaps I have dismissed it as the stuff of film and fiction. But is it possible the degree of an artist's talent has little to do with the ease in which creativity flows? Perhaps all artists, no matter their gifting, struggle to bring their work to the world. Perhaps that is the very nature of art itself, hard-birthed.

I stand, nod a vague goodbye in her direction, and set out across the grassy lawn toward the feast table, with its accompaniment of heaped treasures and gifts.

Will I see Sam before I cross the footbridge?

I scan the guests, looking for the black vest and white shirt stretched across a broad chest. Has he been looking for me since we shared that breathtaking kiss?

The music hushes as I approach the table, but the silence is not for me. At the base of the Tree, on a small platform, a man stands with an open book in his hands.

The party chatter stills, guests drift toward the Tree and the speaker.

He begins reading from the book.

"It was a bright cold day in April, and the clocks were striking thirteen."

I shake my head.

May I present... George Orwell.

I skirt the far side of the table of food, avoiding the attention of the guests trained on Orwell and his reading.

The platform of musicians has emptied, assumedly because the reading will go on for some time.

The distraction of the crowd suits my goal, which is to place my journal on the table without fanfare, summoning all the gifty-ness I have within me, and then see what happens when I cross—carefully—the stone footbridge beyond the marble sphinxes.

But as I slip between the upright piano and the three-tiered trays of fruit tarts on the end of the table, a figure emerges from the shadows beyond the gift table, as if she has been waiting for me alone.

"Here you are at last, K."

"Hello, A."

I brandish the journal in Agatha's direction with a self-conscious smile.

Will she take it from me, begin reading it right now?

She spent many years in Egypt and the Middle East herself, accompanying her archaeologist husband on his digs and researching books like *Death on the Nile*.

My effort in this journal holds little academic understanding of ancient Egypt—I can study and work all of that into the rewrite—but will she agree with that process?

A nervous flutter hums across my skin but then passes, like discharged electricity. The journal is my gift to the Garden. Whether or not Agatha Christie likes my story, approves of my process—finally, none of that matters to me.

And I suddenly understand all the references to generosity I have heard here in the Garden. To write scenes that may be cut from the final version, to rough-draft, to take the risk of doing hard work that may come to nothing, to be recklessly extravagant with your work—paint, clay, words, notes, whatever the medium—knowing some of it, even though it was so hard-won, will be wasted… this is an act of generosity and love toward your audience.

Agatha's smile widens, as though she reads my mind, and she holds out an empty palm.

I place the journal into her hand.

"It's only the beginning. But I didn't want to waste time."

"Hmm." She nods, running a hand over the embossed cover. "No time is wasted, if it brings you closer to the work you are creating."

"No, I only meant that I feared for the Garden. And for C."

Using a lacquered fingernail, she eases open the cover to the first page. Skims the writing, angling the book to catch the lights strung over the table.

"Egypt?" She looks up and smiles.

I nod, a tightness in my throat. Why does bringing this story feel so emotional? It's not as if I'm giving it up, giving it away. It still belongs to me.

But it's not loss I'm feeling.

The heat in my chest, the thickness in my throat, it's both joy and vulnerability. I am somehow expanded at the same moment I am narrowed by the name which defines me.

Storyteller.

Agatha returns the book to me and moves aside, clearing my way to the table of gifts.

I step forward. The table is still pleasingly arranged in the way I improved the display so many nights ago. I find a vacant space, the perfect size and placement for my moss-green journal, and delicately tuck the book between others like it.

A strange sense comes over me, as though I'm watching someone place a flower or a candle alongside other of its kind at a vigil-site for someone who has died.

But this observance is the opposite.

The Garden holds vigil for life.

The assortment of gifts honors the artists who are present right here, honors their life-giving creativity.

My touch lingers on the journal's cover, but then I let it go. Step away. Glance at Agatha before scanning the Garden.

What am I expecting? Some kind of fairy-tale swirl of pixie dust? A *swoosh* of magic restoring life to the flora and Charles Dickens to the party?

I see nothing, feel nothing that is changed. Orwell is still reading, the guests still enraptured by his frightening vision of a world still thirty-five years into his future and more than thirty-five in my past.

Agatha's hand is warm on my back. "That was well-done, K. Your story, though still small, and perhaps not what you wish it to be, is a tiny part of the world of Story that has been and is now and will be. You are now part of stirring the world awake." She studies my profile. "And now you are also ready to go deeper."

Right.

I've nearly forgotten. The writing of my new story's beginning, the offering of it on the gift table, it's all felt like the final battle. As though I've at last conquered all my demons and performed the impossible feat.

But with this one word—*deeper*—Agatha reminds me that my superhuman effort has only been the first step, my necessary initiation, into my real quest, whatever that might be.

"The footbridge?" I want to make sure my next attempt isn't a repeat of the cottage.

She only smiles. "I'm off to listen to G.'s mad predictions." She pats my arm. "Good luck, my dear."

She slips past the feast table and into the gathered crowd beneath the Tree.

I turn away from the community, toward the centaur-guarded path that leads to the marble sphinxes and their bridge.

Fitting that it's sphinxes standing at my crossroads. Coincidental, given the story I've written of my intrepid travel-poster character stumbling into Egypt. Just like the coincidence that I seemed to have been assigned a mentor who is one of the leading writers of mysteries set in Egypt.

Too coincidental?

A chill raises the flesh on my arms. It all fits too perfectly.

But I hadn't even written the story yet, didn't even have the idea for it when I first met Agatha. When I first saw the sphinxes.

It matters little now, I suppose.

After a last fruitless glance to see if I can spot Sam, I square my shoulders for the task at hand and begin toward the path.

The voice of George Orwell fades to a deep drone. The trees on either side of the path murmur in the slight breeze, and the gravel answers in a crunch underfoot as I walk.

I walk slowly through the woods lit only by stars now, no desire to repeat the previous teeth-rattling crash into something I never saw coming.

The man-headed lions focus into sharp relief against the dark woods.

I stop beside the statue on the right, run a hand over the pharaoh's striped marble headcloth that extends down its back to melt into the haunches of a lion.

Hesitant steps onto the footbridge now, walking along the right side, my hand on a stone rail.

What will *deeper* entail?

Agatha implied I could have gone *through* the cottage, assumedly to something else on the other side. Would it have been an enchanted forest, perhaps at the edge of some medieval kingdom?

Shouldn't I have been told the purpose of this journey? Issued my quest before I cross?

Up, up to the apex of the bridge. I hesitate, scan the water below. It flows forward and away from me on the right. I step to the left wall of the bridge and follow the water as far backward, where it must originate at the Tree, as one of the four streams.

Ahead, the bridge descends, and I can almost make out more statuary at the other end.

And lights. Lights on the other side.

I exhale, relief slowing my pulse. Walking into the dark unknown is terrifying. But if there are lights, there must be… something. People, perhaps. Another path, or a building.

I nod once, courage filling me, and push forward, hands extended and trembling.

No invisible barrier sends me home this time. I descend to the end of the footbridge.

Sphinxes.

Two of them, at the end of the bridge, mirror-images of those I left behind.

Or did I?

A moment of disorientation sweeps me. Will I step off the bridge to the path beyond and find it leads me back to exactly where I left?

Perhaps it's a magical bridge that doubles back on itself,

and my entire test was only to find the courage to cross it, entitling me to rejoin the Garden.

I put one foot in front of the other, step from the bridge to a darkened gravel path, push forward toward the lights.

But it is flaming torches that greet me, not party lights strung over a food-laden table. There is no reading by George Orwell, no crowd gathered before a Tree. This area is as much a Garden as I left behind, but it is silent.

I pass immediately through a small courtyard bordered by the torches to a deeper darkness beyond. Huge white flagstones lead me between beds of narcissus blooms and tangled jasmine.

Above me, a million silver stars wheel across the blackest sky I've ever seen. I tip my head back and back, drinking in the spectacular display.

When I can no longer hold my head at this angle, I return to my limestone path, run a hand along the tiny white flowers, peer ahead to see where it might lead. How much can one empty lot in the middle of the city possibly hold?

The path continues into the darkness to a stone wall but leads my eye above the wall to the horizon, to three sharp silhouettes barely visible against the ebony sky.

I draw up short, gasping, hands thrust outward, grabbing for support that is not there. Trace the lines of the three massive shapes once more and again.

This cannot be. It cannot be.

THIRTY-TWO

See! The winter is past;
the rains are over and gone
Flowers appear on the earth;
the season of singing has come...
Arise, come, my darling;
my beautiful one, come with me.

~ Song of Songs 2:11-13

Despite everything—from the sphinxes, to Agatha Christie, to my own travel-poster story—I never expected this.

The smoky horizon lies on the far side of a desert turning purple in the darkness, and along the curving line of earth against sky, these three shapes rise, pointed and solid and triangular. Familiar from every poster of the place I've ever seen—from my very own poster urging me to see the "Mysterious Wonder of the World!"

It would seem that moments after passing out of the Garden located impossibly on Chestnut Street, I am in Egypt.

The iconic three pyramids greet me, like travel guides as I step off a plane.

Except I have stepped from a Garden.

Or was it through a vintage travel poster on the wall of the Book Emporium?

I wish Sam were here to see this.

The pyramids have stood in the desert of Giza for nearly five thousand years, though in my present they perch on the chaotic rim of the vast and crowded city of Cairo. Will I be taken sightseeing to the monuments, perhaps with a group of European travelers on their Grand Tour, seeing the world? I scan this new garden for my elegant poster-people from the shop.

Will my wisteria dress, ripped at the waist and revealing my knees and legs, seem inappropriate—

My gut tightens, followed by a missed beat of my heart.

The twirly dress is gone, replaced by a white linen sheath, fitted scandalously close to my skin, falling to jewel-sandaled feet.

Gold bands, six of them, climb above my elbow, encircling my upper arm. My ears feel heavy as well, and my wandering fingers find pendants hanging there. A pectoral piece, with three parallel and swooping rows of turquoise, weights my chest.

This is not the early twentieth century Egypt of my travel poster.

The three pyramids in the distance seem suddenly closer, sharper. I shut my eyes, casting aside the poster's images of crumbling steps and only the jagged capstone left on the peak of the Great Pyramid. See instead the three monuments as scholars say they once were, covered smooth with gleaming white limestone, capped with an overlay of a gold pyramidion to catch the sun's rays.

From somewhere in *this* garden, music plays. Not the classical or operatic or even jazz I've enjoyed in my Chestnut Street Garden, but raucous and ancient party music on instruments I don't recognize—a foreign mixture of strings and drums.

Closer than the music, a rustling across the stone path at my back spins me in the direction I've come.

The footbridge, with its guardian sphinxes, is gone. In its place is an immense and sprawling multi-storied building aflame with torches inside and out, squared entrances glowing like otherworldly portals.

Outlined by the light spilling from of one of these entries is the figure of a man, bald and bare-chested.

"There you are, Kepri. Why are you hiding yourself out here?"

This cannot be happening.

My head spins in a dizzy wave of déjà vu mixed with disbelief. The words are so like T.S. Eliot's first greeting. And seem to be spoken in English. Imply that I am recognized and known here.

"I—I was—"

I can think of no explanation, have no idea what is expected of me.

"She is asking for you again. Come quickly."

He turns and slips through the greenery to the left, soundless as he veers off the main path.

I follow, my steps as hesitant, as though my entrance into this new garden is the first time I have used these legs.

He outpaces me, twisting through narrow paths between leafy palms and glossy shrubs.

The music grows fainter, as though we are leaving a party.

I try to hurry. What will happen if I lose him?

How am I to get back to Chestnut Street?

Torchlight flickers ahead, indicating a wider space, perhaps.

I stumble into a little clearing in the garden—another small courtyard with a tiny fountain in the center—and pause at the edge.

My guide has stepped across a black-graveled square to stand behind a lounge chair veneered in ebony, on which a woman reclines.

The man is now stone-faced, staring at nothing, hands behind his back and shoulders set in the ever-ready posture of a bodyguard.

I do not miss the short dagger strapped at his waist, above the white skirt knotted there.

The woman lies along the length of the chair, propped by luxuriant cushions, head lolling as though she dozes.

Is this woman the "she" who has been asking for me? She does not appear to care that I've arrived.

Do I greet her? Wake her?

I glance to the guard who brought me, but his face reveals nothing, and he does not make eye contact.

For the first time since I stepped through the iron gate on Chestnut Street many days ago, a stab of true fear spikes through me, far greater than what I felt when Frank Baum first urged me deeper. I have no control here, no knowledge of how to act, and no idea how to return to the familiar. I have never initiated my return to my apartment above the bookshop, which feels a million miles from this place anyway.

I shift my weight from one foot to the other, fingers twisting against the fabric of my dress. Silence seems my best option.

But it lasts only a moment.

The woman opens one heavy-lidded eye, blinks and tries to focus, then waves me over with a languid hand.

"There you are. You must not leave me like that."

I take a few hesitant steps forward. Though perhaps to turn and run would be smarter.

"Come. Sit." Her head drops back against the cushions once more.

There is no other chair in the little courtyard. Only torches lining the perimeter and a large bronze basin of water on a pedestal.

I approach, then lower myself to the gravel.

The dress is impossibly tight around my legs. I drop to a hip, propped on one hand, legs awkward with pea-sized gravel poking holes in my skin.

I glance at the guard, whose stoic disregard has faltered, and whose eyebrows are lifted at my undignified posture.

Is the woman sleeping again?

Am I her companion? Meant to sit at her feet while she naps?

Who is she?

"You may begin."

The words are mumbled, barely audible, but she is speaking to me, this I do know.

I swallow, lungs constricted. Glance at the guard.

He's gone back to staring at nothing.

"Where would you like me to begin?"

The woman sighs, as dramatic and put-out as an aging film star lounging in her dressing room. "If I knew where stories should begin, I would not need a Storyteller."

Seriously?

I'm eyeing that dagger again. My position on the ground, wearing a dress made for a mermaid, gives me no latitude for a quick getaway. I struggle to my feet once more.

The woman blinks up at me. "You are not leaving?"

"No." I feel the heat of the guard's glance. "No, just getting more comfortable." I straighten and step to the side, closer to the path where I entered. "What kind of story would you like me to tell?"

She waves a languorous hand. "I do not care. Only make it… absorbing. That is what the others cannot do. Why I have brought you."

She brought me here, somehow?

I study what I can see of this garden. Clearly, the little courtyard where she holds me is a small part of a larger area —nearly a park, it would seem—running the length of this magnificent building. Is it a palace? What era? Old Kingdom? Middle? I don't know enough Egyptian history to place the clothing or architecture. But if we are near the pyramids, and the building is royal, then we must not be in the New Kingdom period. By that time, the center of government had moved south to the area of Thebes.

What am I doing running through history lessons? None of this is real. It's all part of some test. My "deeper" journey into the Garden. My wonderment at the entire scene has addled me.

And yet it's like a wish fulfilled, really. My desire to travel, to see Egypt. I've finally done it, and somehow done it in costume, in character. Like international tourism rolled into a participatory dinner theater.

"Why are you smiling? What do you know?"

She is half-sitting now, studying me.

"What? Nothing—I—I am glad to be here. That's all."

"Do you know something?" Her speech is slurred. "About my Storyteller?About my baby?"

I thought I was the Storyteller. And... her baby?

She swings her legs over the elongated chair, her eyes only slightly more alert.

Has she been drugged?

I glance at the guard. Surely he can see she is unwell.

He has shifted his position to stand behind her again. His hands are at his sides now, not behind his back. As if he might need ready access to that dagger.

I shake my head and hold up a palm. "I don't know anything."

Her eyes are painted with the parallel lines and looping scroll familiar to anyone who loves ancient Egypt, but they are narrowed in suspicion toward me now, and her full, poppy-painted lips are tight.

She is younger than I thought. About my age. Her hair is the color of gleaming onyx and hangs in a multitude of narrow braids to her bare shoulders, brushing a pectoral piece much more ornate than the one I am wearing, studded with turquoise and beads in faience and coral, shot through with gold. Everything about her speaks wealth and privilege.

I am suddenly aware of being the "hired help" and what displeasing my employer might mean in this ancient society.

"I am—I think—" How do I get out of here?

Maybe just go.

"I will return. In a few minutes. There is something I need to retrieve, to be able to... tell the story."

I bow my way out of the courtyard. Why am I bowing?

You are ridiculous, Kelsey.

But all of this is ridiculous.

I clear the little courtyard, push back into the leaf-lined path where I entered, and begin to run, or at least as fast a jog as I'm able in this dress.

Where to run? Acting on instinct, I move toward the music. Perhaps it's the hope of my familiar Garden party, or only a desire to lose myself in a crowd, but where there is a gathering, there may be a chance to remain unseen.

I slip through low-branched olive trees, along torch-lit paths that smell of smoking oil and are lined with chiseled stone benches, turn a corner into a wider avenue with two facing rows of small sphinxes, like a gauntlet of menacing stone. Ahead, the music swells and a gathering of people clogs the end of the avenue where two sycamore trees frame an opening to yet another garden.

I trot toward the crowd, slip to the side of the tree-bordered entrance, then along the backs of the people, all of them facing inward, clapping in rhythm with a single drumbeat that pulses under the melody of a gaily plucked stringed instrument.

I wiggle into a gap in the circle, joining the group of perhaps thirty or forty as if I'm one of them. And certainly, I'm dressed to match. If this is a costume party, it's the most zealous one I've ever attended.

Oh… It seems not all of us have costumes.

The five women dancing inside the circle are stripped naked of all but jewelry.

My fists tighten at my sides, and my breath escapes in a rush. What kind of exploitation is this? Are they slaves? Forced to entertain wealthy partygoers, despite the humiliation?

I skim the circle of faces lit by the flicker of flames, laughing and clapping. Women and men. But the dresses of many of the women are white linen bands over their shoulders, dropping to tight swaths of fabric that only begin under their breasts. And the faces of the dancers—pure joy.

Images of painted murals of ancient Egypt flit across my memory. Women in all states of dress—and undress—in ceremonial and public events. Perhaps my assumptions, brought from the twenty-first century, have no place here.

As if to underscore, a boy of perhaps eight or nine years darts into the circle, also completely naked, with a long braid swinging from the right side of his shaved head.

A young woman at the perimeter yelps in outrage, grabs the boy by the shoulders and steers him away from the dancers.

The boy kicks up his heels on his way out, and the rest of the circle erupts in laughter.

A moment later, my own arms are grabbed from behind.

"Hey!" I try to spin but am held fast.

The face of the guard who found me at the edge of the garden is at my shoulder, eyes glittering with malice.

"What do you think you are doing, Kepri?"

My voice hisses through gritted teeth, low and angry. "Let go of me."

He releases his hold but does not back away.

The heat of his bare chest radiates against my skin, and his oiled head reflects the torchlight.

I bolt.

Across the circle, through the dancers, like the mischievous boy.

The dancers break apart and pause.

A gap opens on the other side of the circle, confused faces parting to allow me through.

Hopefully the gap will close. Keep the guard inside a moment longer.

Can I escape this series of gardens? Get alone somewhere to figure this out?

Ahead, through a tiny space in the shrubbery, a half-wall separates the enclosure from the desert beyond.

I run. Push through plants that scratch my arms and snag my dress.

Reach hands for the low wall, ready to vault like a gymnast.

And a moment later, I'm on the ground, forehead and knees throbbing with the force of whatever invisibility has knocked me backward.

Like the footbridge. I cannot leave. But then why, why am I not waking up in my apartment?

Rough hands grab under my arms and haul me upward.

I blink to clear the disorientation, too stunned to fight.

"Did you want to get eaten by jackals, you fool woman?"

I turn, wriggling from his grasp. "Whaa—what?"

He juts his chin toward the wall, the desert. "Running to what?"

I pull in a few shaky breaths. "Not to anything. Just away."

"Away?" He pulls me closer. "From me, or from her?"

He's too close for comfort.

I brace my palms on his chest and shove.

He drops his arms, confusion crossing his expression. "You are a mystery tonight."

No kidding.

"I—I wanted to hear the music."

He glances back to the party which has not missed a beat since my exit.

"What makes this night any different than any other?"

"They do this every night?"

He shrugs. "You have not been here long enough to see how it is. The king is plagued with the oracle's prophecy that he will die in only six years. Menkaure looks to turn six years into twelve by making every night as eventful as every day."

Menkaure.

I shift my attention to the three pyramids, still visible under the starlit sky.

Khufu—the Great Pyramid.

Khafre—his son, buried in the second largest of the three.

And Menkaure—the grandson, the third, and considerably smaller, pyramid built to be his tomb. From here, it appears to be finished. Ready for its eventual resident.

My guard draws closer again, whispers against my ear. "But the Son of Re's misfortune is our gain, eh? We have many nights—"

I push him away again.

Whoever this *Kepri* is, I can't tell if she'd welcome this attention or not.

I'm playing it safe.

"I am exhausted. I will be better able to perform my duty in the morning."

The words sound like I've read them from a script, but the exhaustion is real. When is the last time I've slept—truly slept, not just awakened in my bed after another party in another Garden?

He growls, low in his chest and a little threatening. But who knows, maybe Kepri would find it sexy. This guy is hard to define.

"It's been three months since Rekhetre's misfortune, and

she still must have the physician's help to find rest." He wraps tight fingers around my wrist. "You had *better* perform your duties well, or perhaps your fate will be that of the Royal Wife's last Storyteller."

I breathe through a bit of panic and nod.

"Come." He pulls me back toward the party. "She has not dismissed you yet."

I let him lead me for a moment, then twist my arm from his grasp but follow.

Back through the winding paths of greenery, back to the dark gravel of the little courtyard with the woman's chaise lounge.

She is still there but with head thrown back, mouth open, snoring.

My guard draws up short, flexes his shoulders and nods. "She will sleep the night now." He turns on me with a smile.

A smile that is either leering or flirtatious. I can't be sure.

"Then I must sleep as well." I'm swaying on my feet now, the energy draining out of me by the second.

He frowns and shrugs. "Do what you must."

He's not moving.

Does he guard the queen all night?

Where do I sleep?

I stumble away, back down the path, and sink to the first stone bench I find. I'll just rest here for a few minutes, curled up on the cold stone, then search out a better place—perhaps I have some enchanting bedchamber in the palace.

Why Egypt? How can any of this "deeper" disaster possibly help me save the shop? The Garden continues to hold out hope then snatch it away, taking me further from my goal.

My thoughts jumble in the precursor to sleep, but one thought rises above, and I clutch at it—the certainty that when I awake it will be to the alarm on my phone, in my bed above the bookshop.

The image of the Egypt travel poster floats behind other muddled images.

One more thought as I drift…

Be careful what you wish for.

THIRTY-THREE

Follow, poet, follow right
To the bottom of the night
With your unconstraining voice
Still persuade us to rejoice;
With the farming of a verse
Make a vineyard of the curse,
Sing of human unsuccess
In a rapture of distress;
In the deserts of the heart
Let the healing fountain start,
In the prison of his days
Teach the free man how to praise.

~ from *Another Time* by W.H. Auden

"Kelsey, wake up!"

A shake to my shoulder, then another. I groan and pull away, eyes still closed.

Everything hurts—hip bone grinding against something unyielding. Arm asleep and numb under my head.

I pry my eyes open to a burning sun.

"Kepri, you must wake up. The morning meal is beginning!"

Kepri. Not Kelsey.

I am still here.

Is this a classic sort of quest, in which I must pass some sort of test in order to be released?

I push myself up from the stone bench, on which I've apparently spent the entire night, and moan once more in the hot sunshine.

Is it always this hot? Even at this hour?

The girl doing the shaking is only about fifteen, dressed in the same type of sheath-dress I'm wearing. Her face is elaborately painted in swirls of black kohl and glittery sparkles of gold fleck her copper skin.

I reach two fingers to the skin beneath my own eyes. Am I wearing makeup like that?

"What is wrong with you?" She frowns and jams fists against narrow hips.

Oh, where to start?

Her petite face is scrunched into a frown. She has a thin, whitish scar wandering from her nose to ear, like a back road on a map. "Did you have too much to drink and sleep out here all night?"

My tongue is thick as paste. No words emerge.

"Come." She places a hand under my arm and hauls me upward. "Let's get you cleaned up and into the banquet hall before Rekhetre notices your absence. She's sleeping late herself, a blessing for you."

I follow, still wordless.

My escort passes into the garden, along winding stone paths that lead us through palm and pomegranate trees, the latter heavy with bright red fruits too large for my palm.

A quick glance above and beyond the garden wall reveals

the daytime outline of the three pyramids rising like the sails of three great ships out of the desert. The gold pyramidion on the cap of the largest pyramid reflects the early morning sun, brighter than a hundred lighthouses. I blink and turn back to the path, golden spots dancing in my vision.

Do I need to retain a memory of where I first entered this place? I'll never be able to retrace our steps.

We follow a path roughly parallel to the sprawling building complex.

When we reach the end, the girl ducks under a squared opening much smaller than the grand entrances glowing with torchlight last night.

What is the hierarchy here? Is she my servant? Or simply a fellow staff member helping out a colleague?

A few feet inside the shadowed entrance, she pauses at a narrow stone doorway and waves me into the chamber, the motion like that of an impatient kindergarten teacher.

Perhaps I'm *her* servant.

It's a small bedroom with a reed-slatted bed a few inches wider than my body pushed against the mud brick wall. The carved stone headrest at the top would give me a stiff neck, but I wouldn't refuse some time to try it out. A three-legged stool in the corner holds a red earthenware jug and a rag the color of dry sand.

I stand in the center of the room, clueless.

She sighs—more of a huff of disgust—then crosses to the jug, wets the rag, and hands it to me. "Wash your face, at least."

I rub the wet rag against my cheek, then pull the cloth away. Still beige, no makeup. The water is tepid but refreshing.

"Here." She hands me a dress identical to the one I'm wearing.

I drape the rag across the top of the jug, set the dress on the narrow cot, and slip out of my current outfit.

The girl watches, lips downturned.

Am I blushing? It feels like junior high gym class, changing clothes in front of a crowd.

I struggle into the second version of the sheath dress, then turn to her.

She nods once. "We must hurry."

Down the hall, deeper into the building, which must be a palace. The halls twist, walls tight together and unadorned. A few minutes later, we break into an enclosed courtyard, open to the sky, in what seems to be the center of the palace.

I slow as we emerge, falling behind her rapid pace across the square.

The garden here steals my breath. Like the stars in last night's sky, the lush fronds and woody trunks of palms set amongst granite columns the breadth of trees and painted in intricate geometrics of peacock blue, jade green, and cardinal red form a tableau that is at once unearthly and yet more vivid and true than anything I've experienced.

In the center of the courtyard, a small lion-headed fountain bubbles into a pool brimming with blue lotus. How do they create fountains without electricity?

At the sound of the water, I'm hit by powerful thirst. I should have taken a drink from the jug when I had the chance.

"Come!" My young escort is glaring from the other side of the courtyard.

I hurry across, trailing fingertips across a bed of orange poppies, taking in all I can of the garden before I'm forced to leave it.

More hallways, but these are frescoed with bright murals —white lotus flowers floating in a reed-banked river, jackal-headed gods and horned goddesses, scenes of boat-making and feasting. I'm scanning, head bobbing left to right, touching the walls as we pass.

Ahead, a broad, squared entrance into another chamber looms, and a rising river of conversation flows toward us.

We pass under the lintel—painted in more bright hieroglyphs—and into a spacious hall filled with long tables. A series of wooden stools with woven seats like wicker line each table.

Women, dozens of them, mill about the chamber, talking, laughing, some of them eating from food they carry in their hands.

Along the walls, tables hold all manner of fruits and breads and vegetables, from piles of figs and cucumbers to bowls of lentils and chickpeas. The air is heavy with the scent of onions and bread, and my stomach growls in response.

The girl who has led me here turns and nods. "Take your place."

I glance at the lines of stools filling up with women and head toward the closest table.

"Not there!" The girl hisses in my ear. "This table is for Khamerer-nebty."

Playing dumb seems like my best option. How much trouble can this young girl cause me?

"Khamerer-nebty?" Not sure I got that right.

She huffs her little exasperated sigh again. "Can you keep nothing in that head of yours? Khamerer-nebty is the Chief Wife. These are her tables, her girls. Rekhetre is only second wife. She will sit there." She points to a table across the hall. "With her ladies. And you."

"And where, exactly, should her Storyteller sit?"

She rolls her eyes. "What do I care where you are seated?"

Right.

"Just keep away from Khamerer-nebty's ladies. They will claw your eyes out as soon as look at you."

The crowd is dividing, slowly, but the change is obvious now.

"They are rivals, then? Khamerer-nebty and Rekhetre?"

"What do you think? Khamerer-nebty's son will take the throne after Menkaure. Rekhetre's child—well, you know what has happened."

Do you know something? The drugged woman's words to me last night. *About my baby?*

No, Rekhetre, I know nothing.

But something tells me I need to find out.

Opposite our end of the chamber, a woman in white sweeps in trailed by yet more accompanying women and a few beefy men who look like guards.

The crowd parts for her, and she assumes a seat midway down the table which my new friend says belongs to the Chief Wife.

So, this is Khamerer-nebty. She has a high forehead and wide cheekbones and a pleasant expression that belies the nastiness assigned to her ladies-in-waiting. Two women sit on her left and two on her right while others hurry to bring small jugs and fresh bread to lay before the new entrants.

My mouth waters at the sight of the crusty loaves. How long since I last ate? You can only get so far on protein bars and stale cheese crackers.

I turn to ask my companion if I should help myself to the buffet, but she has disappeared.

No one's attention is focused on me. I drift to the food table. No stack of plates at the end. I fill my hands with two small loaves of bread and as many purple grapes as I can hold before I cross to the far side of the dining hall, to Rekhetre's long table. I choose a stool near the end, no one yet sitting on either side. Hopefully no one chatty will join me.

A repeat of Khamerer-nebty's entrance occurs moments later, this time the second wife, her retinue, and more guards.

Rekhetre is a younger, slightly more petite, version of the Chief Wife, and she enters with similar fanfare, though less of a commanding presence than her rival.

Khamerer-nebty watches Rekhetre's entrance with narrowed eyes.

Did the Chief Wife intend to arrive second in some sort

of late-to-the-party power play that was bested by her rival, Rekhetre?

Rekhetre's arrival appears to be a signal. All across the chamber, women scurry to be seated.

I'm joined on either side by women who are older than I, but everyone is silent.

Servants rush to place food in front of Rekhetre and her women. And then a horde of new servants pours from the hall's entrance, flows down the side of the chamber where the food tables are still piled high and begins grabbing every tray and hauling them to the dining tables, laying them down the centers in front of all of us.

Relief. My little pile of bread and grapes is already gone, and my belly's still complaining of hunger. Directly in front of me is a tray of cucumbers and melon. I can make a meal out of that any day.

On my left, a woman who looks to be in her fifties leans close.

"You're the new Storyteller? Is she sleeping any better?"

I fumble with a chunk of melon, take my time to chew and swallow, smiling in apology at the delay. How am I to answer? Is my suspicion of her being drugged correct? And if so, do her ladies know it?

"I—I haven't had much time with her yet."

She nods, as if my answer satisfies. "Well, prayers to Isis that you're as good a teller as Ekisi-betta. Even the physician Bahadur has not been able to help."

This is madness. How can I get out of here?

At the touch of a heavy hand on my right shoulder, I startle and spin.

It's last night's guard, who seems inordinately interested in me.

"What are you doing down here?" His voice is low but threatening, accompanied by a fierce scowl. "She wants you up there. Next to her."

"Now?" My pulse thuds. Am I supposed to come up with a story *right now,* in some kind of ancient improv exercise?

"Now."

He hauls me to my feet without ceremony, half-drags me down the table, and deposits me on the stool at Rekhetre's side.

She is picking at a small date cake and does not acknowledge me.

I glance at the bodyguard. He nods and flicks his eyes in her direction. A clear indication that I am to begin my profession immediately.

Perhaps this is the ancient equivalent of the constant distraction of our ever-present devices. Does a Storyteller entertain at all hours of the day, a streaming service that began thousands of years ago?

But this is not going to work. I have no stories, I don't even know how—or *if*—to address this woman. If I am being tested, I'm not going to pass.

The bodyguard stands at my left elbow. I lean back, head turned over my shoulder to whisper to him.

He bends, still with the scowl.

"Listen," I allow a bit of pleading to enter my voice, "I'm not very good at this, telling stories. I'm not even sure why I was brought—I think there would be more qualified—"

My excuses end in a yelp when he wrenches me to standing once more and pulls me from the table.

I trip over my feet and topple against him.

He shoves me upright and yanks me toward the wall of the dining chamber.

"What are you doing?"

"I'm not a Storyteller—"

"Then what lies did you tell to bring yourself here?" His face reddens, eyes boring into mine.

I inhale a shaky breath. Glance to the other women. Is anyone watching? But who would come to my rescue?

His fingers tighten around my upper arm, digging the

gold bands into my skin. His voice is a hiss. "Rekhetre has been inconsolable for three new moons, and we have waited two for you to arrive from Punt. Now you tell me you are not a Storyteller?"

He cares for the woman, it's written on his face.

"Sadiki?" Rekhetre is calling, her voice a murmur. "Is there trouble?"

My captor glances her way. Releases my arm.

"No trouble, lady. Your Storyteller is ready now."

He pushes me forward, his mouth grazing my ear. "Do your duty or we have no use for you here."

THIRTY-FOUR

We want to see with other eyes, to imagine with other imaginations, to feel with other hearts, as well as with our own... We demand windows. Literature as Logos is a series of windows, even of doors. One of the things we feel after reading a great work is "I have got out." Or from another point of view, "I have got in."

~ C.S. Lewis

After the guard's admonishment, I tumble onto my stool beside Rekhetre and grab for the stone cup set in front of me. Some kind of liquid has been decanted into it, and I'm thirsty enough to drink anything.

The cup contains wine, albeit diluted to taste like grape-scented water. I gulp it down, slaking my thirst in part, and glance at a serving girl with a jug.

She senses my meaning and brings more.

I sip this one with more care. The last thing I need is to get too tipsy to think.

Rekhetre continues to use a bit of bread to push a paste—perhaps lentils—around a stone platter, eating little.

Is she waiting for me to launch into a story? She seems unaware of my existence.

I take the opportunity to fill up on some kind of heavily spiced meat, roasted and still dripping with juices, and finish the watered wine.

But Rekhetre soon tires of the meal entirely and pushes her stool from the table with a deep sigh.

Sadiki is at her elbow in a moment, his body wedged between me and the royal wife.

"You are finished, King's Wife, Blessed of Re?"

"Yes. I have no appetite. I will go to my father's temple this morning. Come to my chamber when all is ready." She stands, then glances down to meet my eyes. "Bring the Storyteller. She will accompany me to the sacrifices."

Three other women stand alongside the royal wife and follow her from the dining chamber.

Sadiki grabs my upper arm—again—and pulls me to my feet.

I twist away. "That's unnecessary."

He raises an eyebrow. "Is it? I get the impression you are reluctant to fulfill your duties."

I raise my chin to meet his gaze. "To her father's temple, then?"

I have no idea where this temple might be. But Sadiki doesn't seem the type to let me find my own way.

"Follow me." He pivots toward the doorway and leaves me behind in three quick strides.

I trot to keep up, still awkward in this tight dress.

We exit the dining chamber opposite the way I entered, but the halls look much the same—frescoes of fish and fowl, with hunters stalking, arrows at the ready.

Sadiki pauses to bark orders at various men we pass in the halls, covering everything from the arranging of a litter to transport Rekhetre to a mortuary temple, bread and beer to be sent with her, and notification sent ahead to have a priest and a ram ready.

I grimace at this last instruction. Will I be forced to participate in some bloody ritual?

We emerge from the palace complex into a different garden, with another half-wall surrounding it.

I take in the horizon as far left and right as I can see, but there are no pyramids. We must have come out on the other side.

"Stand here." Sadiki points at the ground, as though he expects me to step on that bit of gravel and remain inert.

I fold my arms over my chest and stare him down.

"Argh!" He throws his hands heavenward and stalks to a cluster of men at the next squared doorway into the palace.

His gestures, most of them pointed in my direction, speak volumes.

Several of the men glance at me, nodding.

And then he's back, scowling as usual.

"You will attend the sacrifices at the mortuary temple with Rekhetre, God's Wife and Blessed of Re. Do not think to step away from her presence. You will be watched." He moves in closer, his breath warm on my cheek. "I expect to hear of her willingness when you return, so choose your words carefully."

"Willingness?"

His eyes narrow. "Rekhetre must send word to her husband that she is ready and cheerful to come to his bed tonight. Menkaure, Lord of the Son of Horus, has waited long enough."

Wow.

"And if she does not?"

"Then her Storyteller has failed to bring her happiness and set her mind aright."

I lift my shoulders in a tiny shrug. I need more information, though it seems like a dangerous game to pursue.

Sadiki pulls back, his lips curled in a snarl. "You think you are above punishment?"

"No story I am able to tell can control Rekhetre's actions."

Sadiki's hand flashes through air like a striking snake.

The slap across my cheek knocks me sideways.

I spin on the man, hand to my face. Mouth agape and stomach clenched in fear and pain.

"You will speak of the Royal Wife with respect!" A vein running from above his left eye back over his bald head bulges blue-green against his dark skin.

I have committed some breach of etiquette, perhaps with my familiar use of her name? But I have never been slapped by a man in my life. It takes all my restraint not to knee him in the groin.

He leans in once more. "If she does not return from the temple with word that she will visit her husband tonight, you will be cast out. And we will see how your confidence serves you when you have nothing but a city which despises you and the wide desert beyond."

Sadiki disappears into the palace, but one of the group of men he's instructed is at my side before I have time to think about sprinting out of here. This one is bald and bare-chested as well, but with aging crinkles at the corners of his eyes. When he smiles, he reveals a gap where an upper canine should sit.

He extends a hand toward the garden wall and half-bows. "This way."

More polite, at least. Even if I'm still some kind of prisoner.

Beyond the wall sits what appears to be a small, square tent. The fabric is white, but heavy crimson tassels dangle from each upper corner, connected by swags of braided ropes in orange and yellow. From each swag hangs a series of jingly copper pieces, roughly circular like coins.

We pass through an opening in the half-wall, and I trip over one of two heavy wooden poles.

This, then, is the litter Sadiki called for.

I glance at the man accompanying me.

He pulls aside the curtain of the litter with a flourish, as though I am royalty myself.

Do I thank him? The wrong word can get you slapped around here.

I settle for a quick bow of my head and a smile and climb inside.

The heat dissipates immediately within the white cocoon, and I sink into cushions in teal and peach and heather, my eyes fluttering closed for a moment and the tension in my shoulders loosening a notch or two.

What am I doing here? Threatened with exile if I don't convince a pharaoh's wife to "entertain" him? If the Garden in the empty lot beside the bookshop has only been an entrance, as the Gardener implied, then this here, this crazy place I've landed, is meant for me. Some sort of test I'll need to pass before I return. Though I have no way of knowing this for certain, every story I've ever encountered assures me.

To be ushered into this deeper place took a willingness to give the Garden the beginnings of my story as a gift without thought of my own need. And a readiness to push through the resistance that meets all creative work, which makes it feel too difficult to achieve. But I found both and brought my gift—a story of a woman accidentally falling into ancient Egypt.

What must I learn to leave this place?

Must I write my way back to the twenty-first century?

The litter rocks slightly, as though a hand has braced against it, and the curtain opens.

Rekhetre crouches her way inside and lowers herself beside me.

She's more alert than I've yet seen her. Perhaps at breakfast she was still sleeping off the effects of the ancient version of Ambien.

Her smile for me is fleeting and only politeness, then her chin is tucked against her chest.

Without warning, the front of the litter vaults from the ground.

I grab Rekhetre's arm with a gasp.

The back of the litter lifts to match the height of the front.

I snatch my hand from her arm. "I am sorry!" If speaking her name earns a slap, what does grabbing the royal arm get you?

But she laughs, a light and airy sound, and produces the first smile I've seen.

"One would think you had never been lifted in a litter, Kepri."

I shake my head and shrug at my own foolishness.

"You are more serious than my last Storyteller." She begins this announcement with a smile, but the final word emerges choked and broken.

"What was her name?" I smooth a cushion's rumpled fabric, my tone casual.

The litter begins to move, a jolting but silent ride on the shoulders of unseen servants.

"Ekisi-betta. And Renpet loved her mightily. The Storyteller did not deserve what happened to her."

The answer is whispered from a place of grief, and her head is turned to the opening of the litter, where shards of the palace garden flash past.

Renpet must be the baby she asked me about last night. *Do you know something... about my baby?* Is there confusion about Renpet's whereabouts?

"We will make a sacrifice for Renpet today. Pray to the gods for a safe return."

Where does a baby go?

And what happened to my predecessor?

Now is not the time to press for more information. Rekhetre's cheeks are wet with tears.

For a Storyteller whose sole duty is to make the royal wife cheerful, I'm failing miserably.

Am I expected to begin a story now? My mind's a blank.

But Rekhetre is silent again.

I will wait until asked.

We continue without speaking, and before many minutes there is a pitch forward and a jolt backward as the litter is lowered to the ground.

The curtain is swept aside, and a woman's hand extends through the opening.

Rekhetre grasps the proffered hand and is pulled to the outside, to the servant girl with the white scar across her smooth cheek.

I am left to struggle through the cushions on my own, to make my way to standing.

But the view is well worth any struggle.

I turn a circle, aware my jaw has dropped.

We have been deposited in the walled outer courtyard of a temple. Behind us, two boats with square white sails float in a sparkling harbor abutting the courtyard. A narrow channel of water flows out of the harbor, to a canal beyond, presumably leading to the Nile.

But it is the area beyond the temple which staggers the imagination.

To my right, the Great Sphinx itself stares impassively across the desert, its face still intact, and its blue-and-gold-striped nemes headpiece glowing with fresh pigment. Below the massive pharaoh's head and lion's body, a swarm of bare-chested men wield stone hammers and copper chisels at the paws, which are still being hewn from a single piece of solid limestone.

The three pyramids hover over us, the middle pyramid linked to the Sphinx by a stone causeway ahead of us, and the third and smallest pyramid to our left. This third is Menkaure's pyramid, and it's clear now that it is unfinished. There is still a series of steps from the bottom to halfway up the base, where the smooth limestone facing obscures the steps all the way to the top. From this distance the men working on it look like a throng of ants building their hill.

What was I expecting?

I will go to my father's temple.

Rekhetre's words led me to believe we would visit some small temple within a city.

But no—of course. Menkaure's wives were probably also his sisters, or half-sisters, at least.

The massive funerary complex and middle pyramid built to honor and bury Menkaure's father, Khafre, are monuments built to Rekhetre's father as well.

She is walking forward, toward the causeway.

I follow.

The servant girl, whose name I've learned is Oni, is at my heels.

We walk in silence, leaving the temple at the harbor behind us, advancing on another temple ahead, at the base of Khafre's pyramid.

We reach the entrance hall in minutes and pass through to a columned court containing various tall niches with life-sized statues of the dead pharaoh tucked into each.

The acrid smell of burning tar reaches me, pricking a nostalgic memory of childhood bicycles and neighborhood friends riding the hot summer streets.

We cross to a deeper chamber, under a lintel inscribed with painted hieroglyphs—crowned falcons and cobras and vipers—in the oval of a cartouche.

Inside, a man stands immobile beside a flaming altar, his white linen dress and white sandals immaculate, a leopard skin fastened by a strap over one shoulder and hanging to his thighs. He is dark-skinned, heavily bejeweled, and ancient. The smell of roasting meat is thick in the air.

Thankfully, it would seem we've missed the animal's execution.

The priest bows deeply from the waist, arms hanging

before him as though he would touch his toes, in acknowledgment of Rekhetre.

"God's wife."

"You have laid the sacrifice?"

He dips his head. "As you instructed."

Do I sense some defensiveness?

He meets my glance but quickly looks away.

Rekhetre approaches the altar. She does not require me to join her.

The priest turns to face the altar with her.

"You will say the prayers for my child."

He immediately begins uttering something in words I cannot decipher.

A chill rises on my arms, across my neck.

Minutes pass and still the priest's intonation continues.

Rekhetre's back is to me, but she sways on her feet.

I am mesmerized by the chanting and by the royal wife's slow and rhythmic dance which mirrors the dance of the flames.

And then it is over.

The priest's voice cuts out, sharp and quick.

Rekhetre shakes herself as though stepping from a stupor. She turns, nods once to the priest, glances at me as she passes, and exits the temple.

I hurry to follow.

She is crossing the courtyard in long strides. But at the perimeter, she sinks to a stone bench as though her strength has failed.

I hesitate, then slide onto the bench beside her.

"Will it do any good? Any of it?" Her voice is a bare whisper, pleading.

I grasp her hand, a deep sympathy welling inside me for this young mother.

She studies our clasped hands. "Tell me a story, Kepri."

I lift my eyes to the harbor and canal, to the little village on our right that was likely built for the workmen creating the great monuments on this plateau. To the Great Sphinx who posed riddles to the Greek Oedipus.

"Will you tell me your story, instead?" I broach the question carefully. "Sometimes it can help to tell of the things that hurt us most."

She shrugs. "There is little to tell. Nothing to know. It is three months since someone stole my child from me, and took my Storyteller on the same night. They are both dead, I am certain. And I am tortured by it, knowing my baby's spirit is lost, with no body to embalm and bury. Without the body, I cannot even hold to the hope of our meeting again in the afterlife."

"Why would someone—"

"Every royal child is a target. And a threat to all other royal children."

Oh, that is horrifying. Has Menkaure's other wife, perhaps Rekhetre's own sister, had this young woman's child murdered to avoid any chance of seeing him placed on the throne?

I wrap an arm around her shoulders.

She leans into me, weeping. Clasps my other arm around her and rests her forehead on my shoulder.

"I fear—" Her voice is broken. "I fear I cannot live without Renpet."

What can I do in the face of this kind of grief? Does story have the power to heal even this pain?

"I will tell you of something wonderful," I say, whispering the words over her head.

She sniffs and waits.

"I will tell you of a woman who once walked through a special place—a magical garden—and when she emerged, she found herself far, far away. Not only in distance, but in years."

Rekhetre lifts her head, gazes into my eyes.

I nod. "Yes, she found herself many centuries removed.

Into the *future*. A future holding mysteries and wonder. And the things she witnessed were far beyond her imagining."

"What things? What did she see?"

I smile. "I will tell you, but not here. Not now. Should we return to the palace?"

It's a classic storytelling technique, the cliffhanger. Perhaps inspired by my location and the proximity to the Arabian lands of *One Thousand and One Nights,* where Scheherazade wove her tales, night after night, to keep the king awaiting the next installment and her head still on her shoulders.

Rekhetre shakes her head. "I want to sail." She glances beyond the wall, as if certain to find someone.

Oni appears. She must have been waiting for such a signal.

"Send word to the palace. I will take a barque to Swenett and return in a few days. And I wish for Bahadur to join us."

Bahadur. Where have I heard that name?

Ah, the physician. The one who administers the drugs I fear she has come to rely upon.

And returning in a few days? A trip upriver will mean missing Sadiki's deadline and Rekhetre's expected appearance in her husband's bedchamber.

And what will that mean for me?

THIRTY-FIVE

To me the meanest flower that blows can give
Thoughts that do often lie too deep for tears.

~ William Wordsworth

Rekhetre's impulsive decision to sail the Nile is followed by a sun-baked stroll from the Mortuary Temple of Khafre, past the temple's small harbor, and along a canal toward a larger harbor at the edge of the Giza plateau.

The four servants and the empty litter follow behind as we walk.

I glance back at the litter with its cool interior several times, sweat beading on my neck.

Rekhetre does not speak, sinking again into her wordless despair. Perhaps a riverboat cruise is the best thing for her.

Sadiki's warnings about my exile notwithstanding, how can I, in good conscience, urge her to put on a happy face and show up at her husband's bed? But she already has one dead Storyteller. I'd prefer not to make it two.

I shield my eyes and squint at the square-sailed boats in the harbor ahead. "Where is Swenett?" I've never heard of the location she named as our destination.

She frowns in my direction. "How strange you are. You cannot have come from Punt without passing through Swenett, where the Nile opens to the Two Lands."

I run this information through what I know of Egypt. The "Two Lands" are Upper and Lower Egypt, and the Nile is considered to begin far south of us, in Aswan. "Swenett," then, must be Aswan. We will sail past the Valley of the Kings, though at this point Egypt is still burying their kings in pyramids and hasn't yet dug out the valley across from Luxor.

"Of course." I smile. "Swenett." I offer no other explanation for my stupidity, and she asks for none.

We reach the harbor, perspiring through our dresses.

Servants stand at the ready beside a low-slung boat with a high, pointed prow and a square cabin in its center.

At the water's edge, a man wrapped in an elaborately pleated and tucked square of linen waits for us, head held erect and the piercing eyes of a clinician trained on Rekhetre.

Bahadur, I presume.

He wears a pouch crossed over his chest with leather straps. At our approach, he bows deeply. "Wife Blessed of Horus, I am told you wish me to accompany you upriver."

Rekhetre nods faintly, as though she is already under the influence of whatever he carries in that pouch. "I wish to rest."

He glances to me with a blink and a slight crease between his eyes.

He does not trust me.

Why?

Two servants approach, hands extended, and Rekhetre allows them to lead her forward, to where the boat has been brought to the shore's edge.

I take a step to follow, but my arm is grabbed above the elbow.

"I do not know what game you are playing." Bahadur's voice is a hiss in my ear.

"I only want to help."

"Do you think it will help any of us if she does not return for days? Sadiki is most displeased with your carelessness. But I am wondering—"

I turn my head, bringing my face to his, and wait.

"I am wondering if you are only the next one sent to cause trouble. The last one has taken the royal child. Perhaps you are sent to destroy the royal wife as well."

I pull back to study him.

"Rekhetre's Storyteller *took* her baby? I thought they were both abducted together."

Bahadur glances at Rekhetre, at the servants settling her into the prow of the boat on a small cushion.

"She chooses to believe this nonsense. No one could have taken Renpet but the Storyteller. She must have been paid to kill the child." His expression darkens in my direction. "And now perhaps you have come to assure no other heir is born to Rekhetre?"

"I want to help her heal." Which is true, oddly. Whatever this place is, however I got here, the desire to ease Rekhetre's pain drives me as much as figuring out how to get out of here. How can that be?

Bahadur laughs, an ugly and derisive sound. "And how do you suppose you will help her?"

I look to the young woman, who is now watching us both, and smile. "Perhaps by telling her a story."

Another laugh. "Ah, yes. A *story*. As effective as any medicine, I am certain."

Is his sarcasm misplaced? Am I far too confident in the power of Story?

"Perhaps." I pull away, head for the boat.

Bahadur is right behind me, his voice still harsh in my

ear. "Sadiki speaks of casting you from the palace to fend for yourself in the city. But you deserve no place in the Two Lands. Once we return, you will be exiled to the killing sands of the west, if I have any influence."

Okay, *psychopath.*

I step from the floating dock into the narrow boat, find my footing, and advance to the prow where Rekhetre sits.

"May I join you?"

She extends a hand in acquiescence. "Bahadur?" Her attention is on the physician. "Prepare a draught? I wish to sleep."

I sit beside her and touch her arm. "Perhaps you would prefer to hear more of my story?"

Her eyes roam my face, as if trying to read the story there. "Will it help me forget?"

Such a question. I have pondered it often. Do we merely distract and numb ourselves with stories until the pain subsides on its own? Or is there some way that this thing we often call *amusement*—literally "without thought"—burrows its way into our souls and actually helps us make sense of the pain?

"Not forget, I do not think. But… endure."

She nods and inhales, a breath going deep into her chest.

It is a good sign when someone is able to breathe again.

Bahadur advances on us, a small stone cup in his hand.

Rekhetre waves him away and leans back against her cushions.

"Tell me your story, Kepri."

The physician's animosity radiates as he backs away, his face a mask of bitterness.

The slaves behind us take up oars on each side of the boat and begin to row us out of the harbor and into the canal.

I retrace and amplify the beginnings of my story about the woman who steps out of her palace garden and into a far future, centuries hence.

Rekhetre closes her eyes, but her features are alert, listening.

We slip along the marshy canal, catching the attention of barely clad women at the banks washing linens and of men raising buckets of water with levers.

And then the canal merges into the Nile itself. Rekhetre's slaves raise a white sail, and I leave off the telling of my story to absorb the wonder of sitting in this boat as it skims the blue-green Nile River.

"Continue." Rekhetre nudges my leg with her toe.

As we catch the warm breeze and slide past the patchwork of farmland and the entrances of irrigation canals, with the pyramids fading to sandy smudges on the horizon behind us, I tell of the wonders my character encounters.

I tell of litters that move along the ground without any help from slaves, even some that fly through the air faster than birds.

Lanterns that burn without flames.

Large, chilled crates able to keep food from spoiling for many days.

Bahadur sits behind us, his back to the small cabin in the center of the boat. Each time I glance at him, his eyes dart away in an unsuccessful pretense of disinterest.

"You are even better than my last Storyteller." Rekhetre grants the compliment without opening her eyes. "Ekisibetta spoke beautiful words, made me see beautiful things in my mind, but her stories were not so… intriguing."

I try to hide a smile, embarrassed by the pleasure her words give me. The world of the bookshop, with all its frustrations, seems so far away. Here in this place, weaving a story that eases the pain of a woman I like very much, feels more real, more *right.*

The story unspools as I tell it, created moment-by-moment as I speak it out.

My traveler, despite all the wonders she sees, grows homesick and sad for what she has left behind.

Her child.

This last addition surprises me as much as Rekhetre, who sits upright and eyes me carefully, as though I may deliver a wound.

"Does she go back, then? Back to her child?"

I shake my head. "She cannot. She cannot find the way back."

The story develops into my traveler's quest to return, through cities and countryside, meeting people with occupations she has never known, wearing strange clothes and eating strange foods.

As if on cue at my description of the foreign foods, pizza included, a slave approaches with a basket and begins to unpack it onto a cloth spread at our feet.

Crusty bread and warm beer, figs and fish, raisin cakes. It is a veritable feast, somehow delivered to the boat even though Rekhetre gave little notice of her impromptu trip up the Nile.

Bahadur comes to stand over the slave spreading the meal, watching the proceedings as if fearful she will be poisoned.

When the slave begins to slice through an avocado, Bahadur growls and grabs at the fruit.

"Not that, you fool! She cannot eat that!" The physician hurls the offending fruit into the Nile, where it hits with a splash and then drops silently to the depths.

I smile at Rekhetre. "Not your favorite?"

She puts several fingers to her lips. "I enjoy them, but they make me… itch. My lips, my eyes."

Interesting. I meet so few people with an avocado allergy like mine.

Rekhetre digs into the meats and vegetables with more relish than I've seen her attempt anything.

Perhaps I am truly making a difference. The thought warms me.

At her urging, I join in the meal, biting into roasted duck.

We share a laugh at the dripping grease, the sticky juices running from our chins and fingers to the woven cloth. A slave brings a wet rag to each of us, bowing away as we wipe the juice from our skin.

"I would hear the rest of your story now, Kepri. How your traveler finds her way home."

"I will return to her, but first you must hear of her child, still in Egypt."

Rekhetre sucks in a breath, but nods.

And so, I tell of a little boy who lives a charmed life, enjoying all that his bountiful land holds, and who is given magical glimpses of his mother from time to time, so that he knows she is safe and having wonderful adventures—and he is reassured they will be together again, one day.

"But when?" Rekhetre's eyes hold deep need for an answer.

But it is an answer I cannot give her. I shake my head slowly. "He does not know. And his mother does not know. Perhaps only after they have both lived all the days they are meant to live. But he is happy. And she can be happy in her new home as well, if she chooses to be."

"Without her child?"

"Yes. There is always the loss, the empty space she will feel, but she does not have to keep chasing a past that cannot return. This empty space can be accepted, can be endured, and she can move forward, and be happy again, with all the wonderful things her life may yet bring."

"Almost, I can believe you, Storyteller. That there is yet good to come for your traveler."

In her smile, I feel the power of my story. The power of all Story to heal and bring meaning.

Bahadur approaches, scowling at me. "You fill her head with nonsense." He bends to Rekhetre. "You would like to rest, surely?" He has the ever-present narcotic in hand.

"In a moment, Bahadur." She turns to me. "I understand

the tale you are telling me. And what it means. Do you believe my child is happy somewhere?"

Questions of the afterlife—Egyptian or otherwise—are not my area. I bite my lip and study the passing shoreline.

"Sometimes," she begins, "sometimes I think about Ekisi-betta, the way she loved my baby. The way she wanted a child of her own but was barren. And I wonder..."

Her eyes take on a faraway look, as though Bahadur has already drugged her.

"I wonder if perhaps they have only gone away together. To live somewhere else and be happy together."

So, not the afterlife, then. Rekhetre's speculation is much more practical.

"You think Ekisi-betta may have taken your baby from you, for herself?"

"I think, perhaps, I can *choose* to believe this, and then I can choose to—how is it you said?—move forward."

It's a start, I suppose. Better than despair.

Rekhetre rises to her knees, turns to the slaves. "I have changed my mind. We will return."

Bahadur flicks a hand to the slaves, as if his additional command is needed to set them turning the boat. "You are ready, then, my lady, to meet your king as he wishes?"

She sinks to the cushions. "I am ready to return to the palace, Bahadur. But I will never risk this pain again. I shall have no more children."

The physician's burning glare turns on me, as if I've convinced her to refuse her husband.

In truth, it might be good for her to have another child. But that is her decision.

Rekhetre accepts Bahadur's draught and arranges herself on the cushions to sleep away the return trip.

The slaves lower the sail once we've turned to ride the current, then settle back at their oars.

With the heat of the afternoon and the rocking of the boat, I don't need medicinal help to find a nap appealing. I locate a pile of braided rope to use as a pillow and curl up against the hull of the boat, tucking half my body into the relief of some shade.

My mind drifts and spins as sleep approaches, flying over thoughts of Ekisi-betta—spiriting away Rekhetre's child—and of Rekhetre—and her avocado allergy.

THIRTY-SIX

I coined the word 'eucatastrophe': the sudden happy turn in a story which pierces you with a joy that brings tears... it is a sudden glimpse of Truth, your whole nature chained in material cause and effect, the chain of death, feels a sudden relief as if a major limb out of joint had suddenly snapped back... this is indeed how things really do work in the Great World for which our nature is made.

~ from *The Letters of J.R.R. Tolkien*

I wake with the full import of my sleep-addled thoughts slamming me like the wall at the top of the footbridge—invisible, unexpected. And shocking.

Is it—is it possible?

I rise from the makeshift bed, rubbing soreness from my shoulder where it rested against the boat's planks and rolling the tension out of my neck. A hand to my cheek, which bears the braided imprint of the rope coil.

Bahadur and Rekhetre also sleep.

Rekhetre might be out cold until tomorrow with whatever the doctor ordered. But Bahadur stirs, propped against the small cabin, his eyes closed.

The slaves still wield the oars, taking us back to the harbor, though out of the six of them, two are taking a break.

Perhaps with Rekhetre, myself, and Bahadur all snoozing, they've decided to rotate and let the current take us downriver.

The sun is low on my left, but still bright enough to hurt my eyes when I scan the horizon. The pyramids rise out of the desert not far ahead. We are almost there.

I reassemble the scattered fragments of pre-sleep thoughts, a prickly sensation scrambling up my legs and across my arms.

Bahadur suspects that the royal wife's previous Storyteller—a woman who painted beautiful word pictures—abducted Rekhetre's baby in order to remove a royal heir to the throne. Rekhetre chooses to believe the woman took her child because she had none of her own.

I lumber to standing, cross the deck to the prow, and brace a hand against the curved wood that rises above my head. In the dusty distance, the temples and buildings are coming into focus.

This woman, this Storyteller, has disappeared, no one knows where.

Ekisi-betta. *Elizabeth.*

And our picnic lunch—Rekhetre's unusual avocado allergy. Just like mine.

Are allergies passed down from parent to child?

The boat turns slightly, throwing the shade of the prow over me, and I shiver, even in the heat.

Time works differently in the Chestnut Street Garden, this I have seen. The longer I stay, the less time passes outside the Garden. Could it work the same here? Could the three months Rekhetre's baby has been missing from the palace be nearly *thirty years* in a bookshop?

My breath shallows, and my hand creeps to my heart, as if I fear it's stopped, but it has only slowed to a fraction of its normal rate, along with the pace of time here.

One problem. There is one huge problem with this fantastical, impossible theory my brain has handed me.

Rekhetre's child was a boy.

Right?

She *said* boy, didn't she? Or did I only assume?

I chase back over all our conversations, but how is it possible to ascertain what *truly* was said versus what one remembers?

A royal child is always a threat.

This is one statement I clearly remember. Did the idea of a power-grab for the throne cause my—somewhat sexist—assumption the child was a boy?

No, surely she said *he, him, boy.*

I turn back to Rekhetre, still curled on her cushions. Sleeping the sleep of the drugged.

You are E.'s girl, are you not?

We were so happy when you were given to her.

I need to know. I need to know right now.

Bahadur. He is moving, shaking sleep from his mind, crawling forward to stand. He stares at me, as though angry I've seen him in a weak moment.

I cross to him, inches away, so neither the slaves nor Rekhetre will hear my desperate question.

"The child. Rekhetre's child who was taken. Was it a boy? Or a girl?"

He yanks his arm from my grasping hand, which I'm unaware I've laid on him.

"You think to question me about anything? You are nothing but poison in the Blessed Wife's ear!"

"Bahadur, I must know—please! A boy or a girl?"

His face reddens at the same moment his eyes go dark. "And now you address *me* with the familiarity of a member of the royal family?"

He raises a hand.

I jump backward. Sadiki's slap this morning still stings my pride.

I look to Rekhetre. Surely, she will give me an answer. In the short time we have known each other, it almost feels as if we have become friends.

As if we share some... connection.

My mouth is like cotton. My legs shaking. This cannot be true.

I stumble to her side, kneel beside her.

"Rekhetre", I shake her arm. "Blessed Wife, please, can you hear me?"

Bahadur is there in an instant, kicking at me.

"Remove yourself from her!"

I topple backward and brace my hands behind me on the boat's splintered deck.

This is madness. Such a simple question, and no one will answer me.

The slaves.

I scramble backward, crab-like, until I'm out of range of Bahadur's feet, then rise to my knees, stand, cross the deck to the first slave.

"Rekhetre's child—" the words are a croak, as if I've crawled across the desert to ask them—"boy or girl?"

His eyes widen and he licks his lips without breaking the rhythm of his rowing. Then glances to Bahadur.

He is smart enough not to answer.

I look to the next slave in his place along the hull, but his focus jumps to the riverbank.

I'm getting control of my desperation, barely. I breathe deeply of the marshy air and try to slow my pulse.

This impossible thing—if it's true—will remain true until Rekhetre wakes from Bahadur's potions.

I will wait. And then I will know.

I return to my place against the hull, marshaling my

thoughts to hold, to pause, to not run away to fantasies that cannot, cannot be true.

We finish our excursion in silence, float past the mortuary temple, and slide into the palace harbor under a desert sunset. The sand is aflame, a persimmon carpet stretching from the darkening cerulean blue of the harbor to the palace beyond.

Bare-chested slaves run to greet our incoming vessel, lighting torches at the water's edge. A boy of no more than ten years jumps into the water to grab a lead rope and guide the boat until its port side skims the stone quay of the harbor.

Bahadur is helped from the boat by two men who secure his arms below the elbow and lift him with care. He bends to speak to one of them, with a hateful glance back at me, then disappears into the darkness beyond the torchlight.

Rekhetre still sleeps.

But within minutes she is borne to a waiting litter, carried with gentle hands as if she is a sick patient, rather than a queen.

I am invited to join her for the silent return to the palace. I follow through empty and unadorned halls, perhaps the back entrance and the servant's domain, then into her bedchamber.

I keep my head down, stay out of the way, speak nothing. Will they allow me to remain with her until she wakes?

When she is settled onto her sleeping couch, and a supple fox's skin tucked around her, the slaves back out of the chamber, heads nodding to me as though they have transferred the care of her into my hands.

I pull a stool to her side, settle on it, and watch her face for any sign of waking.

With the early rising, the sun-baked trip on the river, and the nap of unknown length, I have lost all track of time. Beyond Rekhetre's squared window opening the last light is fading, but what time of year is it? Are the days long or short?

My stomach is empty, this I can say. Our picnic lunch feels long ago.

But I dare not request food. Better to remain unseen until I get my answer.

The stool has no back. My shoulders slouch, then tire.

I slip from the uncomfortable perch to sit on the floor, braced against the carved lion at the head of Rekhetre's long bed.

Time crawls, and the chamber darkens. Across the room, the slatted stool and wooden stand covered with cosmetics disappear first, then the woven floor coverings and footstool near the bed, and soon I can see nothing but a crescent moon, waning through the open window.

Will she be frightened to awaken in such darkness after falling asleep on the boat?

I move to the foot of the bed, to give her space to adjust to my presence.

But her wakefulness arrives slowly, and I am whispering to her long before her eyes flutter open.

"Bahadur?"

"No, it's me. Kepri."

She tries to rise, her arms shaky.

I help her upright, dare to sit on the bed beside her.

"Kepri—" Her voice catches, and she clears her throat, then tries again. "Kepri, I need Bahadur. I cannot sleep."

A wave of compassion rolls over me, powerful enough to bring tears to my eyes.

I want to fight for her.

"Rekhetre, you have been sleeping long. Let's talk now, and I will help you. You don't need Bahadur, you are strong."

She shakes her head in silent protest.

I wrap an arm around her, as I did at the temple when she cried against my shoulder. Before I knew.

"Rekhetre, I must ask you something. And I am sorry to

speak of it, to remind you of your pain, but it is about your child."

She exhales softly. "*Remind* me? As if I have *forgotten?*" Her voice rises in pitch, loud in the darkness. "It is with me every moment. Like a—like a jackal with his jaws around my heart."

I swallow against the seizure in my throat, hot and tight.

"Your baby. I—I am sorry I have not been told—was it a son? Or a daughter?"

In only the moonlight I can see her blink up at me.

"Renpet. Her name was Renpet. Named for the goddess of time."

Goddess of time. The oxygen escapes my lungs.

It occurs to me that all my life I have waited for this moment. Unaware that I believed it would happen but waiting all the same. Even with The Letter, lying in a drawer, unsent to the adoption agency, and Gran's insistence that my questions would be better left unanswered. I have somehow known I would one day meet my mother.

But never, in any fanciful story I have told myself as child or woman, has the meeting been like this.

I am trembling, a twig caught in a raging river. I am both empty and filled, broken and whole.

And what to say to this young woman—younger than me—about the daughter she has lost?

Can I explain that I am the traveler in the story I have woven for her? Gone off to a faraway future? That I have not left my child behind, but my mother? That I have somehow returned to her, nearly thirty years older?

Will we somehow make up for so many missed birthdays, not with the glittery packages and red curly bows of my childhood fantasies, but… somehow?

A swish of footsteps outside the chamber is followed an instant later by the entrance of a man.

Rekhetre stiffens in my embrace.

Has the king come for her already?

Worse. It is Sadiki's face that comes into focus, striding toward us.

"Great Lady. The king is requesting your presence now."

She huddles closer to me.

I grip her like she is being taken to her execution.

"Tell my husband I am ill."

Sadiki glowers at me. "He will not wait."

Is this guy loyal to Rekhetre or not? But perhaps it is his loyalty that makes him fear for her if she refuses.

She raises her eyes to him, looks him fully in the face.

I have rarely seen her so clear, so focused. "Sadiki. I *cannot* have another child. I *will not.*"

The words are raw and honest.

Her guard blinks, his shoulders fall. His expression softens to pity, then to a nodding acquiescence.

"I will tell him you are ill."

A reprieve. Not a solution.

"But you," his eyes bore into me, compassion gone, "you cannot be here. Remove yourself to your own chamber immediately."

I glance to Rekhetre. Can I wait until morning to explain my identity?

She nods at me, already sinking to her bed.

Her skin has paled, and if her illness is feigned, it is believable.

I will take the night to think about how best to explain. Perhaps with another story, guiding her to the truth gently.

I follow Sadiki to the chamber door, pause and look back at her prone form.

"Storyteller?"

The word breaks my heart. "Yes, Blessed Wife?"

"Send for Bahadur."

THIRTY-SEVEN

"The books or the music in which we thought the beauty was located will betray us if we trust to them; it was not in them, it only came through them, and what came through them was longing... For they are not the thing itself; they are only the scent of a flower we have not found, the echo of a tune we have not heard, news from a country we have never yet visited."

~ C.S. Lewis

"Kepri, wake up!"

My eyes open in an instant.

"What is it?"

Oni is bent over me on the narrow cot where I first changed my clothes yesterday morning, where I've finally fallen asleep after leaving Rekhetre

It's still dark—the middle of the night—but torchlight from the hall illuminates her silhouette and enough of her face to reveal something terrible. Shock? Terror?

I push to sitting, then stand. Grab her arms.

"Oni, what is it?"

"They are coming for you!"

"What?" I glance at the open doorway. "Who is coming? Why?"

But the stomp of sandals in the hall sends more fear into her eyes. She looks left and right, as if to hide, but there is nowhere in this tiny room.

Instead, she backs herself against the wall, just beside the door, as if she can remain unseen.

Two armed men round the corner, march into the room, and grab my arms.

"What is going on?" I try to twist away, search their blank faces.

"Oni, what has happened? Where are they taking me?"

I am met with silence and dragged from the room.

Rushed down the hall, I can barely keep up with their pace.

Across the midnight-dark courtyard garden.

Is that weeping coming from the shadows at the edge of the garden?

Through more unlit halls, then pushed toward walnut-colored double doors ahead.

As if anticipating our arrival, the doors swing open on stone sockets.

Inside, two more guards secure the door.

I am shoved inside the throne room.

My attention travels to the dais at the far end, a raised platform with a ramp leading to it. The throne sits atop this platform, the side of which is covered with red and blue reliefs of bound captives of various races on a background of yellow.

Braziers burn hot and bright in all corners of the room, striping the floor with light and reflecting off the gold leaf wrapped around the four granite columns that support the vaulted ceiling. The smell of spicy incense stings my eyes.

A bevy of women stand at the left wall, wailing as though they are being tortured.

And this must be Menkaure on the gold inlaid throne, crowned with the double crown of Upper and Lower Egypt, gripping the crook and the flail and fanned by dark-skinned Nubians wielding ostrich feathers. He is the image of an iconic seated statue of Egypt's pharaohs come to life. His face is stern, or perhaps angry.

Two men stand before him, their backs to me, but at Menkaure's heated look toward the doors, they widen and turn, as if inviting me forward.

Bahadur and Sadiki.

All this because Rekhetre has refused to come to Menkaure's bed?

These two warned me I'd be exiled if she didn't comply. But right now, exile doesn't sound so terrible.

Except for the stomach-clenching desire to tell my mother that her daughter is not lost, not dead.

"Ask her."

Sadiki's words are for the king, but his snarl is meant for me.

I raise my chin, ready to answer whatever question, and stride forward.

"Ask her how she tried to abduct the royal wife, and when that failed, how she killed her."

My knees turn to water. I stumble.

"Wha—?"

No one moves.

Even the weeping women at the edge of the room cease their keening.

"What are you saying?" I search Sadiki's face.

Bahadur shakes his head in disgust.

The king leans forward, his arms draped over his knees. He is angry, yes. But it is anger born of shock, even grief.

My head swivels, feeling loose on my neck. "What has happened? I don't understand."

But I don't want to hear the answer. Cannot bear it.

Bahadur turns on me. "Do not pretend you know nothing. Rekhetre, Blessed of Re, is dead. At no one's hand but yours."

"I did not—she is *dead*?" The word emerges as a hoarse whisper, as though barely scraped from my throat.

I cannot breathe.

I bend over double, hands on my knees, sucking in air.

No tearful reunion. No birthdays with fancy gifts and shared laughter.

"Ignore this ridiculous ruse, my king. This preposterous display of grief. She is no more saddened than she is surprised." Bahadur's accusation echoes and bounces from the throne room walls.

My legs give way, and I'm on my knees.

Weeping for the mother who never knew me.

"The Storyteller was the last one to be present in the royal wife's chamber, my king."

"No." I croak the word into the darkness. "No, she told me to send for Bahadur. I told the servants outside her chamber when I left."

I lift my head, still kneeling, to face the king. "She wanted more—more of his sleeping draught—"

"And you gave it to her, didn't you?" Bahadur's voice is ice. "After you stole it from me as I slept on the boat. The boat you tried to use to take her from us. You gave her all of it! Enough to kill her!"

I swipe at my tears and inhale, clamping down on my grief and embracing my outrage.

I stand again, shaking my head. Seeking Menkaure's eyes.

"She was alive when I left her. She wanted Bahadur brought."

Menkaure looks between the three of us ranged in front of him like an impossible choice.

"Why would I kill her?" My voice trembles. "I—I loved her."

The pharaoh turns to Sadiki, as if the bodyguard holds the answer.

"I cannot say, Majesty, Divine Golden Falcon. She was found on her bed, an empty cup, smelling of her usual sleeping draught, at her hand."

"Did she—did she appear—forced?"

Sadiki's glare turns on me. "No. There was no indication of any sort of struggle. But perhaps her Storyteller convinced her—"

"Perhaps Bahadur left her with too much!" My voice rises, high-pitched.

The women grieving at the edge of the chamber remain silent.

The physician Bahadur holds up a hand as if to silence me. "Ridiculous. The royal wife was very familiar with the quantity needed, and the dangers of taking too much. Even if I had left more behind—"

"It was intentional." These words—this realization—slips from me like an exhale, like all the air siphoned from my lungs.

All three men stare at me.

"She knew you would force her—that she would be expected to bear another child. She told you—" I whirl on Sadiki, jab a finger in his direction—"she *told* you she would not have another child, couldn't bear the idea of another loss, of giving her heart to another—" My breath fails me, words strangled to nothing.

"You accuse *me*, then, Storyteller?" Sadiki rises to his full height, chin lifted.

"Why not? You hang about her like a—like a mother hen! You should have known how desperate, how despairing—"

"And that is why we brought you! To distract her with your stories!" Sadiki's words are heated but laced with grief.

"Pah!" Bahadur's scoffing derision is like an arrow shot into the conversation. "Stories she tells of a woman who lost her child!"

Menkaure shifts forward. "Is this true, Storyteller?"

I breathe out for a beat, glancing between the three men. "No. I mean, yes, but not like that—it was meant to be a hopeful tale—"

The king is on his feet, glaring down on me. "You were to help her forget the past! Not cause her to dwell in it, to live all of it over again!"

Heat rises in my chest. "You think she would ever forget? That a mother *could* ever forget the loss of her own child? Then you are a fool! There is no forgetting, there is only healing. And that was what my story was meant to do! To begin, at least, the healing."

I have not been unaware of the gasps of the women at my disrespect, nor the way Sadiki and Bahadur have taken a step backward, as though to distance themselves from whatever lightning strike I have earned.

"Healing." Menkaure repeats the word with a touch of sadness, but mostly scorn.

And for the first time—how has this not occurred to me yet?—I realize this man is my father.

"Healing," he repeats. "Well then, you have failed, Storyteller. You have failed utterly."

I try to suck in a breath, but the air catches somewhere between my lips and my chest, leaving me empty. Hollow.

I bow my head, and all the heat drains to the tiles beneath me.

"Yes." I squeeze my eyes closed at the pain of it, at the utter unchangeableness of all of it, and the forlorn desolation of being un-mothered once again. "Yes. I have failed."

My words spill like hard marbles, rolling and echoing through the silent vault of the throne room, left to reverberate as a pronouncement of guilt.

"Take her," Menkaure finally says.

Where or to whom, I don't know, as I will not open my eyes against the sting of tears.

But then my arms are gripped, and his meaning is clear.

I open my eyes to the hold of the two guards from the doorway.

I am being dragged backward, off my feet.

I do not care.

"She should be executed."

This from Bahadur, his eyes on my throat, eyes like razor blades.

It is a perfect tableau. The three men arranged in angry symmetry, with Pharaoh at the center, higher on his dais, and the physician and bodyguard staring down the desperate and tear-stained woman near-to-fainting in the grip of two stone-faced guards. The huddled group of mourners at the wall, wide-eyed and whispering.

We all hang suspended here a moment, waiting for the artist to sketch us quickly, to be painted later.

And then the moment breaks, and Menkaure waves me away, away from his presence.

"Confine her until I make my decision."

Is he considering Bahadur's suggestion that I be executed?

The cold wriggle of fear in my belly gives me strength enough to gain my feet.

"Majesty—" It may be my last chance to defend myself.

But Menkaure is shaking his head, turning away, dropping to his throne to sit half-turned, his forehead propped with stiff fingers.

And the guards do not wait for his attention.

THIRTY-EIGHT

One of the strange things about living in the world is that it is only now and then one is quite sure one is going to live forever and ever and ever... One knows it sometimes when one stands by oneself in a wood at sunset and the mysterious deep gold stillness slanting through and under the branches seems to be saying slowly again and again something one cannot quite hear, however much one tries.

~ from *The Secret Garden* by Frances Hodgson Burnett

"I can walk!"

There is no need to drag me backward through the palace halls.

We swing an arc in the throne room, near to the double doors, and I am marched into the hall beyond.

I take no notice of the halls we pass through. They are dark and silent, most of the torches extinguished at this hour. What difference does it make where they take me?

Confine her.

A prison? Am I to be sentenced? I suspect it will be release or execution, with no hope for anything between.

My lack of concern for the location of my confinement flees when the two guards force me down a series of stone steps into near-total darkness.

Not down there.

"Where? Where are you taking me?" I struggle backward, pulling upward like a plant seeking sunlight.

A rough jerk downward and my feet slip under me.

I fall, hard, tailbone jarring against the stone. Pain slices like a serrated knife up my spine.

"Get up, woman."

"I—I cannot—"

But they lift me to my feet, drag me downward.

The tunnel is lit by the sparks of agony firing behind my eyes.

We come to an alcove, most of it hidden by a partial wall as high as my shoulders. Shadows dance on the ceiling above.

And then I am being lifted, between the two guards, up and up the side of the wall.

No, *no*! My lower back screams in fear, a scream that boils up and explodes out of my chest. "No!"

But I am above their heads, scraping across the top of the wall, sliding toward the abyss. Falling.

I land with a bone-crushing *thwack* on a stone floor.

Whimper. Curl into the pain. Lie still.

Breathe, Kelsey.

Breathe through the pain. Ride the crest of it. Refuse to be dragged under.

Shadows on the roof above me still. Shapes on a cave wall.

Real? Only shadows? Shadows of something real? Or is there nothing left that is real?

The guards are gone, long gone, and I lay like a coiled snail, knees drawn to my chest.

The light grows brighter—a wavering, shaky oval, dark shadow above, almond-shape of white eyes above it.

"You are hurt."

The eyes, the face, bend to me.

An elderly man, circular terracotta oil lamp in his palm, kind eyes.

I say nothing.

He touches my head, a light stroke of my hair.

The gentle touch dissolves my restraint. What begins as a moan emerges as a sob, the pain in my soul far deeper than the pain in my body.

His *ssshhh* is protective, fatherly. "Come, let us get you up."

I shake my head. "I fell. My—my tailbone—"

"Yes, but we can't let you grow stiff, my girl, or you will never want to move again. Come, sit, yes, that's right. That's good. Now we will stand. Walk a little."

He is right.

The spasm loosens slightly. I am moving.

We pace the floor in short trips, the entire length of the cell no longer than twenty feet.

"Better?" He squints across the lamplight, studying my face.

I try to smile. Nod my head.

"You must try to move a little every hour you are awake. It is the only way."

He leads me to the wall, helps me lower myself. Slow, painful, a last drop to the floor that brings fresh tears.

"Now." He slides to the floor beside me. "Tell me your name."

"Kels—Kepri. My name is Kepri."

"Ah, the new Storyteller. Tell me, how does the royal wife fare? Still seeking oblivion through Bahadur's *care*?" He leans on the final word, sarcasm tainting it.

"She is dead." I drop my chin to my chest.

He sighs. Remains blessedly silent.

Later, I do not know how long, perhaps I have slept, I whisper out the words that are too entangled in my mind to process.

"I thought... I thought the most difficult thing would be rejection of *me.* That the work I might create, the story—it might reflect poorly on me, cause others to shun me. Or mock me. Or simply ignore me. I was willing. Willing to take that risk for the beauty of the story and to honor my own creativity."

He is nodding, a slow movement of his angular chin, his shoulder touching mine.

"But this—this is so much more than any slap in my own face. This is... *failure.*"

"You believed you could heal her."

I study his profile. "How can you know this?"

He smiles, not at me, but a sad smile into the darkness. "Because I am her musician." He inhales. "*Was* her musician."

I find his hand and clasp it. "What is your instrument?"

"The harp, to soothe a disquiet soul. And my voice. To remind her of beauty and goodness."

"Yes. That is what I tried to do as well."

"We both have failed, then."

We let the silence play out before us.

In a faraway life, a Gardener spoke to me of risk. But this risk is far greater than I imagined.

And I see it now. Even after the artist overcomes reticence to share the work, conquers fear that the work has no value, no great quality, and is able to bring it, to show it, to *give* it, even then there is danger that the work itself will go astray. That the song will not soothe, the story will not heal, the painting will not speak. To have created, and to have that creative thing fail, is a different sort of pain. Like the pain inflicted on one's child rather than one's own body. Outside, and yet... more grievous.

"Will they execute us both?" I finally ask when I can think no longer on the failure.

He does not answer at once.

"Perhaps."

How can I explain to them? When they come for me, I must tell one last story. Must convince them that I am Renpet, taken by Ekisi-betta, to be raised in a far-off place where time advances differently and a child ages and returns a grown woman. But what possible proof could I offer to corroborate such a claim?

An avocado allergy? I nearly laugh into the darkness.

But what choice do I have? It is one last story that might save my life.

They do come for me, hours later. Perhaps it is morning. Impossible to tell in this place. My new friend, Ihy, has kept me walking at intervals, and my tailbone is bruised but functional.

A three-legged stool is tossed over the wall, its legs lashed to a cracked seat that looks unable to hold my weight.

"Don't get any ideas, old man." The warning is issued by an unseen voice on the other side of the wall.

He needn't have bothered. Ihy hasn't even risen to his feet.

I step onto the stool, test it, then raise my upper body above the wall.

One last look at Ihy, a nod of gratitude.

His wan smile in the tiny lamplight is small comfort.

And then the guards haul me over the wall, catching me before I hit the floor, to my great relief.

In the upper halls, the morning light is pale and early, as though the sun has not fully risen.

Menkaure has apparently not considered long before making a decision about my fate.

I am returned to the throne room, tossed to the floor in front of the pharaoh's dais.

In front of my father.

He does not look as though he has slept. He rises slowly, towers over me.

I stay on my knees.

"Kepri of Punt, Storyteller to Rekhetre, Blessed of Re, whose *ka* has retreated to the west, you have been found guilty of treason."

Treason? This sounds very bad.

"Because of your warped and dangerous stories, the royal wife has given up all hope of living and has taken her own life. For this, there is but one recourse, to restore ma'at in the Two Lands."

Ma'at. The ancient Egyptian understanding of truth and justice, a balance that must always be held. A balance I have violated with my failure.

"You will be executed at sunrise, your body thrown into the waters without burial."

To be unburied, with no hope of afterlife, is the more serious part of the sentence to the Egyptians, I know. But execution? This cannot be happening.

And sunrise? It cannot be more than a few minutes away.

"Divine King, if I may be permitted to tell one final story first—"

"Your storytelling is over." He flicks a hand in the direction of the guards and turns away to his throne.

They descend on me like hungry vultures.

"Wait!" I try to twist from their grasp. "Wait—you don't understand! She was my mother—Rekhetre—and you are my father!"

Menkaure spins back on me, his teeth bared. "Silence! I will hear no fanciful stories!"

"I know how it sounds—she was younger than I—but you must let me explain—"

But I am halfway through the throne room doors, then all the way out and the doors close. I have failed again.

My strength forsakes me for an instant, my body limp between the guards. But then I'm back on my feet. Scrambling and twisting.

To no avail.

Back through the halls once again. Across a courtyard.

I glance at the flat white of the sky, paling toward sunrise. Fear lodges first like a solid stone in my gut, then runs like molten lava heating my veins.

Another hall, then outside the palace walls to the garden that seems a million days ago.

It's unfair, all of it. Such a worthless, futile cheat. As though I've run a marathon under a blistering sun and then seen the finish line evaporate moments before I reach it.

That ridiculous Garden and its promises of finding my true identity. I see the faces of Eliot and Agatha Christie, of Baum and even of the Gardener, making promises they will not keep. Delivering false assurance that truth can be found.

But I allowed it, God knows, I allowed it. I let them bully me through the Garden, across the footbridge, to this terrifying moment when all of it will be taken.

My chest burns at my own cowardice. Too weak to know myself, too fearful to refuse.

Too desperate to belong.

I am dragged through the half-wall to the outer road beyond, with the pyramids staring down at me and the Nile and the desert to the east glowing brighter with a pinkish dawn, too fast, too fast.

Then the sun itself rockets over the horizon, launches across the desert, ignites the gold-tipped pyramid.

And I am tossed to my knees before a bloody stone block.

A sandaled foot crashes against my back, thrusts me forward. My chin slams the stone. My eyes a fraction from the blood of the last execution.

The guard's intake of breath.

My own to match, inhaling shock and courage.

The whirr of a blade through air.

And then, darkness.

THIRTY-NINE

The only words that ever satisfied me as describing Nature are the terms used in the fairy books, "charm," "spell," "enchantment..." A tree grows fruit because it is a magic tree.

~ G.K. Chesterton

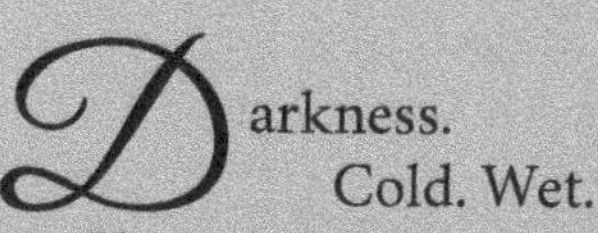

Darkness.

Cold. Wet.

Shivering in the wetness.

Too dark for heaven. Too cold for hell.

I am dead but aware.

A hand to my chest—breathing. Fingers to the back of my neck—dry. The wetness is not my own blood, then. The damp chill seeps upward from the ground beneath me.

Too damp for Egypt.

I force my eyes open, my breath shallow and pulse racing at what I might find.

A flicker of light, beyond where I lay.

Flames.

The *edge* of hell, then?

And this a... grassy area at its entrance?

"Kay?"

A voice from the dark distance.

"Kay, what's happened? Are you unwell?"

The voice, deep and worried, much closer.

And then it all snaps into place, and I am sitting upright, too fast, dizziness knocking me back down to an elbow in the grass at the base of the stone footbridge, and Sam kneeling, propping me with a steady arm under my shoulders.

"I'm not dead."

He chuckles, but in the concerned sort of way someone laughs when they think you might be delusional.

"You're not dead." He raises my shoulders higher, until my weight shifts and I am steady, then removes his arm. "What happened? Did you faint?"

My turn to laugh. *Faint* sounds like something a fragile, Victorian woman might succumb to. A fainting spell. Far cry from a beheading.

My laugh turns a bit manic and ends in a snort of hysteria.

"Come on, let's get you up out of the grass."

I'm on my feet, I'm in my wisteria dress, I'm alive.

"I think you need something to eat. Maybe a drink."

"Yes." By all means, yes.

At the marvelous table beside the towering live oak, Sam loads a delicate china plate, requests a glass of white wine, then catches my eye and inclines his head toward a bench near the base of the Tree.

He holds the wine and doesn't speak as I eat—salty caviar on wafer-thin crackers and *crème fraîche* on cucumbers—not asking questions, not problem-solving. Smart man.

When I've polished off the last cracker and drained the glass, he only smiles.

"Feeling better?"

"Yes."

I slump against the back of the bench, exhausted beyond all ability to think. Again, the question of how long it's been since I've slept is unanswerable. Sam has mentioned nothing of my absence, so perhaps it's only been minutes in this place, with time slowed here just as it is once I return to my life.

Nearby, the table of gifts shines like a beacon of creative prowess. In the center, the warm yellow wall in Van Gogh's *Cafe Terrace at Night* glows with a brilliance that is both enviable and unrivaled.

"Not every artist is a genius." The words emerge like a sigh, like a resignation, even though they feel more like accusation. "*I* am not a genius."

Sam takes my hand, curls my cold fingers into his large palm. "Nor am I."

I doubt this is true—he is here in this Garden, after all—but it doesn't answer my inherent question.

"So, what then?"

He says nothing.

A glance at his face reveals a sad smile, sympathetic eyes.

I shake my head. He does not understand.

"It is one thing to write a story—make a piece of art—and know that you could have done better, that this thing you created did not live up to your expectations of it, but you have learned, and the next will be an improvement upon the last. That is failure, and it is hard. But it is another thing entirely to realize you simply have limitations. That your talent will *never* measure up to your expectations, to your desires. That you simply do not possess the genius to create something great."

The words have come in a rush, the most I've spoken since I lost my head in Egypt.

Sam still holds my hand, but he looks away, as if I've struck him with my words.

"Yes." His agreement holds a bit of rancor. "Yes, that is a

great disappointment. And I have seen artists destroy lovely things in the wake of that great disappointment."

I let those words ride in the night air of the Garden for a few minutes.

Lovely things.

Were they deceived, these artists Sam speaks of, into thinking their lesser works were worthless? Deserving of destruction?

Did the deception lie in believing that *only* works of genius deserved life?

I created a story I believed would heal Rekhetre. It failed to heal her. But the greater pain is the certainty that I do not possess the *ability* to create such a thing, no matter how much I might long for it.

"We can only do our best." Sam's tone has softened.

"It may never be enough."

"No. It may not."

Across from our bench, a series of men are filing toward the platform carrying trumpets, saxophones, and trombones. Another seats himself at the drums. A moment later, they strike up "Chattanooga Choo Choo" in classic big band style. A *whoop* of appreciation goes up from the sophisticated party guests, and within two minutes, swing dancing has broken out on the lawn.

The pink sunrise of ancient Egypt is a million miles from here. Was it even real?

My parents? Truly?

And if so, what was the purpose of this *going deeper*—only to break my heart?

"I don't suppose you'd like to dance?" Sam's voice is quiet but playful.

"Uh, no." I glance at his profile. "I'm sorry. It's not—I don't know how to dance like that, and I'm not really feeling up to it."

A couple approaches the food table, a bulky man in a jacket and vest with a high-starched collar and handlebar mustache, and a younger, pastel-wearing woman tugging on his sleeve, laughing. The man shakes his head and seizes a plate.

"Of course." Sam folds his hands together. "I was only hoping to cheer you up."

The woman at the table is pleading. "D., come on, you never want to dance with me."

Her companion is focused on the food.

"Sorry, girl, you know I've two left feet, and you'll not see me making a fool of myself out there."

I lean forward, catching her attention. "S. will dance with you."

She shoots a glance at me, then at Sam, eyes lighting up. "Will you?"

"I—I'm—" He turns to me with a look of accusation.

"Go dance." I tilt my head toward the party. "I'm fine here."

The truth is I am far from fine, but I need time to process all that has happened, all I've discovered.

The man circles the table, plate in hand, nodding at Sam. "Happy to keep your lady company while you're getting me off the hook."

I force a smile.

Sam sighs and stands, to the sound of the woman's little squeal of delight.

My new bench-mate settles in and starts on the series of tiny fruit tarts on his plate. "I'm D.," he says around bites of cherry and cheese.

"K. Nice to meet you."

"Oh… K.?" He ceases chewing. "You're E.'s girl, then?"

The question is like a slap to the face. It was never an easy answer, given her title as "Gran" despite being my adopted mother. But now?

I nod, studying the dancers. The way Sam effortlessly swings his partner left and right in some kind of jitterbug I could never match.

"M. signed some of her books in E.'s shop once."

I try to straighten, take another squinting look at the woman dancing with Sam. "Did she? I wasn't aware we'd had any signings with female authors."

"Oh, I'm not surprised you didn't know. I mean—" he leans in and lowers his voice—"she's not well-known. Just a local sensation for a little while."

Should I admit I thought everyone in this place was famous? I can't be blamed for that assumption, given the handful of luminaries I've met, from T.S. Eliot to Charles Dickens—

"C.! Has C… returned?"

How to explain?

"Who now?"

"The author. Ebenezer Scrooge? David Copperfield?"

Déjà vu, explaining Dickens to my Creative Writers of Tomorrow.

"Ah, C., yes, of course." D. waves his fork in the direction of the dancing. "Just saw the man over there, I believe, talking with R."

I close my eyes. At least I've solved one problem.

And the Garden? I reach a hand to the nearest shrub, a Japanese Pieris. The glossy leaves reflect the lanterns strung over the table, a healthy emerald green.

I'm unsure if it was my journey to ancient Egypt or simply the courage to bring my story-journal, but it seems I've restored what I nearly destroyed.

So it is only my own life in shambles now.

I've done what they asked. Gone deeper. Embraced my role as Storyteller. But I've come back with no answers to my immediate bookshop problems and a devastation about my identity that I'm not sure I can manage.

"Such a lovely shop, as I remember." D. is back at his plate, moving on to the blueberry tart.

I fish around my mental list of descriptors to define this guy, but my thought processes seem a little scrambled.

Besides, why am I always trying to control people with definitions?

"Yes. Yes, the shop is lovely." At least for now. Until it's swallowed by Blackburn's monstrosity.

"That Beaux-Arts facade. Such elegant proportions."

"Beaux—?"

He grins. "Sorry. Architects always believe everyone is just as fascinated by building styles as we are."

"You're an architect?"

"Guilty."

Thus far in the Garden, I've met only writers, painters and sculptors, and musicians. Perhaps, as Van Gogh said, my notion of the expression of creativity is too narrow.

I've always loved the front of the bookshop, with its Classical Greek and Roman influence. And been vaguely aware it was once part of a larger structure, before the theater took over. I should look up D.'s "Beaux-Arts" once I'm home.

At the thought of home, a deep fatigue begins in my limbs and spreads. My eyelids flutter, and I try to cover a yawn with a hand.

D. chuckles. "I thought you seemed a bit done-in, my girl."

"I guess I've had a long day."

"Hmm. Been deeper?"

"What?" The question jolts me upright.

He waves the fork again, this time in the direction of my face. "You have that look about you. Someone's who's recently gone deeper and lived to tell the tale."

I search for words, lips parted. "Does—does *everyone* go... deeper?"

"Of course. Eventually. We all must learn."

Right.

"Thankfully, we come back here." He nods toward the party. "I sometimes believe surrounding yourself with other likeminded creatives is the only way to keep overcoming the fear, to survive the disappointment."

I scan the party guests, thinking about Judy Garland, the dangers of isolation.

Sam and M. are kicking their lower legs in mirrored movements, laughing with the music and with the joy of being part of the general dance.

D. and I watch in silence, and suddenly someone else has joined us. D. gives up his seat to allow the Gardener to lower himself beside me.

D. drifts off without a word, as though the meeting has been prearranged.

Once again, I sense the impossibility of guessing anything specific about this man, the man without even a first-letter designation.

"You could have warned me." I speak the words softly, though not without a touch of bitterness.

"Ah, but I did."

I sigh. "The greater risk you spoke of, after I found the courage to bring my gift?"

"There is much ugliness in the world." His attention is on the music and dancing, a strange counterpoint to the words.

I put a hand to the back of my neck. "You're telling me."

He is silent a moment, then shakes his head. "I do not speak of violence, though that is part of it. I speak of what is the opposite of Beauty, an attack on it. I speak of evil. The acceptance of ugliness as normal, and the hopeless despair that ensues from accepting such a thing."

"I'm afraid I did nothing to defeat evil." I risk a look at his face.

He is studying his own work-worn hands but smiling. "You have done everything."

"How? What have I done?"

"Your stories, my girl. All the stories—" he sweeps a hand across the party guests. "When stories go out from you all, the words are like magic, like fire. They speak worlds into existence, they are words made flesh. You take up the call to defeat the evil as you *Story* it back to its dark and joyless and silent place."

"But… she is dead. I failed."

"And you are embarrassed by your failure?"

I shake my head. "No. Not any longer. I am simply heartbroken."

"Yes, that is the greatest risk. Disappointment over our limitations. Even harder than the reception of a shortsighted world who does not reward our efforts."

It feels mad to be speaking of such sadness with the dancers swirling before us and the big band still tapping out "Chattanooga Choo Choo," and yet this mixture of joy and grief is part of what I know to be real.

"I feel like such a small part of it, though."

"Yes." He braces hands against his knees and pushes himself to standing. "Yes, you are a small part of bringing back life through your creativity. But we can be both small *and* important. Some of the best things are."

I look up but he is already walking across the grass.

The music quits, Sam and his dance partner return, laughing and flushed.

M. hugs Sam in a burst of giggling thank-yous, then flits away.

Sam lowers himself to the bench, taking the Gardener's seat. "How are you feeling?"

How do I get out of this place? I've never learned how to end my time in this Garden intentionally. Do I need to knock myself unconscious to escape?

If I'm here much longer, leaving might not require a blow to the head. The flames of the globe lights are already swirling in my vision.

"K.?" Sam's leaning in, studying my face.

"Sorry. Tired. Have you gone deeper?"

He looks away from my abrupt question, the movement quick and evasive.

I sigh. "I don't recommend it."

"I'm not sure it's avoidable."

"Yeah, you might be right." I close my eyes and lean my head back a little.

"So, what now?"

"Now I suppose I try to use what I've experienced to better push into the work I'm meant to create."

It's a lofty answer. What I do *not* say is that I'm more likely to return to my apartment and spiral into a dark place as I contemplate my dead mother—dead *parents,* really, since Menkaure's days are long over by now—and the truth of having been stolen from my family by the woman I thought had my best interest at heart.

So, yeah. That, too.

If I actually knew how to leave.

"Let's walk." Sam stands and offers me a hand.

I make good use of it, pulling my exhausted body upright.

"Shall we take a turn about the Garden?" I ask, another little hysterical laugh escaping.

"Brontë?"

"Jane Austen."

"Ah."

Sam offers me a chivalrous arm, which I also accept, because all of this is getting to be several shades of ridiculous.

We walk a circle around the grassy lawn, just inside the vine-covered marble columns. The relief of companionable silence.

We come upon the spirited and smiling jazz pianist—B.—who warned me of the part I played in the Dickens Disappearance.

The big band's still playing and she's focused on the music platform, tapping fingertips against a giant urn of silvery eucalyptus. She glances our way as we approach.

"Will it be your turn again soon?" I ask.

"What? Oh, perhaps. It's better they keep the real talent

up there, though." She shrugs, with what seems likes real humility and not a bid for affirmation.

"You have talent." I give her the affirmation anyway. "I loved your playing."

She squints up at me as though trying to determine if I'm honest.

"Hmm. Room for everyone, then, I guess."

We're joined by another, a man I've not yet met. His full and wavy dark hair, along with a thin mustache and pointed strip of a goatee, seem to indicate someone from the fifteen or sixteen hundreds.

His attention is on Sam. "It's time." His comment is spoken nearly as an aside, quiet and casual.

B. wanders away, toward the music.

Sam glances at me, lips parted with an intake of breath, but then an exhale and a head shake.

"I—I'm happy to stay here with K. At least for a bit."

My gut clenches. Is Sam being taken from me? Even with all the people I've met here, I've only felt at ease with him.

"Apologies, my friend. It is, of course, your choice. But you must come now, or choose never."

Is this Sam's "deeper" requirement? What happens if he chooses *never*?

But I guess we won't know, because Sam's looking at me with an apology in his eyes.

"I'll meet you... after."

By which he could mean *in a few minutes,* which might be days or weeks wherever he is going.

I nod but grab his hand. "Thank you."

He frowns.

"For watching out for me, talking with me."

"I'll see you again, K."

"I know." By which I mean, *I have no idea,* but I don't want to argue. I can't explain why this feels like goodbye, but I sense it is my last time to wander this amazing place.

He squeezes my fingers, then pulls me closer and kisses

my cheek. "I'll see you again," he whispers against my ear, the tone determined.

"Good luck." I pull away and smile.

He shrugs and turns to follow the mustachioed man.

I watch him go, those wide shoulders fading into the unending twilight of this place, until I can no longer make him out.

Then I turn and find the nearest bench—past B.'s urn of greenery and leaving her behind—and sink into a fatigued slump once more.

The big band ensemble has given way to a small chamber orchestra playing a piece I recognize as Tchaikovsky. The strings are like a mournful lament, matching my growing sadness.

I am so tired.

I'll just close my eyes here for a moment.

FORTY

What if you slept
And what if
In your sleep
You dreamed
And what if
In your dream
You went to heaven
And there plucked a strange and beautiful flower
And what if
When you awoke
You had that flower in your hand
Ah, what then?

— Samuel Taylor Coleridge

I wake in the pre-dawn coolness of my own bed.

For once, I am not surprised.

Eyes still closed, I take a slow inventory of my mind and body.

I've slept for some time, feel well-rested. But the trauma of my near-execution swims under my consciousness, as though it's waiting to surface and sink its jagged teeth into me.

Yeah, what therapist is going to work through a *beheading* with me? I force back the hysterical laughter that's becoming a disturbing habit.

What else?

Sadness, a deep sadness. It began to smother me in the Garden and now feels like a weighted blanket, pinning me to the bed.

Can I stay here all day?

Depends on what day it is, which is not a given any more.

I spent how long—about thirty-six hours?—in ancient Egypt. Left my apartment on Wednesday evening. Is it too much to hope that time has moved *backwards* and I can repeat my Wednesday off?

I grope for my phone, check the display.

Thursday morning.

Considering it feels like I've slept all night, it would seem my time in Egypt amounted to nearly nothing.

And really, what was the point of any of it?

The red circles of notifications show I've missed two text messages and a voicemail.

I thumb to the text messages first, then sit upright.

Ms. Willoughby, please call AdvantaCare at your earliest opportunity.

Both messages identical, as if auto-generated.

I play the voicemail on speaker, shoulders hunched over my phone.

"Hello, Kelsey, this is Dr. Petrakis at AdvantaCare."

Her voice has that sad, forced-to-give-bad-news tone.

No, no, no.

"I need to let you know that it appears your grandmother's had another stroke. We've moved her to the Acute Nursing Care wing and we're monitoring her closely, but I think it would be best if you headed over here as soon as you're able. Ok, Kelsey, thanks, bye."

I'm throwing the blankets off before the message ends. I jump into jeans and a sweatshirt, check my face, swipe a brush through my hair, grab my keys, and run downstairs in less than two minutes.

The drive to AdvantaCare is a blur, I'm unable to think past *get there, get there, get there.*

A rush through the check-in desk, my scrawled signature in the sign-in book illegible, the buzz of the security door, and flying down the hall, asking for the Acute Nursing wing, smashing the elevator button six or seven times before the doors chime open.

Upstairs, outside the elevator, three nurses look up from the hexagonal station in the center of the open space.

"Elizabeth Willoughby. Where is she?"

A young woman slides toward me from her side of the desk. She looks about sixteen, though that can't be right.

"Are you family?"

"Yes. I'm her daughter."

Despite the girl's age, she's learned to affix that medical sad-smile on her nodding face.

"She's there, in 7B. You can go in."

"Is she—how is she?"

More sad-smiling. "Elizabeth's doctor will be making her rounds soon, and you can speak with her when she comes in."

Room 7B is a quick ten-step journey but feels like a mile.

I pause at the door, gasp in a shaky breath at the sight of Gran's slight form, motionless in a bed, machines beeping and whirring, tubes and wires attached.

The room's a double, but the first bed, nearest the door, is empty.

I cross to Gran's bedside, pull a chair from under the window, and take her hand in mine.

A pulse-oxygen monitor is clipped to her bony index

finger. I follow the lead up to the screen, see some numbers but have no idea what any of them mean.

"I'm here, Gran. It's Kelsey." My voice breaks at the end, a little catch in my throat to match imminent tears.

She doesn't open her eyes, doesn't react to my presence.

Is this how it will be? Gran slipping away without a warning, without a chance for me to say goodbye? Without a chance to ask questions—about the Garden, about Egypt, about where I really came from?

I want to understand. I *need* to understand—who I am, and what it means, and why, why she did what she did—to Rekhetre, and to me.

An unexpected surge of anger, followed by a swell of guilt, brings the tears at last.

She loved me. Raised me as best she could. Gave me everything I needed and so much more. How can I be angry? It's so... disloyal.

I realize I need more than questions answered. I need somehow to also say *thank you.* To say *I love you*.

And yet the anger remains.

"Oh, Gran, please wake up." I lower my forehead to her frail hand, tears falling onto her skin.

Time slips along, heedless of pain.

The promised doctor arrives, another woman who seems too young for her position. I must be getting old.

She introduces herself, but I don't register her name.

"How are we doing, Elizabeth?" The doctor's all business, touching Gran's skin, checking the monitors above her head.

Why does it annoy me to hear younger people address Gran in such a familiar way?

She turns her attention to me. She wears no makeup and has very thin lips, which she pinches into a tight slash of concern while tilting her head toward me as though communicating something.

"Well, as you heard, your mother's had a stroke."

I nod, swallow painfully.

"She hasn't regained consciousness. At this point, it's impossible to know if she will."

More nodding.

"Do you have any questions?"

Questions? Oh, if you only knew.

"Uh… what are you doing for her? I mean, like—what kind of treatment?"

Another head-tilt and significant pause. "Well, Elizabeth is ninety-four, as you know."

I see the math playing through her head. How can I be the daughter of a ninety-four-year-old? I don't explain. Nor do I acknowledge my obvious awareness of Gran's age.

"Yes. So." She's nodding.

So much nodding here.

"We are continuing the medication she's been on for some time, of course. No need to stop that. Her dementia is progressing, and this latest stroke will hasten things, of course. Of course this is just part of the process."

Please stop saying *of course.*

"She is dying, then? Is that what you're saying? And she may not wake up before… before that happens?"

"I'm afraid that's where we are right now. Yes."

"Right. Okay. Thanks."

She circles the bed and touches my shoulder. "Let me know if there's anything you need, okay?"

I half-smile at her attempt at empathy.

She disappears, on to give the next family the news they are hoping for or dreading.

I sit with Gran's hand still in mine as the morning outside brightens into a hot spring day and visitors begin buzzing in the halls.

A nurse passes through, checking the monitors, smiling at me, moving on to the next patient.

The room is mostly silent and chilly and sterile, nothing like Gran's room downstairs, with her paintings and her music. It seems unfair.

I can relieve the silence, at least. Perhaps she can hear me.

"I've been back to the Garden, Gran."

Her features do not change.

"It was quite a trip this time. They kept telling me I had to go deeper, so I did. I'm thinking that's something you might have done, too. Ancient Egypt, perhaps?"

Should I tell her the story of my adventure?

A twinge in my chest, like tiny spikes digging into my heart. What good would a story do? What good do any of them do, despite the Gardener's lofty sentiments? I couldn't save Rekhetre, and I'm not going to save Gran by weaving together some words.

"I met some people there. In Egypt, I mean. A young mother. Mourning the loss of her child."

The steady beep of the monitor is like someone poking me repeatedly. Can't we turn the volume off? I should have asked the nurse.

What would Gran say if she could hear me tell of Rekhetre's assumed suicide? Would she feel guilty for the part she played? Or is there some explanation I'm still not understanding? One I may never understand?

The losses are piling up, choking out something inside me.

Gran.

Rekhetre. My mother.

The Book Emporium—only days away from the Taking now.

Even the Garden itself, which I suspect I will never reenter. The people I met there.

Sam the Sculptor.

I lay my head against Gran's arm and drift into half-conscious reminiscing.

The morning wastes away.

My phone buzzes with a concerned text from Lisa.

I step out of the room to call her, apologize for the lack of contact.

"I'm closing the shop for the afternoon, Kelsey." Lisa's voice sounds tear-filled. "I'm coming over."

We can't afford to lose the afternoon of sales, but I don't argue.

She arrives in thirty minutes, fresh tears on her cheeks as she enters and crosses to Gran's side.

"I'm so sorry, Kelsey. She is… such a special person."

"She is. Yes."

Lisa strokes Gran's hair in a moment more tender than any I've seen from her. "I can never repay her for everything she's done for me."

More guilt jabbing my insides, now at my frequent annoyance over Gran's illogical loyalty to Lisa. Or perhaps it was loyalty to her dead friend, Lisa's mother. Even so, it all seems quite noble of Gran now, rather than foolish or gullible.

Lisa swipes at her tears. "I hope I can at least thank her once more. Will she wake up?"

"They can't say. But Lisa, she knew you were grateful."

She looks at me sharply, her expression a little wary. As if I've revealed a secret.

If she and Gran had secrets together, they are likely to remain a mystery.

Just like all the secrets Gran has kept from me.

A woman enters the room, slows at the sight of Lisa, then proceeds.

She's an aide from Gran's wing downstairs.

"Hi, Ms. Willoughby. They sent me up here—"

She glances at Gran, pauses, as if she feels bad about intruding.

"It's fine. What is it?"

"I'm sorry. It's just that they've made the decision to… free up her room downstairs for another incoming resident. Keep her here until…"

Lisa bristles, arms across her chest. "That's a little fast, don't you think?"

"It's okay, Lisa." I try to loosen the tension in my neck. "Is there something you need me to do? Papers to sign or something?"

"No, nothing like that. Just—when you have a chance—her things, in her room—"

"I'll be down soon."

She escapes with a grateful expression.

Lisa shakes her head with a huff. "Unbelievable—"

"Can you stay with her? It won't take me long. But I don't want her to be alone."

She softens. "Sure. I'll text you if anything changes."

It takes only about ten minutes to assemble all of Gran's personal possessions in her former room. The little Monet and Cézanne reproductions from the wall, the bedside lamp and speaker. Her clothing, folded into neat pastel piles on the bed.

A drawer reveals a few things I don't even remember bringing—a book of Wordsworth, some old jewelry, a photo album.

I add this last item to the stack on her bed, then open the album cover, drawn to wander through photos I haven't seen for years.

A younger Gran at the entrance of the Lyceum Theatre on Broadway. Then on the deck of a ship, holding her hat against the breeze tugging at her hair—the Greek isles, wasn't it?

I turn the pages quickly. I'll come back to this book again, but for now, I don't want to be down here too long.

One more page turn, and a photo catches my eye.

It's Gran and another woman, taken perhaps thirty years ago. Gran looks about sixty, and the other woman about the age I am now. They're smiling, arms linked, under a "Grand Opening" sign. It's the Rhythm & Wonder Music Shop, on the other side of the empty lot.

Gerry—I think that's his name—runs the shop now, since

his mother's retirement. This must be her in the photo. Something about her seems familiar.

I bend closer to the photo, study her face.

A slow beat, like a premonition, pounds in my chest.

When the recognition comes, it changes everything.

FORTY-ONE

We name ourselves by the choices we make, and we can help in our own naming by living through the choices, right and wrong, of the heroes and heroines whose stories we read.

~ Madeleine L'Engle

I can't leave Gran.

Not yet, despite the photo now pulled from the album and tucked into my back pocket.

Most of her belongings are in the trunk of my car, and I've brought her clothes up to her new room in Acute Nursing Care.

Lisa has gone, making me promise to text at any hour if Gran wakes up. She returned to the shop before three o'clock to intercept my Creative Writers of Tomorrow and cancel our workshop for today. She's been pretty great, I have to admit, these past couple weeks. Maybe she senses we can only handle one crisis at a time, so my meltdowns have somehow put her usual mess on hold.

The hours tick past, each one filling up with more questions but no answers.

The cart rolls past with stacks of dinner meals for the floor's occupants but doesn't pause at Gran's door.

How long since I've eaten? The thought of food turns my stomach.

Somewhere around six o'clock, the night-shift nurse wanders in and pauses to study me rather than Gran. He's a huge guy with a buzz cut and tattoos, as if daring anyone to question the matchup between his appearance and profession.

"You're looking almost as pale as her. It's Kelsey, right?"

"Yeah. Just tired."

He busies himself checking over Gran but talks to me. "Nothing I haven't seen before. You need to take care of yourself, too. Stay strong for her."

"Nothing I haven't heard before."

He chuckles. "Touché."

"I just don't want her to wake up alone. Or to miss my chance..."

He leans against Gran's bed, hands on the rails, and looks into my eyes. "Listen, we're checking on her all the time, and if she regains consciousness, we will call you immediately. As for missing your chance—"

He pauses, as though unwilling to speak freely.

"Say it. Whatever it is."

"Okay. She's either going to wake up and be with us for a while, or she's not. But she's unlikely to wake up for only a few minutes and then be gone before you have a chance to get here. Besides, the process of awakening from a stroke-induced coma is typically a slow one. We're talking hours, even days. There'll be time. And you need to sleep."

What I need more than anything, besides Gran's recovery, is to track down the woman in the photo burning a hole in the back pocket of my jeans.

I sigh. "Thanks. For the explanation. It's helpful."

"Go home for the night. Come back in the morning if you feel you need to. But take care of yourself."

"Okay. Thanks."

I wait until he's gone, then lean over her bed, kiss her forehead.

"I'll be back soon. Wake up for me, Gran. I need you."

Thirty minutes later, my car's parked in front of the bookshop, and I'm walking down Chestnut Street. Past the empty lot, slowing enough to glance through the gate, into the gathering gloom.

Then onward to the Rhythm & Wonder Music Shop.

It's closed, not surprisingly. But I had to try. I lean against the glass door, cup my hands around my eyes to peer into the interior.

The walls are lined with hanging instruments of various sorts. A drum set just inside the door catches the reflection of the streetlights.

Beyond, a thin line of light leaks out of a door slightly ajar, perhaps to a back office.

I knock on the glass until my knuckles ache.

A shadow wavers in the line of light behind the door. Definitely someone there.

I knock again.

The light widens. A silhouette appears framed by the light, followed by a muffled call.

"We're closed! Open at nine tomorrow."

"Gerry?" That's his name, right? It's been years. "It's Kelsey—from next door—the Book Emporium. I need to talk to you."

His face is in shadow, and he's not moving.

My chest tightens. I can't wait any longer for answers. "Please—it's important."

And then he's moving toward me. Grabbing a set of keys from somewhere behind a counter.

Thank you.

He unlocks the door, opens it only a few inches.

"What's going on? Some kind of problem? Is this about

that blasted hotel development?" He's shorter than I remember, and his dark hair is graying at the temples.

"No. Nothing about that."

"I'm suing those idiots, just so you know. You oughta do the same."

"Yeah. Maybe. I just need to show you something." I have the photo in my hand, but the streetlights aren't bright enough. "Can we go inside, in the light?"

He glances at the photo, frowning, then opens the door wider and flicks on the light. "This couldn't wait until the morning?"

"No. Sorry." I follow him into the shop, wait for him to turn, and hold out the photo. "Who is this with my—with Elizabeth?"

He takes the photo, holds it up to the light and squints, touches his chest and then the top of his head as though searching for reading glasses, but then shrugs. "It's my mom, obviously."

"Right. Do you—uh—have any recent photos of her?"

"Recent?"

"Yeah, like the last five or ten years, maybe?"

"What's this about?"

I bite my lip. "Elizabeth's had another stroke. She's not doing well. I found this photo in her room at the facility, and I know she was friends with your mom..." I've run out of explanation after hoping something reasonable would occur to me as I rambled. It hasn't.

Gerry shrugs and turns away. "Sorry about your grandmother."

That's it?

But no, he's walked to the left wall of the shop, where a collage of random dollar-store frames hangs between the guitars. Newspaper clippings, photographs.

I hurry to join him.

He points to an article with a headline about the music

shop being passed to the next generation. "This one's from about ten years ago, when she retired."

I step close, lean in to study the black-inked newsprint photo of Gerry and his mother, side-by-side, just like the picture of Gran and her in my hand, except decades later.

My heart rate revs up instantly.

I'm not crazy.

I've seen this woman, this older version of his mother, Beatrice, in the newspaper photo. And I've seen her very recently.

Playing the piano at a Garden Party. Like she's having the time of her life.

"She was a pianist, your mom?" I'm taking in that smile in the photo, the smile I've enjoyed. Envied.

"She played in a jazz band for a while, years ago. Not sure they were any good. She gave it up to run the shop. Smart." He shrugs. "Although she always seemed bitter about her choice."

"And where is she?" I whisper the words. "Where is she now?"

I fear the answer. Even though I haven't heard this news from Gran or anyone else, Bea must be gone, deceased, a ghost like all the others in the Garden, right?

"Now?" Gerry's voice carries confusion. He looks at his watch. "I don't know. Probably watching some BBC show or something."

I close my eyes and inhale a steadying breath.

I knew it. Somehow, the moment I saw the photo, I knew it.

Gran would have mentioned if Bea had died.

But she hasn't.

Which means two things:

One, I was not the only living person at the party.

And two, the party is not some kind of apparition that exists only for my benefit.

"Where does she live? I want to visit her. Can you give me her phone number?"

"I still don't get why this couldn't wait—"

"Can you just give me her contact info? Then I'll leave you alone."

He shakes his head. "Fine. Whatever." He crosses to a messy desk, fishes a scrap from the sea of paper, and scribbles something on it. "Here. Her number."

"Thank you. Sorry to bother you."

I escape without another word and have my phone out of my pocket before he's locked the door behind me.

One ring, two, three. I hold my breath.

And then, voicemail.

I pause just outside the iron gate in the brick wall, run through a half-dozen possible messages before the beep, but still fumble over my words. "Hi—Bea—this is Kelsey Willoughby, Elizabeth's, uh, daughter. From the Book Emporium. Um, I have something really urgent to talk over with you. I mean—not urgent like an emergency, but important. Really important. Um, can you give me a call back as soon as possible?"

I leave my number, hang up, and mentally replay the stupid message I've just left. She probably remembers me as a young teenager, and that message won't prove I've matured.

Will she call back right away? It's about seven o'clock now. How late do people her age return calls?

And now what? Derek, the evening nurse, would probably tell me to go to bed. But I'd toss for hours with all the thoughts rolling in my head right now.

I glance at the gate, debate only a moment, then retrieve the iron skeleton key from inside the shop, return to fit it into the lock, and slip inside.

There'll be no party, not this early, I know that. But for some reason, this empty lot seems the best place to process my thoughts.

I wander for a few minutes, trailing my hand over snarled weeds, yanking back when a thorn pricks my fingertip. The walls of my bookshop and Bea's music shop, bookends to the vacant space, are mildewed and pockmarked. The brick wall hiding me from Chestnut Street is in better condition, newer perhaps. And the back wall of the lot, which I've never thought much about, is invisible behind a mass of vines. On the other side of that back wall, beyond a narrow alley, the small art museum I've visited only a few times glows white under the sun setting from behind me, across Chestnut Street.

What wisdom does this empty lot still hold? Too bad my white marble bench under the magnolia is nowhere to be seen.

It amuses me to pick my way through the trash and weedy brush to reach the place where the bench ought to be.

In its place, the old washing machine of mysterious origins.

Should I? Why not?

With a shrug and an eyeroll at my own absurdity, I climb onto the machine and settle my low back between the knobs and dials, legs poking out straight. Beside me, a frond of unknown weediness dips near my head, its compound leaves quivering in the breeze.

Here I am, tucked between music and books on each side and art behind. Sitting on an abandoned washing machine.

How did Bea get in here? Has she been here more than once, like I have? She's always in that same man's suit and skinny tie, as if it's all been the same evening for her. But then, I'm always in my wisteria dress.

How did she get to that joy I witnessed when she played? Is she experiencing the same revolution of thought as I am—understanding the risk of rejection, accepting the hard work involved to be creative? Perhaps also facing the disappointment over the failure of her art and the insurmountable limitation of her abilities?

Last night, just before I fell asleep on the wooden bench, she made that comment about reserving the platform for the "real talent." She seemed to only half-believe me when I assured her she played well.

What was it she said?

Room for everyone, then, I guess.

Is this true?

I glance to my right, as if I will still see M. swing-dancing with Sam. She signed only a few books at the Chestnut Street Book Emporium. A local author, a signing no one remembers. Was she disappointed by the limited reach of her work? Did she feel as though her limitations—whether time or connections or even talent—disqualified her from pursuing her art?

And how do *I* feel about her? Do I feel she should have given up?

What about Van Gogh and all his lovely paintings, like the *Café Terrace at Night* he placed on the table at the Garden Party? Didn't he die in poverty, his work almost entirely unrecognized and unrewarded? Who's to say the response we see when others encounter our work is the only response it will ever receive?

The sun drops below the buildings across the street, and the temperature of the lot seems to plummet. A bird chirps, as though in greeting to the coming evening. I reach for the hanging branch at my side, strip the series of small leaves like flower petals into my palm, a shower of green teardrops.

Where I came from, whether my beginning was here or in an ancient desert by a river—this may be a riddle which will never have a solution. All that could have been is lost. And I can grieve the not-knowing. But there is one question I can answer—*must* answer.

Who am I now?

And I know this answer. I have known it, perhaps my whole life. Known it but been afraid to admit it, even to myself.

I am an Artist.

I am a Storyteller.

And it cannot matter if I am lauded or mocked, ignored or admired. If I play in a jazz band that was never very good or sign books at an event no one remembers.

In all my fighting—from Charles Diamond Blackburn to the tax office to the Taking—I've allowed Story *owner* to become my identity. Holding on to a shop full of stories, unwilling to write my own. The travel posters were always whispering, urging me to create portals to secret places for readers to step through.

One thing I've learned from my time in the Garden Party: even great artists are insecure.

For some reason, Selena Manning and her bestselling *The Starlight Folio* play across my thoughts.

Yes, probably even her.

The pettiness I've clung to over this stranger's success has been another signpost, pointing me to the importance of embracing who I truly am.

A strange wave of something so unlike the jealousy I've felt at each glance at the horrible cover, each mention of her name, washes over me.

I feel... *affection* for her. As though we are part of the same struggling community who must hold each other up, spur each other on, to keep going in the fight for beauty despite all the risks and all the disappointments. Even in the face of success, which can also be terrifying and crippling, I am sure. Perhaps she also had to risk and sacrifice and even acknowledge that her work is not what she imagined it could be.

I hold my hand aloft, release the petal-soft green leaves in a fluttering shower, watch them float to the ground.

Here in the messy jungle of this vacant lot, between the books and the music and the art, I am pulled into something bigger and greater—a whole community of creatives. And just as this vacant lot of trash has come alive, I recognize that creative people must labor to awaken people to Beauty, to transcendence, to something wholly *Other* than the material existence of the everyday, in which we are so often mired.

Yes, Selena and I have written similar stories. And yes, her story has been devoured by an enthusiastic public while mine has wasted away to nothing. But she is not my enemy, not my rival. Because in some way, we are the same, she and I.

In all the ways that matter, we are the same.

I shimmy forward on the washing machine and hop down to the ground.

Night is falling. The vacant lot is only a vacant lot.

And I have one more phone call to make.

FORTY-TWO

Once again I think my green and wonderful thoughts. Why grow roses? *Ask a dancer why she dances, though her feet be battered and bruised. Ask a painter why she paints, a writer why she writes. The answer is beauty. Not prettiness. Not loveliness. But a beauty so rich and real it is almost terrifying. This is beauty with a voice. This is beauty that beckons.*

~ from *Garden Maker* by Christie Purifoy

By the time Lisa arrives the next morning, thirty minutes late and a bit rumpled, I am deep into event-planning mode.

"I can't believe it," is Lisa's only comment when I tell her about phoning Robert last night and telling him I'll be attending the party he's putting together at the Book Emporium in one week.

I shrug, turn the sign on the door from *The End* to *Once Upon a Time*. "I realized I was being ridiculous. And the lawyer can handle arguing my case at the meeting."

It was much more than that, but opening up to Lisa about my epiphany feels too vulnerable. "Besides, it may be the last event we ever hold here."

Lisa makes a face at me and turns to finish re-stacking the NEW RELEASES table.

What will she do if—when—the Book Emporium's sign flips to *The End* for good? Will another employer tolerate her unreliable-yet-sincere work ethic?

A twinge of fear, for myself as well as Lisa, pings inside my chest. And sadness at the vision of this whole place crumpling under a wrecking ball, from its Beaux-Arts facade, which I'm still curious about, to the back wall of the former theater stage.

Perhaps it's foolish, deciding to attend the party instead of the meeting. But it feels like an important symbol. A declaration of my new identity. A decision to focus on saving myself rather than saving the shop.

I spend the rest of the morning at my desk, trading emails with Robert's administrative assistant about AnaMaria's catering services, how much available parking, where the expected queue of attendees will line up, space for banners, and every other detail that she pops into my inbox. It's a good distraction from waiting for phone calls—both from AdvantaCare and from Beatrice.

When my phone finally does ring, it's an unknown number, so not AdvantaCare.

"Is this Kelsey?"

I recognize her voice. Scratchy like a former smoker, no-nonsense like the woman at the Garden Party.

"Yes. Bea?"

"Hey. It's been a long time."

"Yes. It has."

"Gerry said you stopped by the shop. Says you grew up normal, which is saying something, with that crazy lady taking you in."

She's laughing, and I half-remember she and Gran always had this kind of playfully contentious relationship.

She coughs, away from the phone, then returns. "Wasn't sure that was a great idea, I gotta admit. But you know her. Once she saw what had happened, she couldn't say no."

Something like a *thunk* occurs in my chest.

"What had happened?"

There's a beat of silence. Then a nervous laugh.

"So, yeah, I was surprised to get your phone message last night. What's up?"

I blow the air from my lungs and slump in my desk chair. What is up? Where to possibly start?

"I—I think we've run into each other recently."

"Oh? It's been so long, I'm not sure I'd recognize you."

"Yeah, I didn't recognize you either, at the time. But then I found an old photo of you and Gran and realized..."

This was going nowhere, or at least not the right direction.

"Do you remember the empty lot? Between the Book Emporium and Rhythm & Wonder?"

"Sure. Was always quite a mess in there, if I recall. I was always trying to get Liza to clean it up."

Lisa? Was Lisa working here, back then? But no, Bea said *Liza*—I'd forgotten that's what some people called Elizabeth, years ago.

The name distracted me. Did Bea sound suspicious of my question? Did she sense I'd been in the Garden?

"Have you ever been in there? In the vacant lot?"

"Well, yeah. I just said it was a mess, remember?"

"Right." I push away from my desk, stand, try to pace in my cramped office.

"But, I mean, have you been in there... at night? Seen anything... strange?"

"What, like drugs? People shooting up or something? No, can't say I have. But still seems like a bad idea to go in there at night."

Could I be wrong about meeting her? She doesn't sound guarded or suspicious or evasive at all. But I have to be certain.

"No, not drugs. I mean, have you ever been to a party—a fancy party—inside there?"

"Ha!" Her burst of sarcastic laughter is loud in my ear. "Good for her if the old lady's finally done something with that space. But no, if there's been a party, she didn't bother to invite me."

I sink into my chair again, head braced against my hand. I must have been wrong. The resemblance is uncanny, but she hasn't been in the Garden. And she's nothing like the exuberant woman pounding out tunes on the piano.

But Gerry said she did play in a jazz band…

I shake my head, inhale against the cluttered thoughts.

"Well, we're having a party here at the bookshop next Friday night, if you'd like to come. It's a publicity event for a new bestseller, *The Starlight Folio*."

"That clunker? I tried to read it, couldn't get past the first chapter."

I laugh, despite my disappointment. A week ago, I would have felt a little surge of vindictive pleasure at her bad review. Instead, I was able to tell Robert to invite the author, Selena Manning, if she was willing to go public.

"Well, if you'd like to come, just to see the old place, or whatever, we'd be glad to have you."

"Ok. Take care."

We disconnect, and I set the phone carefully beside my laptop.

There is something more there. Some kind of information about my adoption. What will it take to get it out of her?

The urge to visit Gran is overwhelming, but my early-morning call to AdvantaCare assured me nothing had changed, and they would reach out immediately if it did. I can't stay with her 24/7, and with only seven days until both the Starlight Party, as Robert has taken to calling it, and the hearing over the Taking, I have a million details and nearly that many meetings to deal with.

The week seems to fly when I'm at my desk taking care of tasks and drag when I'm sitting at Gran's bedside. As the nurse Derek promised, the changes to her conscious state happen gradually, giving us all hope that she'll eventually regain alertness.

"I wish you could be there for the party, Gran," I tell her on Thursday night. Only a few to-do items remain on my list, and I'm spending a quiet evening at AdvantaCare.

Her left hand flutters, as it often does at the sound of my voice. No movement from the right side of her body, but that's not surprising, they tell me.

"Robert Dumas—you remember him, right?—says he has some kind of big announcement to make to the public. I don't think she's coming—the author—because she's some kind of recluse or something, but apparently he's going to reveal something about her that nobody knows." I smile, willing my words to penetrate the fog in her mind. "Sounds like your kind of thing, right? A mystery revealed, right in your shop."

Another tremble of the fingers.

I wrap my own hand around hers. "Don't worry, I'll fill you in on all the juicy details."

By six o'clock the next evening, I'm waiting by the front door for Robert to arrive. Everything is in place, including a plethora of "Everything 25% Off" signs we've hung, a head start on the possibility we'll need to liquidate inventory quickly.

The party doesn't start until seven, and Lisa and I have closed the shop at five to make final preparations. Already, a line has begun forming outside the door, many with their hardback books in hand, as though expecting to get them signed.

"I told you this would be good for business." Lisa jabs a thumb toward the line outside the door.

"Yeah, well, we'll see. So far, they're only traipsing in here with books they bought somewhere else."

"Hmph." Lisa shrugs. "At least they know where we are."

Neither of us mention the elephant in the shop—the fact that after tonight's hearing, book sales might not matter.

I scan the Book Emporium, checking and double-checking. The central tables in the main section have been relocated to a storage room for tonight. Now a huge counter claims the central part of the room, stacked with a zillion copies of the newly minted paperback version of *The Starlight Folio*.

At the back of the shop, up the short flight of steps to what was formerly the theater's stage, AnaMaria has set up tables of simple refreshments—spirals of sliced turkey wraps on beds of lettuce and shortbread cookies sprinkled with blue sugar to match the book cover. Robert wasn't shelling out big money for anything fancy, given that the event is free and open to the public, but the business is good for AnaMaria nonetheless, and it was nice of him to let me choose the caterer.

Robert arrives, along with Saanvi and Olivia from my Creative Writers group, whom I've hired for the evening to help at the register.

Yeah, high hopes for good sales. But we'll see.

The two girls are all giggles and excitement over being able to help run the splashy event.

Robert looks sharp in a peacock blue suit and white shirt, unbuttoned at the collar. He eyes the table, the banner, the refreshments at the back. "Everything looks wonderful, Kelsey. I hope it's a huge success for you."

"And for you. Can't wait to hear your big announcement." I glance at the door. "I was wondering if maybe the author herself was your surprise."

He smiles and winks. "Hmm, something like that. But you'll have to wait with everyone else."

And *everyone else* turns out to be quite a lot of people.

When Lisa opens the door at seven, the line streaming in from the street seems unending.

The shop fills with guests—hopefully customers—some alone, some with a companion, and even a few clusters of what I learn are monthly bookclubs who've read *The Starlight Folio* as a group.

I lean against the rail of the stage at the back of the shop, above the heads of the milling crowd perusing tables and shelves, and smile.

In some ways, it's like the Garden Party. Which makes me happy.

Even Charles Dickens is safely back, looming over the BRITISH LITERATURE section from his framed and matted print.

If only Gran could see this. It's also like the old days, perhaps, when big-name authors came here to sign. It's a celebration of books, of writing, of the stories that capture our imaginations and open up new worlds.

I am part of this celebration tonight. I have moved past my petty envy of Selena Manning, who has beaten the odds to gain recognition for her work. But even more importantly, I have begun to step into my own role as a creative artist.

The front door continues to admit new arrivals. We've removed the bell for tonight, knowing it would drive us crazy, although the hum of excited conversation in the shop might have drowned it out.

The latest customer to enter is a big guy, both tall and wide-shouldered, and a little twinge of something like nostalgia hits me, for my conversations with Sam the Sculptor.

The man pauses just inside the door, scanning the shop. He looks at Lisa and Saanvi, both behind the counter, and then seems to lean a little, as if trying to see past the half-closed door, into my office.

Something about the way he moves—I narrow my eyes, trying to get a better look at him from this distance.

The door opens behind him. He turns, then steps aside to allow the next person to enter.

Austin.

I glance at my watch. Austin offered to arrive early to help with any last-minute items. So much for that.

I hurry down the steps and into the crowd, weaving my way toward the front. He's no doubt waiting for me there, assuming I'll be watching for him.

A few steps from the front door, I push past the final group of chattering bookclub members and emerge into the clearing to greet Austin.

And stop with a shock that sends heat blazing against my face.

The man standing beside Austin does more than *remind* me of someone else.

"Sam?" I manage to close my slack jaw with a shake of my head. "What—what are you—Sam?"

He grins. Then laughs. "Hey, K. Good to see you again."

FORTY-THREE

Before him stood the Tree, his Tree, finished. If you could say that of a Tree that was alive, its leaves opening, its branches growing and bending in the wind that Niggle had so often felt or guessed, and had so often failed to catch. He gazed at the Tree, and slowly he lifted his arms and opened them wide.
"It's a gift!" he said. He was referring to his art, and also to the result; but he was using the word quite literally.

~ from *Leaf by Niggle* by J.R.R. Tolkien

In the wake of Sam's greeting and obvious recognition of me from the Garden Party, the general hum of conversation in the bookshop fades to fuzzy background noise.

I stand, mouth agape, with no words.

Beside Sam, Austin looks back and forth between the two of us.

"Sorry I'm a little late, Kelsey. I was caught up at work—"

"What? Oh, Austin. Hi, yeah, no problem." I'm still staring at Sam.

Austin turns to him, thrusts out a hand. "Hey, I'm Austin."

Sam is still smiling over me, and it takes him a beat to even notice Austin's introduction.

"Samuel De Luca. Nice to meet you."

Samuel.

Austin squares off in front of Sam. "And you know Kelsey… how?"

He laughs. "Long story. But you should ask Kelsey." He leans on the last word, his first use of my real name. "She's the storyteller."

A glow begins in my chest and makes its way to a warm smile.

"Oh, I know, believe me."

My eyes cut to Austin and his sarcastic response.

Sam glances at him too, frowning.

It's clear Austin believes my "storytelling" the most ridiculous thing about me.

In the silence, Austin looks between us, as if realizing his mistake, and shrugs. "Sorry."

I can't think about Austin's opinion, not with a party to host and an imaginary sculptor come to life in my shop.

I have a thousand questions for Sam. But not in front of Austin.

"I think I'll wander around your shop for a bit," Sam says. He acknowledges Austin with a head nod, and me with a long look that says more than words.

I swallow against the flutter in my chest. "I'll find you later. Soon."

He moves past me, but clasps his hand around my forearm, just for an instant, as he passes.

I watch him slip through the crowd, graceful despite his size.

Austin is standing at my side. "That guy looks like he could play for the NFL."

"He's a sculptor."

Austin laughs. "Seriously? Wouldn't have taken him for the artsy type."

I'm watching as Sam picks up one of the new paperbacks on the counter and flips it to read the back cover.

"How about me?"

Austin turns to me. "Huh?"

"Me. Would you take me for the artsy type?"

"Sure. You did that tree and everything." He points to my Hobbit papier-mâché. "And I keep telling you, you have talent—"

"I want to write books."

"So then, write books. Everybody needs a hobby."

He's not wrong. Hobbies are good. And there's no shame in having a "day job" while writing books or making any sort of art, is there?

So why does his comment rankle me?

Because he doesn't understand you.

The answer paints itself against the canvas of my thoughts, suddenly so obvious I don't understand why I haven't already seen it.

And because you've met someone who does.

Yes.

Someone who is… real. And alive. Now.

"Austin, do you want to be here?"

He frowns. "You mean, at this party? I apologized for being late—"

"No, it's not about being late. I mean, truly, do you *want* to be here? Tell me, honestly."

He sighs and looks across the shop. "You know books aren't really my thing, Kelsey. But I want to support you."

I smile and take his hand. "That's very kind, Austin. And I appreciate it, I really do. But I don't think we're… going the same direction, you know? We don't care enough about the same things. Have the same interests—"

He pulls his hand out of mine. "Are you breaking up with me?"

I bite my lip, second-guessing myself. The timing is bad, seems ill-advised, given all that's going on in my life. You're never supposed to make life-altering decisions in the middle of a crisis, right?

I glance at Sam, who has ascended to the stage at the back of the shop and somehow already struck up a conversation with AnaMaria.

She laughs at something he's said, head tilted backward.

"Yes." I bring my attention back to Austin. "Yes, I am. I'm so sorry. I just don't think this is going to work out."

His jaw shifts, lips tensed, and he follows my previous glance, back to Sam. "Yeah. I think I get it."

"No, it's not—"

I stop myself. Because it is. At least in part.

"Good luck with everything, Kelsey."

He's saying the polite words, though his face is saying something else. "I'll see you around, I guess."

By which we both know we're unlikely to ever see each other again.

I pull him toward me for a quick hug. "Take care of yourself, Austin."

His shoulders are tense. He pulls away, nods, and escapes through the front door, where the descending sun across Chestnut Street lights up his blond hair for a moment. And then he's gone, up the street toward the future White Orchard Hotel.

I don't hesitate, though the crowd doesn't part itself for me the way it did for Sam. I have to jostle through people to reach the back section and hurry up the steps.

Sam sees me coming, pulls away from his conversation with AnaMaria and faces me fully.

Behind him, AnaMaria's lips quirk into a knowing smile and her eyebrows twitch upward.

I'm moving toward him, faster than appropriate, and only

realize at the last moment it's because I'm wrapping my arms around his neck.

He pauses for only a fraction, then returns the embrace, burying his face against my hair.

"Kelsey."

I pull away, a flush crawling up my neck and into my face.

Sam hasn't let go. "Where can we talk? Or maybe—this isn't a good time, obviously—"

"No! This can't wait." I scan the room, still busy with book-shopping and mingling, every corner and cranny taken up with customers.

Robert has his big announcement to make, but he's told me it won't be until eight o'clock.

"This way." I grab his hand, pull him toward the metal exit door to the left of the stage area. For fire-code reasons, the door's kept unlocked whenever the shop is open.

I push against the bar, slip out into the narrow alley behind the shop, then keep going, to the fire escape steps, which hover about two feet above my head.

"Can you pull them down?"

Sam uses one hand to slide the steps downward and then follows behind as I ascend.

A moment later, we're on the roof, crossing to the east side, in unspoken agreement, to overlook the empty lot.

It's nearly sunset, the time-between-times, but we see only weeds.

I grip the wall with my hands and take a deep breath. Where to start?

"You can't see it from here. It's always like this. Just weeds."

"I know." He inclines his head to the right. "I've seen it from there. From that rooftop."

On our right, the Central Art Museum's white stone shines.

"The museum?"

He nods. "I work there."

"How is this possible, Sam? I don't understand any of it. And how did you know where to find me?"

He leans his forearms on the wall, his attention on the greenery beneath us. "I found you months ago, actually."

I say nothing. The need for explanation is obvious. It's been less than three weeks since I first entered the Garden Party.

"On my afternoon break almost three months ago, I wandered into the Book Emporium looking for something new to read. And there you were, talking and laughing with some teenagers next to that amazing Hobbit tree. I nearly fell over."

"Why didn't you say anything?"

He pushes away from the wall and laughs, deep and full. "I did. After I got past the shock that you were a real person, I said, 'Hey.' I was expecting you to be as surprised as I was."

I shake my head. "I didn't recognize you?"

"You said, 'Can I help you find something?' So polite it knocked the wind out of me."

"I don't—it makes no sense." I'm gripping the wall, fighting against this puzzle with no pieces that fit.

"Yeah, I've been trying to work it out since you saw me at the door tonight. Back then, I assumed you must be some kind of double of the woman I met in the Garden, or maybe you had no memory of it after you left, even though I remembered everything. I kept coming back, every few weeks, wandering the store until I knew you'd seen me but still didn't know me. But then, tonight…"

"The last time I saw you there, in the Garden, was just over a week ago, when they took you away, to… go deeper."

"And for me, that happened six months ago."

We're both silent, staring down over the darkening vacant lot, absorbing this impossible thing.

"Time works differently there." I state the obvious. But it must explain the asynchronous experience we've had of each other.

"Yes."

"Beatrice." The awkward phone call with the former Rhythm & Wonder Music Shop owner.

"I don't know who that is."

"You do, I think. The jazz pianist we spoke with in the Garden. 'B,' she called herself."

"She's from… *now*… as well?"

I point across the lot, to the brick wall opposite us. "She owned the music store, right there."

"Wow. Have you talked to her since you met her down there?" He nods toward the jungle below.

"Yes. She didn't know what I was talking about. But maybe—"

"Maybe it's the same as when I first saw you. It hasn't happened for her. Not yet."

"What does it all mean? Why… and how? I keep trying to figure it out."

He laughs. "I've had six months to try and still have no answers."

"You haven't been back?"

"No. After that night when you last saw me… Well, let's just say there was a bit of trauma."

I reach for the back of my neck, still hearing the hum of a blade slicing the ancient Egyptian air. "Yeah, I get that."

He nods. "I wondered—later. When I came back myself, I remembered finding you on the ground, at the edge of the Garden. You'd just returned from going deeper?"

"Barely. And I'm still trying to figure out what any of it meant, what it was *for*, you know? The whole thing seems rather pointless."

"Failure." The word emerges from him, deep and fraught with sadness.

"Yes, it was that for me, too. Is that what we were meant to learn? That sometimes, all of our creative efforts simply fail?"

Sam turns my direction, reaches tentative hands toward me, touches my arms.

I step closer.

He clasps his hands behind my back, comfortable and familiar. "I want to hear everything that happened."

I nod. "And your story, as well. Later." My gaze drifts over the empty lot. "Do you think we'll ever go back?"

"I don't know. Since that night, I have felt like my time there was finished, somehow. As though everything that was supposed to happen had taken place."

"I feel the same way. I keep thinking about something Bea said to me."

He unclasps his hands from behind my back, but slides them down to hold my hands, waiting.

"She was talking about her own level of talent, not being up to the same standard as the musicians there in the Garden, but she said there was room for everyone."

"Hmm."

"I've always felt like I needed to be some kind of prodigy or something, the literary genius of my generation, for it to be legitimate for me to spend time writing the books I want to write."

"And now?"

"And now it occurs to me that *most* people only get to pursue their creative expression as a hobby. It's the rare ones whose work allows them to make a living, or almost a living."

"I've been down that road as well." Sam inclines his head toward the museum. "I work amidst all that talent every day and hadn't realized how resentful I'd become that my own work wasn't recognized. I thought it would make me a sellout to create pieces that sold for a pittance."

The breeze picks up, the sun inches lower, and we turn to lean over the wall together. I cross my arms against the brisk air. "I met a guy once, a woodworker, at a county fair. He told me he considered himself lucky to be able to carve his pieces every day and sell them to people who put them on their fireplace mantels and front porches. I realize now that even though his stuff will never be displayed at the Met Museum—and perhaps he longs for that recognition—he can and *should* be proud to turn out his pieces for people who enjoy looking at them on their mantels."

Sam runs a hand through his hair and sighs. "Last night I ate at El Tío Sombrero, and there was a man with a guitar strolling around, playing for all these couples on dates and families with young children while they ate their burritos and their chips and salsa. I'm guessing he'll never play Carnegie Hall."

"Right!" I'm nodding now, feeling my thoughts come together. "Perhaps he longs for that. But the limit of his talent, the limit of his life circumstances, will mean it never happens. But that's okay."

"So, how are we supposed to live with that disappointment? How do we continue to take joy in the work, knowing it does not, and likely will never, receive the reception we long for?" Sam's hands tighten to fists on top of the wall. "I know I could do the work necessary to make a living, but it might mean working faster, with less quality than I'm able, or at least to avoid obsessing over unattainable perfection. How do I do that without feeling like a sellout or a hack?"

"I don't know. Perhaps you don't. Although, I'm guessing there is always a gap between what the artist desires to create and the thing created. We have to decide if we can keep going. If we can take the risks and then make peace with the results somehow, stop living tortured and disappointed, full of regret or even bitterness if we haven't been hailed as geniuses. And still, always, *create.*"

Sam's fists flatten, and he breathes deeply, his eyes straying to the museum.

I check my watch, only a few minutes until Robert's announcement. I should get back down there.

"I do know one thing, though, Sam."

He leans an elbow against the wall and focuses on me.

"The world needs more beauty than the Met and Carnegie Hall can provide—much, much more. It needs beauty and creativity on every fireplace mantel, over every basket of chips and salsa. And the largely unsung heroes who provide those things are heroes indeed."

He smiles. "That's beautiful, Kelsey. You should be a writer."

I grin and punch him on the arm.

He responds by scooping me toward him, one hand behind my head, and pulling me into a kiss passionate enough to spirit away my breath and leave me wobbly on my feet.

I close my eyes and lean into the kiss, my first assurance that the connection born in the Garden might extend to the here, the now.

The wind rises, blowing my hair around his head, wrapping us in our own world, and the warmth between us is enough to ward off the chill.

A sharp "hey!" bounces across the rooftop.

Lisa's at the door that leads down to my apartment. "What are you doing up here?" She rolls her eyes. "As if I can't see for myself. Robert's ready to start, and he says you're not going to want to miss this."

FORTY-FOUR

It is the function of all art to give us some perception of an order in life, by imposing an order upon it.

~ T.S. Eliot

Sam and I cross the rooftop and follow Lisa down the steps into my apartment.

Sam's quick glance into the dusky gloom of my living space is casual.

Thankfully, the place isn't a mess.

We take the second set of steps down to the landing just inside the front door.

Lisa grabs my arm before I move toward the crowd. "Hey, that lady from next door was in here a few minutes ago."

"Next door?"

"Yeah, the music shop—the mom who used to own it, before Gerry the Jerk?"

"Bea?"

"Yeah, she was asking all kinds of questions about the

empty lot next door. Seemed like she lost something in there, I don't know. I gave her the key and told her she could go in if she wanted. Hope that was okay. It was almost sunset, so I didn't think she should wait for you."

I glance at Sam, and he's already laughing.

Outside the shop's front windows, the last of the sun's rays disappears behind the shops across the street, leaving Chestnut Street in its moment of magical twilight.

"Yes, that's fine, Lisa. Thanks."

We push a little farther into the shop, joining the crowd.

Robert has already taken the stage near the back of the bookshop. His commanding presence at the rail sends quieting ripples through the space, turning heads toward him.

Sam and I stay behind most of the customers. His solid presence at my back is like an anchor.

Robert's looking across the sea of heads, searching for someone.

I raise my hand in a quick acknowledgment.

He makes eye contact, smiles, and returns his attention to the group at large.

"Good evening, folks. So glad to have you all here to celebrate with us. I'm Robert Dumas, Editorial Director at Sparrow Books, publishers of the book we're here to talk about tonight."

A few cheers and hoots circle the crowd, followed by a general buzz of laughter.

"As you know, we're celebrating fifty thousand copies sold of *The Starlight Folio,* as well as the release of the paperback version. I hope you're all planning to get your paperback copies. They make a great gift!"

His smiling suggestion is met with more laughter.

I'm loving the atmosphere here tonight. To have the bookshop packed out with people, everyone in a party mood, is like a dream.

Why did I hesitate to say *yes* to this event? My jealousy of the author was ill-founded. I can celebrate a good story, no matter the source. Adding stories to the world is not a zero-sum game. Her success does not equal my failure. Maybe I'll even read the book.

"We are here to celebrate," Robert says, "but not to celebrate a book, *per se*. We are here to celebrate the power of Story. The power of words." He chuckles. "Words are losing their magic these days, are they not? Pull down an airplane tray table and find an advertisement. Close a toilet stall and find words on the back of the door."

The crowd laughs with him.

"Words everywhere, shouting, posturing, bragging, crying for our attention and affirmation. In this crazy, noisy world, words are losing their punch. But the stories we love—these stories reclaim that power."

A smattering of applause through the room, though I imagine this is much more philosophy than they'd expected.

"But I promised a big announcement tonight, didn't I?"

More hoots. Someone yells, "Bring her out!" Everyone laughs.

Robert holds up a hand. "I'm afraid that's not the surprise. Selena Manning is not here with us tonight."

The crowd collectively moans, though there are still smiles all around.

"When's the sequel coming out, then?" Yelled from somewhere in the shop.

Robert shakes his head. "Let's not get ahead of ourselves. Or perhaps you'd all like to just keep guessing..."

More laughter, but then they quiet down.

"As you probably know, Selena Manning has not consented to any interviews, either on-screen or written. There has been much speculation flying around the literary world as to the reason. Is Manning a pen name for an already-famous author writing in a new genre? Is she simply guarding her privacy, not wanting to be recognized and hounded in public? I've even heard the one where she's not a real person at all—only some computer-generated artificial intelligence machine that spit out this novel in less than ninety seconds!"

Sam leans down to whisper. "If that thing was written by A.I., then you're done for."

I make a face at him and whisper back. "Yeah, well, ever heard of 3D printing, Mr. Sculptor?"

The buzz of amusement settles around us.

Robert is milking this announcement for all it's worth, holding out the suspense like he's a storyteller himself.

"Alright, alright." He laughs as though he's finally acquiescing to the crowd's pressure, as though he hasn't promised this big reveal.

"Here's the truth: Although Sparrow Books brought this amazing novel to the public six months ago, sparking a phenomenon and raising many questions about the author… not even Sparrow Books knows who the author is!"

Wow. This woman really is reclusive. Does she have some kind of special deal with Sparrow Books? If so, it seems like Robert might be about to reveal her secret identity.

He waves one of the paperbacks above his head. "Yes, Selena Manning is a pen name—and apologies to all the real-life Selena Mannings out there now getting hounded by an eager fan base—but it's a pen name Sparrow Books invented." He opens the book to the beginning and holds up a hand again to silence the murmurs. "This is the manuscript that came across my desk many months ago."

He begins to read from the first chapter, I assume.

The crowd quiets like a pack of kindergartners in a reading circle.

The words are… wait, *what the...?*

My jaw drops, my heart speeds, then slows. The blood in my veins catches fire.

This book is more than *similar* to the story I wrote.

This. Is. My. Story.

"What is it?" Sam's holding my shoulders, turning me toward him. "What's wrong?"

I look down. My fingers have wrapped around his arm, white knuckles glowing.

I shake my head, quick and tense, and release my grip.

Robert is still reading. Every word familiar.

Well, not every word—the main character's name is different. And the name of the bookshop where it's set... also different.

As if someone found my manuscript and plagiarized nearly the entire thing, altering only a few tiny details, as if that would keep her—or him?—from getting caught.

Robert winds down his reading of the initial passage.

A smattering of applause rolls through the audience, but they're clearly waiting for more explanation.

As am I.

Robert smiles over everyone. "Of course, just like all of you, I was immediately hooked. Spent the next couple of hours continuing to read. Knowing I wanted to publish this manuscript. There was only one problem."

He lets it hang, unfinished.

The breath in my lungs turns solid.

"It was unsigned. No author name, no return address. Just a manuscript." He bends to the floor, retrieving a piece of paper from somewhere I can't see. "All we had was this single cover sheet." He waves the page, then holds it aloft to read it to the crowd. "Bobby," he pauses for a look at the crowd. "That's me."

Polite laughter.

"Bobby, I thought you'd love this story and wanted you to have first crack at publishing it."

The crowd murmurs their confusion.

"No signature," Robert repeats. "No return address. To this day, we have no idea who the author is."

"How can you publish something without the author's consent?" someone yells out.

Robert laughs. "Oh, believe me, we had a whole team of legal counsel on this one. We're covered, I assure you. All royalties are in a trust, waiting for the author to reveal herself. Or himself. We really don't know."

A few hands pop up around the shop.

On the far right, under the wall of murals, a teenage girl jumps up, waving enthusiastically. "It's me! I wrote it!"

The absurdity brings laughter, but then it feels like the entire bookshop is waving and calling out.

"No, I wrote it!"

"No, it was me!"

"I'll take those royalties now!"

But I am silent. Feet rooted to the floor, thoughts moving like sludge.

How can this be?

Robert lets the jokes play out before he regains their attention.

"It won't be as easy as that, my friends. Like any good fairy tale, there's a glass slipper that only our fair author can fit. A slipper that no one knows about, except for me."

Sam wraps an arm around my shoulder.

"Kelsey, you're shaking. Are you sick?"

"I—it's—" I stare up into Sam's face. My lips are numb.

"Until we know whom this glass slipper belongs to—" Robert is saying.

I stumble forward, out of Sam's grasp. "Me."

The word croaks out, loud enough for only half-dozen people nearby to hear it.

But they turn as one, and stare.

I lift my chin, suck in a breath. Make eye contact with Robert Dumas.

"Me." Louder this time.

The whole room turns, as though they sense this is not a joke.

"The glass slipper belongs to me, Mr. Dumas. I wrote that book."

Robert squints, head tilted. "Kelsey?"

I take a hesitant step forward, then another.

The crowd parts for me.

I make it halfway before Robert holds up a hand, smiling at the crowd. "This is Kelsey Willoughby, folks. She owns this wonderful Chestnut Street Book Emporium. The first time I visited this shop after reading *The Starlight Folio*, I knew we had to hold this celebration here—

"Audrey Foster."

I call out the name from my place in the center of the main floor, where the NEW RELEASES table has always stood.

Robert's explanation of my lunacy cuts off. His lips part. He studies me as though seeing me for the first time.

"The main character of the book. When I wrote it, her name was Audrey Foster. And the bookshop was The Book Cellar. The title, too—you changed that. It was *House of Dreams*."

A snicker to my right.

"Yeah," I look that direction. "I guess *The Starlight Folio* is better."

It feels as though someone has pressed MUTE on the entire bookshop. The buzz of a halogen light is the only sound that denies we haven't all fallen into a vacuum.

"Kelsey, I don't understand—"

A vibration against my thigh.

My phone's on *Do Not Disturb* for the evening, and only a few numbers can break through.

I pull the phone from my pocket, glance at the display, then lift it with a shaky hand to my ear.

"Yes?"

"Kelsey? It's Jenny at AdvantaCare. Elizabeth's awake. She's asking for you."

FORTY-FIVE

Can you imagine being royalty but being treated like a servant? Can you imagine being the daughter of the true king but being held in low regard and never setting foot in your home country for as long as you live? Can you imagine being destined to reign yet never even hearing your true name?
Of course you can.

~ from *Becoming Myself* by Stasi Eldredge

Lisa assures me that she, Saanvi, and Olivia can handle the line at the register, as customers check out with their paperbacks and armfuls of other books they've found.

Sam insists on driving, which seems like it should be odd but instead feels simply *right*.

And also somewhat bizarre, in the backseat of Sam's Fiat sits Robert Dumas, murmuring words like *astounding* and *unbelievable*.

"It makes total sense now," he's saying, handing a sheet of

paper forward to me. "The way the Book Emporium reminded me so much of the shop in *The Starlight Folio*."

I glance at the scrawled writing, grown cramped and tight as her hands became more arthritic, but still legible. And recognizable.

Bobby, I thought you'd love this story and wanted you to have first crack at publishing it.

Gran sent Robert Dumas my manuscript.

My frantic, fruitless search through my apartment, through the drawer of the half-moon table with the display of pen-and-journal sets in the shop. No wonder I couldn't find it.

"But why didn't she sign it?" I hand the sheet back to Robert. "Why did she never tell me that she sent it to you?"

He shakes his head, sharing my bewilderment. "Has she—has her mind been—"

"Yes. Yes, there's been a decline. So maybe she forgot."

Sam accelerates onto the bypass that will take us to AdvantaCare. "Maybe she didn't want you to be disappointed if they didn't want to publish it."

I suck in a deep breath. "She knew I was really… sensitive… about criticism. So, yeah. That's probably true."

"Kelsey, I have to warn you, there are some legal hoops we'll need to jump through to get all this squared away…"

I wave a hand. "I don't care. Right now, I just need to get to Gran."

"Of course, I'm sorry. And I'm so glad to hear that Elizabeth has improved."

My thoughts seem to hang suspended as we speed toward AdvantaCare. The revelation is too much to take in, a thing too impossible, even at the end of what has become a month of impossible things.

"May I see… the book?"

Robert hands it over the seat.

My hands shake as I flip it open to a random chapter, a

snippet of a scene, and begin reading. Then another, and another.

Unable to take in more, I snap the book closed and return it to Robert.

"Well?" Sam glances at me, then back at the road.

"Yes. It's mine."

When we finally reach AdvantaCare, sign in and get buzzed through the door, Sam and Robert hold back outside Gran's room.

I nod in gratitude and slip into 7B, still bright under fluorescents even though the sky outside is nearly dark.

Gran turns her head slightly at the sound of my arrival.

Her smile is clear, though weak, and her lips pull upward on the left but droop down on the right.

She lifts her left arm off the bed slightly, then drops it.

"Gran." I'm at her side, clasping her fingers in mine. "Are you cold? You feel cold." I pull the blanket at her feet up to her middle.

"Kelsey."

"I'm here, Gran. It's so good to see you awake. To see that smile."

She tries again, though it's still only half a smile.

But I'll take it.

I drag a chair closer, sit with her hand in mine.

Her eyelids flicker and close, but if she's asleep, it lasts only a few moments. Then she's looking at me again, head turned my direction.

I want to sit with her, tell her all the things I've wanted to say, before it's too late. But Robert and Sam are waiting outside the room, and I want to get that out of the way.

"Gran, there's someone else here to see you. It's—it's a little strange—do you remember Robert Dumas?"

It's absurd, asking her to remember a decades-old friendship when she's just awakened from a stroke-induced coma.

But she nods and tries to speak. Swallows and tries again.

The words slur against the left side of her mouth. "He and Melinda just had a little baby. A girl."

Robert must be in his late sixties, so I'm guessing her mind has jumped backward a few years.

"He's outside, come to visit you. He wants to ask you a question."

"Okay." The word is so accepting, so childlike, it brings tears to my eyes.

"I'll be right back."

I bring Robert into the room and wave Sam in, as well.

I want him to meet Gran. There is an inevitability about Sam and me, I think. An assurance that he is going to be important in my life, and they need to be introduced.

But Robert's at her bedside, taking up her hand.

"Elizabeth, my dear, it's been a long time."

"Has it?" She looks between Robert and me. "I don't know."

Robert glances at me. "Perhaps now is not a good time—"

"No, it's okay. I—I don't know how long—"

His forehead creases, but he returns his attention to her, then pulls the cover letter from his attaché. "Elizabeth, do you recognize this letter?"

Her eyes wander over the sheet, barely focusing.

"She's not wearing her glasses." I step forward, suddenly guilt-ridden. "You're right, this is crazy timing."

"Did you publish it?" Gran's looking at Robert, not the paper.

He returns the sheet to his case. "Publish what, Elizabeth?"

Her eyes wander, searching and finding me. "Kelsey's story. About the bookshop. She says it won't be published, but I knew you would like it. That's why I sent it to you first."

There is a collective exhale around the room.

Robert pats Gran's arm. "We published it, my dear. We did. And everyone loved it."

Sam's hand finds my shoulder, a warm and gentle pressure that says more than words.

"That's good, Bobby. And you'll pay her? For her story?"

Robert laughs. "Oh yes. We will pay her."

Gran's hand floats above the bed, fingers searching the air.

I squeeze past Robert and take her hand in mine again.

"Kelsey?"

"Yes, Gran?" Her face blurs on the other side of my tears.

"You be careful with the money."

I laugh. "I promise."

"You can help her. But not too much."

I glance at Robert, then Sam. "Help who, Gran?"

She frowns, the good side of her mouth matching the downward tilt of the stroke-affected side. "Lisa, of course." The words sound frustrated, as if I'm not understanding.

I sigh, try to smile. Even now, with all that's happened, she's still trying to find a way to help this woman who has never done anything to deserve it.

"Okay. I'll help her."

"Not too much."

"No, not too much."

She leans her head back against the pillow and closes her eyes. "Good. She was just a little girl. Much too young."

There is nothing to be said in answer to this. Lisa wasn't what I would call "a girl" when she came to work at the Book Emporium. But then, I guess Gran did know her years ago, before Lisa's mother—Gran's closest friend—passed away.

"You need to rest now, Gran. No more talking, okay?"

Sam and Robert have disappeared again, but I sense another presence behind me.

"Good to see her awake, isn't it?" Gran's doctor is smiling her thin-lipped smile.

I stand. "So, how is she? What does this mean?"

The doctor keeps her voice low, standing so Gran cannot see her. "We knew this was a good possibility, as she's been slowly gaining alertness these past few days. But there's been damage, as you can see. And she's not strong."

I take a deep breath. "How long? Just tell me."

A sympathetic head-tilt. "I'd say we're talking about weeks, not months."

Weeks.

"Okay. Thanks."

She checks over Gran's monitors, exchanges a few words with her, then turns to go.

"You don't need to worry about exhausting her. She'll sleep when she needs to. Stay as long as you like."

When she's gone, Gran's reaching for my hand again. "Don't be mad at her."

"Who? The doctor? I'm not mad. She's fine."

Gran's head rocks against her pillow. "Lisa. Not mad at Lisa."

It's like she's fixated on Lisa. I push down the annoyance that Gran can't seem to focus on herself. Or me, if I'm honest.

"Lisa's fine, Gran. Don't worry about her."

She gives me the weak half-smile again. "Good. Good. You two will be fine when I'm gone."

"Don't say that. We've got some time here, the doctor says."

"Okay." That childlike agreement again. She nods. "But someday. You two will be fine. She needs you, Kelsey-girl." Gran squeezes my fingers. "And a girl always needs her mother."

FORTY-SIX

However many years she lived, Mary always felt that she should never forget that first morning when her garden began to grow.

~ from *The Secret Garden* by Frances Hodgson Burnett

The doctor is correct. Gran will sleep when she needs to.

And apparently, she needs to sleep immediately after making this ambiguous-yet-provocative statement.

I wander out of her room, trance-like.

Sam jumps up from a plastic chair against the wall.

"Do you want me to come back later, Kelsey? To take you home?"

"No." I try to focus on his face. "No, I'm going back to the bookshop. Now."

Robert spends the first few minutes of the drive back into the city chattering about a book tour, interviews, other things I cannot focus on long enough to comprehend.

His enthusiasm eventually subsides in the face of my silence.

Sam reaches across the seat, holds my hand.

I can feel him glancing at me, worried, perhaps.

They must think I'm in shock over my newfound and barely believable celebrity status.

But it's Gran's last few words before falling asleep that ping around the inside of my head.

Sam pulls up to the curb in front of the bookshop, double-parked.

"Do you want me to come in?" His face is hopeful.

"Tomorrow?" I search his eyes. "I need to—can you come by tomorrow?"

"Of course." He pulls me toward him, kisses my cheek.

Robert gets out of the backseat, into the darkness. "And I'll be in touch tomorrow as well, Kelsey. We have much to talk about."

"Right. Okay. Thanks."

The party is over, the customers gone, and the front door locked.

But the lights are still on.

And Lisa is there. Leaning over the counter, scribbling on some paper.

I tap the glass.

She glances up, sees me, and smiles.

Hurries around the counter to the door and unlocks it.

Her smile fades as she takes in my expression.

"What is it? I thought she was awake—doing better—"

"She is. Yes. She's not strong, but she is awake. There's stroke damage. The right side. Her arm. Face."

I'm rambling. I cannot bring myself to say what I must say.

How old? How old is Lisa?

Forty-three. She's forty-three, right?

My mind is refusing to calculate. I push harder.

Forty-three minus twenty-nine.

Oh, dear God. Fourteen.

Younger than Saanvi, than Olivia.

This revelation is yet another impossible thing, though not as impossible as a grieving mother in ancient Egypt. And it explains so much. Gran's unfazed desire to help Lisa, no matter how unreliable or unskilled she may be. Lisa's loyalty to Gran, which has always seemed outsized, even for someone grateful for employment.

"Lisa."

She's headed around the counter again, back to whatever she was working on.

At the single word, she glances at me, smiles, then halts. Smile gone. Grabbing the counter.

She knows.

She knows that I know.

A coldness douses me from head to feet. An emotion I can't come close to identifying.

I think of Rekhetre, in the ancient past, mourning the loss of her child.

And of Lisa, right here in front of me, partying half her life away. As though trying to forget.

But always returning to the Book Emporium. Again and again.

I exhale slowly, trying to find my voice, the words, the strength.

Lisa's eyes bore into mine, searching, asking. Seeking something, desperately seeking something.

"Lisa."

It's all I can manage, and even those two syllables feel choked and tight.

I take a shaky step toward her, where she still hangs on to the end of the counter.

Her eyes widen as if I'm wielding a weapon, something that could destroy her.

Perhaps I am.

"You—you were so young."

Her face crumples. She braces herself, gripping the counter, head down, shoulders shaking in silent sobs.

"I never knew." Another step toward her. "How could I know?"

She's still not speaking, still not looking at me. Her body trembling.

"Why didn't you ever tell me? Either one of you—why?"

She raises her head, the movement sharp and sudden. "What good would it have done? You had a mother. A wonderful mother!"

I close the gap between us.

I want to touch her, to connect somehow, but I'm dizzy with confusion and anger, with something that feels at once like hope and like fear.

I felt it with Rekhetre, but I got all of that so wrong, didn't I? So many false assumptions. I can't get this wrong, not again.

I grab the back of my neck, tight fingers against the ropy tension there. "I don't understand. How? Why?"

She wipes two hands across her face and meets my eyes.

"They were such good friends. Elizabeth and my mom. Even though my mom was fifteen years younger. You know that."

I nod.

"My mom even named me after her, in a way."

How has this never occurred to me? "*Lisa* is a variation of *Liza*."

"Yes. And when—it happened—"

My stomach clenches.

Lisa must read my thoughts. "No, nothing—nothing terrible—just a boy I knew at school, a stupid mistake. But it was right after my mom's diagnosis. They gave her only a few months. And I was only…" Her voice trails off.

"Fourteen. You were fourteen."

She nods, fresh tears flowing. "I didn't know what to do. My mom—she was desperate to help me in the little time she had left." Her voice catches with a strangled sob. "I made her last months a nightmare."

"No, Lisa, I'm sure that's not true. She must have loved you, only wanted the best for you."

Lisa shakes her head, her lips clamped shut, then exhales heavily. "We knew I couldn't keep the baby." She looks at me. "I couldn't keep—you."

And I realize that I am sobbing now, too.

"We wanted to find adoptive parents that would be perfect. But there was so little time, and I didn't know anything, didn't know how to figure it all out."

She presses her fingertips against her forehead. "And then, when it all seemed impossible, there was Elizabeth, offering to solve everything. At first, I thought she'd be too old, that it would make things hard on you. But she came up with the 'Gran' thing. And it wasn't just my mom—I had always loved Elizabeth, too. It would be a way to stay close to you, see you sometimes, maybe. And then, finally when I was older, I was ready to see you more, and she let me work here..."

"I just don't understand why you kept it a secret."

Lisa huffs out an angry laugh. "Really? Have you taken a look at my life?"

"I don't see why—"

"Kelsey, I've been homeless. I have no money. I drink too much—way too much, if I'm being honest. I've had a series of deadbeat boyfriends. I have no education, never had a decent job besides this one." She thumbs the bookshop behind her. "I made Elizabeth promise to keep my secret. You said it yourself. Any mother who would give you up isn't someone you would want to know. What possible benefit would there be to telling you the truth?"

I suddenly see all of it—Lisa's entire life, which has always left me feeling a little superior—in a terrible new light.

There is another story behind everyone's pain, isn't there? A story waiting to be told, waiting to be understood.

Waiting to be redeemed.

"What possible benefit?" I cross the remaining space between us. "Because it is the truth."

I touch her hand until she looks into my eyes.

"Because you are my mother."

EPILOGUE

ONE YEAR LATER

LOCATION—FROM THE STREET:
The White Orchard Hotel, filled to capacity with guests still enjoying its month-long Grand Opening special events and premium service. The hotel and adjoining convention center extend for three city blocks, having taken in the south end of the former Chestnut Street, both its shops and the very street itself.

To passersby, walking down the newly diverted street, peering through the glass-fronted hotel entryway or catching a glimpse of the lobby as the massive revolving door rotates past, the hotel is at once a marvel of modern architecture and a throwback to a more golden age.

Ornate sculptural decoration integrates seamlessly with arched windows, pedimented doors, and grand entrances.

A testament to progress amidst a hat-tip to the past.

INSIDE—REVEALED:
A continuation of the exterior design, from the wide marble staircase ascending from the lobby, across an

atrium striped by a warm sunset streaming from the lofty windows.

The smooth sound of a piano drifts across the space from somewhere unseen, beyond the potted trees and leather chairs, perhaps, or past the entrance to the Paradise Bar. Is that *Happy Birthday* someone is playing?

But as lovely as the interior of the White Orchard Hotel might be, guests and tourists alike have already established a pattern of gravitating toward the far end of the hotel, wanting to see something unusual.

Something wonderful.

Perhaps even a little magical…

~

"*Happ—y—Birth—day—to—you...*" The last lines of the song overlap with applause and a few cheers, and I hold my hair in one hand as I lean in to blow out candles on the towering three-tiered cake covered in white buttercream with emerald-colored vines tendriling up and down the layers.

AnaMaria has outdone herself for my thirtieth birthday.

I grin in her direction as the smoke curls upward and mouth a *thank you*.

She returns the smile from the round bistro table where she sits with her grandson, along with William and his wife Sara from The Groove, the shop which is no longer.

In fact—I look around at our location—The Groove was once right here, right where a dozen scattered tables now sit among lemon trees I've set into stone planters, against a backdrop of a living wall of cascading greenery, amid overflowing pots of bougainvillea and astilbe. A fountain at the back right accompanies the hum of conversation with the sound of trickling water.

And all of it glowing warm under a criss-crossed string of lanterns, each one a small, fiery globe.

It took me a long time to find those string lights.

But they were the perfect finishing touch to this "garden" inside the hotel.

An oval wooden sign hangs above the metal arbor that forms an entrance to the dining area, carved with three simple words: *The Secret Garden*.

"Are we going to eat this cake or just look at it?"

The words whisper against my ear as an arm circles my waist.

I lean my head back against Sam's solid chest.

"Happy Birthday, sweetheart."

I smile, eyes closed.

"Oh, and I'm sorry, but I forgot to get you a gift."

"Very funny." I hold up my left hand, the diamond flashing a reflection of the globe-lights. "I think I did okay this year, as far as birthday gifts go. Maybe thirty's not so bad."

"Good." He punctuates the word with a kiss.

From across the garden party, my Creative Writers send up hoots and moans.

Sam waves a hand at them. "Oh, get over it, all of you."

I've renamed them, these kids, and the new group of students who've joined us this year. No more Creative Writers of Tomorrow—they don't need to wait for their creativity to be validated or recognized.

No, we are all the Creative Writers of *Today*.

They think it's a stupid name.

It's a miracle, really, that this group still meets every Tuesday and Thursday, climbing their way through the wardrobe to exchange stories and encouragement.

I glance up at the Chestnut Street Book Emporium, still standing. Inside the White Orchard Hotel.

Such an impossible thing.

Sam says I wove together a fantastic story when I made my presentation, first to the city and then to the National Register of Historic Places. The story of the old theater days, and then its new life as a bookshop, of famous authors signing there—even a few authors who only attained local fame—and the Beaux-Arts facade designed by a world-renowned architect when the theater was built. It was enough to convince the board that it should be deemed a "registered historic district" which could not be Taken by the city in the name of economic development.

And ever the opportunist, when Charles Diamond Blackburn heard the news, he jumped in with a delightfully innovative plan to incorporate the Book Emporium building *inside* of the hotel.

The very thing I kicked against for so long has wrapped me inside of itself and become the answer.

It doesn't hurt business, Blackburn says, that Selena Manning owns the place.

Between the publicity around the "Cinderella story" of the unknown author becoming a bestseller and the extra foot traffic the hotel brings, the bookshop's financial troubles are a thing of the past.

And yes, the book royalties didn't hurt, either. But while imagination *can* sometimes pay the bills, I've realized we must stop asking it to. The convenient *deus ex machina* resolution to my own financial crisis bothered me for a few months, but in the end, it turned out the money from *The Starlight Folio* wasn't needed to make this lovely dream of the Book Emporium's new life come about.

I've also set aside a nice chunk for our honeymoon—a trip around the world, to all my travel-poster locations. Egypt first.

The vacant lot still lies on the other side of the far wall, untouched. This garden area beside the shop, where The Groove once stood, is served by AnaMaria's baked-goods-and-coffee kiosk, which has more than made up for the reduced traffic to her Sunny Side Up Diner.

I laugh, thinking of Austin's idea to create a high-end coffee shop. When he stopped by a few weeks ago, to introduce his new girlfriend, he made sure she understood it was all his idea.

"Go," AnaMaria waves me away from the cake. "Go socialize. I'll get this served."

"Thank you." I give her a little hug. "I was afraid Sam was going to start digging in with his hands."

"I still might."

AnaMaria swats Sam's chest, then applies her attention to cutting through the layers.

Another friend strolls over, gives me a quick hug.

"Thanks for the song, Bea."

The former Rhythm & Wonder Music Shop owner accompanied the party guests as they sang *Happy Birthday*, but I know she has more music planned.

"Oh, you're welcome, honey." Bea rakes a hand through her spiky gray hair. "Wait until you hear what else I've got. My favorite piece, from my time with you-know-who." She winks with a dramatic flourish.

You-know-who is none other than twentieth-century jazz great Bill Evans, Bea's music tutor in a Garden Party we once attended.

I see Bea here in our own version of the Garden Party once a week, when Sam and I host a get-together of assorted creatives in the area, a gathering for feasting and laughter and much-needed mutual support. It takes a community, this creative life, this risk of rejection, disappointment, failure as we give of our time and our energy and our work in generosity, without demanding affirmation or reward. Believing that creativity is first and foremost a gift to be given, not a commodity to be traded.

AnaMaria hands me the first slice of cake and a fork. "Is your mom coming?"

The casual question still gives me a jolt, even after all these months.

"I'm here, I'm here!"

Lisa rushes into the fray, nearly hidden behind a giant,

red-wrapped box with a glittery pink bow, and lands a kiss on my cheek.

It's been a strange year getting to know this woman in a different way, transitioning from employee, to friend, eventually to something like an older sister. Not sure I'll ever fully relax into *mother*. But it's a relationship that doesn't need defining. I've come to love her. And learned that over the years, in her strange, stand-offish, guilt-ridden way, she has always loved me.

I'm still deciding whether I want to track down my biological father.

And what of my bizarre trip to ancient Egypt? If not to find my parents, what was the purpose? I suppose I've made peace with the difficult lesson the Garden needed to teach me… hard as it might be, we cannot let even the complete failure of our creativity stop us from creating.

The cake is getting passed around, Bea's started pounding "Autumn Leaves" on the piano, and the party is drawing attention from hotel guests who smile as they walk past.

I pull away a bit, wanting to just observe.

To see my friends, my community, my *family*, enjoying this impossible garden I've created inside a place that should not be able to hold it.

Just outside the front door of the bookshop, a bronze plaque is mounted beside an acrylic glass-covered poster. The poster contains vintage shots of the Chestnut Street Theatre, the original bookshop, and a beautiful photo of Gran in her thirties—bohemian dress, braided hair, and all.

I insisted on the plaque, which dedicates the bookshop and its adjoining garden to the woman who raised and also loved me. I miss her still, every day.

And the other Garden?

Oh, we've been back, the three of us, to chat and mingle with "the greats." Even though we are not the greats. Which makes no difference at all.

Because despite achieving overnight bestseller status, I'm

already mired in self-doubt and fear again, trying to produce the sequel everyone seems to want, and panicking that I'll never be able to get it right.

And I've realized something. In the life of any artist—no matter their talent—every new work is a choice in which the magic must be denied or the magic must be embraced.

This isn't an embrace as one grips the arms of a friend. No, this embrace is the frantic grip on a life preserver after a night adrift at sea. It's the desperate lunge toward water after a day adrift in the desert.

But sometimes, the magic is denied. And then the artist dies.

Not physically, of course. But something in the inmost being, where the artist was knit together for such a time as this, goes silent and dormant and dead.

Why should such a thing happen, you ask? Why would anyone refuse the life-raft, pour the life-water into the sand?

Because the magic is terrifying.

For an artist—whether she be poet or painter, singer or storyteller, dancer or decorator—the magic is wild and unknown and altogether frightful.

Because even though the magic is life, it is also death. It is Sirens wailing their song of beauty while we dash ourselves against their rocks. The magic is a headlong run into the light, which may turn out to be an oncoming train.

There is the death of denial, and there is the death of embracing, and either one is death and both are death, and so, what's an artist to do?

That is the choice. It comes to every one of us, in whatever beauty we pursue. To continue as an *aspiring* artist, doing our making safely on the side—dipping the toe, coloring in the lines, delivering the expected.

Or to face our drowning, thirsting desperation and fling ourselves into the wild, even as an amateur—a lover.

And lest you think you can simply avoid this choice, you must understand avoidance is still a choice.

But I get ahead of myself.

Because before the artist is forced to choose, there must be a moment of clarity. For some of us, I'm embarrassed to admit, it takes a bit more persuading for us to see. But the choice must come, with the two courses laid out. Two roads diverging in a yellow wood… or on a yellow legal pad or yellowing ivory keys or a palette of yellows.

Yellow. The color of cowardice.

But also of sunlight.

You choose.

WANT TO READ KELSEY'S STORY?

Kelsey finally worked up the courage to bring a gift to the Garden.
Would you like to read her story, inspired by the bookshop's travel posters?
I want to give it this classic-style murder mystery, free!

As a university math professor, Audrey knows how to solve problems. But the one problem she can't solve? The whereabouts of her brother, missing for seven months.

When a vintage travel poster advertising a Nile riverboat cruise—tacked up in the back hall of the restaurant where her brother was last seen—reveals a startling anomaly,

Audrey stumbles into an adventure too classic to be real, but too real to be a dream.

Now she's trying to rescue her brother, return a stolen Egyptian artifact, and solve a murder, all while navigating the unfamiliar world of Egypt one hundred years in the past.

Sure, she wants to get home. But danger, mystery, and a dash of romance—who could resist?

THANK YOU

Hello Reader Friend!

Thank you for reading *Nightfall in the Garden of Deep Time.* I hope it was meaningful to you.

If you enjoyed the book and would like to share it with others, I have two requests:

1) **I would so appreciate it if you would post a brief review.** You can find all the online retailers where it is currently available for reviews here:
https://books2read.com/u/bQjgww
You could also post a review on Goodreads if you use that platform.
And you could also copy your review to my website, which would be so lovely of you!
https://tracyhigley.com/nightfall

2) If you enjoyed the book and believe your friends might also, I have a number of **super-easy ways to share it.** Please check out this page for shareable graphics, other creative ideas, and also a VIDEO of me sharing my heart with you:
https://tracyhigley.com/share-NGDT-with-others

Thank you!
~ Tracy

READ THIS NEXT!

Looking for more adventure?
I think you'll love my trilogy ~
The Time Travel Journals of Sahara Aldridge
beginning with *A Time to Seek.*

WHEN TIME TRAVEL IS A FAMILY TRADITION, A GIRL COULD GET HERSELF INTO TROUBLE.

Sahara Aldridge never asked to be a time-traveler. She inherited the crazy ability from her parents before they died, and she's not at all certain she wants it.

For one thing, time traveling is dangerous.
And for another, there's a line of unscrupulous people who would use Sahara's gift for their own gain, if they could. Including Giada Moretti, who just happens to the aunt of the most attractive man Sahara's ever met.

Now Sahara is careening through time, on a desperate search for the truth about her family.

She needs to get control of this thing and discover how it all went wrong, before Jack Moretti leads her into a future even more dangerous than the past.

But the truth just might be more of a shock than learning you can travel through time.

Dear Reader,

Thank you for going on this adventure with me! I hope you greatly enjoyed *Nightfall in the Garden of Deep Time.*

You can find lots more about ancient Egypt on my website, along with travel journals of my trips there.

You also might be interested to read more about the writing of this book, and see some of the places that inspired it. You can find the Story Behind the Story here: https://tracyhigley.com/ngdt-the-story-behind-the-story

And in case you're curious, here's more than you want to know about me…

I've been writing stories since the time I first picked up a pencil. I still have my first "real" novel—the story I began at the age of eight during a family trip to New York City.

Through my childhood I wrote short stories, plays for my friends to perform (sometimes I had to bribe them), and even started a school newspaper (OK, I was the editor, journalist and photographer since no one took that bribe to join me). Then there were the drama years of junior high, when I filled a blank journal with pages of poetry. {{*sigh.*}}

In my adult years I finally got serious about publishing fiction, and have since authored nearly twenty novels.

When I'm not writing, life is full of other adventures—running a business, spending time with my kids, and my favorite pastime: traveling the world.

I started traveling to research my novels and fell in love with experiencing other cultures. It's my greatest hope that you'll feel like you've gotten to travel to the settings of my books, through the sights, sounds, smells, colors, and textures I try to bring back from my travels and weave into my stories.

I'd love to hear your thoughts about *Nightfall in the Garden of Deep Time,* or ideas you have for future books I might write. Get in touch with me at tracy@tracyhigley.com.

Now, onward to another adventure!

READING GROUP GUIDE

NOTE: QUESTIONS CONTAIN SPOILERS

1. Have you ever wished for a portal to somewhere else? Where would you go?
2. Do you consider yourself a creative person?
3. If you are creative, do you feel embarrassed or insecure about your creativity?
4. How familiar were you with the characters Kelsey encounters in the Garden?
5. In what ways have you struggled to bring something creative to life? What obstacles have you faced?
6. How did you feel about the Chestnut Street Book Emporium? Have you ever visited a bookshop like it?
7. Do you agree that every creative person plays a critical role in the world? If so, what do you feel is that role?
8. What were you expecting when Kelsey finally went "deeper" into the Garden? Ancient Egypt? Something else?
9. Have you experienced discouragement in areas of your creativity?
10. Where do you think Sam went, when he was drawn into his "deeper" adventure? How about Bea?
11. How did you feel about the two big surprises in the last few chapters?
12. What are your thoughts about this quote from the book: "We create, not to be affirmed in our talent, but to serve. We create, regardless of the limits of quality or the reception our work receives. We create, because we must."

BOOKS BY TRACY HIGLEY

The Seven Wonders Novels:

Isle of Shadows

Pyramid of Secrets

Guardian of the Flame

Garden of Madness

So Shines the Night

The Time Travel Journals of Sahara Aldridge:

A Time to Seek

A Time to Weep

A Time to Love

The Books of Babylon:

Chasing Babylon

Fallen from Babel

The Lost Cities Novels:

Petra: City in Stone

Pompeii: City on Fire

The Coming of the King Saga:

The Queen's Handmaid

The Incense Road

Standalone Books and Short Stories:

Nightfall in the Garden of Deep Time

Awakening

The Ark Builder's Wife

Dressed to the Nines

Broken Pieces

Rescued: An Allegory